Wired For Magic

JANET ROBERTS

Human Authored™, Reg #: 7650176, https:// authorsguild.org/human

Wired For Magic

Copyright © 2025 by Janet Roberts

PB ISBN: 978-0-9973896-9-2

Ebook ISBN: 979-8-9990268-0-4

All Rights Reserved. Written permission must be secured from the author to use or reproduce any part of this book, except for brief quotations in critical reviews or articles.

NO AI TRAINING: Without in any way limiting the author's exclusive rights under copyright, any use of this publication to "train" generative artificial intelligence (AI) technologies to generate text is expressly prohibited. The author reserves all rights to license uses of this work for generative AI training and development of machine learning language models.

This books is a work of fiction. Names, characters, places and incidents are the product of the author's imagination or are used fictitiously. Characters in this book have no relation to anyone bearing the same name and are not based on anyone known or unknown to the author. Any resemblance to actual businesses or companies, events, locales, or persons, living or dead is coincidental.

Cover design: Larch Gallagher Designs

Author photo: Mariah Treiber Photography

 Formatted with Vellum

Angela Hudson Smith
(1957-2025)

You are missed, my friend.
This book is for you.

*"You've always had the power my dear,
you just had to learn it for yourself."*

Glinda, The Good Witch from The Wizard of Oz

Rowan

Rowan needed to run lean and unfettered now.

They'd fought a bit about the original artwork and the dog. For the dog's sake, it was best she'd lost that battle. He was too old to be constantly on the move in the way she intended for the foreseeable future. It was surprising, when it came right down to it, how simple it was to dismantle the trappings of a relationship, to divest oneself of its many pieces and parts for the reward of exhaling and walking away.

Her name was not on the lease. Her mail was delivered to a post office box. It had been a good place to settle for a while—until it wasn't. Great sex, not much substance in Rowan's opinion, but wasn't that what she always went for to protect herself? Loving her required tolerating both the constant threat from her stalker and an inherited magic she had a less than competent understanding of—and pointed lack of control. The latter of which she usually worked hard to hide. What Rowan longed for and what she believed attainable regarding her love life had been on a collision course for a long time. What man would agree to live this way? None was the answer Rowan supplied without ever asking her partner of the moment. If she were honest, she probably chose men she was incapable of falling in love with.

Unfortunately for Peter, he was one of those men. Their relationship had revolved around passionate weekends before she flew out for a photo assignment until the pandemic illuminated the fact that they could not survive the daily togetherness of quarantine.

Rowan took one last look at the slim remains that constituted what she considered worthwhile belongings, packed in a pathetically small number of boxes, before rolling down the door to the rented storage compartment and locking it. This wasn't the first time she'd been on the move, traveling light, but it was the first time she'd decided running away wasn't her best or only choice. She headed north until she reached the London Underground, where she slid into a mix of students and professionally dressed office workers in the queue to scan their phones, Oyster cards or tickets for a ride on the District Line. Her thick, straight, dark brown hair was in a ponytail, her backpack in place, her hand tight on the handle of a small suitcase, mask covering her mouth and nose.

As a nearly six feet tall former supermodel, hiding was difficult. She wouldn't miss the pandemic, but covering her face in public—oppressive and exhausting for millions—had been a temporary gateway to the freedom of anonymity she desperately needed. The COVID-19 pandemic had made hiding in plain sight easy. Now, with the end of 2022 a few short months away, nearly everyone in the U.K. was vaccinated. Rowan could still mask up, but she wouldn't blend in easily anymore.

She'd chosen to layer dark colored clothing today, wearing a long-sleeve shirt, covered by a hoodie, and finally a puffy, down-filled winter jacket. It offered warmth and a little bulk to give her a slightly different shape that she hoped, coupled with the mask, would provide a bit of disguise. She planned to head home to the United States while she could still manage a small level of incognito. But there was one important stop before she left the U.K.

Rowan exited at Holborn, taking the mile-long escalator ever upward from the bowels of the London transportation system until she surfaced and headed toward Covent Garden. The air was brisk and cool but comfortable for early November. Much milder than it would be in the U.S. at this time of year. Minutes later, she tucked herself into the back left corner of a small Greek restaurant and unzipped the coat and hoodie but kept the mask in place and hood up. Her chair angled away from the window without losing sight of the street beyond. She'd scanned the sidewalk on her way, eyes seeking anyone looking faintly suspicious—a lurker, a too casually positioned watcher, someone who reappeared along her path as she moved forward. Occasionally, though less often, she was recognized from a magazine cover. Many prominent fashion publications had once displayed Rowan's image and now stood as reminders that her past life negated the hope she could easily go unnoticed.

Her stomach responded to the heavenly aroma coming from the kitchen, rumbling its noisy need. In the years spent entirely in front of a camera, she'd had to forego baklava and keep the portion sizes of moussaka and spanakopita relatively small. Lightheaded with hunger today, Rowan ordered dolmades, baked feta cheese, and hot tea, watching the passersby and the antics of a fat chef in the sandwich shop across the way as she waited for her food to arrive. By the time the bite-sized, stuffed vine leaves full of rice, herbs, and ground meat, followed by cheese and tea, were placed in front of her, she was ravenous. There would be no wine today. Rowan needed to keep her wits about her. She removed the mask to eat. With the exception of a few young teens hunched over laptops, oblivious to a world outside social media, the restaurant was empty. Although it was a relief that no one watched her a bit too closely, she was sure Jarrod was aware she was in London. Rowan had spent the last three years running from Jarrod Marrone, the powerful CEO of Marrone Industries.

Rowan had discarded a highly lucrative career due to his obsession with her. She'd embraced freelance photography in its place, taking an assortment of assignments under the pseudonym "Nora Edwards" that kept her on shifting ground and hidden from the public eye. Since moving to the other side of the camera, she'd made a point of dressing down to display a bland, quietly unassuming look. Photography, and living light out of a suitcase, paid the bills and allowed her to keep her savings intact. The earnings from her runway days were collecting interest in a Swiss bank account, barely touched.

Rowan loved being a photographer. Her life focused on capturing the perfect shot. Only she was aware that each photo might have fallen flat, emerging dull and uninspired, if her natural ability to capture the best shot weren't powered by a special level of intuition. *A good eye plus a bit of family magic,* she often said to herself when others complimented her work. She might be woefully undertrained in the extent of her magical abilities, but she could channel her gift to see what others could not. It was one of the few things her mother, Elin, taught Rowan before her untimely death when Rowan was barely thirteen.

Despite using a pseudonym, the recognition her photos engendered created danger. Working locally during the pandemic took her outside her trusted circle of nomadic photojournalists. Somehow, Jarrod had connected her with the London newspaper publishing her work. When he offered to run a wide range of expensive advertisements in exchange for an in-person meeting with her, she'd resigned. She'd loved those human-interest assignments, loved learning every inch of the city as she photographed it.

"Don't resign, Rowan. I can make sure someone is with you when you meet with him." Her editor obviously didn't buy her assertion that Jarrod was a stalker, a dangerous man.

"You put him in front of me and I'm going to, at a minimum, punch his lights out. Pretty sure that's not what you want." Rowan watched the editor's eyebrows raise with surprise. She'd always been low-key, quiet, very private.

An explosion of rage had filled her as she walked out of the newsroom. Yet another job she loved over, gone. Her anger was focused as much on herself as on Jarrod. Rowan's frustration that her fear of one man combined with ignorance about how to use her magic to stop him grew. She was tired of running like a frightened rabbit. No one was going to hand her the power to create change; she must stand up and take it. If she wanted a career she loved, a man she could put down roots with, and a life lived in the open, she had to stop Jarrod's madness. To do this, Rowan needed to confront herself first. Pull up her big girl pants, as she should have done long ago, and like an electric car, plug herself into a power station for a super charge of her magic.

Amusing, since my power station is a couple thousand years old. Rowan chuckled. Her magic would have to be firing at one hundred percent and warp speed to rid her life of him.

After that, she would head to the one place where the training she'd alternately wanted and avoided waited for her. Maya, her mother's sister, had often nudged Rowan to come to her for magic training, but she'd declined, claiming she wasn't ready. No more fleeing, folding to fear. She needed Maya's training. Her strategic plan coupled with her brother's expertise would get her to Maya safely.

"Replacing fear with knowledge is empowering, Rowan." She could hear Maya's often spoken refrain in her head.

The phone in her pocket played a quiet jazz tune. Rowan

checked the screen and smiled, tapping the green button to answer.

"Hey, little brother." She kept her voice low.

"Hey there, big sis." Griffith Campbell had the deep register and tonal quality of a sportscaster, but he was a software geek, a cybersecurity expert.

"Ready for me to head back to the U.S.?"

"Ro, are you sure you want to take the risk?"

She imagined Griff, running his hands through close-cropped dark brown curls, hopping back and forth in a habitual dance that indicated he was nervous and wired for action.

"It's not safe for me anywhere, Griff," Rowan said. "A couple of thugs tried to corner me on the Tube platform two days ago. I was able to slip into a train car before the doors closed, and they lost me."

"Are you sure Jarrod sent them?" Griff asked.

She shivered, thinking about the man who'd grabbed her arm on the train platform. She rubbed the bruise on her right arm that remained from the grip of his meaty fingers.

"The big one said, 'Mr. Marrone would like to see you.'" Rowan heard the annoyance in her voice even as her stomach churned at the memory. "Thank God for that self-defense course I took, and the people on the platform who called for help or tried to intercede."

"Did you kick them in the nuts, Ro?"

She couldn't tell if Griff was amused and not taking her seriously or if he asked out of honest concern.

"As a matter of fact, I screamed and bit one of them," Rowan answered with a small white lie. "That got the attention of others waiting for the train. A woman hit one of the thugs with an umbrella, and a guy with a security guard jacket grabbed the other one by the arm. It was enough for me to slide through the open train doors and keep them from following me. It was frightening, Griff!"

Rowan refrained from telling him that as she screamed, arousing attention from others on the platform, she'd used her magic to slam the two men in the solar plexus with an invisible force that knocked the wind out of them, giving one a knee between the legs. Biting had not been necessary. She'd watched from the train as it pulled away and more people on the platform got involved. Griff was skeptical of magic in general and hers specifically.

"Okay, okay, I get it. Jarrod is one sick bastard. What I don't get is why you won't let me talk to him." Griff said, his voice tight and exasperated. They'd had this argument before.

"Because I can handle this myself, Griff. He wants my . . . my inherited abilities." Rowan sighed, frustrated. "I don't need a protector. I need to stand up to him . . . stop him."

"If you truly had 'inherited abilities' or magic or whatever you're calling it these days, you would have kicked the shit out of him already instead of roaming the world, hiding," Griff said. "You said you injured him pretty badly in Paris."

Of all the people in this world, it was Griff who loved her best and who carried the same silent pain at the loss of their mother. In many things, they understood one another completely, but not on this subject. How could she explain to her brother what she struggled to explain to herself? Yes, she'd inherited magic from their mother. When she was in imminent danger, she reacted without thinking and her magic simply happened. She was at a loss as to how to manage her powers and unsure of the extent to which she could call on magic to protect herself. She needed Griff's technology skills to implement her plan.

"What happened in Paris was a clear indication that I can't control this gift. It probably scared me more than it scared Jarrod," Rowan said. "Maybe I should have gone to Aunt

Maya then, but I convinced myself that he would give up over time. You know all this."

"I know that he hasn't given up. I know I don't believe our family is filled with magical women," Griff said. "What I think is you should stay put and I should have a word with him, maybe kick his ass a little bit."

Rowan sighed. "You're not going to get arrested for assault and lose your job over a battle that is mine to fight. When I get home, I'm going to see Aunt Maya and learn what I should have agreed to allow her to teach me long ago."

Rowan waited out the normal silence. Their mother had said Griff was named for generations of Welsh princes and kings who, Rowan assumed, consulted with druids and had faith in mystical powers. *Her* Griffith lived in denial. She didn't want her brother interacting with her stalker. Just as Griff wanted to protect her, Rowan believed she needed to keep her brother safe from Jarrod. She sensed this in much the same way she intuited the best photos to take or predicted imminent danger to herself. Griff labeled her an overly protective older sister. He'd respected her wishes thus far, mostly because she'd convinced him any action on his part would increase, not decrease, the problem she faced. The task before her required an untested—and rarely unearthed—inherited magic she had an uneasy acceptance of but terrified her. For Griff, anything not grounded in his own reality existed only in his sister's imagination.

"Let's not argue. But I can't deny what's obvious. I can hurt someone when I'm angry by touching them, I can sometimes move inanimate objects, and a special intuition tells me the best photo shot. I need to hone this magic before I confront Jarrod," Rowan said.

She avoided discussion about the blue quartz necklace their mother left to her. Griff would completely shut down if she told him she occasionally used the stone to contact her mother's ghost and, at times, to confirm her own intuition about people, impending danger, and more. Unlike Griff, Rowan still viewed ghosts, magic, or anything she couldn't see, touch, and find in the real world as undeniable, even in the face of her own abilities. At age thirty-two, Rowan's acceptance of the passing of years since her mother's death hadn't lessened the longing or weight of that loss. Elin Edwards Campbell's violent ending refused to sit quietly in a dark corner of her mind. It sprang up unprompted, wrapping her in a dark veil of dread as a warning that if she couldn't learn to control her powers she, too, could lose her life.

Rowan touched the stone hanging from a silver chain around her neck. Mined in Wales, handed down through the generations, it was her only channel to Elin. She used it sparingly, but it comforted her. By her calculations, she was the tenth generation in her family to carry a genetically bestowed gift. Unfortunately, hers came from a mother who hadn't lived long enough to embed in her a deeper understanding of the source of this power and, more importantly, how to manage it.

Griff visited Maya fairly regularly, whereas Rowan's appearances had been rare, especially after Jarrod began stalking her. She told herself keeping a distance from family protected them. But, in truth, Maya looked so much like Elin it hurt. And then there was the issue of the spiritualist community in Western New York state where her aunt lived, surrounded by spirits, whispering voices that apparently only Rowan could hear. She shivered thinking about it. Yet when she spoke to Maya, an intuition—a feeling of undeniable union—rolled up in her like a soft wave coming in with the tide, wrapping gently around her body, calling her to come home.

"Ro, I've seen that jerk's sick obsession with you, and I think I'm a better safeguard than a bunch of family voodoo."

The stubborn tone in Griff's voice indicated she'd better veer the conversation in another direction.

"I won't tell Aunt Maya you said that," Rowan answered with a laugh, lightening the mood. "Every step you've taken to set up my trip home the way I requested is shielding me from danger, Griff. Are you worried a part of my plan will fail?"

"No, it's a good plan," Griff said, his tone softening. "Nearly everything's taken care of on my end. I'm still working on your actual ticket home."

"Great! No one is better than you at manipulating technology." Rowan chuckled.

"Text me when you're through security and again when you leave the airport." He was all efficiency and business, the frustration gone from his voice as quickly as it had flared.

Rowan smiled. They were very different from one another. She held anger at a low simmer for a long time, while Griff blew like a volcano and then moved on. "I will, I promise."

"Tell me again where you're going first? I worry when I don't know where you are."

"Swansea." She waited, knowing what he was thinking before he spoke.

"Wales." The resignation in his tone rendered his opinion.

"I need to sit with the standing stones, Griff, no matter..."

"Don't tell me about some ancient druid ruins you think are a witchy hot spot. I'm going to tell myself you're visiting Mom's family or touring old castles. Please be careful!"

"I'm avoiding family. It's an obvious place to look for me. If I tour an old castle, I'll tell you all about it when I'm back in the U.S. I can't wait to see you again!"

"Ditto that, sis."

Rowan ended the call and set the phone down, prepared to drink her tea and wait. One hour, and she'd head from

Paddington Station to Heathrow on the express train, but not to board the seven-hour flight back to the United States. Not yet. That was the plan—*her* plan. Griff initially objected, insisting she come home immediately. After going through security with her U.S. passport, she'd change her clothes, put on a wig, then pass through security cameras as a different person when she left the airport without boarding the plane. They'd page her name and, eventually, someone would realize she wasn't on the flight. Hopefully, the idiots working for Jarrod either weren't savvy enough to figure it out or wouldn't want to admit to their boss they'd lost her again. Her goal was to return to Paddington Station and board a train to Wales while Jarrod was busy tracking her supposed flight to Chicago. Griff booked her on the flight she'd chosen, but was now working on her actual flight home, reserved under another name, that departed in a week. It was an added benefit that her brother was a white hat hacker for a major airline. He promised to try to check her off as seated on the Chicago flight after takeoff, providing he could work through internal controls without suspicion, but he couldn't commit to it.

No matter what Griff thought, an internal pull to visit the ancient standing stones whispered to her at night with an intensity she couldn't ignore. It was a place Elin had visited each time they came to Wales, quietly rooted to a spot under its capstone while Rowan played nearby. Afterward, Rowan often sensed a change in her mother. Thinking of Elin triggered a reminder to check in with Maya.

> Rowan: Will be in Wales tomorrow.

Rowan waited to see three ellipses dancing on the screen. Maya was in her late fifties, with a disinterest in modern technology that left her slower when using it than others her age. Her resistance, coupled with Rowan's constant traveling for work, lowered the amount of communication between them, but Maya was always there, waiting.

> Maya: Gather strength, re-arm yourself and your magic, then come to me.
>
> Rowan: 👍

Maya had been adamant in her insistence that Rowan could not face Jarrod until she first visited the ancient stones. Hopefully, the detour before returning to the U.S. would prepare her to train with Maya. Rowan touched the stone around her neck and wished fervently that it had the power to eliminate her hesitancy around her ability to summon and control her own magic.

> Maya: Be careful. Stay safe.
>
> Rowan: 🛡️

She smiled. It would be good to see her aunt and join forces. Long ago, her mother tried to explain to Rowan that her magic was a gift—tried to guide her—but she'd been resistant.

"I don't want to be different. I want to fit in, to be like my friends," Rowan had said.

"You don't have a choice, Rowan. Your powers are a gift. They are your destiny." Her mother's assertion that she was unique in this way had never meshed with reality to Rowan's teenage self.

"I don't believe you. That's my choice." Rowan had turned away, the sound of her mother's sigh echoing in her ears as she left the room.

Over the years, incidents occurred when she did things—or her body did things—that were inadvertent, unexplainable, and usually outside her control. The day Elin died, she'd magically guarded Griff from a strange man at their door. Her abilities had stunned the police officers who delivered her mother's blue quartz necklace.

"Be careful," one police officer said, pointing to his hand which was wrapped in a bandage. "No one at the station could safely touch that thing."

"I'd bury it and forget about it, if I were you," the other officer said, crossing himself. "Strange—maybe evil—describes that stone."

They waited, curious, watching as Rowan opened the box, removed the necklace, placed it around her neck, and closed the clasp. She'd rarely been without it since.

"The stone is your conduit to speak to your mother," Maya told her, weeks later. "Only you can safely wear it."

As a young girl, Rowan convinced herself that, without the stone, she was an average person, powerless and vulnerable in the face of danger. It helped her to maintain a thin veneer of denial about the deeper power she carried that needed no stone to unleash. Anxiety that she would never be the warrior her mother had been held a grip on her, at times bordering on a panic attack. Yet, avoidance and denial were no longer choices. Jarrod was obsessed and relentless. She accepted she might have to fight as her mother had done.

Rowan touched the blue quartz lying between her breasts. November meant it would be dark by late afternoon, making it easier for her to move unseen in the clothing she'd chosen. The gray London sky was melding into pre-evening dusk. Rowan left a tip on the table. She double-checked the small, belted pouch around her waist before zipping up her coat. Her alternate U.K. passport was there. She'd lifted it from her great-aunt Alice's well-worn Bible while attending a family wake in the Welsh village of Nevern following the elderly woman's death. Alice had been fastidious about keeping her passport current, perhaps waiting patiently, prepared for that holy call to find a grail, a mission, a destination that never alighted on her pious soul or her simple, lonely life. When the stone thrummed lightly against her chest the minute she touched the passport's outer cover with its royal seal, Rowan had stolen it without thinking twice.

Amongst her many connections in the world of photography were a few shady characters who altered passports. One, a friend she trusted to ask no questions, made the fix for her. Alice's passport now held a photo of Rowan with a blond bob, green contacts covering her blue eyes. The expensive wig and new birthdate on the finished product looked realistic. She'd paid a little extra for an accompanying birth certificate, and for a separate driver's license and credit card issued to Bryn Davies, which she planned to use for a short time. The credit card was dangerous, but she couldn't rent a car without it. She hoped to pay the final bill in cash when she dropped off the car. She'd save Alice Edwards for her flight home. Until then, she needed to practice mimicking the beautiful, lilting accent of her mother's people.

Mask up and hood forward to hide her face, Rowan slid open the front of her backpack and transferred her U.S. passport to her coat pocket before slinging its straps onto her shoulders. A slight drizzle had begun, accompanied by a damp breeze. She shivered as much from the shifting weather as from apprehension. A lot depended on Griff successfully booking Alice Edwards on a flight home, then safely picking her up at the Pittsburgh airport.

It was three blocks to the Tube, and then the Heathrow Express train at Paddington. She'd purchase a paper ticket with cash instead of using a phone or credit card. A ride share would require use of her credit card. A cab or train allowed her to use cash, but a train allowed her to blend in with the crowds. Once she left Heathrow, headed back to Paddington, then on to Wales, she'd make the transition to Bryn Davies. As

Bryn Davies, she had a smartphone with convenient apps connected to easy pre-payment options, backup burner phones, SIM cards, cash, Visa gift cards, and one credit card for singular use only.

The hood and mask hid her face but stymied her peripheral vision. She glanced side to side, rain mingling with tiny beads of sweat collecting on her forehead, and then moved quickly. The sooner she could meld into a large crowd, the better. Rowan was a block from the subway entrance when she ducked into the doorway leading to a small coffee shop. Two big, muscular men in tracksuits and running shoes, puffy down ski vests their only concession to the weather, were scanning the crowds heading into the Tube.

"Shit," Rowan mumbled. She could see a black cab moving slowly nearby. She'd have to take a cab to Paddington or maybe all the way to the airport. The two men were now moving inward, out of the rain, to watch from behind the subway doors. Rowan glanced at the cab again. It had no registration tag in the window. The windshield wipers were thumping as the driver talked to someone on the phone.

"You're not a London cabbie, asshole," she muttered, stepping into the coffee shop and heading for the bathroom.

"Ma'am? Tha''s faw customers only," the barista said, leaning forward, a lock of purple hair falling over a pierced eyebrow, the Cockney accent defining his East End roots.

"A tall Americano with room," Rowan answered, slapping a ten-pound note on the counter. "I'll be out to get it in a few minutes."

It was a single restroom, one toilet and one sink. She locked the door. How had they found her? She searched her backpack slowly for any type of tracking device. Nothing. She'd packed it herself. It had to be her phone. In her hurry to leave the apartment, followed by her focus on loading and then locking the storage unit, had she shut down GPS and any apps she didn't absolutely need to avoid enabling someone to track her via phone? Rowan opened her settings and cursed. The GPS was on. She shut it off, then ran a check of her listed apps, closing or deleting anything she didn't need. A strange app called "Find My Kids" appeared in the list with no icon on her phone screen. What was that doing there? Having no memory of downloading it, she deleted the app, re-checked twice to ensure it was completely removed, and powered the phone down. Hopefully that would throw them into the dark long enough for her to adjust her plans.

"Is there a hotel nearby?" Rowan asked the barista, picking up her coffee from the counter. She settled herself at a corner table away from, but with a view through, the window. The coffee shop was empty. She was the only customer.

"Sure, abou' a block wes' ov 'ere," he answered, focused on cleaning the espresso machine, barely looking at her.

"Can I use the back door? You know, the rain and all, maybe the alleyway is quicker?"

"Yeah, i''s a bad rain ou' 'here" He was looking at her now, assessing, considering.

Rowan sipped her coffee to partially cover her face, concentrating on the barista. In an effort to engage her interest, Maya once told her that her powers included mental telepathy. She'd tried it and found her aunt was correct, but it left her with a splitting headache. Desperation convinced her to endure a bit of head pain now. Her plan would collapse if she didn't get to the airport quietly, unnoticed. Rowan pushed hard from within her mind to the barista, sending what she hoped were powerful thoughts that would shift him to the ally she needed in this danger-fraught moment.

"Okay. You takes the back door an' then knocks on the door across the alley. My friend works in the shoeshop an' she'll let ya through to the hotel. Best of British," the barista said, rubbing his left temple as if his head hurt.

That was quick. She rubbed the mild tension in her own temples. Years of walking the London streets photographing the homeless and destitute had familiarized her with the city's many dialects.

"Perfect. Thank you." Rowan watched the barista text someone, presumably the friend next door.

"All good. Le''s go," he said, his smile showing crooked teeth.

A warm kinship with him washed over her. He was very young. She'd love to photograph him, but there was no time for that now. Rowan stepped through the back door where she found herself under an overhang in an empty alleyway. The barista pointed to a plain beige metal door directly across and slightly left from where they stood. Before she could move, the door opened and an attractive woman who appeared to be around Rowan's age leaned out, waving to them. Rowan bolted forward, heart pounding, scooting quickly past the woman and into the shop.

"Welcome, glad to help you escape from the rain," the woman said. Her glasses gave her a quiet bookish appeal, and the soft mellow tones of her voice with its familiar lyricism and elongated vowels were a welcome sound to Rowan's ears.

"I think he likes you," Rowan answered, flicking her thumb in the direction of the alley with a smile and a wink. A soft warmth emanated from the quartz lying against her breastbone.

"Ahh, yes, I'm the focus of his obsession for now. A teenage crush." She laughed, giving Rowan an eye roll.

The word "obsession" created a small sense of nausea. "Be careful. I have someone obsessed with me, and it's frightening."

"He wants to date you and can't hear 'no,' is it?" She was now walking Rowan through shelves lined with shoes, the smell of polish and leather mingling with the slight mildew-laden odor of the old building.

"Perhaps at one time," said Rowan. "Now his solitary goal is to possess me. To own me and my . . ."

"You and your magic?" the woman answered knowingly, eyeing Rowan with concern.

"Why would you say that?" The reference to magic startled her.

"Have you told the police?" the woman asked, avoiding the question.

"Yes, once . . ." Rowan shook her head at the memory. "He's powerful and it was useless."

"Would you take my mobile number in case you need me?" They'd reached the front door of the shop. Rowan scanned the sidewalk outside. The hotel was directly across the road, a line of black cabs parked against the curb, waiting for customers. The woman turned toward Rowan and her blouse shifted open, revealing a blue quartz necklace, smaller but similar to Rowan's.

"You assumed magic earlier. Is it because we have this in common?" Rowan smiled, pointing to the woman's necklace. Her own much bigger stone, easily seen after she unzipped the top of her coat, must have prompted the question.

"I was a small child when I saw that," the woman said, pointing toward Rowan's chest. "Not long before my mother brought me to London to live, after Dad died. She was saying good-bye to her friend, Elin, who was visiting from the U.S."

"My mother." Rowan's simple response must have resonated with the woman who stopped, eyebrows raised.

"Are we of the same clan of women?" Rowan asked. "You said they were friends, and yet my stone is reacting to you much like it does with my Aunt Maya."

"We are part of a line of magical women," she answered. "My mother always told me Elin was a direct descendent of the source of our magic, while the women in my family are several levels removed. My magic is helpful, but not as powerful as yours must be if you are Elin's daughter. Yes, we're part of the same clan—distant cousins in a way."

"If our mothers were friends, we can't be strangers. I'm Rowan . . . Rowan Campbell."

"Ahh . . . Rowan Campbell from the covers of Vogue and Sports Illustrated? I thought you looked familiar. My younger brother was devastated when you disappeared," she said with a laugh. "I'm Catrin. But everyone calls me Cat." Cat pulled out her phone. "I'll order you a cab, on my credit card. That should leave no trace of your travels."

"Cat . . . thank you," Rowan fished two twenty-pound notes from her backpack and handed them to Cat. When their fingers connected, energy moved through her arm to Cat. Cat's softer, milder energy ran up her arm in return.

"Is it to the old druid stones our mothers favored then . . . where you're headed?" Cat asked.

"Yes. How did you know? Have you been there yourself?"

Cat nodded affirmatively, her phone to her ear as she ordered a taxi. "He'll come round in about fifteen minutes."

"Any advice?" Rowan asked, knowing Cat understood she meant Pentre Ifan, the standing stones Rowan planned to visit. Cat was silent for a few seconds.

"Get a car or taxi and go off the A487 to a lay-by on the west side of the road where you can park. Follow the signpost to the footpath leading to the site." Cat eyed her casually before adding, "If you don't want to be seen, there's a longer hike through farmland. But honestly, I wouldn't go that way this time of year. You could get lost in those woods while hiking back to your car."

"Will I be safe there?" Rowan asked.

"Yes, anything you need to fear comes from humans, not

from the standing stones," Cat said with a smile. "Your necklace and the goddess will be with you."

"The goddess?" Rowan shivered. This day was getting stranger by the minute. Maya had never mentioned a goddess, but then Rowen's resistance to participate in magic training kept the door to many discussions firmly shut.

"My mother referred to that spot as 'Croth Ceridwen.'" Cat smiled, her eyes somewhere far away, lost in a memory.

"Forgive my limited understanding of Welsh, but what does that mean?" Rowan asked.

"The womb of Ceridwen, our most famous goddess from which, I believe, you are directly descended and I'm connected distantly. I doubt you'll see anything ghostly," Cat said, patting Rowan's shoulder reassuringly. "I feel warm and safe when I'm there. My mother always said it's the goddess. Take my Welsh mysticism as a comfort."

The kind words filled her and, as she reached out to touch Cat's hand, she smiled despite tears filling her eyes. "I believe we are destined to be friends, Cat."

Minutes later, slouched down in the back seat of the taxi, Rowan smiled, surprised that she'd instinctively tossed her usual cautionary ways aside with Cat. She savored the momentary lift from habitual loneliness that came with a new friend. Cat's magic was softer, gentler than Rowan's. It created a sense of balance between them that Rowan liked. If she was able to return to Wales after confronting Jarrod, she'd have a friend who both shared and understood her mystical heritage.

Jarrod

The phone call came in while Jarrod Marrone lay naked in the dark early morning hours upon his black, seven-thousand-dollar Bernhardt bed on the third floor of his suburban Pittsburgh mansion.

"Get out!" he said to the Rowan Campbell look-alike astride his torso.

"Gladly," she responded, pulling on her clothes and leaving at a near run.

These paid escorts were never satisfying, and the last few times, he'd gotten too rough in his frustration. The girls were beginning to refuse assignments to him.

"Speak!" he told the caller.

"We almost had her." The male voice on the other end sounded nervous, his normally deep voice rising a notch or two.

"What do you mean 'almost,'" Jarrod snapped.

"What can I say, boss? She gave us the slip." Jarrod could hear Derrick, his head of security shuffling, coughing slightly.

"And you couldn't find her again? We're tracking her phone." Jarrod's people had convinced Rowan's drunk and angry ex-boyfriend to drop a tracking device on her phone for a one-time generous payment. When they approached him again, he was sober and refused to provide more assistance, despite a second, substantial cash offer. Another man she'd permitted inside her body, inside her mind. Another man he automatically hated.

"She shuts it off when she's not using it," Derrick replied. "And we suspect she found and removed the tracking app. She stayed in her apartment for a week until she finally went on the move today. She must have been packing, because she left with boxes in a taxi, then shut off her phone. We don't know where she dropped the boxes." He paused. "And . . . I suspect she has a burner phone."

Jarrod was tempted to fire the man and his whole crew, but they weren't the first to fail. Rowan had an innate sense for impending danger.

"No hesitation or second guessing my instructions that might have caused this?" Jarrod's former head of security had quit after stating he wasn't in the business of kidnapping. Not the word Jarrod would have chosen. He merely wanted her in the same room with him, to talk to her, show her he had feelings for her and win her over. But she wouldn't come of her own volition despite his efforts, and he wasn't willing to give up. There was more at stake here than his desire for her.

"We got her flight information. The ex got a bit chatty in a pub after a couple beers," Derrick said, skirting Jarrod's question. "We planned to intercept her before she got to the airport but, like I said, she gave us the slip. She should be arriving at O'Hare later today."

"I want to know her plans. Is the ex-boyfriend good for more information?" Jarrod envisioned Chicago's big, busy O'Hare airport as a place where it was easy to lose a tail. He wanted information on where she was headed after she landed.

"His last words to us were 'Fuck you, asshole.' He's

evidently sorry he helped us. Not that I think she shared any plans with him or that he'll ever hear from her again. He's worthless."

"You think she's using a burner phone?"

"I'm sure of it. She still uses her phone at times, but the ex-boyfriend said she may have multiple burners. Some that she buys, others that her brother provides."

"Ahh . . . Griffith. I should have known." Jarrod closed his eyes, clenching and unclenching his fist in frustration. "Call me from O'Hare. Keep me updated."

He hung up the phone and lay there remembering how tracking her in the past had been more difficult in some countries than in others. Initially, she primarily photographed models from her old work community who were fiercely protective of her. Over the last two years, she'd shifted to freelance assignments in war-torn countries where he couldn't even find an internet signal, let alone an investigator willing to follow her.

Jarrod had tried, once, to introduce himself to Rowan, showing up at a Paris runway show where she was one of the supermodel stars. The pictures he'd seen didn't do her justice. Beyond her physical beauty, there was something intangible he couldn't define. He became obsessed with her.

He'd approached her at the Paris after show party. She'd worn a flowing, off the shoulder black Armani gown with simple jewelry that showed off a stunning blue quartz necklace. He learned from one of the models that Rowan only removed it for runway shows and modeling shoots where she wore whatever jewelry was assigned to her, locking the blue quartz away in a safe. Later, he became convinced it was a talisman of some sort, perhaps even the source of her magic. He desire to possess that stone was equal to his desire to possess her.

Short, with slightly thinning light brown hair and plain

features, he was under no illusions that he was physically attractive to women. It was his wealth and lifestyle that resulted in mild, albeit often short-term, success with the female species. He'd been sure, with the type of monied circles she was part of, he could impress her, easily seduce her with the lure of power and money as he'd done with other women. Yet, Rowan coldly ignored him. Jarrod winced at the memory of the moment he'd boldly reached out to touch her hand and experienced a burning sensation. His scream still echoed in his head. Her physical response to him, visceral and abrupt, should have left him hating her. Instead, the immediate look of shock on her face told him the subliminal force she emitted to push him away was superhuman. It was his first inkling that Rowan had magical powers. Whatever she'd attacked him with, it had frightened her. She ran from the room, leaving him writhing on the floor, his hand a bloody mess. When he left the Paris emergency room, bandaged, medication alleviating the pain, he contemplated the benefits of having that magic under his control. His initial lust moved to an overwhelming drive to own what she'd wielded against him. As partners, they could be a power couple beyond all power couples who had come before them.

"Ahh, Rowan. You marked me for life. I'm yours and, one day, you'll be mine." Jarrod rubbed the scar on the back of his hand, a habit enacted often throughout the day.

He was the adopted son of the late Paul Marrone. Adopting him was his mother's idea, not Paul's—a fact that instilled a deep level of insecurity in Jarrod. His parents' loveless, miserable marriage. His mother's shrill accusations followed by that slam of the front door as his father left their home, left Jarrod with a paranoia that his singular hold on Marrone Industries could be challenged by a biological child one day. He'd navigated between their icy silences and avoidance of one another until his mother died of cancer, and a year later he left for college, rarely returning home. Shock but little else filled him when Paul died in a fiery car crash with Rowan's mother, Elin.

It wasn't until later, as an adult, he'd come across information that turned his early paranoia into a deeper concern that his father had sired a child. He had no interest or intention of sharing his inheritance with anyone else. Jarrod spent long hours obsessing over the accident, concluding—without a shred of proof—that Rowan was the love child of Paul and Elin. Once he'd seen her photos, his concern moved to lust and onward to a diabolical plan to solidify his ownership of Marrone Industries and have Rowan too. They weren't blood relatives, he reasoned. She was fair game.

"We'll be a powerful alliance, Rowan—you, me, and your magic," Jarrod mused to himself. "Too bad you won't come to me willingly. That's unfortunate. But gradually, you'll see the wisdom in an alliance. I think you could love me too, but if not, you'll love what the power of our partnership brings."

Jarrod closed his eyes, shaking off the image of he and Rowan together and crashing back to the present. "Goddamn Griffith."

The fact that Rowan's instincts kicked in whenever he hunted her, as if she could smell him, sense him, and manage to avoid him, made finding her hard enough. But obviously, she'd told her brother and they were working together to thwart his efforts.

"I wonder why she's coming back to the U.S." Jarrod reached for the small remote control on his nightstand. He pressed a button, and the splashy but dark-toned contemporary painting on the wall, facing the bottom of his bed, moved to the left revealing a blown-up photo of Rowan on the runway, in a bikini.

"You and me, Rowan. We can own the world." He'd take

her now, like he would anything else he wanted in life. A gilded cage waited for Rowan Campbell.

Never taking his eyes off the photo, he imagined himself owning her, possessing her, the heat from her that had blistered the skin on his hand shifting to the heat of being one with her.

Griffith

"What's new, Henry? How's the job?" Griff paused. He didn't want his voicemail to set off any alarms. "Give me a call if you want to grab a beer and catch up."

When Henry Hudson sent his life and career spiraling downward, his friends scattering like frightened mice to avoid the taint of his fate, Griff stood by his mentor. He made the trek to the state prison to visit him. He spoke for him at his parole hearing. He tapped his contacts in cybersecurity to get Henry part-time work after his release, and even put down the deposit plus several months' rent on an apartment in an older neighborhood to give him a place to live. Griff owed a lot to the middle-aged man whose information security class had sparked a life-changing passion for cybersecurity inside him.

Griff was aware he was considered an up-and-coming rock star in cybersecurity, while his peers viewed Henry as washed up, career ruined. In Griff's opinion, the man made a mistake and paid dearly for it. No part of Henry's fall from grace had changed his skills, yet without immediate family to take him in, back child support payments hanging over his head, and a criminal record, he was adrift when released. Griff empathized.

A motherless child at an early age, he'd floated from one major to another in college while his father focused on his second marriage. He heard from, but rarely found himself in the same city or country with, the sister he adored who traveled the world.

Today he was glad he'd kept quiet when, nine months earlier, Henry's joyous text to Griff about the new full-time job he'd been offered, complete with benefits and good pay, rocked him to the core. It had taken immense self-control not to beg Henry to decline. Now Henry was right where Griff needed him to be, working for Jarrod Marrone. Griff respected his sister's right to call the shots since she would face Jarrod, but his opinion about her claims of magical powers hadn't changed. She'd created a fantasy in her mind that kept her feeling eternally connected to their mother. Griff was going to infiltrate Marrone Industries quietly, in case things didn't go according to Rowan's plan. Hopefully, she'd appreciate his actions later.

His phone pinged, signaling an incoming text message.

Henry: Dive Bar at 6:00 tonight?

Griff: 👍

Griff smiled. Dive Bar & Grille on the edge of Pittsburgh's Regent Square neighborhood was good. Not his usual hang out, but better than places Henry had chosen in the past. He'd put his foot down and made a safe neighborhood and clean interior a requirement.

Henry: Meet u at the bar.

Griff would need to tread lightly to reassure Henry that the request he planned to make wouldn't endanger his friend's job.

"Griff?" Gemma's light, childlike voice floated across the room. He shut the laptop to darken the monitors sitting on either side and turned his chair toward his office door.

"Hey, gorgeous! You leaving now?" Griff stood and walked toward her, wrapping her in a hug.

"Taxi will be here any minute." She smiled and gave him a soft, sexy kiss. Like Rowan, she nearly looked him in the eye. A sensuous floral aroma surrounded her.

"I'll walk you out. Call me when you get there." Griff took the handle of her suitcase and followed her into the hallway of his condo.

"When I get back . . . let's talk about moving in together." Gemma was looking at him with enormous brown eyes that usually melted his natural reserve.

Griff shrugged, noncommittal, as he transferred the suitcase handle to her. "We'll talk when you get back. Have a safe trip."

Gemma pressed the elevator button. "Maybe I'll see Rowan there? She's still in London, right?"

"I'm not sure since she and Peter split up. She might be traveling." Griff avoided direct eye contact, looking up at the numbers over the elevator as it climbed to the tenth floor. His lie wouldn't go unnoticed. He always knew exactly where Rowan was.

Seconds before the elevator doors closed, he caught Gemma's look. He expected the usual sad, frustrated downturn of her mouth. What flashed across her face was new—anger.

Gemma Gallucci was a fairly successful fashion model, not at the level Rowan had reached but earning a decent living. Griff had been amused when she'd approached him at a party a year earlier and, instead of flirting with him, introduced herself as a "huge fan" of his sister, asking if she could meet the once popular ex-model, Rowan Campbell. Griff told her she could if she agreed to go on a date with him. Despite his normal commitment-phobic ways, he'd found himself caring deeply for Gemma. He admired how hard she worked, giving a big percentage of her pay to her struggling extended family in Albuquerque. He loved that she had a wide variety of interests—books, museums, jazz and classical music—and little to no interest in how beautiful she was or whether she always left the house fashion-ready. She was all but living with him, by his standards. She kept clothing here, stayed with him most of the time when she wasn't off on an assignment, and vacationed with him.

"I like her!" Rowan had said when he'd finally introduced the two in London.

He wasn't sure if it was Gemma's family baggage—her parents' bankruptcy and money needs, her siblings with their addiction issues and legal troubles—or Rowan's decision to confront Jarrod with Griff's help and force an end to the stalking that fueled his reluctance to move to a permanent living situation.

Griff returned to his home office and sat quietly for a few minutes. The room was his sanctuary: walls painted a soft slate blue, gray carpet, and an assortment of Rowan's best photos arranged across three walls. The fourth large window offered a view of the city of Pittsburgh with its familiar bridges, rivers, and mountains. Gemma respected his privacy and the sensitivity of the work he did in this room. As she became more comfortable in his home, he'd find her in here looking for office supplies, but she never touched his laptop. He'd logged her in to check her flight and assignment schedules last week when her own laptop crashed and her phone battery was nearly dead. He'd been surprised at his own ease and level of trust when he stepped out of the room, leaving her alone in order to call a local store to order her a new laptop. Yet, he was unable to commit fully, keeping a level of space between them that he was surprised she still put up with. Distrust and paranoia went hand in hand with his profession. Unlike Rowan, who wanted a permanent love relationship so badly she was willing to confront Jarrod, even if it proved dangerous, Griff always vacillated, uncertain.

And then there was Maya, kind, caring, and strangely distrustful of Gemma for no logical reason. He'd developed a deep connection with his aunt as an adult. He found her resemblance to his dim, faded memories of his mother comforting. Maya had tried to step in during Griff's childhood, despite his father's lack of interest in keeping a strong connection. As he grew older, he taught Maya to use a cell phone and they texted, opening up a relationship for both he and Rowan with their aunt. She'd never been overly enthusiastic about anyone he dated, but her reaction to Gemma was downright weird. He chalked it up to Maya's belief, like Rowan's, in magic and worse—in Griff's opinion—that the powers they claimed to have were descended from medieval times and gifted only to the women in their family. The entire concept was nuts. Bonkers. He'd openly called it "sexist," which got both of them all fired up. Despite their differences, he loved Maya and Rowan unconditionally.

Griff's phone buzzed, the word "private" with no number displayed on the screen.

"Griffith Campbell," he answered, fairly sure of the caller's identity.

"Hey Griff, it's Rick Stafford. Any progress on Marrone Industries?" Rick's son had been a friend of Griff's in college. Rick tried to recruit Griff into the FBI's cybersecurity team, but Griff preferred to work for an airline. He liked the idea of less danger and free tickets.

"I'm meeting the friend I told you about tonight."

"You still sure you can trust him?"

"Yes. He owes me a lot. But he also needs the job. We'll see what he'll agree to."

"Update me after you meet with him."

"Will do." Griff disconnected the call. He'd update Rick, but if he thought for a minute Henry would be caught up in any federal action against Jarrod, protecting his friend would become the priority.

At a summer barbecue, several months earlier, Griff had cornered Rick, sharing his belief that Jarrod was dangerously obsessed with Rowan. Rowan would be furious with him, but he hoped Rick could help. Unfortunately, it appeared Jarrod needed to successfully break the law on U.S. soil before law enforcement could step in. When Rick called him a few days later to say he was in Pittsburgh and wanted to meet, Griff assumed it was about Rowan. But over coffee at Margaux in East Liberty, he learned there was an ongoing federal investigation into Jarrod's activities. Rick thought Griff's tech skills could be useful to his team.

"You have guys with as much experience as, if not more than, I do," Griff said.

"I'm not saying I don't trust them, but there have been information leaks. I want an outside, private contractor—meaning you—reporting only to me," Rick answered. "We think Marrone has a lab in the basement that's off limits. We inserted someone on the cleaning staff, but they were unable to get the names of employees with access. When our agent tried to use a key card in the elevator, it not only didn't work, someone reported the attempt, and they were fired."

"And you're not sure whether someone on your team tipped Jarrod's people off, getting your agent fired?" Griff asked.

Rick nodded, affirming the possibility, but stayed silent.

"Can you tell me what you think Jarrod is up to and why?" He'd been certain then that he'd get little information until he signed an NDA, but he wanted a clear idea of what he was being enlisted to do.

"We think whatever he's developing will disrupt the upcoming elections. Possibly a deep fake, but we're not sure. It came up accidentally in a separate investigation of one of the senators."

"I have a contact at Marrone Industries with expertise in deep fake technology." Worry for Henry had risen in Griff as he'd watched Rick sit, silent, the wheels seeming to turn in his mind.

"You think your contact is involved?" Rick had looked concerned, his mouth downturned, his brows furrowed.

"He's only been there nine months. If this is the project he's working on, I doubt he knows its intended use . . . although he'd be smart enough to suspect," Griff had answered. "Listen . . . he's out on parole, and he struggled to find full-time work until this job came along."

"And Marrone picked him because he knows that." Rick sighed. "Can you convince him to help you help us?"

"Maybe, if I present my sister's situation," Griff said. "But I won't let him feel blindsided later. I'll tell him I'm helping a federal agency . . . keep the information slim. I doubt he'll like that. He has a well-developed aversion to law enforcement. But I'm sure he won't tell Jarrod."

"Can you approach him soon?" Rick had asked, anxiously tapping his fingers against his coffee mug.

Griff watched the late summer sunlight cascade through the tall windows of the old building, touching the displays of local artwork scattered across the walls. He'd decided, in that moment, to wait. To slow Rick down and give him time with Henry before launching this delicate request. "I need to be hired by you first. NDA in hand. Paperwork done. Then a little time to talk with him over a few casual meetings before bringing this up. I want to check out his situation first."

Griff had paused, watching for a negative reaction from Rick, but the man remained quiet, expression impassive. "He's a good guy. Made mistakes, but his ethics are solid."

Rick nodded then stood to leave. Griff stood with him, offering his hand.

Taking a deep breath to shake off his worries about involving Henry in efforts to bring Jarrod down, Griff remained in the coffee shop after Rick left. He'd tapped his contacts app, touched recent calls, and chosen a name.

"Hello, Griffith! How are you?" Griff smiled at the familiar voice with its lyrical, singsong Welsh tone. She was the only person who called him Griffith. "Hello Aunt Maya! I'm good. I miss you."

"Well, you know where I live. It's a nice, sunny day and only a few hours' drive. You're always welcome."

Griff rolled his eyes, thankful she couldn't see his reaction to the community of psychics and mediums in Western New York where she'd lived since before he was born.

"She's coming home." Griff didn't elaborate.

"She'll come here, straightaway, from your place." It was a statement, not a question.

"You spoke with her about her plans?" Griff was surprised.

"No . . . we texted. But I sensed, prior, that she plans to confront Jarrod and needs my help."

Griff sighed. Maya and Rowan and all that magic crap again.

"Don't make that noise, Griffith!" Maya's voice was stern. "You choose to deny all you like, but don't be disrespectful."

"Sorry, Aunt Maya. I do respect you." Griff hoped his tone was repentant enough to satisfy her. That had been three months earlier when Rowan first introduced her plan to him.

"She's headed to the standing stones in Wales first, at my insistence," Maya answered. "Selfishly, I'm thrilled I'll see her again after so long, but I'm also worried. Coming here is dangerous."

"We have a plan. I'll get her a ticket under the name on her fake passport."

"The passport she stole from her great-aunt?" Maya surprised Griff with this statement.

"Does the family think she took it?" He had no contact with the remaining relatives, most of whom were second and third cousins. Hopefully Rowan wasn't compromised.

"No, I figured it out when they mentioned the theft to me," Maya said. "I covered for her, telling them it couldn't be Rowan because she has her own U.K. passport, which is true. She has dual citizenship via Elin, but I assumed she wouldn't use anything with her name on it to return to the U.S."

Griff sighed at the memory of their conversation. He turned his office chair to look out over the city. The winter sun, bold and bright despite the cold air sparkled across the river.

He'd ended the call when Maya headed in her usual direction, which he liked to avoid. "What about you and what's her name?"

"Her name is Gemma." He asked himself then, as he did now, why he never made the time to introduce Gemma and Maya in person. He wasn't sure he'd ever even mentioned his aunt to Gemma. "Things are the same with her, Aunt Maya. I am going to bring her to meet you one day. You can't dislike someone you've never met. Remember, it's my life. We discussed this before."

"And I told you my instincts about people are rarely wrong. Text me when your sister arrives."

"Will do. Love you . . ." Griff had ended the call before it got any weirder.

Sitting in his office now, watching the sun sparkle across

the river, he thought about the look on Gemma's face as she left. He needed to take action, make a decision.

Rowan

The trains at Paddington Station sat in solemn, parallel lines, dark green, sloped, the bullet-shaped front with a splash of yellow sporting the GWR label. Seasoned travelers conversed in multiple languages as they hurried down the platform to match their tickets to the correct car. Rowan tucked herself into a seat in the quiet car, the disguise that had kept her safely hidden from Heathrow to Paddington in place. She'd decide whether to remove or keep it when she reached Swansea. Minutes later, the train pulled away from the station and Rowan exhaled a sigh of relief. Her car was sparsely populated. No one paid an unusual amount of attention to her. Most were bent over their phones. Her eyes rested on a good-looking man about her age, his headset in place, phone on the table in front of him. A wave of loneliness swept over her. If she were able to be herself, no disguise, no stalker, she could think of a way to strike up a conversation. He raised his hand to scratch his head, the gold band on his left hand evident. Rowan turned away, gazing out the window, envying whoever waited at home for him while she suppressed the longing for human warmth and intimacy.

Dark clouds hung over multiple rows of five- or six-story, modern glass office buildings and low one-floor warehouses. Rain-streaked windows slightly muted Rowan's view as the train sped forward. Here and there the odd, ancient structure in need of repair sat amidst its contemporary neighbors, occupying land it had graced for generations. Graffiti from young, talented taggers brightened the somber gray walls lining the tracks.

Gradually, urban construction gave way to a landscape of rolling hills and green farmlands dotted with sheep and separated by low, time-worn stone walls. A rugby or lacrosse field appeared, empty now due to the weather. Rooftops on many older homes made Rowan think of Mary Poppins, her favorite childhood movie, and she murmured "chim chiminey, chim chiminey chim chim cheree" with a smile. Three elderly people, seated around a table two rows up and across, chatted quietly in Welsh. Rowan closed her eyes for a moment, rolling back to her childhood. The echo of her grandmother and her mother chatting during breakfast filled her.

Each train stop told a different story about Wales. After Swindon, hedges squared off property lines while leafless oak trees stood in a macabre spectacle of unity, stoically performing their duty of separating one open field from another where no walls had been built or hedges planted. Large warehouses in each city along the route mixed with the drab sky to create a mildly depressing scene. Once the train crossed the border from England to Wales, each stop displayed a sign with her favorite word "*Croeso*" — "Welcome" in Welsh. A warmth encircled her. Despite the many years since her mother's death, she sensed Elin nearby.

Rowan had had little interaction with the remnants of family still living here. Her Nain, as she'd called her grandmother, died when she was seven or eight years old, and her only uncle passed away the same year Elin died. It had been good to reconnect at Alice Edwards's funeral. Her childhood memories were encased in yearly trips, where the plane and train rides were more exciting to her than spending time in a small village.

The train slowed to a stop at Cardiff. Large modern offices and the rugby stadium lined up against historic buildings visible as they approached the platform. Rowan loved the retro-meets-progress sensation of Wales's capital by the sea, a stark comparison to Port Talbot which appeared frayed and holding its own by a shoestring.

She planned to take a taxi to a small B&B in Swansea. She'd called ahead and learned they were virtually empty. Although the proprietor urged her to book with a credit card, Rowan's vague excuses about not being sure exactly which day she might arrive resulted in an agreement to accept payment in cash or gift card. Tourist traffic was slim this time of year, making her stay welcome income. As Bryn Davies, she would pick up a rental car in the morning. With any luck, the rain would ease by tomorrow, making driving unfamiliar roads easier. Rowan yawned and envisioned a good night's sleep ahead, a luxury she hadn't enjoyed in a long time and of which she was in desperate need.

An hour later, carrying a backpack and wheeling a small suitcase, she checked into a B&B. It was clean and off the main thoroughfare. She'd choose street parking later to separate the rental car from her location. Locking the door to her room, she pulled a Brinks security bar from her backpack, a purchase she'd made a long time ago upon the advice of a friend, and positioned it under the doorknob for safety. It was a relief to shed her disguise. She stripped to her underwear, pulled an oversized, well-worn T-shirt over her head, and washed her face. Minutes later, tucked under a thick comforter, she closed her eyes and gratefully sank into a warm and peaceful sleep.

She awoke to the sound of rain pummeling down,

running across the windows. The digital clock on her phone said five a.m. It was dark and the bed was cozy. Rowan closed her eyes and let the rhythm of the rain lull her into a half sleep. Its steady sound was a song that harkened back to her childhood visits, snuggled next to her mother's body, safe and loved. She relaxed, inhaling a rare sensation that she was cocooned from daily problems. What was it Griff said? "Off the grid," that was it. Rowan was off the grid for a while. It wouldn't last. She'd absorb and cherish these few hours, perhaps days, before she pulled out her Alice Edwards passport and headed back to the States.

Four hours later, showered, deeply rested, and full of a breakfast bigger than her normal protein bar or bagel, Rowan stood in the shadows beside the B&B, checking out the street. Two elderly women walked by with their dogs, the soft singsong cadence of their voices touching her ears as they spoke in Welsh. Although she couldn't understand the words, the sound filled her with memories and the stone tingled against her skin.

Seeing nothing suspicious, Rowan used a burner phone to call for a taxi. Hood up, mask on during the taxi ride, she lowered her face to avoid any security cameras at the rental office, although she saw no visible signs of surveillance. Rowan chatted up the rental agent a bit, stating she was born here and trying to relocate far away from a difficult ex-husband living in the U.S., then offered her driver's license and credit card. She sincerely hoped the card was not ripping off an actual identity and would emerge as fraud when entered. The address was her post office box in London to ensure legitimacy.

The woman, whose name tag said "Bronwyn," nodded in understanding and said, "Welcome to your home country."

Rowan accommodated her request to pull down the mask temporarily and allow a check of her face to the Bryn Davies license. She noted the agency had both a handwritten log and a computer. The woman typed the credit card number into the computer. Rowan exhaled with relief when there were no questions. The card must have passed inspection. In the log, Bronwyn wrote "Mr. B. Davies", and the type of car rented. Rowan smiled. Passing her off as a man was clever. Her mother always claimed her people were the best in the world at closing ranks and protecting their own, but seeing it happen was heartwarming.

One hour after leaving the B&B, Rowan drove a small black Honda Civic, its GPS disabled, to a convenience store where she stopped to pick up fruit, protein bars, and bottled water. She added wine, cheese, and crackers for later. There was no telling how this day would evolve or how she'd feel when she returned. Rowan didn't drive often, preferring trains or taxis. She set the GPS on her burner phone for her destination and pointed the car north. A familiar tension lay across her shoulders as she focused to avoid slipping to the American side of the road. She'd forgotten how the high hedgerows encased narrow roads, creating an experience similar to that of a tunnel or a maze. As a young girl, she'd imagine a minotaur appearing suddenly in their path, despite her mother's explanation that this was a myth—and Greek, not Welsh, at that. The memories that rolled back with each turn in the road threatened to distract her.

"To the left, to the left," she said, mimicking the Beyonce tune in an effort to remind herself to stay in the correct lane. Occasionally, she repeated GPS instructions aloud. An hour and several wrong turns later, she stopped in Newport to eat, use the bathroom, and add enough gas to last until she returned to Swansea. Rowan expected her late afternoon arrival would place her in the space between light and dark signaling the onset of the day's end. She hoped to be the lone visitor at that hour.

At about three-thirty, she turned onto the A487 from

Newport and slowed down, inching up the hill, watching for the gate to Pentre Ifan. There were no cars; the small inlet from the road was empty and open for her to park. Rowan pulled in and turned off the car, sitting quietly for a moment. The dolmens were evident in the distance. Although they inhabited very little space amidst the broad landscape, they stood tall and imposing, their color reflecting the diminishing light of the gloaming. Elin had called it "the witching hour." Rowan shivered at the mild thrum of the blue quartz against her chest. Hesitation replaced certitude.

"Come."

She experienced rather than heard the word. It was her mother's voice. She shook her head as if to remove a tangle of cobwebs. Her hand lay on the stone. She didn't remember using it to call for her mother. Was Elin's voice merely Rowan's imagination? Slowly, she opened the driver's side door and stepped out, locking it behind her. The wind was mild but cold, making her glad she'd layered her clothing and replaced the hoodie with a thermal runner's jacket. She lowered the thick, warm knit cap on her head to cover half of her forehead and her ears. The wooden gate looked well kept, new, with clear signage around it. Closing it behind her, she began walking along the path toward the ancient Druid standing stones, wondering if it had been used for ceremonies or was a burial chamber. The literature she'd read was inconclusive. The yellow gorse and primrose to her left were still in bloom. Rowan stopped and closed her eyes, a memory coming back to her in which she was much smaller, closer to the ground, and touched those flowers. She inhaled the remembered sensation of her mother's hand in her own.

Rowan opened her eyes and surveyed the rolling hills and farmlands, the distant mountains, spreading outward from this spot. The pungent aroma of sheep excrement floated on the breeze, mingling with the scent of flowers and a freshly mowed carpet of green grass. A sudden, comforting sense of belonging moved through her. The stone around her neck was becoming warmer, its energy not uncomfortable but stronger than usual. Rowan touched it lightly, concerned.

She moved forward, the sky above the dolmen continuing its path to twilight. "*Gwyllion,*" she recalled her mother saying when dusk began, "it's when the spirits and night-wanderers are out and little girls should be inside, in their beds." Exactly where Rowan would love to be right now, but she needed all the power she could gather for the task ahead. She prayed this place would instill confidence in the often-faltering belief in her own abilities. Running away must stop. Rowan had to fight the evil that Jarrod harbored inside himself which manifested in an obsession for her. She shuddered, hugging herself as her mind willed her heart rate to slow down and allow her body to relax. Determination to embrace her magic, believe in it fully, filled her, partially quelling trepidation.

The ancient bluestone structure was smaller than its counterpart, Stonehenge, believed to have been built from the same Welsh resources. Yet, Pentre Ifan's stones were massive. Rowan's research, confirmed by the information signs at the entrance, showed the capstone on top weighed sixteen tons and sat balanced on three upright standing stones positioned in a triangle, hovering, tilted forward toward the shorter of the tripod holding it. At first glance, the capstone looked as if it could easily slide forward. But it had stood, immobile, for over five thousand years. One larger standing stone stood slightly apart and behind the structure. Smaller stones encircled the primary structure, creating an enclave. Larger stones lay like markers a few feet away in an uneven but deliberate perimeter. On a distant but visible mountaintop were what looked like two rounded piles. Rowan guessed a closer inspection would show the origins of the stones she now stood in front of. She found it awe inspiring to imagine early inhabitants moving massive boulders from the mountain peak down to this flat land without modern equipment, then arranging the stones in their current formation.

"Must have had help from the fairies," Rowan said to herself with a laugh.

Welsh fairies were not the elfin, Tinkerbell stereotypes of Hollywood fame. According to her Nain, the late Gwyneth Edwards, they were tall, graceful, beautiful beings who resided in bogs, marshes, meadows, streams, woodlands, and valleys. Her Nain, the Welsh word for grandmother, died not long after Griff was born. Following her death, Elin traveled to Wales less often. But Nain's voice was cemented in Rowan's brain and, even now, at age thirty-two, her bits of folklorish wisdom rolled up inside her granddaughter unbidden.

Rowan stepped around one of the stones on the perimeter. Instantly, she heard a faint, soft musical voice and wordless singing. She glanced right and left, then out toward the farmhouse in the distance, but only the sheep and mountains, aglow with the setting sun, lay before her. Hands shaking, she tucked her cell phone into a jacket pocket, then curled the fingers of her right hand around her necklace stone. It continued to radiate a gentle energy into her chest. The humming or singing remained at the same decibel level as she stepped forward, then halted in front of the circle of stones around Pentre Ifan. Her necklace shifted to a stronger pulsating rhythm against her chest. It wasn't painful, but it scared her. The only time the stone did more than a mild energy vibration was when she used it to call for her mother—its only real power being as a conduit. This level of activity combined with the strange humming was new to her. Perhaps her mother was nearby.

"Take a deep breath. You'll be alright," Rowan said aloud to the sheep, the hills, and the soft green carpet of grass surrounding her.

Despite her qualms, the place was familiar to her. The country was littered with standing stones, stone walls, and castle ruins made of stones, but she was more certain than ever that she'd been to this very spot before. Rowan shook her head to clear her thoughts. She was here today because she hoped that in this place she, like her mother before her, would strengthen the power source for her magic. It wasn't enough that in a moment of panic or rage she could point a finger or push her hand and arm out and hurt someone. In a quiet moment, she could move an object, intuit a good photo shot, or sense when danger was nearby, but that was no help in fighting a stalker. Rowan needed magic that was strong and reliable, not sporadic, and fully charged for the training that lay ahead. Once her power was at its best, Maya would teach her to summon and control it at will.

Still, her more practical nature caused her to hesitate, unsure if approaching the structure would result in help or harm—or perhaps nothing at all. Slim memories of visiting with her mother coupled with Maya's insistence a trip to these stones was necessary didn't seem like much to count on. The idea of turning back, depositing her scared, cold body into the rental car, heat turned up and radio on, rose inside her.

"Oh, Nain, I wish you and Mom were here," Rowan called out, her voice a light echo off the standing stones. "I'm afraid."

The wind moved across her like a cashmere scarf, wrapping around Rowan's shoulders, rustling the hair peeking out from below her hat. With it came remembered words, as clearly as if her Nain were standing next to her, *"You were named for the sacred berries of the rowan tree. Their magic will protect you against the fairies and spirits who curse others."*

Rowan took a step forward. Something squished under her shoe. She looked down to see tiny orange berries scattered in a circle around her. Crouching down, she picked up a handful, recognizing them instantly as rowan tree berries. Straightening to a standing position, she scanned the wider area. Not a rowan tree in sight. A tree would need to be fairly close to have the wind scatter the berries to where she stood. Even then, they wouldn't fall in a perfectly symmetrical circle around her.

"Hello, Nain," Rowan whispered. She was not alone. Her unease dissipated as an intoxicating peace crept through her. Nain, who always claimed to have named her, was with her now. Even if her concerns returned, Rowan was safe.

Taking careful steps, she moved into the hollow beneath the capstone, then turned slowly, her senses on heightened alert, hoping the prehistoric monument would hold firm for her. Her necklace was becoming uncomfortably warm now and beginning to radiate an unusual glow through her jacket. An odd, electrical wave of energy ran up her legs from the ground. One of the two larger standing stones was cold and smooth against the fingertips of her left hand, a sensation diametrically opposed to the current immediately coursing through her arm and across her shoulders when she touched it. Keeping her left hand on the stone, with her right hand she opened the top of her jacket and released the light from her necklace. It bounced off the rocks and spread a glow like a beacon across the grass at the very moment the sun made its final drop beyond the mountain. Only a few stars twinkled in the cloud filled sky. Her necklace lit the immediate space around her. Rowan's disconnect from her own body was strange, ethereal, as if she were levitating, but when she looked down at her feet, they were solidly planted on the dirt below. Despite a temperature drop in the sun's absence, her body was warm and filled with odd sensations. Rowan waited for pain, headaches, heart palpitations, but nothing came except the energy coursing through her at an increasingly quick pace.

Only the glow from her necklace and her phone, which she'd removed from her pocket, provided light. Hopefully the experience of recharging herself would be much like an electric car at an EVR station, filling her genetic battery.

Deciding she'd absorb this sensation for another ten minutes, if her arm didn't tire, and then leave, Rowan checked the time on her phone. Four o'clock. Seconds later, the glow from her necklace stone receded and a brighter light appeared. It moved toward the opening in the stones. She tensed, believing it belonged to curiosity seekers, perhaps tourists or hikers.

"Damn," Rowan muttered. "How will I explain to strangers what I'm doing?"

She glanced at her phone. The flashlight was still on, though it was much fainter than the necklace had been. Looking up, she blinked once, twice, then stared in disbelief. Before her stood what must be an apparition. A woman, with flowing reddish hair streaked with gold as if the very sun radiated from her head. She lit up the night sky, the glow cascading to white robes with a Grecian flow, cinched across her middle by a hand-tooled gold belt. Stunningly beautiful, she was smiling kindly. Every part of Rowan strained to deny the image that her eyes continued to signal to her resistant brain.

Before she could close her eyes, sure the image would disappear into the misty air when she re-opened them, a line of apparitions appeared, stretching out behind the woman. Rowan cried out, realizing one was her mother, and tried to step forward, but a force, strong but not visible, prevented her from moving from where she stood.

"Mom?" Rowan called out.

Her mother's ghostly image smiled, causing a strong bolt of longing. Rowan let go of the standing stone and reached out both arms. Her mother didn't move, but the force of her love hit Rowan hard, wrapping around her, nearly causing her to drop to her knees. Once she managed to catch her breath,

Rowan stared at the apparitions in awe. Nain stood next to Elin, and behind them were the women of her family, familiar to her from old photo albums.

"I am Ceridwen, although some might call me Witch." The words must belong to the elegant, ethereal woman standing in front of her. Rowan heard them in her head although the woman's mouth never moved. It appeared no one could speak to her in a normal way, but she could take in their thoughts. Had she fallen asleep without realizing it? Maybe recharging had spawned a mirage, a waking dream unleashed from her subconscious. She pinched her thigh, hard, wincing at the pain. She was awake. The bizarre experience should have left her frightened, but instead, a deep sense of serenity flowed through her.

"You carry our collective power. The power of many, bestowed by me."

Rowan shivered, more from the cold than the words entering her mind. She hugged herself, noticing the veins in her hands beat a visible pulse beneath her skin. As she stared at the apparition calling herself Ceridwen, a small memory of herself at age five emerged. She was sitting at the kitchen table in Nain's house, listening as her mother told the story of a goddess with the same name. A "special story" her mother had said. One which all the women in Rowan's family enjoyed.

"Why are you here?" Rowan was thankful no one could see her, on this lonely hill, seemingly talking to herself. Her instincts told her it was very likely only she could see these spectres.

"You may no longer avoid your birthright. Maya will train you to use your powers and to understand the responsibility you carry." Although the delivery was soft, the tone was firm, as if an order had been given.

"I'm trying to stop one person," Rowan answered,

shaking her head from side to side. "I'm not seeking a life mission."

The apparitions were no longer smiling at her. Rowan's mother looked sad. Ceridwen, the self-styled Witch who might be an ancient Goddess or a figment of her imagination, looked stern. Rowan's logical mind couldn't quite accept that she'd spoken to a ghost other than her mother. It was easier to believe the energy from the stones had created a hallucinogenic state.

"We've coddled your ambiguity for too long at your mother's request. That ends now. Leave and go to Maya."

"No, no . . . Mom," Rowan cried out. "Please, stay with me. Talk to me. Help me."

She tried to scream the words, but her voice rose no higher than a tiny yelp. Her mother shook her head, a sad smile on her face.

"We were there when you first fought Jarrod. And then you ran. Again, when you fought the men he sent. And then you ran. I have allowed this because you had no mother to raise you, but no more."

"Is this my responsibility? To stop Jarrod?"

Ceridwen's laugh was like clear bells pealing from a church tower across the land. *"It is your responsibility to use your powers for good, and to continue the line of women, passing your magic along, training your own daughter. In return for embracing what you were born to achieve, you will find the love you long for."*

Rowan was irritated with this demanding, holographic image before her. "I'm in charge of my life. Whether I choose love, choose motherhood, choose broader responsibilities . . . this is my choice, not your demand."

Silence settled across the lines of ghosts, the tension between Rowan and Ceridwen crackling with heat.

"I'm relieved you are finally embracing your own inner

strength and taking control rather than running in fear. For this, I will ignore your insolence. One day you will be the most powerful among us if you allow yourself to fully open the doors to your magic."

"More powerful than my mother or Maya?" Rowan could not shake the impulse to make it clear she wouldn't take orders from this supposed goddess or easily believe her words.

"Your mother was a most powerful witch, but she married the wrong man. She had to hide her magic from him, thus failing to hone her craft to a point of perfect control. It cost her her life. Maya's magic was never as strong, and her mistakes put a burden on your mother that landed her in an untenable situation."

Rowan saw Elin drop her head in shame. "You're entitled to your opinion. But I'm not going to listen to you talk about my mother this way."

Ceridwen smiled. *"Lucky for you, you're the one most like me. I took orders from no one. When you fully understand and embrace your power, your magic will grow. But it will never grow greater than mine, and only I can strip you of your magic . . . which I will do if you continue this frivolous, childish refusal. The world waits for you, Rowan. Stand tall and do not fail."*

As suddenly as they appeared, the ghostly women left, absorbed into the mist.

Her necklace lay dark and still. Rowan sobbed, wailing like an abandoned toddler for her mother. Lights appeared outside a farmhouse. Squatting down, one hand on the dirt, the other on her stone, she gulped in the cold evening air over and over again to steady her shaking body. Worried someone heard and might have reported her, Rowan zipped her jacket tightly, stood and, using her phone to light the way, moved quickly back to the car. A thousand emotions ran through her. Once inside, she turned up the heat and waited, working to center herself until she was confident she could drive. A desperate need to call Griff collided with the knowledge that not only would he never believe her, he might lose confidence in her sanity. Had the stress of running from Jarrod, the ever-present grief at the loss of her mother, and often being alone and lonely too much caused her to hallucinate? No . . . no, what she had seen was real, and despite the utter weirdness of the experience, it explained a lot. Gaps and empty spaces within her closed. Rowan was changed in a way she could not describe. She touched torso and limbs that were, outwardly, the same, but inside her body sang of renewal, of an improved and stronger psyche and body. As she let skepticism and denial fall away, a fierceness took over that was bigger than herself, that connected her to the centuries behind her with ropes of ancestral steel.

She unzipped her jacket and wrapped her hand around the stone. It was never a sure thing, but she had to try. "Mom, please speak to me. I need you." Silence. The stone was cold.

She visualized Maya in her mind's eye. Although Rowan sent a text here and there to Maya, and at times initiated a video call, she hadn't seen her aunt in person since she began running from Jarrod. Maya was the key, the way forward. She'd lived in a spiritualist community for over thirty years. Rowan knew exactly where to find her.

Rowan

It took all the concentration and effort Rowan could muster to drive back to the B&B in the dark. Her hands gripped the wheel in an effort to stop the shaking that started the minute she loosened them. She talked to herself in an ongoing, jumbled flow of words, desperate to believe she hadn't imagined seeing the mother whom, for two decades, she could only speak to using her necklace stone. Hearing the dead she could accept, but seeing a phantasm seemed, logically, to be a hallucination born of longing.

While high hedges skimmed past her like monstrous looming shadows and red lights caused her to twitch with impatience, she faced the inevitability that she could no longer straddle a line in which she only accepted in her mind and heart as much of her magic as made practical sense. The stone allowed her to speak with her mother at times. Anger and panic triggered rare, violent but justifiable reactions meant to protect herself. Magic heightened her native intuition, making her a better photographer and helping to parse those who presented danger from those she could trust.

"Mom . . . Elin . . . was it you? Did I see you? Does that

even make sense?" Rowan's teeth chattered between words. "How can I tell this to anyone? No one will believe me if I can't fully believe it myself."

The miles fell away, and soon road signs agreed with her phone's GPS that she was near her destination. Rowan envisioned a hot shower, then a glass of wine—maybe the whole bottle—with the comforter pulled high around her until she reached a level of exhaustion that would finally shut off her mind and allow her to sleep.

"Will you come to me in my sleep, Mom? I need you. I need to understand." Rowan struggled to anchor herself firmly to a world that made sense.

The only response was the GPS signaling a left turn that took her to the B&B. She parked one street away and quickly exited, still trembling and talking to herself. It was highly possible she teetered on the edge of a mental breakdown.

Once inside, she stripped and hopped into the shower, standing, arms crossed over her chest, head down as if in prayer, while the hot water beat upon her head, back, buttocks and legs until her skin was pink on one side and white on the other when she emerged. Instead of crawling into bed, she sat for a long time in a comfortable armchair in her room, a glass of wine and another of water next to her, a Welsh wool blanket across her lap, breathing slowly. She willed herself to a state of calm, her mind reduced to a pace where she could think without a descent into chaos. The shower had loosened her muscles to a point where she was no longer unsteady. She'd set out cheese, crackers, and a protein bar. They would suffice as both dinner and padding in her stomach to absorb the wine. She needed to think, not lose herself in alcohol.

Had she truly seen and heard what she remembered? Seeing a mythical fourth- or fifth-century goddess right out of *The Mabinogion* and, behind her, Rowan's dead mother could only be labeled a fantasy. But a fantasy brought on by what?

Once she'd discovered, in her teenage years, that the quartz stone could help her speak to her mother, she'd gradually come to terms with her loss. Seeing her mother as a ghost was another thing altogether. Rowan's throat constricted, and her eyes watered. Images from today sat squarely before her, refusing to fade into her imagination, demanding a reckoning, an acknowledgement from her. Memories of Elin always stayed in a place in her mind where she could both access them and maintain control. Tonight, she'd reverted to a screaming child. It was impossible her experience was more than a hallucination, yet it was equally impossible that she could have imagined anything this intense in such startling detail were it not real.

She gulped the rest of the wine and then crawled into bed, praying sleep would come quickly. Hours later, the sound of rain coming down steadily, hitting the roof and running along the gutters, woke Rowan. Disappointment washed over her. Her longing to see her mother in her dreams hadn't come to pass. Swinging her legs over the side of the bed, she sat up, fighting tears, a deep pain still pulsing inside her. The necklace lay next to the wine glass. Rowan walked to the table and picked it up, wondering if she should try, once more, to speak with Elin. Choosing morning meditation might be a better solution to help ground her. It was how she often began her day, but she suspected she'd struggle to focus.

"Mom? Can you please speak to me?" Rowan held the stone against her heart, its vibration encouraging, and waited.

"Yes, my sweet child. I'm here, but our time will be short." The familiar voice resonated in her ears only. If anyone else was in this room, Rowan would seem to be talking to herself.

"Was last night a hallucination? Did I see you? If I did, then the rest of it was real as well." Rowan kept her voice low, unsure if there were guests in the room next door.

"It was real. Do you remember playing near those stones as a child?"

"I had small flashes of memory walking up the path to Pentre Ifan. It was strangely comforting." Rowan's muscles relaxed. She'd been standing, tense, and now she seated herself in the armchair, pulling the wool blanket across her legs.

"I know seeing us, seeing me, was shocking. You cannot defy Ceridwen. From whence comes your power is the place you should most respect. We are all conduits of a larger power . . . of God. Even Ceridwen." Elin had never spoken to her in this way. Their conversations in the past had centered around Rowan's loneliness and fears followed by Elin's love and reassurance that she was always with Rowan in spirit. The limited times her mother pushed her to take ownership of her magic, Rowan sidestepped and ended the conversation.

"I'm still confused. I went there to recharge what limited magic I have, trying to prepare to confront Jarrod. I don't understand what she meant by my responsibilities." Rowan was half afraid the answer would only deepen the disorientation she struggled to shed.

"Your magic is not limited. It is unlimited. Put your responsibilities aside for now. That will come later. Like me, you'll go through a terrible trial from which you may not emerge alive. Remember, using your powers for good can mean actions that will seem the antithesis of good. You are here to do more than rid the world of Jarrod, but, for now, focus on stopping him. Maya will help you. I'll do what I can to protect you. Elin's voice was fading. She would be gone soon.

"I love you, Mom."

"My love for you is endless, Rowan."

Rowan closed the clasp on the necklace and settled it against her chest. A slight vibration from the stone mixed with her own intuition created a tingle that ran up her spine like a harbinger of danger. She checked the burner phone for the time. Six a.m. No voicemails, but there was one text message. Expecting Griff, she was startled to see it came from Bronwyn at the car rental.

> Bronwyn: Call me, please.

Misgiving crawled through her. She had to stay in Wales a few more days while Griff completed the steps they'd agreed on that would allow her to leave the country safely. Seeing that message signaled a problem that might require a new location.

Rowan pulled out clean clothes, changed, then repacked her small suitcase and backpack. She filled the coffee maker with water and inserted a coffee pod. She had no intention of sitting downstairs having breakfast this morning. A protein bar would suffice. She'd prepaid for three nights. She'd leave the key and a note, then head out. Rowan sat down to wait for the coffee and check the bus schedule to Mumbles, a small village nearby. She'd been there once while on a photo shoot at the Gower Peninsula and vowed to return one day.

"Today is the day, Mumbles," Rowan said to herself. It looked like the buses ran from Swansea to Mumbles every half hour, although the walk to the bus station would take forty-five minutes, maybe longer. Instinct said the car was no longer an option.

Rowan walked to the coffee machine and poured a cup, then hovered in silence near the door, listening for any unusual noise as she sipped the hot liquid. Next, she moved to the window and positioned herself near the left edge, out of sight, continuing to drink and watch the street below. Everything was quiet. Photography had taught her the art of patiently waiting, keeping as still as possible, to get the perfect shot. It was easy for her to stand motionless except for the hand that lifted the coffee mug to her lips. After fifteen minutes without seeing even a dog walker braving the rain, she was sure she could leave. Unfortunately, the long walk to the bus station would leave her vulnerable if Jarrod's goons were, in fact, here and looking for her. She was ready to turn away from the window when a small white truck pulled up and began unloading food and supplies for the B&B.

"Perfect!" Rowan smiled.

She called the car rental office, planning to leave a message. Instead, a quiet female voice answered. Rowan was sure it was the same woman who'd rented her the car.

"Hello, this is Bryn Davies. Is this Bronwyn? I believe you sent me a text?" Rowan waited. She could hear footsteps as the phone was taken to another location.

"A man was here yesterday afternoon," Bronwyn whispered. "He was looking for a woman named Rowan, but the picture resembled you. I assumed it was your ex-husband and thought I'd best leave you a message."

"What did you tell him?" Rowan asked.

"That I hadn't seen anyone who looked like the picture, and no one named Rowan had rented a car." Bronwyn continued to keep her voice low, an indication that she wasn't alone.

"Thank you! I think it might be best to put the keys under the mat and leave the car. Can you have someone pick it up?" Rowan gave her the street and the location where the car was parked.

"I've got an ex of my own," Bronwyn answered. "I can pick it up on my lunch hour, fill the tank, and park it round back without any fuss."

Rowan thanked her again and hung up. She removed the Brinks security bar, folding and sliding it into her backpack, knowing it could double as weapon of defense if necessary. She headed down the back stairway. A door leading to the kitchen was ajar, revealing the front desk clerk with a clipboard apparently checking a list against the boxes offloaded by the driver.

She quickly dropped the key at the empty front desk and slipped out the side door, leaving her suitcase near the passenger side of the truck. She pulled up her hood and jogged out into the rain, keeping close to hedges and higher stone walls until she reached the rental car where she slipped the keys under the mat along with thirty pounds—a thank you to the kind woman whose actions might be saving her life. The streets were still empty. She made it back to the truck as the driver was closing the rear door.

"Hello sir," Rowan called out, giving him her best smile. "It's miserable weather. Would you be so kind as to give me a lift to the bus station?"

"Ahh, well, I have one more delivery." The portly driver, bits of gray hair peeking out from his cap, sported a silver wedding band that had become tighter with weight gain and age.

"Oh, I see." Rowan gave him what she hoped was a sad, disappointed look. She was rewarded when he blushed, and then his eyebrows scrunched with concern. "I need to catch an early bus, and I can't be sure a taxi will arrive in time. The walk looks to be about forty-five minutes."

"Miss, you can't walk that far in the rain with your suitcase," the driver answered. "I'll tell you what, hop in and we'll swing by there. I can't be late for deliveries, but with this rain they might throw me a bit of leeway."

"Thank you, sir," Rowan said, hopping into the passenger seat and settling her suitcase between her legs and backpack on her lap, snapping the seat belt in place before he could change his mind.

A broad-shouldered, muscular man appeared in her line of vision at the same moment the driver shifted into reverse. Outfitted in attire that mimicked a mobster movie straight out of Hollywood, a black jacket, gold chain shining from his neck through the open collar, tight black jeans and running shoes, hair either wet or slicked back with gel, he set off every alarm for danger possible inside Rowan. She ducked her head, pretending to search her backpack while hiding behind it. The truck shifted into drive and moved a few blocks along the street.

"Did you forget something? We can go back." Rowan looked up and into the kind face of the driver who, unbeknownst to him, had come along at the perfect time.

"No, no. Everything's fine. Making sure I didn't forget my toothbrush, but it's there, way down at the bottom." She smiled at him, keeping her back to the passenger window until they turned onto a busier street.

Ten minutes later, Rowan entered the crowded shopping area connected to the Swansea bus station. She stepped into a shop catering to tourists and bought a cap prominently displaying the Swansea Swans local rugby team. Tucking her hair under the cap, she raised the hood on her jacket, then added an open umbrella before stepping outside. A quick survey of the entranceways to the bus station revealed no one suspicious or out of place. How had they tracked her? Rowan fingered the Bryn Davies identification, wondering if she should throw it out or keep it to use in Mumbles. Odds were slim that she could check in with a cash-only payment, using a fake name, and not provide identification. She had three days before Griff sent her flight arrangements.

The bus was there, people onboarding, but Rowan held back, watching. She planned to be the last to board. Suddenly, to her left, she heard childlike voices arguing. A harried looking man, balding but probably no more than forty years of age, was working hard to corral three small, unruly children while holding a fourth in his arms.

"Enough! All of you. The bus is leaving soon. Stay together and with me." He gestured toward the bus to

Mumbles and began herding the children through the entrance from the mall and shops into the bus terminal.

Rowan moved quickly to walk with him on the other side of the children. He gave her a surprised, somewhat worried glance.

"Can I help you? They seem quite the handful. I'm heading to Mumbles myself." Rowan smiled at him, put down her umbrella but kept her hood up. She hoped a woman with a cap and hoodie didn't seem strange to this middle-aged father.

He eyed her a bit suspiciously for a moment, then relief flooded his face, and he nodded. "Thank you. If you could walk behind us and keep them from running in another direction that would be a great help."

Rowan happily joined the family, pretending they were a unit. The children cut her a glance now and then, remaining wary but more subdued. To anyone watching, she hoped they appeared comfortable with her. Once lodged in bus seats, Rowan moved to sit a row behind the two older children.

"My wife will meet us there and give me a hand," the man said, tucking the smallest onto his shoulder to sleep. "They're quite a lot to manage on my own."

Rowan smiled and nodded, sliding her mask on as if guarding against illness. A scan of the people on the bus left her with little to worry about. Many were speaking in Welsh or a mix of Welsh and English. Several wore hats sporting local rugby team logos. She opened her phone and searched for a bed and breakfast in Mumbles, landing quickly on a few. The question of whether she could continue to use her Bryn Davies identification haunted her. Had they seen her at Paddington on her way to Heathrow? The disguise should have prevented her from being identified after she left the airport. When she never appeared in Chicago, Jarrod must have assumed she was still in the U.K. Did her mother's family make Wales an obvious location choice? They must be checking car rentals, hotels, and B&B's.

Thirty minutes later, Rowan sat at a picnic table situated in the middle of what appeared to be a park filled with a variety of colorful items to climb upon. It was empty, the weather too cold for little children. She was fairly well concealed by a large tree that lent an enormous shadow. Swansea Bay and the sea beyond sat behind her; boats docked on a concrete platform near the water awaiting their next adventure, and equipment and supplies left by a construction crew lay idle. Obviously, work was being done to the breaker walls. Across the road and straight ahead, a short alleyway ran between two restaurants and dead-ended at the front door to Patrick's Boathouse B&B, its Juliet balconies giving it a sweet, welcoming air. The website said it offered a choice of six large en suite bedrooms and multiple payment options.

The clear bell sound of a text message interrupted her thoughts. She pulled the phone from her pocket, assuming it was Griff. It was Bronwyn.

> Bronwyn: B&B turned same man away. TY 4 £30. I'm a single mum.

The man wouldn't give up easily. He was being paid to find her. Rowan was sure he'd try to hack the computer or look for a guest log. She hadn't signed in or filled out the little book near the front door where other guests gushed about the benefits of their stay, leaving their name and hometown. Rowan looked at Patrick's Boathouse again with a sinking feeling, then eyed the park, wondering if she could sleep outside until Griff found a solution. Her normal level of confidence that she could keep ahead of danger was turning into desperation coupled with anger. Could she employ her magic to talk a hotel clerk into a cash payment using her fake identification? How to stay safe for three days weighed upon her. Rowan considered waking Griff to discuss her options when her phone pinged again.

> Bronwyn: My cousin owns B&B. Bryn Davies was never there.

In that moment, Rowan recognized how tight her shoulders had become as she'd sat, frozen, immobile, filled with worry and uncertainty. Knots developed in her stomach, the inception of panic that chased her often and which she worked hard to elude, making her nauseous. She exhaled, trying to create a sensation of release throughout her body.

> Rowan: TY Bronwyn. We'll meet one day for a cup of tea.

> Bronwyn: It's Bron. Ask for me at the B&B when ur able to come back safely.

> Rowan: Bron . . . know anyone at Patrick's Boathouse? Need 2 book privately.

> Bronwyn: brb.

Rowan stood and stretched, confident Bron, true to her text, would be right back. She watched the rhythm of the water as she waited, the cold, damp air making her long for a warm room and a hot drink. Rowan wasn't sure how it looked to the villagers, a lone woman in a dark hoodie, huddled in the park with a backpack and suitcase. Her research had shown limited, if any, police presence. Unlike in London or large U.S. cities, she wouldn't be reported immediately as homeless, a vagrant to be questioned or shooed away. She said small, silent prayers and waited. Minutes ticked by but her phone remained silent. Worry crept in followed by angst as she visualized herself sleeping outdoors. Should she wake Griff in the middle of the night? Just then, her phone pinged.

> Bronwyn: Done. Ur checked in as me. Pls transfer £600. code 2 key & dongle coming.

> Rowan: TY. Transfer address?

She'd worked with Griff to set up e-transfer options that were as private as possible. It was for emergencies, of which this qualified. Once she issued payment, she'd jot down Bron's number, then destroy the SIM card and toss it in the park trash can. She had more SIM cards available to replace it.

> Bronwyn: 1964: code. key - 1B. morgan13@gmail.com. Be safe.

Perhaps Bron had been stalked before. It was obvious she was no stranger to men better avoided than confronted. Rowan sent an electronic reimbursement, followed by a text to Griff asking him to monitor her e-transfer account in case it was compromised. Rowan removed the SIM card, placed it on the ground, and crushed it with her foot, grinding a rock onto it for good measure before throwing it in the trash can. Backpack in place, she grabbed the handle of her suitcase and headed toward Patrick's. The front door was at the top of a small alleyway. She extracted an electronic card and room key from the lockbox, waved the card in front of a pad, heard a click, and opened the door. A challenging row of steps in front of her indicated this would not be a place for the old and feeble to stay. At the top of the stairs, a laundry room sat to her left and a door on her right led to a hallway. She paused. Someone could easily hide in the laundry room if they were able to get in. Rowan sighed, shaking her head. She was too tired, wet, and cold to deal with the possibility now. She extracted the Brinks tool as a precaution and headed upward.

Her room was off the right side of the hallway. Opening the door, she stepped into a wildly colorful environment painted lime green with a hot pink couch and pillows and, more importantly, a clear view of the alleyway to the front door where she could easily see anyone approaching. She placed the deadbolt and chain locks in place, adding the Brinks tool for extra safety. Reaching into her backpack, Rowan pulled out the phone, inserted a new SIM card, and texted Bron a quick thank you.

> Rowan: TY, Bron. Cwtch.

Rowan loved the Welsh word for "hugs" which could be interpreted beyond that to encompass any warm feeling of caring. A few minutes later, Bron's reply surprised Rowan.

> Bronwyn: Ur stone necklace is very old. If it came from ur mother, we will protect you.

Rowan's chest tightened. She wasn't sure what Bron meant or who "we" referred to. Meeting Cat, then Bron, followed by her experience at Pentre Ifan had heightened her curiosity about this network of women who believed in her magic. Women who automatically understood things about her that she was newly realizing and endeavored to shield her from harm. She took a deep breath before responding.

> Rowan: Mom died. I was 13. Someday u can help me understand?

> Bronwyn: 👍

Tears filled her eyes at Bron's kindness.

> Rowan: I hope we can be friends one day.

Hot water appeared quickly in the shower, and she let it run down her hair and body, expelling today's tension. The sound masked the long, pulsating sobs as longing for her mother enveloped her. This new vulnerability, internal walls descending and emotions she'd tucked away reappearing, was nearly as frightening as seeing ghosts and the anticipation of facing Jarrod. Finally, exhausted, she dried off and dressed in an old T-shirt and sweatpants, then crawled under the thick comforter on the double bed. Instantly, there was a sensation like arms curling around her body from behind, coupled with the smell of lavender. Yet, the space next to her was empty. Rowan closed her eyes, smiled, and gave in to a peace she had not enjoyed since she was a child.

When she awoke, it was dark outside. The curtains were open, but she'd left no lights on in the room. She stood and stretched, refreshed.

"I love you, Mom. I miss you, but I can feel your love," Rowan called out into the empty room.

Her affirmation was met with silence. The stone lay dormant. But the warm, maternal sense she'd experienced before falling asleep remained. Rowan looked out at the alley. A couple walked by on the sidewalk where it opened to the street, holding hands. Palpable, painful bands of loneliness tightened across her chest. A restaurant, hopefully filled with locals, might help. Plus, she was hungry, having missed lunch. She needed to be around people. A shot of courage mixed with need fueled her forward. Closing the curtains, she turned on a few lights and looked through her suitcase. A change of clothes and a little make-up would do it, but to be safe, she'd wear the cap and put on a mask. Once inside, she'd find a private area in the restaurant and then remove the mask when it was safe to do so.

Rowan had walked a few blocks when the sign for Gin & Juice appeared. She crossed the street and stepped into a corridor open on both ends, the opposite side leading to the beach. The entrance to the restaurant was tucked discreetly to her left. She took the stairs, noting there was a lift for an alternate exit if needed. At the top of a winding three flights of steps, she found herself in a quiet, sparsely populated room. Beautifully decorated in Victorian style, the tables were tucked in semi-private pockets along the right and left walls, softly cushioned and booth-like. Ahead, where the few clientele out at this hour were seated, was a glass-enclosed front section facing the bay and ocean beyond. It was definitely too exposed for Rowan's taste. Along the right-hand side, facing part of the beach, was a rectangular area with small tables partially hidden by plants and a dividing half wall. Should a problem arise, she'd be trapped in there. Ultimately, she chose a table along the wall in the main room where she could see who came up the stairs and entered the restaurant and the bar but remain somewhat hidden by plants, pillows, and low lighting. It would be easy to tuck into the ladies' room and then into the lift, leaving quickly if needed. She removed her mask, keeping it close by, and lowered her hoodie but left her cap on.

Rowan stirred the Purple Haze cocktail she'd ordered—a mix of Boe Violet Gin, elderflower tonic, lemon, beetroot, lavender, and sugar. Her drink stopped halfway to her lips when a tall, good-looking man appeared at the top of the stairs. Her eyes tracked him over the rim of her glass as he scanned the room, then leaned against the bar and spoke to the bartender. His wavy, dark hair moved to curly in places. His ruddy cheeks were more wind burned than the result of aging. She found herself wondering what he looked like under that casual navy Patagonia pullover, what sounds he would make if she unzipped those worn jeans fitted to what appeared to be a lean, muscular frame. She imagined what he smelled like, what it would be like if the warmth of his skin collided with hers. Rowan shook her head and struggled to regain control of herself. A hookup with a stranger was out of the question. And yet, he looked familiar. She was overwhelmed with the irrational intuition that she'd come into this restaurant on this day at this time because fate meant for her to meet this man.

As he headed in the direction of her table, Rowan realized it was Huw Evans. Excitement flooded her the same way it had when she'd met him, pre-pandemic, at a pub during a photo shoot in Switzerland. Shame mixed with amusement as she remembered thinking, at the time, *I could leave Peter for him in a heartbeat.* She'd downed a shot of whiskey either due to guilt or for courage before speaking to him. Now, like then, Rowan couldn't keep her eyes off Huw. Whomever he was meeting at the restaurant tonight hadn't arrived yet. Still partially hidden in the corner of the hightop booth, her stomach clenched as loneliness mixed with desire. She took a steadying sip of her drink.

"Hello!" He smiled at her and passed her table, then stopped and doubled back. "Rowan?"

"Could it be Huw with a W?" Rowan smiled. "How long has it been?"

"Too long." He slid into the booth across from her. The smells of his aftershave and shampoo, a musk and citrus combination, overwhelmed her senses. "I'm meeting a couple mates here for a beer. Would you like to join us when they arrive?

Rowan shook her head. "Thanks, but no. I'm here to eat and run. It's good to see you, though."

Huw studied her in a way that made her skin tingle. "Well, they tend to stand me up. Maybe it will end up only you and me."

Rowan sipped her drink and sent a fervent plea to the universe that his friends wouldn't show up.

The waiter appeared, greeting Huw like an old friend. He ordered a local craft beer without looking at the menu. Rowan was curious as to how many friends he meant, how many people would crowd into this space, and whether she should leave. She hesitated, struggling with her longing to stay and her ever present inability to trust. She couldn't let her desire get in the way of keeping her guard up.

"You'll be doing good if those two louts show up." The waiter called back over his shoulder. He and Huw laughed in unison.

Good, only two friends.

Her necklace hummed, warm against her chest, confirming her intuition that she was safe here with Huw. Her mind continued to warn anyone could be a threat, but her heart pushed her to relax and enjoy the moment.

"I remember you saying you lived in a small village on the coast, but not that it was this village," Rowan said.

"Mumbles . . . born and raised." Huw said. "Are you staying in town?"

"Yes, for a few days, then back to London." Rowan imagined taking him back to Patrick's Boathouse with her. A warm flush rose from within. She was sure her cheeks were visibly pink even in this low lighting. A little food and another drink, then she'd head back to the B&B alone.

The waiter appeared with Huw's beer.

"Could I order the creamed leek and potato halloumi," Rowan asked. Tasty and least likely to result in a gorgeous man watching her making a mess with her food. She smiled, thinking how Griff would tease her endlessly about that if he were here.

"Burger and chips for me," Huw said.

Rowan lowered her face to sip her drink again, hiding an ear-to-ear grin. She tingled with pleasure that he'd written off his friends and was now focused on her.

"Still with . . . hmmm . . . what was his name?" Huw's mouth curved into an amused smirk.

"Nope." Rowan returned the smile, crossing her arms over

her chest. "How about you? Still with . . . uhh . . . whatshername?"

Huw let out a deep belly laugh and shook his head. "Nah . . . that barely made it past three months. I tried texting you, but apparently you'd changed phones. I had no other way of finding you."

Startled, Rowan was suddenly more tongue-tied teenager than worldly woman. He'd tried to keep in touch with her. She'd given him the number to a temporary phone she used when traveling. They'd texted a few fun, flirty messages while he took a group of people on a hike and she remained in Lucerne. When she left, she'd tucked the phone away, writing him off as sexy, fun, and, like her, in a relationship with someone else. Then Covid came and confined her to London. She'd had no use for that phone and had thrown it away while packing to leave Peter.

"It looks like my mates have abandoned me this evening and it's just the two of us."

The deep, rich tones of his voice coupled with his lyrical Welsh accent made Rowan's skin tingle. All thoughts of keeping her guard up rolled away gently like the tide in Swansea Bay.

"Sounds great to me."

The vibes between them were stronger than she'd experienced with any other man. She hoped the food would arrive soon. Alcohol was weaving its hazy effect across her. Her logical mind struggled with her emotional center to write off these feelings as a symptom of her rootless life, while every part of her body responded in opposition to such a notion.

"You know what I remember clearly about our brief encounter in Switzerland?" Huw's gray-blue eyes twinkled in tandem with his smile. He ran his fingers through his hair in a way Rowan longed to do.

"I'm afraid to ask. I'd had quite a few drinks that night."

"You caused a sixteen-ounce glass of beer, set down for someone else who'd already left, to move along the bar and land in front of me." Huw was obviously unperturbed by what he'd seen, speaking as if it were both humorous and normal.

"I did no such thing. You were drunk and you obviously suffer from an oversized imagination." Rowan had been pretty intoxicated herself.

"No, you pointed your finger at that beer and it moved!" Huw was laughing now. "I said, to myself, 'not only is she sexy, she's a witch.'"

Rowan smiled despite a level of discomfort. She'd been reckless and impulsive that night. She remembered now. The way he'd made her feel had triggered a drunken desire to show off. She carefully changed the subject.

"You know, my mother was born not far from here," Rowan said. "She met my father while visiting her sister, who had moved to the U.S., and ended up marrying him and staying. But I came here with her often, as a child, to visit my grandmother."

"Are you visiting with your mother on this trip?"

"No, no . . . she died when I was thirteen." Rowan's eyes grew misty.

Breaking down into tears yesterday, and now this display of emotion, belied the tough woman she strove to be. However real or imagined, the belief that her mother's presence hovered nearby daily since she'd arrived in Wales was changing her, softening her in a way she wasn't sure was helpful. "I'm on vacation. I don't have a lot of family left here."

"Sorry about your mother. I lost my father when I was twenty." Huw was leaning on the table now, arms folded. She inhaled, breathing in every sensation he exuded, and reached for his hand. Desire flowed through her in a way that made her want to throw caution out the door. The waiter appeared with their food, his mouth curving upward as she pulled her hand away.

Huw tapped his drink and hers. "Refills for both, please."

The break caused by the waiter brought a moment to steady herself. Rowan calmly cut the grilled halloumi into bite size pieces she could eat without danger of spinach or cheese ending up between her teeth.

"Are you still leading groups of hikers?" Moving the conversation to Huw eased Rowan's tension. Eating and listening put her in a safe space where she could slow the pace of her heart and its crazy, instinctive reaction to him.

He pulled out a business card and pushed it toward her. She loved that he used the traditional Welsh spelling of "Huw." Apparently, the hike in Switzerland had been part of an actual business he ran which offered guided excursions.

"I was born in Wales. Went to uni here to become a software engineer and then took a job in Belgium with a large corporation," Huw said as he squirted ketchup on his burger and cut it in half. "I'd been hiking with my father since I was a child. He ran weekend outings for local tourists when it fit his schedule. In Europe, I used every opportunity to hike somewhere new—Switzerland, France, Spain. I even walked trails in the Grand Tetons while on a business trip to the U.S. Hiking kept me connected to my father after he was gone."

"Did your job bring you back to Wales?" Rowan couldn't fathom how such a large life could be pared down to existence in a small village.

"In a way it did. I got tired of corporate life," Huw said. "My mother was facing medical issues. I guess you could say that, and the pull of my roots, brought me back about five years ago. Then I gradually turned the pleasure of hiking into a business."

He broke eye contact, shifting his gaze to the table. Intuition told her there was more to his career change than he'd shared.

"Are the hikes you guide primarily outside the U.K.?" Rowan doubted a hiking business was any more lucrative than photography. Unlike Huw, she had the savings from her modeling days and owned no property to maintain or car to repair.

"About fifty percent are here and the rest are week-long hikes in other countries throughout the year. Mumbles is an expensive place to live. It attracts people who can afford either the local hikes or the out of U.K. getaways." Huw lifted one half of the large burger, ready to eat and listen. "And what about you?"

If she wanted to keep things going with Huw, she'd have to offer a level of truth to gain his trust. Still, she didn't know him well enough to be confident that he wouldn't innocently share details about her with others. Once she left the restaurant, she'd never see Huw again. It was a fluke, a few minutes of flirting and fun.

"You already know everything about me," Rowan said, her tone light, joking. "I'm a freelance photographer. I'm an American with a Welsh mother. I'm single."

She paused and winked at him, watching with pleasure as his face flushed red, his mouth quickly chewing what appeared to be a messy but juicy burger.

"I tried to look up your photography online after we met," Huw said, once he'd swallowed and could speak again. "I couldn't find you anywhere online."

Rowan was moved by the lengths he'd gone to find her. Any other man would have triggered in her the sinking feeling that she had yet another stalker, or a crazy fan from her modeling days. "Hand me your phone."

Huw popped a French fry in his mouth and pulled a

phone out of his pocket, handing it to her. She quickly typed into the search bar and pulled up her website.

"Wow! These are amazing!" He slid his finger left, carefully considering each photo.

"I publish under a pseudonym, and I keep the website name a bit difficult to connect with me," Rowan said. "Long story. Most people get the address from me or through my friend who manages the site."

A friend had built a website that displayed her best work, complete with a secured form through which customers could order prints of her photos. Anyone wishing to hire her was required to fill out a separate form, but ever since Jarrod tried to engage her services, the website content was changed to display "Not taking new clients." Rowan considered herself a photojournalist specializing in human interest shots of people and places, often intertwined with global events. She worked only with people she trusted, even if it lowered her income. All acceptance of assignments and communication were done online, through a management company owned by the same friend who handled her website, and the payments were deposited in an account under her pseudonym. She gave no interviews and allowed the friend to describe her as "reclusive" and "private" to anyone who pushed to meet her.

"Why don't you use your real name? I mean you've won awards for many of these photos under a fake name." Huw's eyebrows knitted together. "You're an incredibly beautiful woman, Rowan. Why isn't your picture front and center here?"

"It's for my safety." Rowan watched Huw's eyebrows arch, concern evident on his face and in the way he shifted his body back into the booth. "There are a lot of weirdos out there. Me? Unfortunately, I have a stalker."

"Like a crazed fan from your days as a model?" Huw looked worried, either for her or for himself.

"No. Worse. A powerful man who wants me and, let's say, my ability to move a glass of beer across a counter."

She waited for a response or a change in expression. Instead, they ate in silence for several minutes. Rowan readied herself for whatever excuse Huw would make to get the hell out of the restaurant. It was as honest as she'd been with anyone besides Griff in a long time, but it came with risk. Sadness rolled across her. Silence sat between them as she waited, worried he would leave. Then Huw leaned slightly forward, beer in hand, and locked his eyes with hers. She was unable to interpret whether his body language messaged acceptance or rejection, but she was sure he'd made a decision.

Rowan looked down at her half-eaten meal, her appetite gone, then up at Huw. "I wouldn't blame you if you get up and walk away. But every part of me is hoping you'll stay."

"I don't want to walk away from you," Huw answered, his gaze gentle but not pitying. "How long before you leave? I assume you're not here permanently?"

A deep sense of relief washed over Rowan. It was astonishing how much his words mattered. The most he could be for her was a one-night stand. She had to be clear about that for him and for herself. "I'm not sure yet. He tracked me to Swansea, which is why I came here." Rowan pushed her plate away from her, moving her drink into its place. She needed to be cautious when answering. "My brother's making flight arrangements for me."

"And the stalker . . . he's here in Wales?"

"No, he's in the U.S. His hired thugs are here . . . looking for me."

"Where are you staying that you believe they won't find you?" Huw's forehead creased with worry lines as he reached out and took her hand in his.

"Patrick's Boathouse. Someone—a Welsh woman—

booked it for me in her name." Rowan curled her fingers around Huw's and squeezed, his warmth reassuring.

Huw was silent. He'd pushed his plate aside and appeared to be thinking. Their flirting had devolved into a heavy conversation. She'd laid a lot more facts on him than was normal for her. Rowan's gaze traveled across his ruddy cheeks to the small beginnings of crow's feet in the corners of his eyes. She shivered with desire. Her hands ached with a need to touch him. The fluttering sensations inside her, fueled by alcohol, were taking over and it both frightened and excited her. Huw looked up. His probing gaze created the sense he could read her mind. Heat ran everywhere in her body.

"Is this stalker after that?" Huw pointed his finger, and Rowan instinctively let go of his hand to cover her necklace.

"Why do you ask?" Once again, people here appeared to recognize her necklace.

"It looks valuable," Huw said with a shrug, as if he harbored nothing more than curiosity. "And I may have heard a few local myths about blue quartz stones like yours."

The corners of Rowan's mouth turned upward in amusement. "Are you one who believes in myths and magic?"

Huw laughed off her question, obviously embarrassed. "My grandmother believed in such things and loved to tell me stories of witches, goddesses, and magical stones when I was a child."

"Maybe you're afraid me and my stone will work a little magic on you?" Rowan gave him what she hoped was a sexy wink.

"I'm afraid that's already been done, Rowan, and now I'm asking myself what you have in store for me next." The very last thing he looked was scared, his face split by a broad grin of what could only be described as anticipation, his arms crossed over his chest, waiting.

Rowan took a deep breath and gulped the rest of her

drink. She was hungry for him, for human warmth, and she was willing to lower her defenses in a way she hadn't done in a long time. She rested her hands in her lap to hide their trembling and looked directly into Huw's eyes.

"We'll have to leave here for you to find out what magical plans I might have for you." She hoped he was unaware of the mix of apprehension and anticipation inside her. Hookups with strangers were not normal for her. She'd had flings with photographers she worked with, then the longer stint in London with Peter that lasted primarily because they were trapped by the pandemic. Rowan's head told her to run, cut this conversation with Huw and disappear. Her entire body and the necklace now vibrating against her heart were telling her the exact opposite.

Huw leaned forward until, if she had done the same, their lips would be touching. "Maybe you'd like to give me a tour of Patrick's Boathouse? All the years I've lived here, I've never had a reason to take a look."

Rowan stepped out of the booth and pulled the hoodie up over her head, then slid the mask over her face. Huw paid the bill, leaving a small pile of pound coins on the table as a tip. Watching her disappear into her clothing like a thief hiding from security cameras might result in him regretting his request. But he said nothing, instead following her in silence. Every inch of Rowan tingled with intense desire unlike any she'd ever experienced. She stayed close to Huw, eyes darting in all directions, looking for anything or anyone who appeared to be suspiciously out of place. He slipped his hand into hers and they walked quietly to Patrick's. She'd give a lot to know what he was thinking and why she was beginning to fold into a sense of safety with him. It made no sense, and yet she was powerless to stop the forward motion she'd set in play.

Once inside, Huw hiked the stairs two at a time, waiting for her at the top. In her room, she relaxed, unzipped the hoodie and pulled off the cap, mask, and hair scrunchie, shaking her hair loose. She heard a hearty laugh and, thinking it was directed at her, turned to look at him.

"Do you think there's enough green in this decor?" Huw chuckled, his amusement lowering the tension but not the heat between them.

Rowan smiled as she turned on a smaller tabletop lamp and turned off the overhead light. She'd closed the curtains before leaving. Huw watched silently, for which she was glad. She wanted him, no words, no explanations. She'd be gone in three days with no certainty of returning. The option to enjoy a leisurely, slow advance to this moment across multiple dates was out of the question. It was a now or never moment. She walked toward Huw knowing her need, her vulnerability, were probably evident on her face, in her body language.

He leaned in to kiss her. She responded, their clothes coming off as they moved onto the bed, connecting skin to skin. A deeper need than lust was being filled. It scared her, seared through her, striking a chord deep inside. Afterward, they both fell asleep, spooned together, breathing as one. Rowan woke up to a room that was dark except for the small table lamp they'd never turned off. She reached for her phone. The digital screen said four a.m. Gently extricating herself from Huw, she padded on quiet feet to the bathroom and shut the door. The glare of the bathroom lights was a shock. She took a long look at her face. She appeared no different than she had yesterday, yet her entire being had been rocked into another universe, into a place she never wanted to leave. Rowan splashed cold water on her face, working to allow her mind to take over from her emotions, then towel-dried herself and took a deep breath. Shutting off the bathroom light, she stepped into the bedroom, turned off the table lamp, and wrapped herself in a soft wool throw laying across an armchair. Carefully, she peeked around the corners of the curtains. The B&B parking area looked the same. Quiet, deserted at this hour except for one car sporting the bright green of what appeared to be a car rental sticker. Not something a local would own. Still, it was a B&B for travelers.

She moved the curtain back into place, picked up her phone from the nightstand, and sat in the armchair. She couldn't let last night cloud her judgment or keep her from staying alert. She checked her phone. No messages. She turned off the sound and texted Griff.

> Rowan: What's up with travel home?

The screen stayed quiet. She heard Huw move, watching his hand reach out into the empty space where she'd been. She pushed down the longing to crawl back under the covers with him. First, she needed to think, and to hear from Griff. Looking down at the phone screen, she waited.

"Are you coming back to bed?" Huw's voice sounded gruff, raspy with pre-dawn sleep.

"Yes, sorry. Used the loo and got caught up checking my phone for messages." Rowan hoped she sounded casual and normal. "Waiting to hear from my brother about travel reservations."

Huw was silent. She could hear him breathing although he made no movement. His arm remained across the empty space. Perhaps he'd fallen back asleep.

"I don't want you to leave." Huw sat up, facing her.

Rowan watched him without responding. Fear clutched her heart, not only for her own safety but for his.

"I mean . . . after what happened between us last night . . ." His voice trailed off.

"What I feel between us is new to me," Rowan admitted.

"And yet you're going to leave." Huw's voice was sad.

"And I'll remember an amazing woman who then disappeared again, leaving me holding only a memory."

"It won't be like that this time." Rowan stood and walked to the bed, crawling in next to him, laying on her side. The tension was coming off him in waves. "I don't want to leave you."

She touched his face softly, then wove her fingers through his, feeling him relax.

"Then don't. Don't leave. Stay and let's see where this goes." Huw kissed her, pulling her closer, leaving only the smallest of spaces between them.

As she relished a different type of magic, Rowan promised herself she would stop Jarrod once and for all.

Jarrod

The dog-eared manila folder lay on his desk. He knew the contents by heart, but surely he'd missed something. Unfortunately, figuring that out would have to wait because Ken Jeffries, the CFO for Marrone Industries, sat in front of Jarrod delivering another difficult quarterly report. Profits were down, and their newest products were stalled in the pipeline following the resignation of the head of product development —the fourth person in that role in three years, all of whom resigned.

"You don't need people who are great with the numbers, Jarrod. That's what you have me for," Ken said. "You need people who are right-brained, innovative. Stop driving them away."

"I'm not driving anyone away," Jarrod snapped, regretting his defensive tone the minute it left his mouth. "I don't handle creative types well. They're soft, weak."

"Well, two of the guys who quit weren't required to sign an NDA or a non-compete. They went with competitors, and they're killing it over there, costing us business." Ken stood up, adjusting the button on his suit jacket. "We're interviewing a replacement. If you bully this one and she quits, I'll be leaving too. I've had enough."

"Enough of what, Ken?"

"You're not your father or your uncle. If you want to get where they were, then grow up."

"Go to hell." He'd lost track of Rowan again. His obsession was spilling over into every part of his life.

"And Jarrod . . . quit chasing after that ex-fashion model. She's not interested in you."

Jarrod clenched the sides of his leather chair and glared at Ken. Having his father's success thrown in his face dredged up painful memories.

"Stick to Marrone Industries business and stay out of my personal affairs," Jarrod snapped. The contents of the folder on his desk were the source of his ongoing belief there was a biological child who could claim a right to half of Marrone Industries. Jarrod believed Rowan was that child and, since they were not related by blood, had convinced himself that once he made her his partner in all ways possible, the threat would be removed. For now, he kept that suspicion to himself, sure Ken would turn against him in favor of any alternative leader.

"You're paying a crew of questionable guys you list as 'security' to jet-set around the world looking for her," Ken replied. "I'm the CFO. That makes your lovesick obsession—and the money it costs—my business.

"I can't elaborate, but I think she's the key to a secret my father and Ray took to their graves," Jarrod shot back.

Uncle Ray took him to baseball games and groomed him for a role in Marrone Industries, the multi-billion dollar software company he and his brother, Paul, created, and attempted to bridge the gap between Jarrod and his father. When Paul died, Ray took over. The plan was for Jarrod to succeed him when he was ready. But as Jarrod took on more senior roles, the employee complaints began. Women labeled him a misogynist and then filed official discrimination claims with human resources. Jarrod subsequently targeted employees who complained, finding subtle ways to fire them.

"And will she improve sales and strengthen the company? She obviously wants nothing to do with you." Ken's face registered an infuriating level of scorn. "You're where you are because Ray died. If he hadn't, I doubt you'd still be here regardless of your last name."

"I took this type of condescending lecture from Ray, but I won't take it from you. One more time and you're out." Jarrod glared at Ken.

"And who will agree to take my place?" Ken said, snorting in amusement. "I'm the third CFO in as many years."

"Get out." Jarrod turned his chair, its back facing Ken, and waited until he heard the office door close. Silence permeated the room.

While his uncle was still alive, Jarrod waited one night until Ray had gone home and then went through his files. He looked for proof, documentation, that offered a reason why Ray was distancing himself from Jarrod, lowering his inclusion in key meetings and access to financial reports. Ray seemed pre-occupied, no longer interested in training him for bigger things. Jarrod planned to find anything he could leverage if Ray attempted to push him out of the company. Discovery of the file in front of him had been a disturbing surprise. Definitely not what he'd been looking for.

Jarrod opened the folder. The original documents consisted of the police report from the car crash that claimed the lives of his father and Elin Campbell, two pictures, and a partially torn piece of note paper with Ray's nearly illegible scribblings. The first picture showed Rowan, looking like a young gazelle, standing on a runway in a clinging black gown. In the second picture, she was seated under a tree with a small boy. An inscription the back said "*Rowan and Griffith, ages 16 and 10*". The police report noted witnesses saw an unexplainable flash of light, its source unknown, which seared the car in two before it burst into flames. The bodies were severely burned, yet a blue quartz necklace survived unscathed. Investigators who touched it singed their hands. It was gently rolled into a container by fire fighters using thick, fire-resistant gloves. Notes showed police officers who delivered the necklace to Elin's family were shocked when Rowan placed it around her neck with ease, closing the clasp. The report concluded the stone retained heat from the fire and, by the time it was returned, it had sufficiently cooled to allow human touch.

"If they'd seen what I've experienced, they'd think differently," Jarrod said aloud, rubbing the scars on his right hand.

Uncle Ray's notes regarding his off-the-record conversations with police officers were more interesting. No one had been able to touch the stone itself, even days after the accident. When Rowan placed it around her neck, it glowed for a few seconds, then became nothing more than a simple necklace with a blue quartz stone. All notes dated prior to the accident were cryptic and in Paul Marrone's handwriting. The notation "*get DNA results for myself and child*" first shocked then angered Jarrod. Next to it, Ray had written the name and phone number of a private investigator ,"*follow up on Paul's work to find heir.*" It was this notation that had rocked his world.

"It's not enough that you've demoted me? Now you think there is a biological heir and they should replace me?" Jarrod said when he confronted his uncle.

"Mind your own business and stay out of my files or I'll fire you," Ray answered. "Focus on improving and you'll have nothing to worry about."

A month later. his uncle died of a heart attack at his home, alone. There was no investigation. He had a history of heart issues. Jarrod seized control of the company and kept his focus on which of Elin Campbell's children might have the power to take part of Marrone Industries away from him. All attempts to find the investigator failed. The man had closed his business and disappeared. Jarrod hired someone to break into the PI's storage container and search his files, but they found nothing regarding Paul Marrone, Elin Campbell, or Elin's children. The notes from the police and Ray about the blue quartz stone necklace poked at Jarrod, eventually leaving him convinced that both Elin and Rowan had above normal abilities of some type. Did that apply to Griffith as well? It appeared Ray thought these abilities important enough to jot down.

Jarrod had taken a day off, long ago, and stood at the edge of the Lower Frick Soccer Field in Frick Park to watch a young Griffith Campbell play. As a child, Griffith displayed no exceptional skills or magical abilities. The boy looked like Elin, not Paul. Jarrod had later hired a hacker to access files at the university Griffith attended, learning he was an exceptionally intelligent student with a higher-than-average IQ majoring in computer science. Changing his focus from Griffith to Rowan led to where he was today. Jarrod flew to France to attend one of Rowan's fashion shows. He hadn't been sure how to confirm whether she was Paul's child, but he had convinced himself an empty-headed model would be no threat to his position as CEO of his father's company. He'd learned the hard way that Rowan did not fit that stereotype.

"Jarrod Marrone," he'd said when he approached Rowan at an after show cocktail party. "Are you free for dinner tomorrow?"

He'd seen the revulsion on her face, her skin flushing red while her eyes displayed a flash of panic that was odd, considering they'd never met. The blue quartz stone hanging from her neck was mesmerizing. He'd touched her hand and, moments later, he was lying on the ground dazed, in excruciating pain. Looking down now at his scarred hand, Jarrod remembered his vow that day to control both Rowan and her magical stone. Over the years, his belief he could win her over, and perhaps marry her, had been reduced to the goal of capturing and owning her in any way possible. He was aware she loathed him. His current plan involved more drastic measures. The costs Ken complained of covered the construction of a very special place. Jarrod was building a cage for Rowan. Just thinking about it made him smile.

Griffith

Warmth, the clink of glasses, and the low hum of voices greeted Griff as he stepped inside Dive Bar & Grille on South Braddock Avenue. He scanned the bar. Henry was seated at the far end, beer in hand, watching a Pittsburgh Penguins hockey game.

"Couldn't wait for me?" Griff patted Henry on the shoulder and then shook the older man's outstretched hand. "Parking was a bitch as usual."

"Can't sit at a bar without a beer in front of me." Tall and lanky with a graying ponytail and sporting a few faded tattoos on his forearm, Henry looked more artsy than tech geek and ex-con. He was a natural fit for the neighborhood.

"Yuengling draft . . . sixteen ounce," Griff told the bartender as he eyed a group of men at the far end of the bar, all within earshot. "Think we should move to a table?"

"You're gonna make me miss the game," Henry grumbled.

Griff pointed to the sparsely populated dining area. "Table or booth?"

He understood Henry's attraction to the place. It was walking distance from his flat. Four televisions screens above the bar covered various sporting events. If there was nothing to watch that suited Henry, a pool table and dart board in a separate room beckoned.

"High-top table. I can see the game with enough space that those guys won't hear us." Henry moved toward one of three high-top tables, taking a seat facing the television screens. "They're pretty loud anyway. Probably can't hear beyond their own conversations."

"How's the job going?" Griff slipped his jacket over the back of a chair and sat down, taking a satisfying gulp of beer. He'd have preferred the empty, comfortable looking booths lining the wall.

"Money's good. I'm managing a smart, young team I like. Boss is an a-hole," Henry said with a smile. "After prison I can put up with anything."

Griff nodded. "How's the food here? Last time we only had drinks, but I'm hungry."

Henry laughed. "Don't worry, food is good."

Griff scanned the menu, then waved a waitress over and ordered fish tacos. "Henry? Drinks and food's on me."

"Bacon gouda burger, medium well, with tater tots." Henry ordered without opening the menu.

Griff loved that, outwardly, he and Henry came across as complete opposites, but inside they enjoyed the same jokes, the same technical topics that put others to sleep, and the same wariness of people. He leaned back in his chair, glass in hand, and took a look around the restaurant. The dining area plus bar was smaller than his living room and kitchen. If the room was packed, they'd have had to take this conversation elsewhere. Tonight, the only occupants were the bartender and the group at the bar, most in muddy work boots and Pittsburgh Penguins hockey jerseys or sweatshirts, their worn winter jackets hanging off the sturdy chair backs. Griff mentally tagged them as regular customers.

White lights, strung across parts of the ceiling, gave a sense of anticipation of a party or upcoming holiday. Although incongruous to the rest of the decor, which alternated between diner-like booths and standard kitchen tables, they created a friendly ambiance. There were twice as many low tables and booths as there were higher tables.

"What's with the lights?" Griff asked.

"Karaoke night. Every Thursday," Henry said, with a chuckle. "You should try it. Singing off key is not only allowed but expected . . . at least by the audience!"

"The more you drink, the better they sound?" Griff laughed. "I'll pass, but I might challenge you to a game of pool one of these days."

They both watched the game until the waitress arrived and delivered their food order.

"It's good to see you, Griff," Henry said, grabbing the bottle of Heinz ketchup on the table and slathering it over his burger. "But a serial texter like you would be more inclined to shoot over one quick line to ask how my job's going."

"I need to talk to you about Jarrod Marrone." Griff shifted in the chair. His foot tapped nervously for a few beats before he willed his body to be still.

"Ahhh . . . the a-hole boss. You aren't gonna make me lose this job, are you?" Henry asked. "Even though I owe you Griff, I can't lose this gig."

"No . . . no. That's the last thing I want to be responsible for." Griff put up his hand as if to stop the very thought. "But I do need your help. Hear me out. If you decide you want no part of it, I'll respect your decision."

Henry began eating his burger, chewing slowly, alternately watching Griff and the hockey game. Griff took a few bites of his taco, stalling as he considered how to proceed. His friend had a lot on the line, but he was willing to bet Henry had seen a few concerning things at Marrone Industries.

"It's my sister, Rowan." Griff took a deep breath, then focused on Henry, keeping direct eye contact to measure his response. "Jarrod Marrone has been stalking her for several years."

Henry's eyebrows lifted in surprise. "If I remember correctly, she's gorgeous . . . and a pretty famous fashion model, right? Doesn't she have the influence to do something about this?"

"She quit modeling after she had one too many encounters with his obsession. She's been living a semi-nomadic life as a freelance photographer while you were . . . well, gone," Griff said.

"Locked up." Henry took a drink of beer.

"She made attempts to engage law enforcement, but he's too well connected. And she can offer no definitive proof." Griff paused. He focused on his food and waited.

Henry nodded but offered Griff no response.

"Jarrod has a crew of thugs with orders to track her. They've tried to shove her into cars, chased her down city streets, followed her on the London subway. It's nuts." Griff shook his head, his face hot, flushed with the fury that rose in him each time he imagined everything his sister had been through. "She's done running from him. She's coming home . . . back to the U.S. . . to confront him."

"Let me get this straight," Henry said, setting his sandwich down and wiping the residue from his lips and hand with a napkin. "Marrone has been trying to kidnap her, he's too connected for complaints to law enforcement to work, and she thinks marching in and having a talk with him is the way to go?"

Griff nodded. "That pretty much sums it up."

"Is she planning to show up packing—a gun, a taser, mace? What's her defense strategy?" Henry's face registered concern, his mouth in a severe line.

"Try not to fall off your chair. She claims she—along with my late mother and our Aunt Maya—was born with magical powers." Griff shook his head to indicate his own disbelief.

"She thinks she's a witch?" Henry was very still. He wasn't laughing or rolling his eyes. Griff couldn't tell whether his opinion was Rowan's claims to paranormal abilities were valid or that Rowan was crazy. "Well, if she's not taking a gun, she'd better have magic. Otherwise, she's in deep shit. Does she know you're looping me in?"

Griff was surprised at the question. He wasn't sure what he'd expected from Henry, possibly a response more along the lines of a half-dozen reasons why he couldn't get involved. "No. Rowan developed a plan—a pretty good one, I might add—and I'm her tech support. I'll get her on a plane under an alias and help her move around with, hopefully, no visibility after she arrives."

Griff could hear the irritation in his own voice. "She thinks my Aunt Maya will teach her to use this supposed magic against Jarrod. I think that's a bunch of hooey. If I don't develop my own, independent, game plan, she'll end up kidnapped or worse."

He hesitated, glancing at the bar behind him again. The Pens scored and the bar-side crowd went wild. Keeping his voice low, he leaned forward to ensure Henry could hear him. "The feds are looking at Jarrod. He and a politician—not sure which one—are up to no good with deep fake. I spoke with an FBI contact about Rowan. They can't help unless Jarrod grabs her or hurts her, but they requested my help with their investigation. I haven't done anything yet."

Henry suddenly looked pale. A small hand tremor was visible as he reached for his beer. Tiny beads of sweat appeared on his forehead. Henry's aversion to law enforcement, coupled with a desperate need to keep his job, were most assuredly, in

Griff's opinion, creating a mountain of internal stress for his friend.

"What protections will there be for me if I agree to help you?" Henry waved his hand in dismissal as Griff opened his mouth, ready to roll back any negative assumptions. "Don't, Griff. What you're asking can end in a lot of ways, most of them not necessarily good for me. I want assurances from you, not the feds. You know I don't trust cops."

"I didn't give your name. I said I had an inside contact who would need to be protected." Griff looked Henry in the eye, hoping to transmit all the trust his friend needed from him to agree to help Rowan. "No hacking. I'll do that. I'll find a way into the company's system. I'd like to monitor for a short amount of time before Rowan confronts Jarrod. If I uncover information the federal investigators want, then maybe I'll share . . . but nothing will trace back to you."

"That sounds great, and it would work if . . ." Henry's voice trailed to silent.

He appeared to have a comment resting on the tip of his tongue. Griff watched Henry's face carefully close, like plantation shutters aligning against a coming storm. Not even a muscle twitched. His friend had once worn his emotions clearly on his face, but incarceration wiped that clean. He was now a master at hiding his interior thoughts and emotions.

"I'm sure Jarrod wouldn't hesitate to leverage your past against you," Griff said. "If I keep you on a need-to-know basis, it's to protect you."

"You don't understand." Henry crossed his arms over his chest defensively and sighed. "I suspected things might not be on the up and up, but I pushed those thoughts down. No chance I'm making the mistakes of my youth and charging forward as Mr. Do Right."

"Are you saying you already knew about Rowan?" A sliver

of anger emerged in Griff. The Henry he'd always known would have called him immediately.

"No . . . well, yes and no. When I took a cigarette break, I heard Marrone's private security team—who I'm sure are the thugs you've referred to—talking about his obsession with a woman. They never attached a name, and I only caught bits and pieces of conversation."

Griff let out a sigh of relief. "Then what do you mean 'things that aren't on the up and up?'"

"Have you heard of Huw Evans or MyShadow?"

"Yes, of course. Evans is the brilliant designer of MyShadow, an early deep fake app. It's been a few years though." Griff sorted through his memories now. "He dropped out of sight after he sold MyShadow for enough money to live off of for two lifetimes. I heard the buyer lied, telling Evans he could stay on and manage the app development, then reneged on that promise."

"Right." Henry nodded in confirmation. "MyShadow was then resold to none other than Marrone Industries. Jarrod Marrone hired me to run a private, limited access only, lab on the ground floor of his building where young, hand-picked tech geniuses report to me and work to take MyShadow to the next level."

Griff gave a low whistle, stunned. The waitress appeared, and Griff ordered another round. Turning to Henry he said, "After that revelation, I might need to order something stronger."

Once two fresh drafts were placed in front of them, Griff waited to see if Henry would offer more. "I'm guessing you have an NDA?"

Henry nodded, affirmative. He dug into his pocket and placed a handful of change on the table. "Let's say that a penny is 'yes' and a nickel or dime is 'no.'"

"Seriously?" Griff let out a hearty laugh. "This is me, Henry. I always have your back."

"You, yes. The feds, no." Henry lined up the coins and waited.

"You're improving MyShadow and Jarrod's focus is on politicians?" Henry moved one penny over to Griff.

"POTUS? Congress? State elections?" Henry moved one penny, then another one penny, then a nickel, separating each from one another with a space in between.

"The primary elections?" Henry moved one penny.

Griff stared down at the little pile in front of him. "Holy shit! Did he openly tell you he wants to use this to affect the primaries?" A dime moved toward him.

Henry leaned forward, his voice low, gravelly from the cigarettes that calmed his nerves several times a day. "Officially, my job is to improve on software Mr. Marrone purchased that will become a new Marrone Industries product for launch this spring."

"And yet you're in a limited access lab in the basement which, I'm guessing, other employees may not even know exists," Griff said, watching as Henry nodded.

"Are you working with Huw Evans?" Griff asked.

"No," Henry said.

"Will you?"

Henry shrugged. "Not that I'm aware of."

A new level of panic, equivalent to his prior concerns for Rowan, appeared. "Anything else? Anything outside the NDA that I should know?"

"My lab is a left turn and about five or six steps from the elevator. The hallway dead ends a short distance beyond the lab door at a wall with another securely locked door," Henry said. "I don't have the code to open it. The bathrooms are located near the elevator. I came out of the men's room one day and the locked door was partially propped open."

"You looked?" Griff asked. It was a rhetorical question. He knew Henry well enough to bet he had.

"Long enough to see construction crews finishing what looked like a small studio apartment with bed, couch, and a few other things, including a locked door and windows stretching the length of the hallway, making it possible to look into the room and, I assume, out from the room to the hallway. It's a bubble with security cameras," Henry said. "They kicked me out. Told me to forget what I'd seen."

"A cage?" Griff's stomach clenched, a sickening feeling creeping through his middle.

Henry remained silent, noncommittal.

"That bastard." Griff closed his eyes, hands in a fist.

"A couple of Jarrod's private security—as he calls them—go out for a smoke when I do," Henry said. "They don't stand next to me, but there are only a few outdoor ashtrays, all located not far from each other. I can hear them at times."

"And . . . ?" Griff's agitation was spilling over as panic grew inside him.

"They got in trouble with Marrone because 'she'—that's what they said, no names—slipped through their fingers." Henry reached out and grabbed Griff's right forearm in solidarity, gave him a pat on the shoulder, then sat back in his chair. "They waited for her in Chicago, but she wasn't on the flight."

Griff exhaled, relieved the ruse to send them in the wrong direction had worked. Hearing this helped shake off a few of the dark clouds hanging over him.

"That was your doing?" Henry asked, a smile crossing his face.

"Rowan's idea, my implementation." Griff let himself relax a little. "I'm not sure exactly what I need from you, Henry. Information now and then, possibly inside tips on how to access surveillance cameras. We'll have to see."

"Shortly after I started working there, I did a little reconnaissance on all surveillance cameras for my own peace of mind and protection. After I saw the 'cage' room, as you put it, I tried checking cameras there, but they're on a different system and locked down pretty solidly." Henry paused. "I'll help you. I owe you a lot. But no direct involvement with law enforcement. Whatever Marrone is up to with MyShadow, I want to avoid being dragged down with him if he's caught. Regarding your sister, now that you've explained it to me, I can better understand anything I hear."

"That's everything I'd hoped you'd say, my friend," Griff said, reaching out to shake Henry's hand.

"When's she back in the country?" Henry asked.

"Better no one but Rowan and I have the answer to that question." Griff pulled a new phone out of his backpack and handed it to Henry. "Here's a separate phone to use to communicate with me. My first step in keeping you safe. Text me after you set it up."

"Should I assume Marrone knows you, or at least who you are?" Henry asked, tucking the phone into his own backpack.

"Oh, yeah. He knows who I am. I've managed to steer clear of him, despite his efforts to hire me through my consulting business." Griff snorted in a half-laugh, half-derisive sound. "When I shot him down via email, he told a peer of mine he didn't care because I'm nothing but a 'small time, two-bit hacker.'"

Henry roared with laughter. "Boy, is he in for a surprise."

Rowan

Rowan sat on the bench outside the Microlot corner coffee shop next to Huw's warm body, their thighs touching under the thick wool blanket, his arm around her shoulders, a soft knit cap on her head. A deep and delightful sense of belonging filled her, followed by a wave of sadness, knowing she'd soon wrench herself away from this bliss and leave.

"It's great how the coffee shop provides blankets," Rowan said, careful not to burn her tongue as she sipped a steaming latte.

"It's cold and damp here for much of the year," Huw replied. "We're fairly acclimated to it, but nothing like a Welsh wool blanket to fend off the cold and a hot coffee to warm the insides!"

Rowan laughed. She enjoyed watching the locals coming and going, many saying hello to Huw while smiling curiously at her. She hadn't experienced a sense of community in a long time, and never in this way. The tight-knit group of photo-journalists she'd befriended in her nomadic life, her traveling clan, were the closest she'd come. How wonderful it would be to live in this small village where she could be part of an integrated whole in a way that wasn't possible now. It tugged at her heart strings, creating both pain and pleasure. Jarrod had stripped her of this experience. Familiar sparks of anger shot through her, followed by frustration at having chosen to run instead of fighting back. That was about to change.

Even amidst the softening of her heart and mind, and the ease with which she attached herself to Huw, she turned her head left and right regularly, checking for anyone who stood out among the villagers. Someone devoid of a big puffy coat and knit cap who didn't speak in the lyrical cadence of her mother's people. Someone who triggered an instant sense of danger. Rowan remained on guard.

"What were you dreaming about last night?" Huw half whispered in her ear, grinning mischievously.

"What do you mean?"

"You were talking in your sleep. It sounded like an interesting dream."

"Maybe I was dreaming about you." Rowan tried to keep her voice light, as if amused, but anxiety made the muscles in her face and neck tighten.

"Unless I'm now an action figure from Marvel comics with a special place in your subconscious, I think it's highly unlikely." Huw was clearly enjoying himself, unaware of the struggle he'd created in Rowan.

"Okay, I'm curious now. What did I say?"

"Hmm . . . well, your little outbursts weren't constant, but I distinctly heard you say, 'use your powers for good,' which I found intriguing." Rowan's cheeks warmed despite the cold, and she gave a weak laugh as Huw continued. "Then you whispered to me—well, I assume you were talking to me—to keep my sixth sense open because it's a portal to who knows where."

Huw waited while Rowan, embarrassed and uncertain how to answer, sat silent.

"I didn't mean to upset you," Huw said. "I found it entertaining, as though you were dreaming of a Star Wars movie."

"No, no . . ." Rowan smiled, touching his face tenderly. "Sounds like something my Aunt Maya or my mother would say to me. I was dreaming about my mother. That happens sometimes, although less as the years have passed. I don't remember much about the dream except she was in it."

"I understand." Huw kissed her cheek. "I dream about my father at times."

"I'll let you know if you talk to him or say anything strange," Rowan answered with a smile.

"I'll take that as a 'yes' that you'll stay with me while you're here . . . even come back to me after your trip home?" Huw locked his eyes with hers, waiting. "Forgive me for pushing, but you've disappeared on me before."

"I don't want to leave." Rowan sensed what lay ahead was dangerous. Making promises she couldn't keep wasn't the route she wanted to take with this very special man. "I have to confront what—who—I've been running from. You give me a greater purpose. I want to return to you, to this village, and see where the feelings between us might lead. But that confrontation could involve a fight . . . a physical fight. If I lose . . . well, I can't predict what happens then."

Huw stood, lifting the blanket from her lap and folding it. He stepped into the tiny coffee shop and placed it back in the pile to await another customer. Returning, he took her hand and they began walking back to Patrick's Boathouse, their coffee now lukewarm but still delicious.

"You'll be safer in my home," Huw said. It was more statement than request.

Rowan heard the "okay" leave her mouth even as her brain screamed "no" out of fear of endangering him.

"I'm looking forward to spending a few days convincing you that you can't live without me." Huw's smile traveled to his eyes, radiating such happiness that Rowan was sure her heart would burst right out of her chest with joy at any moment. She opened her mouth to answer but was too overwhelmed to speak.

"Good. It's decided. We'll pick up your things and head for my house, straightaway." Huw gave her hand a light squeeze.

While Huw waited, sitting on the hot pink couch checking his phone, Rowan quickly re-packed her suitcase and backpack. Her phone pinged an incoming text. It was Cat, checking in on her from London.

> Cat: Hey. How R things going?
>
> Rowan: Good. Thx for directions. Found Pentre Ifan easily.
>
> Cat: And . . . ur ok?
>
> Rowan: Yes. fine. Can't explain now. Maybe later. G2G.

Rowan secured the backpack across her shoulders and headed for the door, suitcase in tow. Huw was already in the hall, ahead of her, when her phone rang. Griff. The caller ID created both relief and sadness. She put up one finger to Huw, then closed the door, leaving him to wait outside.

"Hey, little brother!" Rowan smiled thinking how Huw, in many ways, reminded her of Griff. The trim, runner's physique, the deep voice that drew her into a familiar, safe haven. "Shouldn't you be asleep?"

"Let's hear a little gratitude to the brother who was up all night for you!" A rasp in Griff's voice despite his lighthearted tone told her he was exhausted. "Ready to come home?"

"Yes . . . no . . . I have a lot to tell you," Rowan answered. "You've put my plan in place? Reservations booked?"

"Thursday, you—as Alice Edwards—get on a direct British Airways flight from London to Pittsburgh," he said. "I'll pick you up when you land. It's the only direct flight available. On and off, no layovers."

Three days with Huw before she'd take a train to London and a plane home to face her destiny. Rowan had decided, long before she closed her storage container in London, that she wouldn't give Griff every detail in her plan. A full-on physical fight with Jarrod was a possibility her brother would never approve of. Any hint that this could occur might make him try to push himself into the driver's seat. She strongly suspected Griff had his own plan involving one or more of his many skills—surveillance, perhaps hacking—that he was hiding from her. She had no objection as long as he didn't go completely rogue.

"What time is the flight, Griff? I'll check the trains in from Swansea." Huw was probably waiting at the bottom of the stairs by now, wondering what was keeping her.

"Flight leaves at noon, London time." She heard Griff's fingers clicking on a keyboard.

"And where will the hunters think I am?" Rowan and Griff's moniker for Jarrod and his crew was created after Rowan admitted the term "stalker" unnerved her. Griff told her "hunter" sounded much worse, even as he'd shrugged and agreed.

"New York. On a flight leaving London an hour and a half before yours," Griff said, his voice determined. She imagined his boyish face, the smile she loved gone, his mouth set in an angry, grim line. "I hope that means they're out of Heathrow when you get there. I won't have enough time to make a change before you're in flight."

"Thanks, Griff!" A modicum of relief washed over her, despite the many hurdles ahead.

"Were you planning to check a bag, Ro?"

"No. Bag overhead, backpack under the seat."

"Good. I added a little more to our plan."

Rowan tensed, waiting, hoping whatever he meant didn't include more people with knowledge of her whereabouts.

"Gemma flies into New York from London on an earlier flight with a different airline. I'm going to ask her to check in a bag with your credentials on it." Griff said.

"Does she know? Gemma, I mean?" Rowan kept her voice calm and casual, trying not to instantly object and push his buttons.

"No, we're operating on a need-to-know basis here, and she doesn't need to know," Griff said, his voice a little harsh in Rowan's opinion, considering who he referred to. "She thinks you're heading to New York on a later flight but can't check multiple bags. I asked an old frat brother in London to pack a suitcase with warm blankets and a pair of boots on the premise you needed them when you arrived. He'll label it with your name, lock it, and drop it at Gemma's hotel. Gemma thinks you'll pick it up at the unclaimed baggage desk when you arrive."

"Wow, Griff! Brilliant!" Rowan was impressed. "Great addition to the plan!"

"You need to follow the same rule, Ro." For a few moments they were both silent as Griff waited, expecting confirmation from her.

"I live by that rule, Griff," Rowan answered. "To prove it, I ran into an old friend here. Someone I met in Switzerland before the pandemic. We shared a meal, and he knows only the essentials—my name, my profession, that I have a stalker."

"What?! Who is this guy?" Griff, no matter how tired he was, could be counted on to perk up when he sensed there was more to a story.

"A nice Welsh guy with a software background who left a big corporation to run his own hiking business here and in other countries." Rowan exhaled the words in a rush. "He's the real thing."

Griff whistled. "Well, he has to be better than the last guy." He let out what sounded like a cross between a snort and a laugh.

"I trust him instinctively—frightening, because I rarely feel that way with anyone but you and Aunt Maya." Rowan wanted to close the topic now and go downstairs to spend what time she had left with Huw. "I'll fill you in when I'm home. Can you text me my boarding pass?"

"If you trust him, he must be a good one." Griff yawned. "Maybe he can help us, if needed. The software skills, not the hiking. After I have a talk with him, of course."

"Of course, what was I thinking?" Rowan laughed out loud. "Can't wait for your seal of approval, Griff. But the answer is no . . . I don't want him anywhere near danger."

"Ooohhh. You're gone for this guy!" Griff was enjoying this too much.

"Goodbye Griff. Send me the boarding pass and information, then get some sleep." Rowan hung up before he could pump her for more information.

Huw looked at her with concern. She was sure her face displayed a jumbled combination of emotions. He picked up her suitcase and opened the door, waiting for her to step outside.

"Apologies. My brother, Griff, called with my flight information and delayed me," Rowan said, avoiding eye contact.

"How long do I have before you head across the Atlantic?"

Huw's soft, amiable tone belied the troubled look on his face. Rowan sighed. She'd have to withhold answers to many of his questions in order to stick with the "need-to-know" rule.

"Three days. I fly out on Thursday." Rowan watched Huw take a deep breath. "Let's make the most of it, okay?"

He nodded, moving forward, her suitcase in tow. They spilled out into the main street and walked a few blocks before cutting up a side street to begin what looked like a tough uphill trek. Five minutes later, Rowan was breathing heavily despite being in what she considered pretty good shape. Everything everywhere flowed uphill. Each street mirrored a mountain path rolling skyward or sliding in reverse down to the bay and the sea beyond. The climb matched any she'd experienced in Pittsburgh.

"How much farther?" Rowan asked, trying to keep her voice from sounding out of breath and failing miserably.

"A few more streets." Huw chuckled. "I was thinking of taking you on a proper hike tomorrow, but by the looks of it, we might need a beginner's trail."

"Hey!" Rowan swatted playfully at his shoulder. "I'm not completely out of shape, but I admit there are muscles I'm working right now that got little use walking the streets of London."

Huw smirked but made no comment. If they continued much longer, Rowan would need to take a break and sit on one of the many low limestone walls. Finally, Huw stopped in front of a stately, three-story townhouse painted gray with white shutters and trim. New, elegant white balustrades lined the gray retaining wall, continuing up the steps and ending as a frontage for the porch. Other, similar, homes in the neighborhood were in various stages of renovation, hinting at what Huw's home might have looked like prior to its upgrade.

Rowan turned to look down the steps while Huw fumbled for his keys. The view from his third-floor window must be spectacular. This home was prime property in a village where real estate often sold for half a million to a million pounds. There was no way he'd purchased his home on what he earned guiding tourists on hikes. Huw held the door for her. Stepping inside, she entered a narrow foyer with a mat for shoes and a long rack with hooks for coats and caps. As Huw closed the door behind them, a beautiful golden retriever ran down the hallway, stopping directly in front of Rowan, head cocked, unsure.

"This is Cooper." Huw stepped in front of her, leaving his shoes on the mat near the door.

Rowan squatted down to let the dog inspect her, hand extended to offer him a quick sniff before she tried to pet him. His wet nose and hot breath against her palm caused a pang of longing for the dog she'd left behind in London.

"Hello Cooper," she said. "You're gorgeous!" He licked her hand and nuzzled her cheek.

"You're gonna love her, Coop," Huw said. Clicking his fingers, he walked back into the house, the dog following. "I'll bet you're hungry, huh?"

"I didn't realize . . . last night, I mean," Rowan quickly unlaced her shoes and stepped out of them. "He must be dying to go out."

Huw smiled. "I texted my sister and asked her to let him out. I don't do that at the last minute very often. I'm sure she'll have a million questions later, but for now he's hungry and will need a walk soon. Otherwise, he's good."

"It's a beautiful home." Rowan turned left into what appeared to be a living room. Its warm brown, taupe, and pale gold colors were like a cascade of fall leaves gently woven across the walls and furnishings. It took her back to October in the Allegheny Mountains. And yet, the decor was decidedly masculine. No paintings on the walls, only stunning, powerful photos of a variety of mountain ranges throughout the world. A brown leather couch and matching chairs complemented a fireplace that appeared modernized while holding on to its historic beauty, an inviting focal point gracing the room with elegance. Two framed photos sat on the mantel. The photo to the left appeared to be Huw in a graduation gown with what she assumed was his mother, and to the right he posed with an attractive woman, his arms wrapped around a little boy.

"Your son?" Rowan pointed to the photo.

"No, my nephew," Huw said, then added, "and my sister."

Rowan was amused by her own sense of reassurance. The little boy resembled Huw. He tapped the graduation photo with his finger. "My mother passed away not long after we met in Switzerland."

"I'm sorry, Huw." Rowan meant what she said. This was a pain she understood.

"How about a tour?" Huw turned and headed into the interior of the first floor.

Like most renovated row homes, Huw's house was one narrow hallway extending from the front door with rooms to the left and right, ending in a large kitchen and dining area that fed outward into a beautifully landscaped patio, several freestanding heaters indicating year-round usage.

"You'll love it out there in the summer," Huw said. "Even in early fall, I get the heaters going and it's wonderful. It's a little too cold now."

"Do you spend a lot of time here and entertain?" Rowan was touched that he spoke of a time when she'd return to share this space with him. Her heart hurt a bit, her eyes watering.

"No, I wish I did," Huw answered. "The house feels empty, lonely at times. When I'm home though, I have my friends over or Andrew—that's my nephew. We call him Drew."

With a grin and wink, he pointed to the ceiling. "Let's go. Best part of the tour is up there!"

Rowan smiled, memories of the night before flashing in her mind's eye. At the top of the stairs, she glanced to the right into what she assumed was his office, its door ajar, and was astonished to see expensive, high-tech equipment encompassing at least half of the room running the length of two walls.

"Wow!" Rowan stopped, standing in the office doorway. "Huw, what did you say you did before you started your hiking business?"

She turned to face Huw, who stood behind her, his hand on her suitcase handle, and watched hesitation cross his face as he contemplated how to respond. Maybe she should have asked him a few more questions before alcohol and impulse landed the two of them in bed. She pushed the thought away, her sixth sense insisting this was where she belonged. Rowan touched the stone for assurance, but it lay quiet against her skin.

"Come on." Huw turned and began walking down the hallway to the left of the staircase, Cooper trotting close to his heels, sniffing the suitcase each time they stopped. "I'll explain after we get you settled."

Normally she'd be overcome with concern. Apprehension would be followed by a need to grab her suitcase and run. Instead, Rowan was filled with a comfortable sense of having come home. She stepped forward, following Huw as if it were the most natural thing in the world to share space with someone she barely knew after years of accepting paranoia as a first and best instinct. She hoped she wasn't getting soft. With that thought came the knowledge that she'd either destroy Jarrod or he would destroy her. The tantalizing longing to be part of Huw's life transitioned to a fierce, warrior-like resolve that it would be she who emerged victorious.

Huw had disappeared through a door at the end of the hallway. Rowan followed, ascending a short flight of stairs to the third floor. She found herself in the master bedroom with a view of the village and bay beyond, its blue-green waters sparkling, the Atlantic Ocean a slim line on the horizon. Two comfortable looking armchairs and a small table sat in front of the window, positioned to make the most of the view over morning coffee. A king size bed against the opposite wall also faced the windows. A cozy dog bed lay tucked at the base of inset shelves filled with books. Rowan eased herself quietly into one of the chairs and exhaled, letting go of her anxiety, imagining a life where she woke up to this view and this man every morning. Cooper laid his head on her lap, waiting to be petted, and she happily complied. Silently, she vowed to call up this moment in her mind whenever she lost faith, lost confidence, or struggled to believe she could ever return here—to this life, this man—and explore a new future for herself.

Huw slid quietly into the second chair, the small table empty between them.

"What a stunning view!" Rowan said.

"It's my favorite spot in the house."

"Better than your office?" Rowan looked at him, eyebrow raised. "That's a lot of high-end equipment. Did you have to rewire the whole house to accommodate it?"

Huw cleared his throat and gazed out the window for a few seconds. Rowan hoped a terrible reveal that would crush the dream she was floating within and send her running wasn't about to roll out of his mouth and into her ear.

"Like I said last night, I'm a software engineer. Even though I don't do that type of work anymore, I'm an electronics addict." Huw's gaze softened and his mouth upturned slightly with pleasure. It made no sense to her why he would walk away from something that obviously made him happy.

"My brother, Griff, is a tech geek, but his home office setup doesn't hold a candle to yours." Rowan waved her arm toward the walls and ceiling. "Are there cameras monitoring us?"

"No," Huw's voice was firm, serious. "I have cameras outside as part of a home security system, with sensors in a couple rooms and one camera in my office. I travel, and that equipment is expensive. But crime is rare here.

"You're welcome to check," Huw added. "Pull books off shelves, look everywhere. No cameras. I'm not a creep. I promise."

"I have no idea why I—a person who is being stalked and has been required to be on guard, paranoid, for years—have a quiet, instinctive trust in you, but I do," Rowan replied. "Don't take advantage of it . . . please."

Huw put his hand out, palm facing up, on the table, waiting. She placed her hand in his. The same tingle she experienced in the restaurant the night before was present, the stone emitting mild, warm energy against her chest.

"Any chance you want to take your coat off and stay awhile?"

Rowan released his hand. Looking down at her coat which remained fully zipped, her backpack beside her as if she were ready to flee, guilt rolled through her. Slowly, she unzipped her jacket and removed it, placing it across the back of the chair.

"Why do I think there's a little more to your story than a software engineer who likes electronics?" Rowan asked. "I find it hard to believe a guy who runs a modest hiking business can afford this view and that level of hardware, not to mention the Natuzzi leather couch and the beautiful furnishings in your living room."

"After a few years, I tired of big corporations," Huw said, taking her hand again. She turned slightly, leaning forward, her elbow on the chair arm, listening. "I hated the politics, the demand that I be creative, and the bureaucratic roadblocks and lean teams that prevented me from moving projects forward. I left, joining a start-up of young, entrepreneurial people who were on the cutting edge of cloud security and AI."

"Artificial Intelligence," he added.

"I know what it is. Griff's obsessed with it." Rowan was surprised to see a wave of sadness had descended on Huw's face. Griff longed to join a start-up and have the experience Huw described. He claimed it would make work fun again. It was why he ran his own small consulting business on the side.

"For about five years, I loved the work," Huw said. "I advanced to the leadership team and became the equivalent of a chief technology officer, although we were too small to bother with a bunch of weighty titles."

He let go of her hand and began massaging his knuckles, then fingers. Remembering obviously brought a level of stress.

"I developed an app . . . MyShadow . . . that used generative AI to allow people to audio record themselves and attach their voices to an avatar or any picture they chose, inserting the file into a presentation to make it seem as if they were presenting live." Huw closed his eyes. "I was young and naive. It was fun to play with, but not ready for launch."

"I've never heard of this app," Rowan said. "Granted, I'm not super tech savvy like my brother, but as a photographer I might have found that interesting."

"I filed for a patent for the app in my name only," Huw said, his arms now crossed over his chest, his face decidedly miserable. "There was a lot of infighting at the start-up about whether to stay small or expand, plus ongoing money problems. The CEO was furious with me when he discovered the patent was registered to me, but I'd created it on my own time, often at home with my own equipment. I was fired when I refused to share the rights to the app and the code to re-create it."

"What did you do?" Rowan asked.

"I sold MyShadow for several million to a Netherlands-based competitor reputed to be very ethical on the assumption they'd hire me to manage and further develop it," Huw said, his voice tight, his mouth in a severe line. "After the sale, they claimed they'd never promised me a role at the company. I should have gotten it in writing. MyShadow, in the wrong hands, has the potential to be misused. It's a relief that journalists have stopped attributing it to me, but I'm ashamed to have handed such a brilliant but problematic creation over to the wrong people and become rich because of it. That's when I started hiking. I was set financially, but I needed to heal. The hiking evolved into a small business that pays the bills and cleanses my soul."

Rowan watched him with a pang of regret that she'd pushed him to recount terrible, painful memories. "If you hadn't developed it, someone else would have, Huw."

"The competitor I sold it to was then purchased by Marrone Industries, a U.S. based software company," Huw said. "And no offense to you Americans, but Jarrod Marrone is as devious and unethical as they come."

Even as Rowan pressed her warm hands to her cheeks, her face remained cool, clammy. Her body shivered involuntarily. Silent tears ran down her cheeks. Huw stood and moved behind her chair, squatting next to her, his arm encircling her shoulder. She remained still, frozen, unable to sob or speak despite the tears.

"What is it, Rowan?" Huw asked. "It's as if you've seen a ghost."

Rowan began taking deep breaths, willing control of her body and her mind to return. Jarrod had been mentioned in her presence before, and she'd responded without reaction. The shock of going from softening with empathy upon hearing Huw's painful history to a realization that there might be a connection between Huw and Jarrod, hit her like a fast drop in blood pressure, a vault off a cliff. She separated herself from Huw, wiping her cheeks before turning to face him.

"Jarrod Marrone is my stalker." Rowan kept a careful, even tone, watching Huw's reaction. If he not only knew who

Jarrod was but was somehow aligned with him, she was in danger and needed to leave immediately.

"Oh my God!" Huw looked genuinely astonished. Rowan monitored every move of his face and body with trepidation. "No wonder you've been using fake identification. He's powerful and, well, to put it plainly, he's a really bad guy."

Rowan continued to observe him, silent. He reached for her hand, and she crossed her arms over her chest, glancing at her coat, wondering how quickly she could take her things and go. She silently kicked herself for letting her guard down, for allowing the ravenous fingers of loneliness crying for respite to invade her better judgement.

"Wait, Rowan . . . tell me you're not thinking I'm connected to Jarrod Marrone." Huw looked her directly in the eyes. She could see the hurt on his face, but she had to be sure.

He began pacing the room. His hurt was evolving to low grade anger. He stopped mid-stride, dropped back into his empty chair, and faced her, arms crossed defensively over his chest, matching her own posture.

"Huw, put yourself in my shoes for a minute. He has money, he's obsessed, and he's bought many people in an effort to get to me." Rowan moved her coat from the back of the chair, but she waited, laying it across her lap, loathe to put it on and leave. A deep sense of desperation pushed forward, with it a tightening in her chest and the beginnings of a tension headache. She prayed fervently for a sign that Huw was the man she'd allowed herself to believe him to be from the first moment he took her hand.

"I've never met Jarrod Marrone. I know him by reputation and from former colleagues who interacted with him. Nothing I've heard is good. Nothing I've heard makes me ever want to have anything to do with him," Huw said, his posture softening, a pleading undertone penetrating his voice. "If he'd hired me to hand you over, think how many times I could have done that by now. Seriously, Rowan."

Rowan struggled, her mind screaming "run" as her heart begged her to stay. She laid her hand on the table, palm up as he'd done. He clasped her hand tightly and, as he did, the stone radiated a comforting, warm glow. Did she believe him or want to believe him? She could see his eyes were moist. Was he fighting tears? She gave in to all her senses. The desire to stay overriding the urge to run.

"You believe me?" he asked, his voice raspy, cracking slightly with emotion.

"Not yet," Rowan answered, reaching for her phone. "I need you to talk to my brother."

He nodded agreement, no anger evident, no refusal. "Call him. Straightaway. Whatever it takes."

"I want to believe you, but this thing with Jarrod is dangerous. It's been going on for a long time. I trust Griff one hundred percent." Rowan tapped Griff's number into the keypad. She heard his voice, groggy with sleep, slightly irritated, after the third ring. "Griff? No, I'm fine . . . I think. I want you to meet someone, talk to him and well . . . let me know . . . you know."

"The new guy, Ro? Seriously?" Griff sounded sleepy but amused. "I was up until all hours for you, finally asleep, and you wake me up to have me check out some guy?"

"Right . . . yep." Rowan watched Huw's face. "His name's Huw Evans. He's a software engineer turned entrepreneur of his own hiking tours business."

"Holy shit, Rowan!" Griff's voice exploded loudly, in her ear. He was fully awake now. "Are you talking about THE Huw Evans, as in H-U-W who is a brilliant app developer? The guy who created MyShadow? The very same app Jarrod now owns?"

"Correct," Rowan answered. "Which is exactly why I'm asking you to talk to him."

"How did you meet him?" She could hear rustling and then Griff moving. She assumed he was out of bed and heading to the kitchen to make coffee.

"Switzerland, initially. Two years ago. Then we lost touch . . . or I disconnected my temporary phone and he couldn't find me." Rowan gave Huw an apologetic smile. "He lives here in Mumbles, Wales. We ran into each other at a restaurant."

"Well, I'm impressed you haven't run out the door," said Griff. "You must have it bad for this guy. But I'm also concerned. I heard from an inside connection that Jarrod has unethical, possibly illegal, plans for how he'll use MyShadow. No indication Huw Evans is involved, but no confirmation he's not. Fair warning, this might be a long call between two geeks, like it or not."

Rowan smiled and handed the phone to Huw. "Huw, meet Griffith Campbell, amazing white hat hacker and my brother. He's heard of you, by the way."

"Hello there," Huw said, after taking the phone from her hand, his voice quiet. A smile spread across his face as he listened. He nodded absently in her direction, his focus on Griff.

"Never met him," she heard Huw say, followed by questions in a technical language beyond her casual knowledge of Griff's area of expertise. Rowan picked up her suitcase and carried it down the stairs to the second floor, then headed for the bathroom. She stopped on her way to peer into two additional bedrooms. A decent sized guest bedroom with a double bed, chair, and chest of drawers faced the tiny backyard and patio. A smaller bedroom sported a single bed with a Spiderman comforter, a small chest of drawers, and a number of children's toys. She smiled, imagining Huw and his nephew playing in here. A longing for a child of her own that was surprising and new washed over her.

Located next to the small bedroom was a very modern bathroom. Its black and white parquet tiles and chrome fixtures were well lit by a large window on the far wall and a skylight. The standalone shower was small, but it allowed for a beautiful, white clawfoot cast iron bathtub, its faux antique faucets adding to its charm. For a moment, she envisioned slipping into a hot, relaxing bath, but in the end, she chose a quick shower.

Twenty minutes later, she walked back into the bedroom, hair partially towel-dried, wearing clean clothes and feeling refreshed. Her phone sat on the table next to Huw.

"Wow, that was a long conversation," Rowan said.

"Your phone ran out of juice and we were cut off," Huw said. "I've plugged it to recharge, but you might want to text Griff to say I didn't hang up on him."

She picked up the phone and shot off a quick text to Griff.

> Rowan: Huw apologizes. battery died. recharging now.

> Griff: I think he's OK, Ro. Remember "need-to-know info". Anything suspicious, call me. Going back to bed.

"He's headed back to bed. It's early there." Rowan said with a laugh.

"Feel better? About me, I mean?" Huw watched her, his face serious, his fingers lightly drumming the tabletop.

"Whatever you said, Griff seems to think you're okay." Rowan watched Huw's shoulders relax, his hand still, a smile widening across his face.

"I liked him. I hope we meet one day." Huw stood, stretched, and glanced at the view from the window again.

"I'm taking Cooper for a quick walk, but it's a good day for a hike a little later. Interested?"

Rowan's calves were still stiff from the trek up through the village, but there was no chance she'd admit it to Huw. "I'd love to. I don't have any hiking boots or gear, but if my running shoes will do, then let's go."

"It'll be a beginner's hike," Huw said with a grin. "And my sister is about your size. She left a pair of boots and a warm coat here. We'll see if they fit."

Huw hooked a leash onto Cooper's collar. "Coming with us?"

"I'd prefer to stay here. Dry my hair and maybe take a rest on your bed." Rowan hoped he was amenable. What she needed was to speak to her mother, provided when she used the stone for that purpose, Elin responded. "I didn't get much sleep last night."

She gave him a flirty wink, and he laughed.

"Come on Coop. Let's go for a walk."

Rowan followed him downstairs where he pulled out a well-worn pair of boots, the leather soft and pliable, and a down jacket. She tried them on. The boots fit perfectly. The coat was a little big, but with a sweatshirt underneath it would work fairly well. Waving goodbye to Huw and Cooper, she headed back upstairs and seated herself in front of the window. Hand on the stone, she positioned it over her heart. "Mom, I need to talk to you. Please grant me the gift of your voice."

The stone vibrated, emitting a steady thrum. That was a good sign. In the past, there had been times when no amount of pleading resulted in success. Elin was evasive when asked about the celestial realm and why often, and for long stretches of time, she appeared unable or unwilling to answer Rowan's calls.

You found love. It both warms my heart and makes me

fearful for you. Stay careful." Elin's voice moved like soft music through Rowan's mind.

"Oh, Mom. You're here."

"To return to this love means facing, maybe fighting, Jarrod. Stay alert. Remain tough. My crossover strength is limited. I save it for you."

"I can trust Huw, right?" Rowan wished she didn't sound like a child, asking for approval when she'd made decisions without Elin for years.

"We're forever connected. You grew within me. I'm filled with your need to end this burden you carry. Your uncertainty is a protective shield that I approve of. I can't see your future from here, but I think Huw is good."

Rowan heard Huw open the first-floor door, followed by barking from Cooper, and then the sound of paws and nails scrabbling up each level coming toward her.

"Gotta go, Mom. Love you."

"Wait . . . I apologize for what you'll discover when you visit Maya. Know that our actions were born of love for you and Griffith."

Rowan sighed. What type of cryptic message was that? It left her with even more to worry about. A secret her mother was apologizing for after all these years. Thirty minutes later, they were in Huw's Range Rover—backpacks filled with water, snacks and a few sandwiches—on their way to the Preseli Hills. Every part of her tingled with excitement at the prospect of a day spent with this man. It would help her shake off Elin's remark. Her phone pinged.

Cat: Checking in. Ur doing well?
Rowan: Yes. Met a lovely man. Going hiking.
Cat: Who? (heart emojis)
Rowan: Huw Evans.
Cat: Meg's brother? He's a good one. Go u, Rowan! Say hello from me.

Huw glanced at her. "Griff again?"

"No, a nice woman named Cat who may be a distant cousin of mine, but we've not had the time to sit down and figure that out. She says you're Meg's brother, you're a good one, and to say hello. I met her by chance in London where we discovered our mothers were friends, long ago, and may have been cousins. Small world."

Huw smiled and patted Rowan's knee. "I am a good one. Hopefully, so good you'll come back to me."

Rowan held his hand and looked away, struggling not to cry. She longed to reassure him, but she could not.

Griffith

"Marrone sucks at personal security," Henry said with a laugh. "Which is to your benefit."

"Don't go too far, Henry," Griff warned. "I don't want you to arouse suspicion."

They were seated next to a big hand-painted mural in D's Dawg's finishing off a lunch of burgers and fries. Henry snorted and rolled his eyes. "Seriously, Griff? One of the first things I did after passing my three-month probation period was to gently test my level of access to the corporate system and find reasons to request access upgrades where possible. I look at it as self-protection."

"What did you learn?" Griff placed his napkin on the plate and moved it aside. He'd received a text from Henry, sent from the safe phone Griff gave him, to have lunch and catch up.

"They have an IT staff, but only a few have cyber skills, none in digital forensics. If I dropped a package on a laptop, no one would be the wiser." Henry leaned forward and lowered his voice. D's was always packed. The Saturday crowd of locals looked innocent enough, and disinterested, but Griff appreciated his friend's caution.

"And have you done that?" Griff wondered if the brash activist in Henry lay waiting, despite his prison stint, for the right cause or reason to emerge.

"No . . . well . . . yes." Henry grinned. "I did it to a few members of my team to see if they caught on. They didn't. They're focused on the MyShadow project. Brilliant kids. A bunch of young Griff Campbells."

"Oh, oh. You're in trouble there!" Griff laughed. The waitress dropped a check on their table, and Griff snatched it. "On me."

"I watched Marrone open his phone when he stopped by the lab for a demo of our work. No biometrics. A four-digit code which I memorized." Henry pulled a small notepad out of his pocket and scribbled on it, ripped out a page, and handed it to Griff. "I hacked his email early on, checking now and then to make sure he likes my work, me, etc. He has two accounts—a work account and a personal account. Until I talked to you, I hadn't bothered with the personal email. Turns out it's more interesting."

Henry grinned mischievously. Griff looked down at the piece of paper. It contained four numbers and the name of a phone service provider. He folded it, pocketed it, and waited. "I'm all ears!"

"Keep your temper in check. You won't like it." Henry's smile disappeared, his mouth in a serious straight line. "This is a combination of what I saw across both email accounts. First, personal papers belonging to his father and uncle insinuate that his father had another child who should have a stake in the company. Ray, his uncle, took over the company after the father died. Ray died of a heart attack, and then Jarrod took control. He's a rightful heir to fifty percent of Marrone Industries, if there is another heir, but he's not one to embrace sharing. Ray hired a private investigator to search for Jarrod's alleged sibling, but he died before anyone was identified.

Jarrod apparently harbors concerns that, because he's adopted, the entire company could go to the biological heir, which, legally, isn't correct. Just his paranoia."

"Whoa . . . Jarrod is adopted?" Griff hadn't seen that coming.

"It appears, from what I've seen, that he was adopted at his mother's insistence with limited interest on his father's part. Ray groomed him for a role in the family business," Henry said. "Their relationship fell apart when Jarrod came to work for the company and caused a lot of problems—reports to HR by women, etc.—making Ray want to fire him. Those old emails between them are pretty intense."

"Why am I keeping my temper in check? I'd like to see someone else come forward and challenge Jarrod—maybe kick him out." Griff was puzzled.

"Jarrod thinks Rowan is Paul's biological child." Henry paused as Griff absorbed this news. "He thinks if he controls her and what he calls her 'magical stone,' he'll become more powerful."

"He's more dangerous and deluded than I imagined." Griff's stomach tightened, his lunch rolling around inside as alarm for Rowan's safety grew. "Paul Marrone died in the same car crash as my mother. The car exploded. No cause was ever determined."

Henry's bushy eyebrows knit together. "Do you think your mother and Paul Marrone . . . ?"

"I don't know." Griff shook his head, trying to dislodge the conjecture from his mind. "I was a little kid. Most of the day Mom died is a fairly hazy memory."

"The CFO, Ken Jeffries, is furious that money is spent chasing Rowan while profits are down and new products are stalled in the pipeline. Seems product development employees keep quitting," Henry said. "Four resignations in as many years. Two never signed an NDA and went to competitors."

"You took a look at the CFO's emails as well?" Griff asked.

"I looked at communication between Jarrod and everyone—CFO, security, whoever." Henry nodded affirmatively as he spoke. "Jeffries wants to force Jarrod out, but there's a U.S. senator on the board of directors who quashes his requests."

Henry sat back, arms crossed. "Older emails between human resources and Ray Marrone indicate lots of women filed sexual harassment complaints. Ray was probably looking for a way to remove Jarrod permanently from the company."

"Who's the senator who has his back . . . the guy on the Board of Directors?" Griff asked.

"Senator Harrison Cherrington, III. The news refers to him as Trey Cherrington."

Griff let out a low whistle. "Powerful guy. Appears to have POTUS aspirations."

He'd need to share this with Rick and the FBI team. A small, niggling voice inside said Rick might already know, that this was the piece of information which first cast suspicion on Jarrod.

"Anything else about Rowan?" Griff asked, checking his watch. He had a client meeting in forty-five minutes.

"Marrone hires an escort service and requests women that resemble Rowan. The escort service sent him a warning. I guess he's not a gentleman." Henry rolled his eyes. "Also, he's got a spy somewhere. He refers to his 'source' but no names."

"I should strangle him, that pervert!" Griff could hear his voice rising. His face was hot with anger. A few customers looked over, but the restaurant's noise level was high enough that he didn't think they'd heard him clearly. "Rowan found a tracking app on her phone in London and disabled it. My money was on the ex-boyfriend for that . . . he's a chump. But they split. There's no communication between them. The spy has to be someone else."

"Maybe several people, not one source?" Henry zipped up

his jacket and checked his watch. "I gotta go. I think the answer is in Marrone's personal texts, but I can't access his phone."

Griff remained seated, thinking. "Is there a way to get a surveillance camera or audio device in his office? Behind a vent or in a plant?"

Henry shrugged. "Only been to his office once. No way I can think of for me to do that."

Griff stood, walking out with Henry. "I'll figure something out."

Rowan

She watched the sun rise over Swansea Bay in layers of orange, pink, and golden yellow. It spread fingers of light softly, like a lush inviting carpet across the darkened waters, making the bay sparkle and unveiling a deep blue hue. It had been a magical three days. Her heart valiantly clung to that happiness, but it would, inevitably, slowly sink into a pool of grief over the reality that she must leave today. Huw's soft, rhythmic breathing, periodically interrupted with a snore, moved in time with the waves rolling onto the thin strip of beach within her line of vision.

The woman she'd been when she arrived in this village would be packing quietly now, slipping out the front door to avoid an uncomfortable goodbye, scanning the streets for danger before walking a few blocks and calling a taxi. She'd considered sparing Huw a painful farewell at the train station, but selfishly, she couldn't bear losing even one extra minute with him. It was strange, this unfolding awareness that she was intertwined with another soul in ways far beyond physical intimacy. Despite her heart's unwillingness to comply, her logical mind accepted it was best to put distance between them. Her normal armor had to be reinstalled. Rowan the warrior must return and put Rowan the lover in a safe place. Hopefully, one day, she'd retrieve this better angel permanently—for Huw.

"Rowan?"

She heard the rustle of the bed sheets moving. Turning from the window, she looked at Huw, his eyes sad, shoulders hunched as he took in the sight of her dressed and ready to leave.

"You look different. The clothes?" Huw rubbed his eyes and cleared his throat.

"Wait until you see me . . . I mean see Alice . . . with the wig and tinted contact lenses," Rowan answered, mustering a small smile. They'd gone shopping at a local store for clothing "Alice" would buy. Items comfortable for travel and what one might expect of a local woman in her mid-thirties who liked to dress more for hiking than fashion. Huw insisted they think of every last detail, concerned that she had no idea which items of clothing in her wardrobe had already been caught on a security camera and might give her away.

"The trail trousers look great!" Huw had suggested pants with a surprising number of convenience pockets that weren't bulky like the cargo pants popular in the U.S. She'd topped the outfit with a T-shirt under a soft fleece pullover. Walking shoes with good treads and hiking socks rounded out her new image. Huw insisted the pullover and a puffy winter jacket would give her bulk, making her look like a larger woman than her actual size. Uncomfortable about foregoing her usual ball cap and hoodie, she'd insisted her new puffy coat have a hood. She'd added a headband to hold the wig in place if she fell asleep on the plane.

"You'll be facing snowy weather over there, right?" Huw asked.

"Hmm . . . not sure." Rowan was noncommittal.

She'd refrained from sharing with him the final destination of her flight, telling him it was to protect him. He didn't like it but gave in when she agreed to a prepaid phone used only with him and no one else.

"It's almost time, Huw," she said softly. "I won't hold you to dropping me at the train station."

"Forget it. I want every last minute with you." Huw threw the covers back and swung his long legs out of the bed, checking the time on his phone. "Quick shower and we'll go. We'll grab coffee on the way."

"I can get coffee on the train." Rowan's eyes filled with tears, her voice shaking.

"No way. That train coffee is shit. Obviously, you've never tried it." Huw kissed the top of her head. "This isn't the end, Rowan. We're meant to be."

Before she could respond, he was gone. The sound of water from Huw's shower mingled with her quiet sobs. Rowan tried breathing slowly, in and out, to calm herself before he returned. Thirty minutes later, she was seated next to Huw in his car, dry-eyed, blond wig and green contacts in place, determined to make their time traveling along the A4067 to Swansea positive.

"I might like you better as a blond," Huw said with a wink.

His attempt to lighten the growing sadness creeping upward between them not only eased the pain in her heart, but it also kept her from crying. Rowan smiled in appreciation. Tears made the contacts itch. It would be a relief if the airline crew darkened the cabin to allow passengers to sleep and she could remove them, reinserting quickly in the bathroom before the plane landed.

"I'll miss looking out across the bay," Rowan said with a sigh. "I could spend all day facing the water."

"You will one day," Huw said, his voice firm and filled with conviction in their future together. "Soon."

"This weekend—our coffee spot, hiking, curling up with you and Cooper in the evening—it's not what I expected," Rowan's voice choked with emotion. "You're the first man who I've been open and honest with about my inherited abilities, the life baggage I'm toting around right now, and a whole lot more. I want to stay and see where this goes, but I have remove that baggage first."

Huw was quiet, but she sensed he held in a lot of emotion. Probably being stoic for both of them. She couldn't shift to a tougher way of being with him so close. She inhaled the clean smell of soap and shampoo, doing her best not to let panic set in. Once she was on the train and away from him, the old Rowan would return. She touched her necklace and said a silent prayer.

They waited in the car park at the station, neither wanting to exit. Huw leaned over and kissed her softly. She rested her head on his shoulder and took a deep breath. They'd agreed she would wear her mask in the station and he would purchase a ticket for her at the kiosk.

"Saying goodbye to Cooper, rubbing his furry head, was nearly as hard as this moment with you." Rowan buried her face in his jacket trying to control the sob that came out more like a hiccup.

"So, Cooper's my competition, eh? Want me to lick your face?"

Rowan sat up and gave Huw a smile, wiping the tears from her cheeks and eyes.

"Text me at least once every day," Huw said. "If I don't hear from you after a few days, I'll know you're in trouble."

Rowan nodded in agreement.

"And we call one another as time zones permit." His voice was tender, but firm. He wasn't fully letting her go. She'd be out there alone, but Huw, like Griff, would remain a lifeline, bolstering her courage.

"Do you have Griff's number?" Rowan asked.

"Yes, you gave it to me twice," Huw said.

She turned now, facing him. His smile eased the tension. "Let's go before I decide I can't do it."

She put her mask on, pulled up her hood, then opened the car door and stepped out into the sharp, cold air. She automatically scanned the car park for any signs of danger. She heard Huw's door open and turned to watch him remove her suitcase. She linked her arm in his, hoping they looked like any couple with one person masked due to medical issues or simple caution.

They'd timed it to arrive at the station shortly before Rowan would board the train. Safer for her and no elongating the pain of separation. Rip the Band-Aid off and go, she'd told herself. Ticket in her pocket, backpack in place, and suitcase handle in one hand, she looked into Huw's eyes and hoped hers conveyed, despite the new contacts, how deep her feelings ran for this man.

"I'll be back."

"I'll hold you to that promise." Huw's voice sounded shaky. People were beginning to mill around them, walking past her, choosing the train car printed on their ticket and climbing aboard. Huw wrapped her in a hug then said, loudly enough for others to hear, "Have a lovely trip, honey. I'll see you in a few days."

Rowan hugged him in return, turned away, and began walking down the platform. She willed herself not to look back, to seem like an ordinary woman going on a quick trip to the city. She located the D car, found her seat, tucked her suitcase into the storage area near the door, and placed the backpack at her feet. She had a window seat, which she alternately loved and hated depending on who sat next to her and whether she might need to exit quickly.

Ten minutes later, tickets taken, the train left the station, and Rowan exhaled a sigh of relief. She carefully lifted her mask to sip the coffee Huw had purchased for her. Her car was sparsely populated, the seat next to her empty. There were approximately ten people, most with white or gray hair, and a few young students hunched over their phones and laptops. She slumped down a bit in her seat, watching as the Welsh countryside passed by, still green this time of year. The overhead safety message asked passengers to report incidents—"See it, Say it, Sorted," a pleasant female voice instructed. It was a repetitive message she'd tire of long before the train pulled into Paddington.

Rowan tucked her feelings for Huw into a tiny space within her heart. To return to him, she'd have to morph back into the Rowan she'd been before he crashed into her life, tearing all her well-built defenses down. Her phone pinged.

> Cat: Still in Wales? Heading there later 2day.

> Rowan: No. On the move. C u when I return.

> Cat: Safe travels

> Rowan: When u touch ur necklace stone, think of me. Send a prayer.

Rowan checked again to make sure her GPS was turned off, then powered down the phone. The separate phone Huw insisted be used only for calls to him sat tucked in her backpack. He'd agreed that if anything went wrong, he'd share the number with Griff. She checked the time and the number of stations to Paddington. She could relax a little bit, but only until she stepped off the train and locked herself fully into her Alice Edwards role. She'd practiced speaking with a Welsh accent with Huw. He'd laughed heartily several times, but after a few sessions with him, she was better equipped to convincingly pass for Alice. Rowan partially unzipped her coat and curled her fingers around the stone, willing her mother to be with her, struggling to hear her mother's voice as she moved forward into the unknown. Only silence, broken by the sound of the train wheels against the track and the overhead speaker announcing the next stop, greeted her in return.

Griffith

Griff watched the airport doors from the driver's seat of his Jeep inside the short-term parking garage. He'd love to listen to music, but he needed to keep all his senses on alert. Once Rowan exited the plane into Pittsburgh's A Terminal, she'd be on her way to him. So far, so good. No indication he'd been followed. Rowan claimed her disguise was very effective. He'd wanted to meet her inside, but she pushed back, convinced she was less identifiable without him. Griff acquiesced, tracking her on Flight Aware, then texting her his location moments after she landed. Now he waited, imagining his sister, tired, trying to blend in with a cluster of people as an escalator took them down, past the statues of Rocky Bleier and Nelly Bly and the life-sized model of a 65-million-year-old Tyrannosaurus Rex, to the tram and beyond to the building exits. He wanted to beat the living daylights out of Jarrod for putting her in this situation.

A woman exited, walking toward the garage. She looked rapidly in all directions. If it was Rowan, she'd done a bang-up job on the disguise. She stopped near the hut that housed the garage ticket taker, the barrier lifting to accommodate exiting cars, and looked out across the street behind her before removing her sunglasses to scan the garage. Moving quickly in the direction of his vehicle, she opened the Jeep's back door, dropped the suitcase and backpack on the floor, and climbed in, lying prone on the seat.

"Hello, baby brother!" Rowan extended her hand upward.

"Who are you? Some blond chick pretending to know me?" He laughed, reached back, and gave her a high five.

"Ha ha! I can't wait to take this wig off. It's super itchy. The contacts too."

Griff shifted into drive and moved toward the exit sign. "We're heading to my condo. It has underground parking and a security guy at the front desk. If anyone asks, you're my cousin. As requested, I bought a decent used car for you to drive. It'll be delivered tomorrow."

"Thank you." Rowan shifted the backpack behind her head. He could see her smiling as he turned on the radio, her fingers tapping in time with a classic rock song on WDVE.

"Little brother services at your command," Griff joked. He pulled up to the booth, window down, and handed over his ticket and cash payment. The tinted back windows partially hid her in a dark cocoon of sorts.

"Ro, let's go over your plan, now that you're here," Griff said as the exit gate lifted.

"Hang on. I need to text Huw that I'm safe." A glance at the rearview mirror revealed Rowan pulling a phone from a side pocket of her backpack. She must be gone, over the moon, for this guy. Griff eased onto 376 East, heading toward the city.

"Does Dad know I'm back in the country?" Rowan asked. "I spoke to him a couple weeks ago, shortly before I moved out of Peter's apartment. I didn't mention coming home, only that Peter and I split and I'd call him from my next assignment."

"He heard nothing from me. He's happy in his little life in Erie with Shellebrity." He was rewarded with a laugh from Rowan. Their stepmother, Shelley, who followed celebrities like astronomers followed the planets, was an ongoing source of annoyance and amusement. "You planning to see him?"

"I want to, but obviously that would put me in a prime spot for Jarrod to grab me." Rowan's voice sounded sad. Griff hoped their father, who would be hurt if he learned she was in the U.S. and had avoided him, remained unaware.

"It's supposed to be the mother of all snowstorms up there this weekend and early next week. You'll need to leave before you're caught in it." Griff wished she wouldn't go at all. "Catch a few z's, Ro. It could be forty minutes to an hour, depending on traffic."

Forty minutes later, they stepped out into the garage below his high-rise, luxury condo building downtown. Rowan yawned, stretching her arms and legs. The elevator in the garage let them off on the tenth floor.

"I assume there are surveillance cameras in the building?" Rowan asked, keeping her head down.

"A few. I run regular checks. Jarrod's not spying on me." Griff rubbed her shoulder reassuringly. He'd accessed his building security system the first month he moved in.

"As you taught me, Griff, anything can be hacked," Rowan said, making Griff chuckle.

"Exactly. Which is why I'll be the first alerted if someone other than me hacks into this building. Come on . . . let's go!" They exited, walked a few steps down the hallway, then Griff scanned a card at the pad in front of the door and they entered his home.

Rowan smiled as she took in the familiar space. It had been a while since she'd stayed with him. The living, kitchen, and dining area were illuminated by windows that spanned the length of the living room. Black and silver appliances complemented pale off-white walls, beige and gray furniture with a pop of black in a pillow or rug here and there. Muted, cool colors. The room was a backdrop for a spectacular view of the city. It was the view that sold him on the condo.

Rowan pulled off the wig, tossing it, with her coat and fleece pullover, onto a chair. She kicked off her shoes and rummaged in her backpack, extracting a scrunchie for her hair and a small white case into which she deposited the contact lenses.

Griff watched her, amused, as he removed a bottle of merlot from his refrigerator, grabbed a bottle opener and two wine glasses, and set everything on the chrome and glass coffee table. He stripped off his coat and sweatshirt, then tapped the keypad on his phone. "Calling for take-out from my favorite Chinese restaurant, Ro. Still a Kung Pao chicken fan?"

Rowan gave him a thumbs up. Griff ordered food while opening the wine bottle. He watched his sister close her eyes and lean back into the couch.

"Hey, don't fall asleep yet!" Griff poured two glasses of wine. "We haven't had a chance to hang out together in months, not since Gemma and I caught up with you in London when you were still with what's his name."

He watched as she moved his glass and her own to two heavy black coasters, softly rubbing out the wet circles left on the expensive Arhaus table with her sleeve.

"Peter? Yes, good old whatshisname . . . a faraway dot in my past life." Rowan closed her fingers around the stem of the wine glass and smiled at Griff.

"Right, whatever. What I mean is we rarely get to talk, alone. I want you to stay awake for a while." He pulled a Chainsmokers T-shirt over his head.

"How was the concert?" Rowan pointed to his shirt.

"Oh, great. The company that puts on these concerts hired

me to consult. I did a little business planning and security setup. Some gigs come with a perk or two."

"Free tickets? Good for you." Rowan gave him thumbs up.

"Food should be here soon." Griff looked at her and waved his hand outward like a car model at an auto show displaying the vehicle, making her giggle.

"The city looks spectacular from here." Rowan's face had a momentary look of sadness, making him wonder what image crossed her mind as she spoke. "Thanks for ordering food. I'm starving and my internal clock is off schedule. I need to eat and stay awake to get my body on U.S. time."

Fifteen minutes later, they were happily working their way through containers of Chinese food. Rowan had swapped the wine for water, stating she wanted to try to hold out for a few more hours before her body demanded sleep regardless of her efforts.

"I've got a friend on the inside . . . at Marrone Industries," Griff said. "He gave me interesting information that might explain why Jarrod chases after you."

"I know why he's after me," Rowan said, making a face to show she found his motives disgusting.

"Well, maybe it's because he thinks you're hot. But also, it turns out Jarrod found papers indicating his uncle suspected Paul Marrone had another child who should, rightfully share inheritance of Marrone Industries with Jarrod." Griff dropped the smile, his face serious.

"Sharing is not Jarrod's style," Rowan said.

"He's adopted. Did you know that?" Griff said.

"Jarrod? Adopted?" Rowan looked surprised. "Interesting."

"Yep. And he thinks Paul's child—and his competition—is . . . drum roll . . . you!" Griff watched Rowan turn pale. She coughed in an obvious effort to swallow her food without choking, then took a gulp of water. "My contact hacked Jarrod's emails—business and personal. The obsession is more than lust."

"No way. Dad is my father. I look more like him than Mom." Griff could see Rowan's hand tremble as she rested it on her necklace. "I'll never be a partner of any kind with Jarrod."

"Let me put it on," Griff was eyeing her curiously.

"The necklace? That's a bad idea."

"Come on! What harm can it do?" Griff smirked. He loved to push his sister's buttons.

Rowan slowly removed the necklace and placed it around Griff's neck. "Okay, buster. We'll see how long you last."

"It appears Jarrod wants to improve MyShadow to allow him and a pretty powerful senator to disrupt an election." Griff stood up, admiring the necklace in the mirror, touching the beautiful blue quartz gently. "Jarrod's on a power climb, and he thinks having you improves his odds. Maybe, unlike me, he believes you have magic, Ro!"

"How do you know all of this?" Rowan looked skeptical.

"The feds are watching him. They asked me to help with their investigation. I said 'yes' hoping any inside information would help me help you." Griff noticed his face looked mildly flushed. "Former employees of the senator told investigators they heard enough to suspect he and Jarrod were looking at ways to use AI that are . . . let's say more nefarious than should be allowed. AI regulations are slim to none. The government hasn't put any guardrails in place. My friend was hired to run a secret lab for Jarrod with the objective of leveling up MyShadow."

Griff wiped a sheen of sweat off his forehead. He checked the thermostat. It sat at a cool sixty-five degrees, yet he was hot enough to be combustible.

"Something's wrong, Griff. Give the necklace back to me."

He could see Rowan's eyebrows knitted in concern as she stood and reached for his arm.

Griff turned slowly, his movements unsteady. His face was bright red and puffy. "Oh, shit! What's happening? I feel super weird."

Rowan carefully unclasped the necklace and placed it around her neck. She hurriedly filled a glass with tap water from the kitchen and set it on the coffee table before leading Griff back to the couch, pushing him downward to a sitting position.

"Drink, Griff." Rowan sat next to him, rubbing his shoulder. His hands shook as he gulped down half the glass, then turned to face her.

"What the hell happened?"

"I'm not sure. The stone keeps me centered and has limited powers, but I've never seen anything like this. It was irresponsible of me to let you wear it."

Griff stood and walked to the windows. He could see Rowan following him, her worried face reflected in the glass.

"Aunt Maya told me never to let anyone else wear the necklace," Rowan said. "It's my fault."

They watched the soft colors of the setting sun caressing the outlines of the city, dancing off the river waters in harmony with lights appearing on buildings and across bridges. Eventually, Rowan walked back to the coffee table where she cleared the remains of their dinner.

"Okay, Ro. Maybe you have magic," Griff said, tucking his usual joking, sometimes insolent retorts away. "But I don't want to believe it."

Rowan gave him a shaky smile.

"What happens next?" He sounded, to himself, like five-year-old Griff again, waiting for his big sister to lead the way.

"I go to see Aunt Maya tomorrow, before the incoming storm makes it impossible," Rowan answered. He heard her sigh. She wasn't enthusiastically looking forward to the trip. "Evidently, she can train me to protect myself."

"And I'm supposed to wait around until you and Aunt Maya are done playing magic games?" Griff had no intention of going along with that idea.

"For now, you go back to work. You keep tabs on Jarrod through your contact. You let me figure this out." Rowan gazed at him sadly. "I need your help, Griff, but I want you away from any danger. Jarrod wants me, my magic, and if what you say is true, an inheritance I'm aware of but have never truly wanted. All of which I need to put a stop to on my own."

"I'm trying to tell you that this didn't start in Paris when you burned his hand . . . however you managed to do that. He was investigating you before that ever happened, thinking you're Paul's kid."

"That party in Paris was a turning point for me." Rowan let out a nervous laugh. "Jarrod's touch incited an extreme sense of danger and revulsion inside me. I lost control. It scared me to learn I was capable of seriously hurting others."

Griff reminded himself that this crazy side of his sister was the only thing he didn't love about her. He fought a desire to stick his fingers in his ears before she said anything else.

Rowan leaned her head back and closed her eyes. "For a year afterward, he sent flowers, notes, and emails. I ignored him, returning everything. But you know all of that."

"He doesn't take a hint, and now you think one-to-one confrontation will do the trick." Griff had rebuffed a lot of advances from men and women, and had done his fair number of relationship break-ups with the women he'd dated. Some were more persistent than others, although he admitted to himself none had been anything near what Rowan was dealing with.

Rowan sighed, running her hands through her hair.

"Remember when I called you, frantic because his thugs succeeded in shoving me halfway into a car in Rome until I was saved by *carabinieri*—the police?"

"Yup . . . I remember that call," Griff said. "You told me you were leaving your modeling career. I was furious."

"Modeling was too public, making it too easy to find me," Rowan answered. "I'd already been taking photography lessons. It's been the perfect profession for regular, rapid, location changes. Now I need Aunt Maya to teach me to control my abilities, to help me defend myself."

"You hate going to Lilydale, Ro."

"I hear voices when I'm there. It creeps me out. But I have to go."

Griff watched Rowan wrap her arms across her chest as if hugging herself. He craved a good night's sleep. Tomorrow, he'd sort out what he'd heard and seen, concluding it was a hallucination brought on by too much wine and weeks of sleep deprivation juggling his sister's needs and his job. He was sure of it.

"I talk to Aunt Maya every couple of months. She never mentions magic or other strange stuff. Never." Griff stood, stretched, and yawned. "And I never saw Mom do a magic trick."

"You were a little kid when she died. If she'd lived . . ." Rowan rubbed her eyes, leaving the sentence unfinished. She must be as tired as he was.

"Want to show me where I sleep tonight?" Rowan grabbed her suitcase and backpack. "I'm not sure who's more exhausted, me or you."

"I was thinking the same thing. Follow me." Griff headed down a short hallway, opened the first door on the right, and stepped aside to let her walk into a rarely used guest bedroom. "Ta-da!"

Rowan smiled as she touched the wool blanket he'd

draped invitingly across the bottom of the bed. It had belonged to their grandmother and then their mother. "Nice touch for a bachelor pad."

"A little feeling of home." Griff turned, ready to head further down the hall where the master bedroom was located. "Sweet dreams, Ro."

"Griff?"

"Yeah?"

"Can you check to make sure everything is locked and the alarm system is on?"

Rowan was still sitting on the edge of the bed, waiting, when he returned.

"The alarm system is activated, and blinds are closed," Griff said. "Make yourself at home." He blew her a kiss and kept going. Minutes later, he heard the water running in the guest bathroom. His head had barely hit the pillow when sleep overcame him.

Rowan

"What do you think?" Griff asked, his voice echoing in the nearly empty garage as she walked slowly around a black 2017 Honda CR-V.

"Nice choice!" Rowan opened the driver's side door, sat down, and ran her hands over the wheel in anticipation. The odometer registered 77,000 miles.

"If you're pulled over, say you borrowed my car to visit family," Griff said. "Oil change, inspection, tire check. All done. Registration and insurance card are in the glove compartment."

"What license do you think I should use?"

"Keep using Bryn Davies." Griff looked serious, his mouth set in a determined line. "Better yet, drive carefully and don't get pulled over."

They rode the elevator back up to his condo in silence. Her suitcase and backpack were ready. Griff insisted on making breakfast before she left.

"About last night . . ." Griff flipped eggs, cheese and veggies into a half circle twice to create perfect omelets. "The realist in me thinks wine plus exhaustion created a hallucination."

"We weren't doing drugs, and you didn't have a fever. How could you hallucinate?" Rowan sat on a stool at the corner of the granite-topped kitchen island, sipping a glass of juice. With a smile, he placed breakfast in front of her and then sat down next to her with his own plate of food.

Rowan reached over to touch her brother's head, tenderly rubbing his already messy morning hair. "If it's any consolation, Griff, I wish my powers meant I could wiggle my nose or click my heels and make Jarrod disappear."

That made Griff laugh. Rowan spent the rest of breakfast steering the conversation toward everything but what might lie ahead for her.

"Dad's become more distant," Griff said. "He's totally wrapped up in Shellebrity and her kids."

"I've given up trying to explain the dangers of Jarrod to Dad," Rowan said. "He gets angry and insists it's a matter for the police."

"Did you tell him how that backfired early on when you reported Jarrod and someone, possibly a police officer, tipped him off?" Griff said, mouth in a grim line.

"Yes. He refuses to blame law enforcement. He says Jarrod's informant has to be someone close to me." Rowan sighed. "I trust very few people, making it seem unlikely, but who knows. It's not in Dad's nature to think you can't always trust the police."

"Henry thinks Jarrod has a spy. Maybe that's why his people locate you, no matter how hard you try to be invisible," Griff said. "Whatever he saw in Jarrod's emails made him suspicious. Do you think it's Shellebrity?"

Rowan shook her head. "No. I'm careful with Dad. He only has a post office box address, and I filter what I say, keeping her in mind. Maybe it is someone in law enforcement. I suppose they have better tracking tools."

"Hmmm . . . well, there's a certain Welsh cybersecurity geek you trusted pretty quickly, I'd say." Griff grinned.

"And you? Ready for the next step with Gemma?"

Griff shrugged, avoiding eye contact. "We're good as is, Ro. She has a lot of baggage—family debt and such—that I don't want to take on."

Forty-five minutes later, Rowan was happily driving on the American side of the road. Leaving the torpor of Pittsburgh's rush hour traffic in her rearview mirror was much like finally exiting from the back of a packed elevator on the thirty-first floor. She set the cruise control and rolled forward to I-79 North. It would take her to Erie, where she'd get off onto I-90 and on into Western New York. She figured about three hours on the road, and she'd be there, barring weather or traffic delays. It hurt knowing she'd pass Erie without taking time to see her father. If only he'd stayed in Pittsburgh. But he'd chosen to follow Shelley back to her hometown. Rowan agreed with Griff that, for her own safety and her father's, she shouldn't stop more than was absolutely necessary.

"Pee and petrol only," she'd said to Griff.

Dark, heavy-laden clouds sat on the horizon. Light snowflakes increased to a steady fall, the prologue to the serious storm Rowan was heading directly into. There was no way to outrun it. The infamous snow belt ran from Mentor, Ohio to Edinboro, Pennsylvania and then north. She'd drive straight through that arc and beyond to the region where Buffalo, New York's famed winter storms reached down like a mantle to blanket smaller cities and villages nearby with frigid, glacier like, precision. She might get stuck in Lilydale. She hoped her reclusive aunt wouldn't mind putting her up until the storm passed and the roads cleared.

The half-empty water bottle resting in the cup holder next

to her was a clear indication she'd need to stop for a restroom break. Being a self-proclaimed "wateraholic" meant there was no way out of at least one pause in her journey. She'd have to choose a crowded rest stop and be careful. Two hours into the trip, signs for I-90 exits to Cleveland, Ohio, or Buffalo, New York, appeared. A feeling of nostalgia tweaked the edge of her emotions, thinking about Cleveland. Her first fashion show was held at the Rock and Roll Hall of Fame, its beautiful, tetrahedral glass structure a geometric prism of light, music, and a sense of spiritual magic. Young, impressionable and excited, with her mother as chaperone, she'd had a wonderful weekend. Six months later, Elin was dead.

Tears blurred her vision enough to force her to pull over at the next rest area, its parking lot half full of cars with a few semi-trucks in the mix. The stark, cold air dried her eyes and pushed the longing for her mother into a manageable place. She would have been taken advantage of, eaten alive, if her stepmother hadn't eventually taken over, guiding her, negotiating for her, and keeping her grounded. Shelley wasn't her mother, and their personalities didn't mesh well together, but she kept Rowan safe until she took over her career at age sixteen. Shelley initially objected, claiming Rowan couldn't model without an adult until she was eighteen. Rowan was adamant. Either she be allowed to run her career or she would legally emancipate herself. Her father conceded she could run things on her own as long as she did not drop out of high school and kept her grades up. Years later, when she'd grown up a bit, she apologized to Shelley for hurting her feelings, thanking her for the help she'd provided. What Rowan didn't say was that even then, at sixteen, Shelley's celebrity obsession was embarrassing to Rowan who was, by nature, private and more of a nerdy bookworm. She wondered now how she'd gone from being confident enough to take over her career at such an early age to a woman running from Jarrod Marrone.

Rowan tried to channel her mother now, her dignified presence, her strength, and that calm otherworldly inner light that emanated from her, silently demanding respect. Elin was a warrior. Rowan was a runner. That must change if she were to have a normal life—maybe it would be a life with Huw, but it was too soon to tell.

"I miss you, Mom," Rowan whispered, her hand over the stone. It tingled against her skin.

She stood in the rest area doorway, watching the parking lot for several minutes before pulling up her hood, mask in place, and returning to her car. Thirty minutes later, she exited toward Buffalo. The snowfall had increased. Fat, wet flakes kept her wiper blades moving, but the roads were clear. Although Lake Erie waters might be frigid against the human skin, if the middle of the lake wasn't completely frozen, an arctic blast of Canadian wind could pick up lake water and dump what was commonly called "lake effect" snow in feet not in inches. Rowan wasn't afraid of extreme weather, but she didn't want to drive in it either. In some ways, being holed up with Maya in a snowstorm, roads closed, would create a safe spot to hide from Jarrod. The car shook slightly with the rumble of a passing snowplow. Rowan tapped her phone.

"Siri, call Maya Edwards." Rowan had tried to call earlier, but there was no answer on the landline. Calls to the mobile phone number had gone to voicemail.

"Calling Maya Edwards," Siri's pleasant, not-quite-human voice answered.

"Hello, Rowan." The voice, akin to her mothers in tone and cadence, its lovely Welsh singsong accent still there despite years living in the U.S., made Rowan smile.

"How did you know it was me? Did Griff call to say I was on my way?" The prepaid phone wouldn't have pulled up a name.

"No, Elin told me." Maya's laughter was light, airy. Rowan trembled and gripped the wheel.

"I think I can outrun the storm and be there in about thirty to forty minutes," Rowan said. "Do you mind having a guest for a few days, maybe longer if the storm locks us in?"

"Of course. I've been waiting for you." Maya's voice was calm and confident.

Rowan focused on the road, clutching the steering wheel in an effort to tamp down her nerves. Paranoia about both Lilydale and the training that lay ahead ran through her like a bolt of lightning.

"Rowan, put your fear away and stay calm. We have a lot to talk about, but you need to arrive safely." Maya said. "Like your mother, you're a gifted, talented warrior. First, tackle the weather and the road, then we'll talk about the training you'll need before setting out on the difficult path ahead of you."

"See you soon, Aunt Maya." Rowan heard her voice shaking in tandem with her hand when she reached outward to tap the red button and disconnect the call.

The roads on New York's Route 76 weren't too bad, but the snow was coming down heavier now. Dark clouds created a feeling of dusk despite the time of the day. As she exited onto the county highways, first 127 then 310, snowplows were less prevalent. Traffic was sparse, giving Rowan the luxury of moving the car slowly, pumping her brakes lightly as salt and ice crunched beneath her tires. She turned left onto Frisbee Road with a laugh and a slight sideways skid. It was only another mile now. She and Griff, who loved a game of Frisbee on the beach during family summer vacations to Erie, found the street name funny when they were young.

The plows had done their work on Melrose Drive, but the road was still a little rough. Rowan shifted to second gear until she'd moved through the famed, arched Lilydale Assembly sign, noticing it had changed from the old "City of Light" she remembered to *World's Largest Center for the Religion of Spiritualism*. The old jolt of undefined jittery energy passed through her. As a child, she'd begged her mother to let her stay home.

"Lilydale is weird, Mom. I hear voices whispering."

"Of course you do," Elin had replied with a shrug, amused. "Tell them to be quiet or go away."

Rowan then put her fingers in her ears. Once Elin parked the car in front of Maya's house, she always turned to the back seat and pulled Rowan's fingers back out before exiting the car.

"Someday you'll realize this is who you were born to be," Elin would say, gently hugging her before they walked, with Griffith, to Maya's front door. "Maya misses you and Griffith. Let's make it a nice visit, okay?"

Rowan's fingers twitched, tapping the wheel. Here she was, years later, hoping her mother was right and the strong, mysterious pull drawing her in was more positive than fear induced. Still, the whispers began seconds after she entered Main Street. The uncomfortable sensation was as upsetting as she remembered.

"Be quiet or go away!" Rowan said, loudly, hoping her voice carried into the spirit world.

Gradually, the whispers faded and the positive vibes within her became stronger. The stone hummed against her chest with increasing intensity. Strength rushed through her limbs, tingling the roots of her hair, her toes and fingertips, widening her vision. Power lifted, then expanded from her core like a hot air balloon whose operator had prepared it for flight. What had once frightened her now created a strange sense of safety. She could guard herself from danger. She could shield Griff, too, if necessary.

Although she was turning the steering wheel, the car seemed to pull into an open space in front of a lavender colored Victorian cottage on its own. Rowan had no idea how Maya came to purchase her home, or how she maintained it without, to the best of Rowan's knowledge, participating in gainful employment. Still, her contact with her aunt over the years had been from afar, sending cards, notes, and texts from wherever she landed around the globe, visiting rarely and always with Griff. Perhaps Maya had a private source of income.

Rowan cut the engine and sat for a moment, inhaling the stillness that is Lilydale, a haunted but serene and magical place. Despite not seeing each other for several years, Maya and Rowan were closer now than they'd been while Elin was alive. Rowan had been her mother's girl. When they came to visit, Maya was usually singularly focused on Griff, and Rowan, not wanting to be there anyway, curled up with a book and tried to ignore the confusion caused by crazy, incoherent ghostly whispering flickering off and on. Griff told her Maya had turned down all his offers to pick her up and drive her to Pittsburgh. Her aunt moved to Lilydale the year before Griff was born, and she'd never left. Rowan questioned whether Maya was agoraphobic, but when she asked Griff, he dismissed the idea.

"She's a homebody. She's not comfortable flying or driving long distances," Griff said. "I bought her a cell phone, and we do video calls if I initiate the call."

The front door to the quaint cottage opened a crack. Maya leaned a quarter of her upper torso out, strands of long white hair lifting on the wind making her look positively witchy. Rowan grabbed her backpack and suitcase, locked the car, and approached the front door, her boots crunching on a gravel driveway, its stones buried beneath snow that covered her footprints seconds after she stepped forward.

"*Cariad!*" Maya greeted her with the Welsh "sweetheart,"

kissing her on both cheeks in European fashion. "Come in! I've got water boiling for tea."

"*Ctwch*, Aunt Maya." Rowan wrapped her aunt in a hug. Maya resembled Elin enough that it was both hurtful and heartwarming to see her.

Maya hung Rowan's coat, hat, and scarf on a wooden peg near the door while Rowan pulled off her hiking boots and padded into the kitchen in thick woolen socks. She turned slowly to look around the room and then beyond, into the living room. At first it appeared that not much had changed. Candles burned, emitting a floral scent that mingled in the air with the patchouli potpourri in a chipped porcelain bowl on a side table. Then Rowan scanned the photos on the wall, each large, framed, and showcasing places all over the world. Photos she'd taken, several of which won awards. Oddly, there was no television to bring the outside world to her aunt. Maybe she kept a TV in her bedroom.

"I love your work," Maya said, setting a cup of hot mint tea on the kitchen table. "I don't hear from you as much as I once did, but Griffith keeps me updated."

"I'm sorry. I've gotten bad at staying in touch on a regular basis. Griff gets on me about that. I promise to do better in the future." Rowan inhaled the smell of the tea before sipping. The myriad, comforting scents of Maya's home settled softly like a cloak of nostalgic goodness, muting the tingling sensations, the whispers, and the uncomfortable purpose of this visit.

"Always on the run, Rowan. Call me old, but seeing someone in person is still best. You can tell if they're good or bad by the sight, the vibe, and even the smell of them."

"Well, we shouldn't necessarily go around sniffing people, Aunt Maya," Rowan answered with a laugh.

Maya chuckled. "You get what I mean."

The accuracy of her aunt's words resonated within her.

Rowan had read a few articles that left the impression Jarrod Marrone was ruthless and devious, but they were nothing compared to the feeling, when he'd stood in front of her, of revulsion and danger. She should have come to her aunt long ago with her questions and negative assumptions, rather than live on the run. Regrets were the stuff that sorrow was made of. She'd allow no regrets. She'd fled, she'd built a new career, she'd learned, and she'd grown stronger.

"I've been on the run, Aunt Maya. For a long time . . . running from Jarrod Marrone. Do you know who he is?"

Maya sighed, looking first up at the ceiling then down into the dark waters of her tea. "Well, I think you've been running from yourself too, but we can talk about that later. I saw Jarrod Marrone once, from a distance, when he was a young boy. I've seen him since in various magazines. Even at an early age, from the stories his father told me and my own intuition, I sensed the type of man he'd grow up to be."

"You knew Paul Marrone?" Rowan was surprised.

"Yes." Maya looked reluctant to pursue the topic any further. "Elin tells me Jarrod stalks you."

There it was again, that casual reference to a conversation with her mother. Her dead mother. Rowan could request her mother speak to her by using the stone on her necklace. But Maya? She wore no jewelry and had no crystals sitting about anywhere. How did she do it? Was it a bonus of living in a psychic community? Or was she imagining things as she grew older?

"He hunts me, Aunt Maya. Has for quite some time and it's getting worse. Ever since what happened . . . what I did to him . . . in Paris . . ." Her voice trailed off. "A very close call in Rome caused me to quit modeling. Too visible. Hiding behind the camera works better for me, and it's a lot more rewarding on a personal level."

"You used your powers?" Maya's eyebrows lifted, and she sat back with a look that was both amused and stunned.

Rowan let out a nervous laugh and was relieved when Maya chuckled. "I lost control and burned his hand. Realizing what I could do, and that I couldn't control it, was terrifying. I can't afford to suppress my magic anymore. Jarrod's become increasingly dangerous and, honestly, I want a normal life."

"Well, avoiding your magical abilities was your choice, my dear." Maya stopped, closed her eyes, and took in a deep breath. "That's in the past. You're here now, and I've missed you."

"Does Jarrod know where you are?" Rowan twitched, her nerves on edge at the realization that she could be putting her aunt in danger. "I don't want anything to happen to you."

"No, Jarrod isn't aware I exist. Paul was careful about that. At least not yet, but with what's to come, he'll find out." Maya looked both fragile and fearless. "Don't worry about me. I can take care of myself."

"What do you mean 'what's to come'? Are you saying you're able to see the future?" Rowan was sure Maya had never indicated this was a skill in her magical repertoire.

"No, I can't see the future, nor do I need to. It's inevitable that things set in motion long ago will soon play out. If I could predict how the story would end, I'd tell you."

"Griff has someone inside Marrone Industries who obtained access to Jarrod's email account. Evidently, Jarrod thinks I'm Paul's biological daughter and a threat to his complete control of the company." Rowan watched her aunt closely. "Why would he think that?"

Maya looked both uncomfortable and sad. A tight ball of anxiety formed in Rowan's gut. She hoped she hadn't opened a basket of memories better left in the past. Maya closed her eyes. Placing her right hand on her heart, she began humming a strange but hauntingly familiar tune. Perhaps her aunt had dropped out of their conversation and was now meditating. Things were becoming more peculiar by the minute. At least the whisper of ghostly voices had quieted.

"Aunt Maya, are your powers as strong as my mother's were?"

Maya opened her eyes and picked up her tea, now cold, sipping quietly as she studied Rowan. The ticking of a round, brass-trimmed clock over the doorway, its hands moving forward with the inevitability of time, sounded louder than Rowan remembered. She stood and walked to the back door, gazing through its windows. Outside, the wind picked up then died down, blowing snow into artfully swirling patterns, leaving it to lie in newly formed piles here and there. Rowan waited, knowing the only gateway to the enlightenment she craved was through the tall, slim woman seated behind her, her face slightly wrinkled with time, her body resonating with something stronger than her calm demeanor would indicate to the average person. But Rowan was not the average person. An energy extended outward from her aunt to her, followed by a zap that ran up her spine.

She returned to her seat at the kitchen table. Her body strong, alert. She was sure the sensation was coming from Maya, and yet her aunt hadn't moved beyond lifting a mug to her lips, sipping, and setting it back down again.

Maya reached her hand toward Rowan. Rowan grasped it instinctively, then gasped. A forceful sensation shot up her arm, and the quartz changed in hue from blue to red, its heat nearly burning her chest. "My powers are almost as strong as your mother's, but yours, if you accept them, are beyond both Elin and I combined."

Maya let go. The sensation of falling from a large cliff or deflating like the air mattress she'd once toted in her backpack from Kenya to Namibia, filled her slowly and powerfully. Pain pulsed across her right shoulder, the hard tiled floor cool against her cheek. She'd fallen off the chair. Maya hadn't moved.

"Help me, please," Rowan whimpered like a small child, surprised at the very sound of her voice.

"You have powers." Maya's voice, compassionate yet stern, floated over her. "Use them. Now!"

Rowan wanted to cry, even though the pain was subsiding. "Mom . . ." She called for Elin like a baby, but only the ticking of the clock and the wind outside responded to her plea. She closed her eyes and concentrated.

"Up!" Rowan wasn't sure if she'd said it aloud or silently pushed the words outward from her mind. Her body shifted, moving upright.

"Now!" She was suspended mere inches above the chair. She grabbed its back and sat herself down.

"Stop!" The tension gradually rolled off of her, and things normalized. Rowan was shaking, hard, her teeth chattering. Suddenly, Maya was behind her, wrapping a quilt across her shoulders, holding water to her lips and helping her to take a drink. She exuded a soft, gentle smell of lavender and roses that was identical to Rowan's memory of Elin.

"What on earth was that?" Rowan heard the tremor in her voice. "How did I intuit what to ask my body to do? Why couldn't I stand up?"

"You experienced the strength of your own power when you directly connect with what lies within you." Maya moved to the pantry and returned to the table with nuts, olives, cheese, and a few cookies. "I wouldn't let you stand up. I forced you to use your magic. It was only about a twenty-five percent transmission from me to you, but you'll need to eat."

"I'm not sure I could survive one hundred percent."

"Let's hope you don't have to test yourself and find out." Maya pushed a plate in front of Rowan, and she ate, greedily, like a starving child. "The goal is to help you identify and control your ability, creating ways for you to shield yourself from harm."

"Mom said what I have is a gift, passed from mother to daughter, but it always scared me. I didn't listen to her. I wanted to be like the other kids at school." Rowan no longer trembled, although her shoulder remained tender. The food helped. Now she wanted answers. "I ordered my body to levitate, an action I never considered and had no idea I could do. I don't understand."

"When did you first accept that these powers were part of you? Not what you think now, but the very first time you realized." Maya's face held no expression, but a stillness emanated from her to Rowan that generated a sense of calm. It was as if they were connected by an oddly familiar yet ancient, ethereal force.

"The first time I accepted I had magical powers was when the police brought this necklace to our house after Mom's accident." Rowan answered, touching the quartz stone resting on her sternum. "They said Mom's necklace had survived, but no one could safely touch it. They assumed it retained heat from the explosion. When they delivered it to the house, I put it around my neck without any problem. It terrified me and, at the same time, brought me close to Mom. The sensation was similar to what's emanating from you right now."

Maya leaned forward, extending her hand, palm up, on the table. "We're going to share a lot over the next few days, you and I. You can talk about those tough memories when you're ready. For now, lay your hand on mine. Don't worry, I'll be gentle."

Rowan laid a trembling hand on top of Maya's.

"Close your eyes while I speak, and you'll begin to see your history, your heritage, in your mind's eye." Maya's smile was reassuring. A sense of peace washed over Rowan as she closed her eyes.

"Not all the women in our extended family inherit magic, and many have only rudimentary abilities. Our branch is powerful. Our magic is *Tanwen*—white fire in English—and comes in a direct line from Ceridwen. Men, despite what they believe, do not . . . cannot succeed without strong women. Occasionally, men in our family are born with their own gifts, but never with magic. Even gifted, they are weaker, and in some cases powerless, without us. We balance and safeguard them from themselves and the larger world."

Similar to a silent film, in her mind's eye Rowan viewed women in clothing she'd seen in history books or museums, wearing necklaces like hers. They placed their hands on the heads of boys and men in a gentle fashion. The aura emitted by them filled Rowan with understanding.

"I see my friend, Cat, who I met in London," Rowan said.

"Yes, Cat has a smaller stone, and lesser magic," Maya said. "I know her mother. Cat is a good person and a good choice as a friend."

"Perhaps women should run things," Rowan said with a laugh. "Run the world."

"Sadly, the world—especially the U.S.—hasn't shown itself ready for that epic shift." Maya's voice sounded fierce to Rowan. "Women do, quietly, run the world, but until we stop using our precious energies to rail against the patriarchy and instead use our inner strength to move it aside, until we stop demanding unified beliefs amongst ourselves, elbowing voices unlike our own out of the way, our true power will remain contained, less visible, and fragmented when it should be united."

"That's a tall, complicated order, Aunt Maya." Rowan heard the flicker of doubt in her voice. "If you mean come out of the shadows, take the reins of the game, and turn the world for good, I'm all for that. But fighting for equality is the eternal fight, is it not?"

"Good point." Maya said in a tone that closed the subject. "I'll get off my soapbox now and get back to you, your mother, me, and your own need to use your powers soon . . . very soon."

"Do we need a magic stone around our necks to ignite the power you're talking about? I've often believed that's true for me." Rowan started to remove her hand, but Maya closed her fingers around Rowan's wrist, preventing release. "You're preparing me for a future I can't avoid, but I'm scared."

"You're right. For now, you're safe here. We're blanketed in by the storm," Maya said. "And no, you don't need that necklace to use your powers. It has its purpose, but I've now explained the source of your magic. Next, I'll teach you to harness your power."

"We each have different levels of magic, and we're capable of expanding our magic with practice and hard work," Maya continued. "When faced with an emergency, we sometimes expend all our powers with tragic results, as happened to your mother. More often, we emerge victorious, our magic stronger than ever. This is my hope for you in the battle you'll face."

"What happened to my mother?" Rowan asked, opening her eyes. "And why are only women in our family gifted with magic?"

Maya released Rowan's hand and stood, talking as she walked to the stove and began reheating water for tea. "Occasionally, a boy is born with above average, extraordinary human abilities. Those boys need our magic, at times, to protect them because they have the ability to change the world for good. We haven't had such a person for a while. The result has been increased chaos; voters faced with choices filled with weakness, demagoguery, and even fascism. Corporations—devoid of instinctive, creative leadership options—promote the weak, the mediocre, and the narcissistic. Gifted leaders—men or women—are rare."

"Wow, for someone who doesn't have a TV and never leaves Lilydale, you have an interesting view on the state of society." Rowan was amused and surprised by her aunt's impassioned rhetoric.

"I have a TV upstairs, in my bedroom." Maya winked and smiled.

"And eliminating Jarrod—one weak, cruel man using his power—will make a difference? Are you saying I'm supposed to save the world? Because that's not only huge, but nonsensical to think one woman—me—can take that on." Rowan met her aunt's gaze directly when Maya returned to the table and sat down.

"No, Rowan . . . Griffith was born with extraordinary, but decidedly human abilities. And you—your magic—can serve as both buffer and bulwark for him." Her aunt's mouth was in a straight, serious line, the energy emanating from her hitting Rowan with a new level of strength.

"Griff? He would roll his eyes if he heard you say that. He doesn't believe in magic . . . especially not where his sister and aunt are concerned." Rowan pictured Griff's reaction the day after he'd worn her necklace.

"Griffith has the potential to be a strong, perhaps once in a generation, type of leader." Maya's face had a stubborn set to it. "Your magic, used correctly, can help Griffith fulfill his destiny, and you can move beyond Jarrod and photography to make significant differences, be a positive influence on your own."

Rowan looked away, gazing toward the window, watching the seemingly endless snow fall. Had her reclusive aunt been entertaining fantasies, delusions about she and Griff, until those dreams functioned as reality? Had it been a mistake to come here? She shoved that thought aside. There was nowhere else to get the vital training she needed.

"Griffith will be very wealthy one day. As a leader, with

that wealth, he can change people's lives." Maya removed her glasses and wiped her eyes. "Jarrod believes he can harness your powers for his own intents and purposes."

"I wouldn't help him if he were the last person on earth." Rowan stood, but her legs were weak, her balance uncertain, and she sat down again. "I love Griff, Aunt Maya. He's smart and talented, but you've always favored him. Perhaps you're projecting his future beyond what he wants or is capable of . . . unless there's more you aren't telling me."

Maya stood up, taking the dishes to the sink, then turning off the flame beneath the now whistling kettle and preparing two fresh mugs of tea. "Go into the living room and get comfortable. Take the quilt with you, and I'll bring us both a glass of water along with our tea."

Maya's voice was placid, but her hands quivered slightly as she dropped tea bags into the mugs, their wet strings hanging over the sides. Walking slowly, Rowan touched the door frame to steady herself. Once settled into a comfortable, oversized armchair, its cushion soft with age but its spring and frame still firm, Rowan snuggled under the quilt and relaxed. Outside, the pristine white beauty of winter had settled in.

"So what do you do here at Lilydale to afford this home?" Rowan asked when Maya appeared and set a mug of tea and a large glass of water on the end table beside Rowan, then set the same for herself on the coffee table and settled into a worn, faded brown couch. She remembered Maya's many lectures on the benefits of drinking water when, as children, they requested a sugary soft drink.

"I bake an assortment of items to sell to the tourists through our cafe, and I'm a licensed midwife," Maya answered. "The latter brings in most of my money. I work through a local hospital and local doctors. I had enough money, prior to moving here, to purchase this house outright when homes were selling pretty cheaply."

That answered the question as to whether Maya was agoraphobic. Evidently, she left Lilydale semi-regularly but carefully controlled where she had interactions in the outside world. Clearly, her aunt had created a safe community for herself. Rowan envied her, thinking about her short time in Mumbles the close-knit village. Her longing for Huw intensified.

"I miss being a part of a family." Rowan pointing to a photo of refugees, covered in desert dust, crossing into Jordan that hung prominently on her aunt's living room wall. "It's not as glamorous out there as you might think."

"I love your photos." Maya's smile exuded pride that filled Rowan with joy. "Griffith helped me acquire them."

"You have quite a few," Rowan said. "I'm impressed."

Maya pointed to a photo of a homeless man huddled in a doorway, all his belongings in two small bags beside him. "This one is heartbreaking, melancholy."

"Covid set me free from Jarrod's stalking for a little while," Rowan answered. "I masked up and roamed London's streets chronicling the effects of the pandemic. The homeless, left without throngs of people to panhandle, reflected the mood of that time. It's been the most deeply satisfying work of my career, thus far."

"Feeling okay?" Maya watched her intently.

"Yes, is this magic water?"

"No, it's good old New York tap water." Maya laughed.

"You look like Mom." Rowan wiped her eyes with her sleeve to stop the tears. "Don't mind me. It's nice to see a bit of her in the flesh."

"Elin's always with me, but it's better to have you here . . . in the flesh, as you put it." Maya's multiple bracelets clicked against one another as she pushed a strand of hair from her face, tucking it behind her ear.

"Can you talk to her?" Rowan asked.

"At times I can hear her, but not often. Several mediums here tell me that she's with me, which I find comforting. I sense her very strongly right now." Maya pulled a gently worn green afghan from the back of the couch and tucked it across her lap. "When Elin was alive, we sometimes used a sister telepathy to talk." Maya's smile didn't remove the sadness in her eyes.

"I can use the stone to ask her to come to me, although I, too, only hear her," Rowan said. "And it doesn't always work."

Maya's bangles made soft music as she sipped her tea. "You were your mother's joy, her life. The love of a good mother doesn't die when her body no longer inhabits this earth. It lives on, watching over you, reaching out to protect you. When Elin was alive, I asked her to guard Griffith because I couldn't."

"Why are you exceptionally attuned to Griff? Even when we visited as children it was only Griff you focused on." Rowan hoped she hadn't come all this way only to find a woman lost in ancient beliefs and fantasies about Griff created out of loneliness. Deep compassion for her aunt, a middle-aged woman living alone, no children or partner, filled Rowan.

"I can explain. I owe you that." Maya was very still, yet Rowan perceived a new vigor radiating from her. "Or if you'd prefer to lie down, take a rest, we can talk later. We start your lessons after dinner tonight. You may need to recharge your energies."

"No, I'm ready," Rowan adjusted the quilt across her lap. "And please tell me what happened to cause my mother's death. I've wanted the answer to this question for a long time."

Rowan watched Maya's eyes close, as if she was praying. Was her aunt religious? She'd never considered this and therefore never asked. Would a woman who might identify as a witch also have a traditional belief system? She hoped this conversation would move, soon, out of the mystical talk into something real, tangible, and, most of all, understandable.

Maya began speaking in Welsh, her cadence and accent deepening with the use of her mother tongue. She opened her eyes, looked at Rowan, and smiled. Rowan shifted uncomfortably under the quilt tucked from her mid-section down her legs, waiting, touching the stone now and again for reassurance. An energy and inner light, a type of chi as the ancient Chinese called it, passed from Maya's body to hers.

"That was nice, Aunt Maya," Rowan said, giving what she hoped was an encouraging smile. "I didn't understand, but I think it was a prayer. I've often stopped in churches around the world to sit peacefully, pray, and center myself."

"My mother, your Nain, always started our day with breakfast and that prayer," Maya said.

Rowan silently hoped Maya couldn't sense the concern running through her. Her aunt rambled from one topic to another, first sharp and lucid, then fragmented and shifting from the present to old memories. She wasn't sure how to move the conversation back to her questions about Griff and about Elin's death.

"Weren't you and Mom pagans at heart. Perhaps druids?" Rowan asked.

Maya's hearty laugh filled the room. "Over the last millennium, we've been Christian, as have others who've been called 'witches'."

"Ahh . . . okay. Another topic I never had the chance to talk to Mom about." Rowan smiled, hoping to hide the sadness and mild concern for her aunt's mental state.

"We believe our magic comes from God through Ceridwen to us," Maya explained. "Magic exists all around us, Rowan. Have you never called an event or action a miracle? You've seen its force in the world and sensed it coming from the spiritual world where your mother . . . and mine . . . reside. Now you need to forge a path with your own magic."

Rowan absorbed her aunt's words quietly. She was glad the snow was falling at an increasingly rapid pace. Although she was sure she'd sense danger if it were heading toward them, the weather created the best protective shield she could ask for. Maya moved the afghan aside and stood, walking to the window to survey the darkening skies. Rowan could see from where she had been seated that her car had disappeared amidst the growing mountain of snow. Maya turned on several lamps in the room, then closed the curtains. Rather than feeling claustrophobic, Rowan enjoyed a warm, cozy, cared for sensation.

"I'd begun to wonder if you'd ever show up, ready to take on your responsibilities." Maya settled herself again on the couch, afghan in place. "Neither you nor Griffith are ready for what is coming. I'm here to prepare you, and I'll be there when you need me."

Rowan squirmed, discomfited by the weird, prescient language. Perhaps Maya had lived with mediums and those claiming psychic abilities for too long. Suddenly, there was a tickle on her neck that moved across her shoulders. A cat dropped into her lap, its soft gray fur rubbing against her hand, its green eyes looking up at her.

"Who's this?" Rowan scratched between its ears, and the animal settled on her legs, purring gently.

"That's Maggie." Maya smiled fondly at the cat. "I wondered how long before her curiosity would get the best of her."

"Hello, Maggie." Rowan stroked the warm, purring cat with delight. "I'm glad you don't live alone, Aunt Maya."

"I love dogs too, but at my age, a cat is easier. Good company and less work." Maggie hopped down from Rowan's lap and moved to the couch where she curled up next to Maya. "Your love for Griffith runs deep, Rowan."

Rowan nodded, smiling. She'd adored Griff from the moment she laid eyes on him. "He's exactly what any sister would want!"

"I prayed first because my mother always advised this was the best path to take prior to beginning anything difficult. I know you're wondering why I haven't answered your questions. Why I'm rambling on about everything else." Maya eyes locked with Rowan's. "I hope what I'm about to tell you won't change your feelings for Griffith, your mother, or for me."

Taking a deep breath, Rowan held Maya's gaze without looking away.

"Griffith is my son. Paul Marrone is his father." Maya pulled Maggie into her lap as if in need of comfort.

Her aunt's blunt words sent a shock wave through Rowan, her mind sorting what she'd heard through filters of astonishment and denial. Maya's face remained still, only the tapping of her foot against the floor indicating a nervous concern.

"But I saw my mother pregnant," Rowan said, leaning forward. "I was seven years old. I put my hand on her stomach and the baby moved."

The ticking of a clock on the mantel of the dormant fireplace echoed across the silence in the room, pacing the tension with the movements of its second hand. It rhythmically blended with the faint sound of birdcalls outside, heralding the movement of brave sparrows traversing the snow and cold to seek food.

"That's true. Your mother and I were pregnant at the same time. I was due in January, your mother in February. I'd broken off the relationship with Paul and moved to Lilydale to hide from him." Maya paused, reaching forward to retrieve her tea mug and take a sip. "Maybe I was hiding from the world, I don't know. I'd had an affair with a wealthy, married man and I wanted to start over. Then I found out I was pregnant."

"Why wouldn't you tell him you were pregnant with his child?" In any future she could envision with Huw, she'd be thrilled to announce a baby was on the way.

"I'll get to that," Maya said, her voice a bit tremulous. "Your mother came here nearly nine months pregnant—despite your father's objections—because we wanted to have a reading . . . about the babies. It was off season, and the medium was a friend of mine."

Maya's fingers nervously picked at the afghan, its right corner unravelling in places. Maggie began playing with the loose bits of yarn. "I was conflicted about my decision to keep the baby a secret. The medium warned that Paul's adopted son would harm my child if he became aware of his existence. That solidified my decision to hide Griffith from Paul."

"Then Elin went into labor. I called a midwife who lives nearby. By the time she arrived, I was in labor too. There was a terrible snowstorm, much like the one outside. Griffith was born here, in this house . . . as was your real brother, who was stillborn." Maya stopped speaking, letting the gravity of her words sink in.

"Oh, God . . . that's terrible! Mom must have been hysterical . . . and to go through that alone, without my father." A light chest pain and a flash of dizziness shook Rowan. Tears welled up, spilling over onto her cheeks. She clutched the edge of the quilt and began taking deep breaths.

"She wasn't alone; I was with her." Maya's voice was sad and tender. "The boys looked alike. Your mother and I paid the midwife triple her fee to keep quiet and allow us to fill out the paperwork, switching the boys. The next day we took the babies to the local hospital and had ourselves and Griffith checked while your mother called your father."

"No . . . no . . ." Rowan looked at Maya, pleading, searching her aunt's face for a hint that this wasn't true. "Griff isn't my brother? He's my . . . what? . . . cousin?"

"I did it to protect Griffith . . . and to help Elin heal," Maya said. "Your mother told me she couldn't bear telling you the baby brother you longed for had died."

They sat in silence for a few seconds. Rowan could see her aunt's eyebrows bend in sync with the worry lines on her forehead.

"This isn't what you expected when you came here." A compassionate, comforting spirit of connection traveled from Maya to Rowan. "Yes, Griffith is your cousin . . . and the brother of your heart."

"Did my father suspect anything?" Rowan's mind conjured up a thousand pictures of her father and Griff together, normal and loving, over the years.

Maya sighed, her mouth in a sad downturn. Rowan stood and walked over to her aunt, sitting next to her on the couch and taking her hand. "Your father and I were never close. He rarely came here to visit. Your mother told him I'd lost my baby, and he never questioned either of us. For years, the truth remained hidden, shared by only your mother, the midwife, and I."

"It must have been incredibly hard for you, giving up your baby, worrying about him while keeping such a heavy secret." Rowan patted Maya's shoulder softly.

"If both babies had lived, I'm not sure what would've happened." Maya sighed. "Your mother wanted me to return to Wales with Griffith. But then her baby died, and I instinctively handed Griffith to her. Nothing could be safer than hiding him in plain sight with the person I trusted most, besides myself, to protect him. I had no doubt that Elin would love him as much as I do. And, selfishly, it ensured I'd see him without sentencing him to a life of hiding . . . or being on the run."

Rowan nodded. She understood fleeing a person you feared—the tension, the lack of stability. Griff wouldn't be who he was today without Maya's decision. She leaned in and hugged her aunt.

"I had limited income. Paul would have hired a lawyer to take custody, and I couldn't have my baby raised in a house with his wife and Jarrod." Maya sighed. "Elin planned to explain this to you when you were older, but she didn't live long enough. Your father had little interest in bringing you and Griffith to visit me, especially after he remarried. I was lucky if I spent time with my son once a year until he was old enough to drive here on his own. By then, you'd left home and were roaming the world."

Rowan gave a small laugh. "Have you met Shelley, our stepmother?"

Maya shook her head.

"Griff calls her Shellebrity." Rowan grinned, watching Maya's tension-ridden face relax into a smile. "To be fair, she's nice. But if you met her, you'd understand why I left at eighteen. I'd done only a few runway shows when Mom died. Without a parental guardian, I'd have been forced to quit. Shelley stepped in, and I'm grateful for that, but it was hell taking her with me. She's a celebrity seeker, and I'm a private person by nature. The minute I was sixteen, I told Dad I was either managing my own career or emancipating myself. Modeling wasn't meant to last forever, but it gave me a lucrative way to independence."

"I had no idea you were dealing with that. I should have taken your mother's place a long time ago." Maya cupped her hands around Rowan's cheeks, holding her face steady. They were looking at each other eye to eye. "I owe Elin for hiding and shielding my child. I intend to give all of myself to train you to defend yourself."

Rowan nodded, leaning in to wrap Maya in an embrace. "I always wondered why, when we came here, you focused on Griff. It was a little hurtful to me, but everyone loved Griff. I learned to accept it."

"I love you too, Rowan." Maya said, taking Rowan's hand. "But understand that I denied myself my only child to protect him. I believe he was born to do great things."

"Is that what went down between Paul Marrone and my mother the day they died?" Rowan pieced her memories together, slowly, weaving them into her aunt's story.

"Former friends from my life with Paul visited Lilydale for a reading. I told them I was only there for the day, but I was visibly pregnant. They immediately told Paul. This community helped me to hide when he came looking," Maya said. "After Griffith was born, I went to Paul's office and told him the baby was stillborn, I'd had it cremated and was moving back to Wales. Initially, he was angry until I explained I'd wanted to protect the baby from his wife's fury at our affair. I gave him a copy of the death certificate and returned to Lilydale without providing a forwarding address. He'd never met Elin. I counted on that to keep her and Griffith safe."

"You were having his baby, and he hadn't met your family?" Rowan asked.

"We were having an affair, one which I tried to end several times, but he wouldn't let me go. I'd convinced him any family I had was in Wales. Eventually, his wife found out, paving the way for me to break off the relationship for good. I'd been to Lilydale several times for readings and made friends here. It was my first choice as the perfect place to hide. I was already a certified midwife and that, plus a small job at the local hospital after Griffith was born, brought in enough income.

"I would have kept Griffith if it hadn't been predicted he'd be in danger . . . and your mother's child died . . ." Maya voice trailed off. Rowan watched her aunt's whole body shudder with remembrance of the joy and agony in what must have been an awful night.

"It sounds like you covered all your bases," Rowan said. "How did Paul find Mom and Griff?"

"When Griffith was seven years old, Elin took him shopping for school clothes, and Paul was in the store," Maya answered. "Your mother and I looked alike, which startled him. Elin was in line at the check-out counter, her back to Griffith. Paul squatted down, chatted with Griffith, and got a good look at him. He asked Griffith easy questions and, of course, Griffith shared not only his age, but his birthday. When Elin grabbed Griffith's hand and told him they were leaving, Paul heard her decidedly non-American accent and became even more suspicious."

"But Griff looks like Mom . . . and you . . ." Rowan said, puzzled that a short meeting in a clothing store would be the catalyst for such tragedy.

"As you know, Griffith has one brown eye and one blue eye, and his hair is curly not straight like ours—both inherited from Paul Marrone. When Elin hurried out of the store, ignoring his efforts to speak with her, that did it. Paul hired a private investigator. He discovered Elin was my sister, and then he waved a lot of money in front of the poor midwife, who folded and told him the truth."

"I remember now . . . he came to our house," Rowan said.

"Elin never mentioned that." Maya's raised eyebrows said she was waiting for an explanation.

"She never had the chance. It happened the day she died." Rowan closed her eyes. "It's starting to make sense. Go ahead . . . finish the story."

"No. Tell me what you remember." Maya twisted strands

of white hair, looking anxious. "Your mother always told me everything, especially if it concerned Griffith."

"Okay, okay, calm down. It's a little stressful, the way your internal firepower is flying at me," Rowan said, still trying to get used to both seeing her aunt's emotions and then being assaulted by little balls of invisible raw energy. "It was the day of the accident."

"You instinctively protected Griffith?" Maya must have intuited this despite Rowan's limited response.

"Yes, but I'd done that before when bigger kids bullied him. This was different." Rowan laced her fingers together and took a deep breath. "A very well-dressed man was at the door. He had eyes like Griff, and he appeared to be upset, angry. He demanded to see Mom. When I said she wasn't home, he tried to open the screen door, but it was locked. Then he began shaking the door. Griff showed up behind me, in his underwear, crying and afraid. The man looked down at him and then at me and said 'He's coming with me. Your mother isn't keeping him from me another minute.' His anger was palpable. He looked as though he'd punch the screen at any moment if I didn't comply."

Rowan paused, her voice shaky with emotion from this long-repressed memory . "I raised my hand to ward off a coming attack, and something surged through me. It traveled along my arm, my wrist, and he flew backward off the steps, landing in the yard."

Rowan remembered the man she now realized had been Paul Marrone sitting on the grass in his expensive suit, holding his head and shaking it, stunned. She waited for a reaction from Maya. Her aunt calmly nodded her head as if this were normal, as though it was what she expected Rowan's response to have been.

"I slammed the inside door shut, locked it, picked up Griff, and ran for the phone to call Mom. Griff kept asking me

'Did you do that to that man?' and I kept telling him I had no idea how it happened, but it wasn't me." Rowan wrapped her arms across herself. "For years, I convinced myself it was a fluke. That I have limited to no abilities, that Mom's necklace is the source of my power. I know better now."

Maya looked sad. "Your mother told your father the truth about Griffith that day before she got into Paul's car. She's told me since, when we speak, that she thought she'd use her magic to negotiate with Paul and work it out with your father later. But then . . . well . . . there was no later. Your father pulled me aside at her funeral, demanding an explanation."

"Mom was very calm on the phone. She told me to make sure all the windows and doors were locked, then to take Griff to his room and stay there until she got home—not to answer the door for anyone, even the police." Rowan trembled, touching her own cheek now wet with tears. "Mom entered the house through the back door. She came upstairs, hugged Griff and I, told us she loved us, then went out the front door. I never saw her again."

Silence settled between them, punctuated only by the rhythm of the clock and the sweeping sounds of wind wrapping around the house and soaring through the snow laden trees. Eventually, in a gentle voice, Maya responded. "Paul probably assumed you'd call your mother immediately, like any thirteen-year-old girl, which is why he waited in his car. He planned to hand Elin papers—drawn up by a lawyer but never signed by a judge—giving him the right to a DNA test and temporary custody of Griffith. I believe your mother deduced it was a ruse. She was a very smart woman."

"How do you know that?" Rowan stared in disbelief. "Everything except the stone around my neck disintegrated in the crash."

Rowan was certain Maya was going to completely unravel the afghan before this conversation was over, to the delight of

Maggie who was batting the strings of yarn with her paws. She watched her aunt contemplate how to respond. She hoped her own energy emanated the encouragement Maya needed to continue with her story. If she were to take on Jarrod and protect Griff, she needed the whole truth before she left this house.

"You probably think I'm a hermit of sorts, never doing more than local trips for supplies or midwife requests," Maya said, her hands now still, her voice firm, decisive. "But I did leave Lilydale, several years ago, after Ray Marrone—Paul's brother—left a number of cryptic voicemails claiming he wanted to learn more about Elin's relationship with Paul and asking for information about Griffith."

Rowan watched Maya pause, lifting her head to show an expression of such torment that Rowan pressed her hand to her heart. Whatever had happened in the past now wrapped the gentle, kind woman next to her in a cloak of sadness and regret.

"I panicked, realizing Ray knew who I was and where I lived . . . and that he might uncover the truth about Griffith. I went to see him." Maya sighed, closing her eyes. She looked exhausted. "I hoped to point him away from Griffith. You were living abroad, and your father was remarried."

"I'm sorry for what must have looked like incredible selfishness on my part, Aunt Maya," Rowan said. It was clear her reclusive aunt, burdened with many sad secrets, had been left to manage alone.

"It's alright. The past is where it should be, in the past—that is, until it charges forward into the present, with all its ugliness, and squeezes you like a vise, forcing immediate action or people you love will suffer the consequences." Maya patted Rowan's hand and gave her a small, weak smile. "As his mother, he's my responsibility."

Rowan nodded silently. Her respect for her aunt grew by

the minute. She wanted to tell her it was all going to work out, but she restrained herself and waited, knowing the story unfolding was not yet complete.

"When I met Ray, he was ambivalent about a future in which Jarrod inherited the role of CEO at Marrone Industries. He clearly suspected Paul had another heir. He insinuated Elin and Paul had an affair, called your mother a 'slut.'" Maya's face flushed with the memory. "Furious, I slapped him across the face and, as I did, power surged down my arm. He clutched his chest and dropped dead on the floor."

Rowan gasped, stunned. Her mind flashed back to burning Jarrod's hand with one touch the first time they met and, before that, Paul flying backward into the front yard. It never occurred to her that she could go so far as to kill someone.

"I'd never met Ray. I was unaware of his heart condition," Maya said, her voice carrying a soft tremor. "Only the two of us were in the house that day. I'd taken a taxi from the bus terminal. After I wiped down all possible fingerprints and cleared the red mark on his face with my healing finger, I removed my name from his phone contacts and pocketed a slip of paper on his desk with information about me. I looked for a file but found nothing. Then, I slipped out the back door through a wooded area onto a street running parallel. I walked until I reached a convenience store, called a taxi, and headed back to the bus station."

"You . . . we . . . have a 'healing finger'?" Rowan was on sensory overload now, trying to absorb and sort out everything she'd heard.

"We can do more than defend or attack with these hands," Maya said, smiling and wiggling her fingers. "I'll teach you. It's the wonderful part of the gift we inherited. We can heal. However, doing it in front of others can be dangerous and lead to the wrong level of attention."

"This is overwhelming. I'm trying to process what you've said." Rowan raised shaky hands to her forehead and rubbed her temples, hoping to clear her mind. "You still haven't answered my original question. How did you learn Paul had papers claiming a legal right to Griff?"

"I knew Paul better than anyone. He always used the same lawyer for his personal business, separate from his corporate lawyers," Maya said. "I left my sister's funeral and went to his lawyer's office after office hours. I used a little magic to short circuit the electricity, which turned off the alarm system temporarily. I was lucky. Once inside, I discovered the alarm code on the office manager's desk, along with a computer login and password."

"I put in the code and turned the alarm off. Then I pulled the hard copy file on Griffith with the name of the private investigator and logged into a computer as the office manager. There were hundreds of emails, files, etc. On advice from a friend, I removed the hard drive, making it look like a robbery. They were a small firm, it was an older desktop computer, and it appeared they only backed up manually about once a month or less. I found the backup hard drive too and took it. I reset the alarm. Luckily, I was able to do so before it triggered a call to the police to report a potential problem. I'm guessing they thought it was nothing more than a small blip, an outage that rebooted on its own."

"You stole the hard drive and Griff's file? Do you still have it?" Rowan's astonished expression must have been amusing to Maya, who was grinning. "Clearly, Aunt Maya, you're an enigma to me. I wouldn't have imagined that you, who rarely leaves Lilydale, could or would break into a law office and steal computer hard drives."

"On my own, probably not. The friend who advised me has serious technology skills and comes from a long, ancient line of warlocks," Maya said. "I explained the situation.

Because the request wasn't made with bad intention, he was willing to help."

"You're acquainted with people who are warlocks?" Rowan asked, wondering if she'd taken a wrong turn into a Chronicles of Narnia or Harry Potter dreamscape. For a moment she considered whether her magic could shift her reality to one without an eccentric aunt and devoid of a crazy stalker.

"Information security is the perfect place for a warlock to hide and use his powers for good," Maya said with a chuckle. "You'd be surprised how many there are."

"That poor lawyer. All to cover up Griff's true identity." Rowan tried to seem calm but definitely didn't like what she was hearing from her aunt.

"Before you judge me harshly, Rowan," Maya replied, a dark amusement playing across her face. "my friend removed all references to Paul and Griffith from the hard drives, then hacked into Paul's emails at Marrone Industries and removed the same. Once he'd completely purged any evidence, I sent the hard drives back to the law firm, anonymously. They're still in business with a strange and confusing tale to tell others."

"Very charitable of you," Rowan said, finally relaxing and letting out pent up anxiety with a small laugh. "So, what now? You need to tell Griff the truth."

Maya nodded, her expression one of nervous apprehension. Her aunt was probably worried Griff would be angry, that he wouldn't understand. Griff was obviously the focal point of Maya's life. Losing a future with him over her past decisions would devastate her.

Maya shifted, turning until she faced Rowan. She took a deep breath. "Here's the difficult truth. The only way to stop this madness is for Griffith to claim his birthright and take half of Marrone Industries from Jarrod. If you love Griffith, strengthen your magic and clear the path for him."

A level of frustration rose inside Rowan at Maya's assumption this could be wrapped up neatly and cleanly, with Griff in his rightful place through the use of Rowan's powers. "How, exactly, would Griff claim Marrone Industries without proof of paternity? Jarrod won't give up without a fight."

Maya stood and walked to the window, peeking around the curtains to watch the storm. "I've had a long time to think about this. I can provide the necessary path to prove Griffith is Paul's son."

"Look, Aunt Maya. I'm focused on regaining my freedom and winning the right to live life on my own terms without the threat of Jarrod hanging over my head. This may be about Griff's future to you, but it is about my future as well." Rowan was tired. It was making her sound harsh.

"I do think it's time to get some sleep," Maya said, without turning to face Rowan. "Let's go to bed and tackle your training sessions in the morning."

"Sounds good. I'm exhausted." Rowan stood, grabbing her backpack and suitcase from the spot near the front door where she'd dropped them. "Lead the way."

As she followed Maya upstairs to the guest bedroom, Rowan hoped for a solid eight to ten hours of sleep. She'd need it to handle any training Maya planned to offer.

Rowan

Griff's smiling face on the phone screen the next morning was a welcome sight. Sleep hadn't come easy to Rowan, her mind racing in many directions. She'd insisted on coffee, not tea, this morning, needing fortitude before training. Maya snuggled next to her on the couch and waved to Griff.

"Good to see you weathered the storm," Griff said, running his fingers through hair that resembled a wild bush while sipping his coffee.

"Mmmm, coffee." Rowan raised her own mug in acknowledgement. Her curiosity was slightly piqued as to why Griff had ear buds in when he lived alone, but she said nothing.

"I'm strictly a tea drinker," Maya answered. "But I do keep a small stash of coffee."

"It's good to see both of you. We barely got a flake of snow here."

Rowan stood and walked to the window, turning the phone to show him the winter wonderland outside. "It's stopped, but the plows haven't come through yet."

"Are you safe?" Griff's brow creased with concern.

"I may not be able to get out, but no one can get in." Rowan felt secure, though logically her concern should be heightened now that she was in the same country as Jarrod. "We need to meet somewhere after I leave here. Decide where I'll go next. He must know I'm in the country by now and will be watching your place."

Rowan could see the longing on Maya's face. "Hey, Griff! Talk to Aunt Maya for a minute while I get a refill."

She handed Maya the phone. "Be right back."

"Cupboard to the left of the sink, second shelf." Maya smiled tenderly at the phone screen, listening.

Rowan stood in front of the small Nespresso machine on the counter and opened the cupboard Maya mentioned. As she grabbed a box of pods, she heard Griff's voice, slightly muffled. "Rowan? Ro, where are you? Pick up the phone."

Turning, she faced Maya. Her aunt stood in the kitchen, an undefinable look on her face, hands clenched, pointing to the armchair. Rowan walked back into the living room. Her phone lay face down on the chair. As she reached to pick it up, Maya appeared behind her, placing a hand on her arm.

"Stand against the wall and don't show anything that will give a hint to where you are." Maya's voice was tense, raw. Rowan again silently questioned her aunt's mental state.

"Hey, Griff! Sorry about that. I went to find coffee." Rowan complied, standing against a plain space of wall behind and to the left of the chair. She pulled a pair of small white ear buds out of her pocket and inserted them, preventing Maya from listening to Griff.

"Everything okay?" Griff's concern emanated through the phone. Before she could respond, Gemma was there, smiling and waving to her. She waved back and watched Gemma ask a question, and then heard Griff say "No, not now."

Gemma shrugged, waved again, and appeared to walk toward the kitchen. Griff smiled in Gemma's direction. "Go ahead and hop in the shower, then we'll head out to get breakfast."

"Everything's okay here, I think," Rowan said, tapping her ear buds as Griff nodded in affirmation. She watched Maya pacing in the kitchen, the nervous energy emanating from her creating a mild tingle up Rowan's spine. "Want to explain?"

"You'll have to ask for specifics when we hang up." Griff was avoiding saying Maya's name. "She doesn't trust . . ." Griff bent his head slightly in the direction where Gemma had been standing.

"Have they met?"

"No, she said it was instinct. I figure she's been alone too long and she's getting older. She has . . . quirks." Griff gave a shrug and a smile.

"Gemma isn't aware Maya exists?" Rowan had met Gemma in person only twice. She was pleasant and fun, but it wasn't clear whether Griff wanted to move the relationship to the next level.

Rowan could see Griff glancing at the doorway to the hall where the bathroom and bedrooms were located, checking before responding. "She made it clear to me she had a 'feeling' the first time I showed her a picture of Gemma. She asked that I not talk about her openly to or in front of her. I'd already mentioned I had an aunt. Gemma asked me about her once and I said she lived pretty far away and we weren't close. I left it at that."

"I'll find out more from my end. Where should we meet when I leave here?" From where she stood, she saw no trace of her car, still buried in snow. "Not that I can leave for a few days."

"Give me a little time to come back with a suggestion as to where. You're right. You can't come here. When you leave will depend on the weather. I think you're in a lull and another storm is coming."

"Well, if I can't get out, no one can get in. Lessons with Maya begin today." Rowan could see the power on her phone was fairly low. "I'll use cash and a fake ID to check in somewhere for a few days after I leave."

"I think I have the 'where to stay' solved. I'll explain when we can talk more freely," Griff was walking to the kitchen now, refilling his coffee. "Heard from Huw? Does he know where you are?

"I did a video call with him early this morning. I told him I was with Aunt Maya in a snowstorm but not where." Rowan hated second-guessing the ethics of people she wanted to believe were loyal. Especially Huw.

"I like the guy, Ro. A lot. But information should remain between the two of us . . . and Maya, of course." Griff's face was growing fuzzy on the screen, his voice crackling.

"Griff, my battery's low and reception isn't good. You're fading in and out. I'm going to hang up and recharge the phone. Text me when you have an update." Rowan could see Gemma walk back into the room in a robe, toweling her wet hair.

"Will do. Later." Griff hung up abruptly, the screen going black.

Rowan returned to the kitchen, plugging her phone into the charger she'd left there. The house was old, but the electricity appeared up to date, the wall sockets grounded with new covers. Rowan popped an espresso pod into the machine and started brewing coffee. While she waited, she put a fresh tea bag into a mug for Maya and turned the gas stove on to reheat the remaining water.

"Can we talk about why you dropped the phone and walked away?" Rowan watched her aunt, seated at the table, nervously tap her foot against the floor tiles.

"Yes." Maya nodded. "Tea and coffee first."

Minutes later, Rowan set a mug of hot tea in front of

Maya and sat down across from her, silently waiting, sipping her coffee.

"What do you think of Gemma?" Maya moved the tea bag around in the mug, her hands seemingly unable to be still.

"She's okay, I guess. I haven't been around her in person more than a couple times, but sometimes I see her when I'm on a video call with Griff." Maya wasn't making eye contact as she spoke. "Griff brought her to London with him once, and we had fun."

"I've always had a sixth sense reaction to her that's negative," Maya said. "I get the strongest sensation that it's important she never see me or learn anything about me."

"What has she done to make you feel that way? Maybe, as a mother, you're being overprotective of Griff?" Rowan found it hard to believe her aunt could determine whether a person was trustworthy or not without having met them in person.

"No!" Maya's quick response was fierce. "I saw her picture when Griffith began dating her, and I had this overwhelming certainty she was . . . not honorable. I panicked and told him he couldn't tell her my name or where I lived."

Rowan checked the instinct to roll her eyes, keeping her face neutral. She'd need to talk to Griff about whether they should keep a better eye on Maya or consider finding her mental health therapy.

"How did Griff take that?" Rowan asked. "I mean, I've had moments where I had a bad feeling about someone—usually someone I met in person—and later found out I was wrong, that they were lovely and wonderful to be around."

Maya's eyes flashed with anger, her energy hitting Rowan like a soft punch against her solar plexus. "I'm not a crazy old lady, Rowan! Griffith asked me a lot of questions, trying to pin me down, then he said it was no problem. He'd told Gemma he had an aunt, but nothing further. He usually calls and only uses video when he's alone or in the office."

"I apologize if I sounded disrespectful." Rowan stood, walked to the kitchen counter, and unplugged her partially charged phone. Sitting down again, she scrolled through her photos, choosing one, then laid the phone in front of Maya. "Well, do you have a bad feeling about him?"

She watched Maya stare at the picture of Huw she'd taken while they were hiking. There was no need to clarify where he was. Maya would recognize the mountains; the late blooming gorse and heather nearly gone brown. The kitchen was as silent as the world outside, blanketed in snow without even the call of the birds this morning. It was probably less than a minute, but Rowan was tense, afraid, making the time it took before Maya responded seem longer.

"I don't have a jolting, negative feeling about him." Maya's face relaxed. "He has things from his past to overcome. I think you should slow down, proceed with caution, but I don't think he's a bad person overall."

Rowan nodded, relief flooding her even though the idea that her aunt could suss out bad people by looking at a picture was unequivocally illogical. She plugged the phone back into the charger.

"Who is he?"

"Huw . . . Huw Evans. I met him in Wales and, well . . . I rarely trust people, but it was different with him. When this is over, I'd like to go back and explore a normal relationship with him . . . see where things might go."

"I think when this is over, you'll be very sure who you can trust and who's worth investing your time and love into," Maya said. "For now, there are many lessons I need to teach you in a short amount of time."

"On that note, Aunt Maya, I hope this old house has a modern shower. I'd need to clear my head and be ready to go." Rowan stood, collecting their mugs and placing them in the sink.

"The shower is modern. You'll find it upstairs, at the end of the hallway." Maya wrapped Rowan in a hug.

Rowan closed her eyes, absorbing a warmth emanating from her aunt that had nothing to do with magic. It was love of the kind her mother had dispensed, the kind she missed more than words could describe.

Jarrod

"Our deal is you keep tabs on where she is and notify me and I provide what you need to solve the issues you face." Jarrod kept his back to the office door, his voice low, flexing the fingers of his damaged hand into a fist. "You're not meeting expectations."

He heard the door open behind him. Making a partial turn of his chair, Jarrod watched Derrick enter and walk toward his desk. "Get me a location," he said sharply, then hung up the phone.

"She didn't land in New York, just as she didn't land in Chicago a week ago," Derrick said, folding his six-foot frame into a chair across from Jarrod's desk.

"Your sources weren't great. I have someone with better access. Rowan's in the country. I expect to know where soon." Jarrod kept his voice and, he hoped, his face calm.

There was no benefit in having the hired help begin to doubt him. He needed complete loyalty. Once they picked Rowan up for what they would be told was a meeting with him and found out he intended to lock her away for good—or at least until she agreed to his vision of them as lovers and power partners—he needed that loyalty and silence to stick. Jarrod believed in finding a personal weakness, a vulnerability, and pushing down on it hard, then offering monetary compensation. His current source would cost a pretty penny out of his personal funds.

Derrick nodded, adjusting the Rolex watch on his wrist. He appeared, with his muscular frame in a Brooks Brothers suit and polished Ferragamo shoes, to be a successful businessman. Jarrod watched Derrick shift nervously in his chair, sensing a level of discomfort that was new and concerning. "I run a solid security and protection business, Jarrod. This is a little outside my normal work. I don't recruit snitches in foreign countries to find one woman . . . for any reason."

"You run a bodyguard business. Label it what you like. And you were very willing to take the generous transfer to an offshore bank and step out of bounds by agreeing pick up one woman who, for the past two years, you've been unable to catch."

"Covid made that relatively impossible, although we tried. You know that."

Jarrod waved his hand dismissively. He was in no mood for excuses, however valid. Lately, he'd begun to suspect, from comments he'd overheard Derrick's team make, that his chief of security was considering returning the money, keeping the interest it had accrued, and dropping Jarrod as a client. Normally, he'd fire the man, but he'd done a better job than others Jarrod hired before him. Not that he'd admit that to Derrick.

"This is more than me having the hots for an ex-model who won't speak to me," Jarrod said, resting his hands on the arms of the chair. "I'm developing sensitive cybersecurity products that, somehow, the federal government has gotten wind of. FBI, DOJ. I'm not sure who's running a quiet investigation, but I do have government sources that tell me I need to proceed with care. Rowan has . . . let's say 'abilities' . . . that could be useful."

"That's the source you were speaking to . . . when I walked in?"

Jarrod shook his head. "No. The person I was speaking to is private. I think the information on Rowan's whereabouts should improve. Soon."

"Do you know where she landed?"

"My source thinks it was Pittsburgh. She must have come in under another name. It appears she staged a fairly elaborate ruse, with the assistance of her brother, Griff. Only a suitcase went to New York . . . as did you." Jarrod smiled.

"Is Griff someone we need to put a stronger watch on? Someone to be concerned about?" Derrick leaned forward, hands clasped.

"Griffith Campbell is a small-time infosec guy who fancies himself a white hat hacker," Jarrod said. "He'll never give up an ounce of information on his sister."

"My team believes both he and Rowan keep the father on a need-to-know basis." Derrick's way of leaning forward and looking at him directly, eye to eye, was disconcerting. Jarrod was a small, compact man. Not athletic or with physical defense skills. His power came from money and Marrone Industries, both of which he was working to expand. "Is your new source close enough to provide accurate information?"

"Yes." Jarrod watched Derrick wait for him to reveal a name.

"Anything for me to go on?" Derrick fiddled with his Rolex again and shifted in the chair, but Jarrod didn't miss the flash of irritation that crossed his face. Derrick would keep trying to elicit the information. For now, silence was the only answer he'd receive.

"Nothing concrete. It appears there's an aunt named Maya

who Rowan rarely visits or communicates with. No last name or location yet, but I expect to have that soon."

Derrick nodded. "I'll do a little digging on my end too."

Jarrod turned to face his computer, an indication the conversation was over. Derrick stood, hesitated for a moment as if there was more he wanted to say then, thinking better of it, turned and left the room.

Jarrod focused on reports from his private lab team about their work honing the original MyShadow app. He'd initiate a bidding war, once updates were completed, between private nation state and dark web buyers. He toyed with pushing to expedite results, concerned over the rumors that he was under investigation. But the lab was hidden in the basement of this building, accessible only to a handful of employees who were paid via a shell company set up for this very purpose. He'd hide Rowan right under their noses in a security fortified area they probably had no knowledge existed. He was close to obtaining her. He was sure of it this time. He heard the ping of a text message arriving.

> Source: Maya Edwards. Location: Lilydale, NY.

> Jarrod: Is she there?

> Source: Can't confirm. highly likely. 90% sure. Possibly snowed in.

Jarrod fired off a text to Derrick. The hunt was on and, this time, he would succeed.

Rowan

She lay on the couch, the muscles in her arms and legs mildly shaky, her head pounding. For the past three hours, Maya had forced her to focus on objects and use her mind to make them move. It was one thing to fool around and move a glass of beer on a bar; it was another altogether to move furniture and other heavy objects. As a child, Rowan had loved reading *Alice in Wonderland* and Harry Potter, but the reality when doing it yourself was brutal. Maya left five minutes earlier to walk to the Lilydale cafeteria, open only to residents, and pick up soup and sandwiches for their lunch. Rowan hoped she could sit upright to eat by then.

She pulled her phone out of her pocket to text Griff.

Rowan: u alone?

Griff: Yes, in the office. Maya?

Rowan: picking up lunch from cafeteria.

Griff: Calling you now.

Less than a second later, her phone rang, Griff's smiling

face on the screen. "How are you up there . . . trapped by snow in voodoo land?"

The tension eased as she laughed in a way only Griff could make her do. "My mind doesn't want to believe what I'm hearing and seeing. I've toyed with the idea that Aunt Maya is nuts and heading for a memory care facility but . . ." Her voice trailed.

"Are you lying down?" Griff appeared amused, as if he were catching up on details of a wacky girls' weekend.

"I'm too exhausted to sit up. Roll your eyes all you like, but she made me use my mind to move objects and to disintegrate a piece of wood in the fireplace." Rowan watched Griff roll his eyes, exactly as she'd expected.

"I don't believe you."

"Remind me to use my pointer finger to start a little fire at your house. We'll see how you feel after that." She regretted that she sounded irritated at his disbelief, but the strenuous morning of training had left her with limited patience.

"Let me think about it and get back to you." Griff was looking at his laptop now, multi-tasking.

"I've got to go and call Huw."

"Does she approve of him? Huw? No bad vibes?" Griff shook his head in a way that indicated his belief Maya's 'vibes' were nonsensical.

"Well, she didn't freak out when she saw his picture, but she told me to be careful," Rowan said. "Not a ringing endorsement."

"They should have the main roads cleared by tomorrow and, I would guess, another day or two for the smaller roads," Griff said.

"I hope to leave in two to three days. Ping me by then with suggestions of where to meet." Rowan watched Griff nod, wave, and then the screen went black.

Taking a deep breath, she took out the phone she reserved

for calls with Huw and tapped the only number in the contact list.

"Rowan . . . where are you and how are you?" Huw's voice flowed over and around her soothing, comforting, making her smile.

"I'm fine. I'm with my aunt." Rowan stopped herself from specifying the exact location.

"I've been watching U.S. news. Hopefully you're not stuck in any of the big snowstorms I've seen."

Rowan was glad she hadn't made this a video call. She didn't want Huw to see the look on her face as she struggled between wanting to share every detail and defaulting to an abundance of caution. It was an innocent enough question. "I'm safe and snug at Aunt Maya's. No problems or worries. How are you? I miss you."

"God, I miss you too! I wish you'd let me fly over and help with what I suspect you're planning to do," Huw said. "How long will you stay where you're safe?"

"Hmm . . . a few days I guess," Rowan said.

"Confronting Jarrod isn't something I think you should do alone. Let me go with you—or at least notify law enforcement. Would you promise me that?" Huw's voice emanated a significant level of stress.

"That will be Griff's job. He'll tap a few federal contacts, then come with me." Rowan closed her eyes and wished her magic would allow her to transport herself back to Huw, to his warm, cozy home with Cooper snuggled next to her. "Can we talk about something else? I only have a few more minutes before Aunt Maya returns."

Rowan didn't want to try to explain Maya - her magic and her complex nature - to him right now. "How's Coop?"

Huw described a hike he'd led and how all the hikers fell in love with Cooper, giving him too many treats which ended up in a few accidents to clean up and a very unhappy dog with an upset stomach. When Maya returned and signaled to Rowan that they needed to eat, then get back to work, she reluctantly ended the call.

"What's next?" Rowan asked as she finished her sandwich, scooping wayward crumbs onto her plate. "So far I can start a fire by pointing my finger, and I can move furniture and smaller items by concentrating and reaching my hand outward."

"Next you learn to move sharp objects you might need to defend yourself, and you learn to turn off electrical systems," Maya replied.

"Hmmm . . . can I turn off security systems?" Rowan could see the merit in this training if she could slip in and out of Marrone Industries without alarms going off.

"No, sorry. Our magic isn't as modern as the new technology around us," Maya said, with a wry grin. "You can't dismantle security systems. You can short circuit electrical wiring. Also, if the stone on your necklace is taken from you, then you can't call upon your mother to come for you. She'll have to do that on her own if she's able."

Rowan quietly absorbed this information while Maya stood, walked to a small closet, and removed a dartboard along with several sharp knives. She hung the dartboard on a hook on the far wall in the kitchen. "Ready?"

Rowan nodded. Standing, she approached the knives and reached for one.

"No, don't touch them." Maya stepped between Rowan and the knives. "First, look at the dartboard. Stay three to four feet back from it and focus on the bullseye. Center your mind in line with it."

Rowan stood for a few minutes, and as she looked at the bullseye on the board, it appeared to expand, making the target easier. But when she dropped her gaze and looked back at it again, it had returned to its normal size.

"Step to the side and let me show you." Maya stood about four feet away from the dartboard. She hovered her hand over the knives and one rose in the air. Without touching the knife or looking at it, she said, softly, "Go!"

The knife hurtled through the air and landed in the center of the bullseye. Rowan gasped with amazement and excitement. "Let me try!"

"Never take your eyes off the target, even as you move the knife. You should get a mild tingle in your hand when the knife is ready for your command. Then, as if you were having mental telepathy with me, you tell the knife to go for the target in your line of vision." Maya paused, eyeing Rowan thoughtfully. "A word will spring up. Mine is "go." You'll have to discover your word as your train. But it will be the command your magic requires to make the weapon move and hit the target."

Rowan shivered with nervous expectation. She focused on the bullseye. As it expanded before her, she hovered her hand over the knives. The moment a tingling sensation rippled through her hand, she instinctively looked down at the knife, and it clattered back onto the tray.

"Oh, I messed up!" Rowan flexed her fingers, working to get a normal feeling back. "I'm sorry Aunt Maya. Let me try again."

"It takes practice, Rowan. I didn't expect perfection the first round," Maya said. "Unfortunately, we don't have the luxury of several months to get you trained and ready. Try again!"

Rowan inhaled deeply through her nose and exhaled from her mouth. She concentrated again, staying focused on the target as the tingle spread across her hand. The word "now" sprang up in her head. The tingling in her hand increased. "Now!"

She heard a whoosh of air followed by a thud. She closed

her eyes, and when she opened them, the knife was in the dartboard. She hadn't hit the bullseye but wasn't far off.

"What did I do wrong that I missed the bullseye? It was expanding in front of me." Disappointed, Rowan was filled with the desire to try again.

"You hesitated too long after your hand and mind told you it was time to go." Maya patted her shoulder. "It's timing. This takes practice. But you were close and, if it were a human, you would have hit them."

Rowan ran through the exercise several more times, each time doing a little better but never hitting the bullseye.

"You're getting tired, Rowan. I say we rest and then, when it's dark outside, we'll work on how to disrupt an electrical system. In other words, how to turn off the lights and, hopefully, the security cameras, when necessary." Maya nudged her shoulder. "Having fun yet?"

"It's tough, but I understand better how to channel my magic and how to control it." Rowan hugged her aunt. "Thank you."

"I promise to teach you a few somewhat raunchy but fun tricks before you go. Your training can't all be dark and serious lessons."

"I'm not tired. Teach me now." Adrenaline-fueled exhilaration overcame Rowan.

Maya looked thoughtful. She raised her left hand, palm outward, and faced Rowan's stomach. Suddenly a mild gut punch followed by nausea hit Rowan. She ran to the kitchen sink and threw up a small amount of her lunch.

"I take it back," Rowan said, after rinsing her mouth multiple times. Still clutching her stomach, she sat down. "I'll skip hands-on training if that is one of your 'fun tricks.'"

"That was mild. I truly didn't want to hurt you, only to help you understand what you can do if needed." Maya sat across from her.

"If you think that I'll do that to you, forget it." Rowan sensed a steadying vibe coming from her aunt to her. Her muscles loosened and she became more relaxed.

"Thanks!" Maya laughed. "I prefer to explain to you what I did and how to do it. Hopefully, you won't need this particular resource. In the same way you focused on the bullseye, you focus on a portion of someone's body—try to make sure it's only one of the bad guys, okay?—and then put your left hand up, palm flat, facing the area you want to disrupt. Be careful to avoid vital organs, especially if you're going to push hard with your powers. Unless, of course, your life is threatened. Then fight with everything you've got."

Rowan nodded, thinking through the instructions, imagining implementing them on Jarrod or one of the men he'd often sent after her. "I can give someone a gut punch and possibly make them throw up? Why did you refer to it as a fun trick? It's mean-spirited."

"Well, you can aim a little lower," Maya said with a grin. "And perhaps they'll wet their pants like a baby."

"Or I could make their hair stand on end . . . even fall out." Rowan laughed so hard that Maya joined in. They were giggling like schoolgirls. "Did you do that to someone . . . make them wet their pants?"

"No, Rowan, your mother did it to a bully who picked on smaller kids when we were young," Maya said. "I was there, and when he claimed she'd used black magic to make it happen, we denied it together. We had an aunt who was a little crazy and would teach us things like this when our mother wasn't around."

Rowan stood and began walking toward the stairs. "I'm going to lie down for a little bit." She turned in the doorway and gave Maya a smile. "Thanks for adding that to my bag of magic tricks, Aunt Maya. I'll be heading into a veritable building filled with bullies. It might come in handy."

Griffith

"Let's spend tomorrow together," Gemma said. "Maybe check out the science center or a museum."

Griff stood with his back to her, adding cheese then flipping one half the eggs in the pan overtop to create an omelet. He answered without turning, not confident his face wouldn't give his thoughts away, arousing her curiosity.

"Sorry, babe. No can do." Griff busied himself with a second omelet for himself, hers nearly done. "I've got a ton of work to finish later today and tonight, then I'm out of town for a few days."

"Griff, it's the weekend. Can't you take time off?" Gemma sounded irritated.

"Speaking of work. Did your laptop crash again? I saw you trying to log in to mine." He slid the omelet onto a plate and placed it on the kitchen island in front of Gemma, adding utensils and a napkin. "You know where the orange juice is."

"I couldn't find the charger for mine, and it was close to dead," Gemma said, her tone nonchalant. "I needed to run a quick search. Don't worry. I couldn't log in to yours. I used my phone instead."

"I wouldn't have much of a career in cyber if anyone could sit down and log into my laptop, would I?" Griff hoped his voice offered no reflection of the disturbing feeling he got whenever anyone touched his technology. "If your new laptop stops working, let me know."

"Where are you going for a few days? I'm not working for the next two weeks. I can go with you." Gemma's eager smile increased his discomfort.

"I'm going to see my dad. It's been a while." Griff kept cooking to keep his back to her. It was an innocent enough question. She was his girlfriend, after all, his steady plus one. She'd often gone with him to see his father.

Griff turned, setting his omelet down on the counter and pulling up a stool. Now opposite Gemma, the marble-topped island between them, he could see she'd barely touched her food and was staring at him, her mouth in a straight, angry line.

"I'll make it up to you, I promise." Griff kept his eyes on his breakfast. "You're off for a few weeks, right? So, I'll be gone a few days and then, providing there's no work emergency, we'll make plans for a day together."

Gemma shrugged in defeat. "Alright. Give me the spare keycard in case I get back before you do."

Griff's shoulders tensed. He set down his fork and picked up his coffee. Part of him had, subconsciously, accepted it would eventually come to this, but he liked the ease of their relationship with no strings attached. Cutting the strings harshly meant losing Gemma for good. Sadness filled him. If timing had been better, he might have given it a try, overcome his trust issues and moved her in. But with Rowan's current situation, that was impossible.

"I'm not ready for you to move in, Gemma. I'll call when I get back." Griff jumped a little, coffee splashing on his hand, as Gemma slapped her hand on the counter, obviously furious.

"It's been a year, Griff. Either we're moving forward or we're not. I think you should trust me by now." Gemma's face flushed a deep red, but an emotion more akin to panic was reflected in her eyes.

"This is on me, Gemma. I have trust issues." Griff took a deep breath before continuing. "When I get back, let's talk through where we're going with this relationship."

"Do you love me, Griff? Because I love you." He could see tears forming. His stomach tightened with guilt at the pain he was causing.

"I do love you, in my way. You deserve someone whose level of feelings is equal to yours. I'm not sure, yet, that I'm that guy." Griff paused, reaching across the counter to take her hand. "We've been pretty much fun—exclusive but no commitment discussions—for a year. All of a sudden, you want to move in together. I need a little time to think."

Gemma sighed, pulling her hand away. "Breakfast was great. I'm taking a shower, then I'll be on my way."

"Next week," Griff said, watching her walk toward the hallway. She waved her hand in either agreement or dismissal —he wasn't sure which—and kept going.

Griff stacked the dishes in the dishwasher. As he wiped down the counter, he bumped Gemma's purse, hanging off the back of her stool, and it fell, its contents spilling onto the floor. He quickly scooped lipstick, wallet, hand lotion, and pens back into the purse. A lone piece of pink paper lay nearby. Curiosity drove Griff to look at it before returning it to her purse. It was a warning, the first step before an eviction notice. She was months behind on her rent.

"What does she do with all her money?" Griff mumbled to himself, returning the paper to her purse. No wonder she wanted to move in with him. It had to be her family again, with their business bankruptcy and one brother in a drug and alcohol rehab facility, sucking her dry. He'd assumed she paid her bills before handing money over to them.

His phone pinged, signaling an incoming text.

> Henry: Need to talk.

Henry. They'd loosely planned to meet in a few days, after he picked up Rowan and tucked her away safely. Griff had a friend who lived two blocks from his condo and was out of the country for a couple weeks. He'd asked Griff to feed his cat while he was gone. It was a perfect hideaway for Rowan.

> Griff: What's up? Can it wait a few days?
>
> Henry: No. Very important.
>
> Griff: Swamped with work stuff. leaving 2morrow.
>
> Henry: 2morrow morning? Pamela's. Strip District.
>
> Griff: 8:30 a.m.

Henry sent a thumbs up emoji. Griff no longer heard the shower running. He walked back to his bedroom, and Gemma stood there, naked and vulnerable. She stepped toward him, and he sucked in his breath and closed his eyes. It was tempting to take the easy route, to make love, to tell her to move in permanently. But he needed privacy. Rowan's situation, getting her back to Pittsburgh safely, overrode everything else. And, although he'd taken today off, he had a ton of work for one of his consultancy clients.

"Tempting as always, Gemma," Griff gave her his best smile, then picked up the towel onto the floor next to her and wrapped it around her. "But I wasn't kidding. I have a big report due on my consulting project, and I need to get moving on it."

Gemma sighed. "I might not be interested when you return."

The warning note in her purse indicated otherwise. Behind on rent with nowhere to go meant she'd be interested. The question was, would he? Griff's empathy for her and deep concern might not translate into taking on fully cohabitating. It required an inspection of the depth of his own feelings that he couldn't do with her standing in front of him, no clothes, dripping wet.

"I'll walk you out when you're ready." Griff turned and left. What he needed was a cold shower, but for now, it was better to sit in the living room and wait.

When Gemma appeared, dressed, thick dark hair pulled into a ponytail, curly wisps escaping around her face, Griff's heart clenched. He wrapped her in a hug.

"I'm sorry I hurt your feelings today. I don't want to do that again."

Gemma reached up and gave him a passionate kiss that was more like a Hail Mary pass considering her desperate situation. Griff opened the door and she walked through, suitcase trailing, to the elevator.

"I'll call you when I'm back from my dad's," Griff said. With a tight, forced wave and a smile, he closed the door and leaned against it, exhaling. He hoped the pile of work on his desk would erase the look of sadness he'd put on Gemma's face.

"You're a selfish bastard, Griffith Campbell," he said aloud. Yet the words rang hollow, more remorse-driven than true as he focused on the next steps needed to help his sister.

Rowan

Rowan woke from a sound sleep. A whisper in her ear that laced its way into her dreams pushed her to open her eyes. Silence, periodically broken by the noises from the boiler heater or small old house creaks and groans, surrounded her. The stone around her neck vibrated slightly. Her phone screen lit showed the time—2:00 a.m. She'd crawled into bed after an evening of magic lessons confident she was safe, tucked into a snowstorm at Maya's home and stronger after four days of lessons that revealed magic she'd only dreamed she was capable of before coming here. She sensed danger.

She heard Maya tossing and turning, which was unusual. Rowan slid out of bed and stood to the side of the bedroom window, hidden by curtains. Everything was quiet, still. The roads were clear. Mounds of snow created by the steady push of the plows flowed unevenly on either side. The moon and stars stood bright in a cloudless sky, allowing a good view that revealed no human movement. Her car appeared intact.

Wait. Her car. She hadn't touched the piles of snow burying it from view. She rubbed her eyes and took a second look. It was completely devoid of snow, brush marks on the hood indicating someone had carefully cleared away the layers of white powder, even digging it away from the wheels. Rowan could see the entire vehicle. She flattened her back against the wall next to the window. Maya stood, silent, in her bedroom doorway.

"Danger is nearby." Maya turned and walked toward the stairs. Rowan could hear her soft footsteps descending. She moved forward to follow.

Maya stopped on the small landing and waited while Rowan spoke in a whisper. "Someone cleaned all the snow off my car."

Maya nodded and continued down to the first floor. She checked all the doors and windows. "He's not in the house. The danger is outside."

Rowan closed her eyes and willed the trembling in her hands and stomach to be still. She was stronger now, trained to use her magic. She could defend herself if needed. "Whatever happened, it involves my car, Aunt Maya."

Maya lifted the receiver to the blue landline phone on the wall and dialed. Who would answer immediately at this hour? Maya spoke too softly for Rowan to hear but, within minutes, lights went on across the street and next door. A handful of women emerged, spilling out onto the snowy landscape, long winter coats over pajamas, winter boots and woolen scarves across their faces. Maya, also, was dressing for the outdoors, sliding her feet into boots and tucking her wild white hair up into a knit hat that she pulled down over her ears and half of her forehead, then wrapped a thick scarf across her face.

"You stay inside, Rowan and don't stand in front of the window. I've been mentally prepared for something like this—be it you, me, or Griffith—for a long time." Maya rested her gloved hand on the front doorknob. "If they're still out there, seeing you confirms what they think they know."

Then the door opened, a frigid gust of wind hitting Rowan head on before it closed and Maya was gone.

Rowan sat down in the darkened living room and covered her body with Maya's old afghan, curling her feet underneath her, the armchair at a distance that hid her but allowed a view to the activity around her car. The women split into two groups. Two men joined them. One group began walking the grounds, the second inspecting her car. The only light came from the full moon and a few flashes from mobile phone screens or the phone's flashlight feature. One of the men lowered himself onto his back, despite the snow, and partially slid beneath the rear of the car. He repeated this motion around the entire perimeter of the vehicle and emerged from the area under the driver's side door with a small object in his hand. Rowan let out a gasp, sure it was a tracking device.

A burst of freezing cold air hit her as the front door opened, then closed. The man she'd been watching appeared in the doorway to the living room, the back of his Carhartt jacket and knit cap covered with snow. It was hard to tell where his long hair ended and the snow covering him began.

"Rowan?" His gentle, wrinkled face emitted a warm smile. "I'm Tom. Could I have your car keys, please?"

"Oh, sure." Rowan unfolded her legs, ready to stand. Tom held up his hand, indicating she should stop.

"Point the way. You stay hidden in that chair."

"They're in a small basket on the kitchen counter with Aunt Maya's keys." Rowan watched Tom step into the kitchen and listened to the soft jingle as he sorted keys in the basket. Obviously, he'd been here before. "You found a tracking device, didn't you?"

Tom paused before he headed back to the front door, keys in hand. "Yes. I'm checking the inside now. I don't think they tried to force the doors open but one never knows." He gave her another warm smile. His entire demeanor exuded an air of confidence that was instantly comforting.

"Thank you, Tom. Being in the freezing cold at this hour in the morning instead of your nice warm bed must be difficult." Rowan gave him her best smile in return.

Tom nodded and then opened the door. There was a whoosh of cold air, the thump of a door closing, and he was gone. Rowan fought the urge to call Griff. Waking him up without having concrete answers to provide would drive him crazy. Let him sleep. Keeping herself wrapped in the afghan, she crouched down and moved through the shadows, away from the window, into the kitchen where she dug into her backpack for the phone she used to call Huw only, thankful for the time zone difference that meant he was awake.

"Rowan?" She could hear him moving around.

"Hey! Are you busy?"

"Popping the last few items in my backpack before leaving. I'm leading a small hike this morning." The sound of Huw zipping the backpack, followed by an expectant bark from Cooper, told her they would head out the door soon.

"Sounds fun! I won't keep you then." Rowan closed her eyes, willing him to stay on the phone with her and reassure her even as she fought feeling weak and needy.

"Are you alright? It must be what . . . three in the morning there?" Huw's deep voice emanated a quiet concern. All background noise had ceased. Rowan envisioned him standing still, worrying lines appearing on his forehead while Cooper sat panting, looking up expectantly.

"Ahh . . . well . . . it appears someone may have planted a tracking device on my car. Maya and her neighbors are outside checking the area and the car." Rowan struggled to keep her voice steady.

"Did you see the person?" Huw quieted Cooper as the

dog whined, anxious to leave. "I mean, how did you figure this out in the middle of the night?"

"I woke up because . . ." Rowan hesitated. "It was instinct. I sensed something was wrong."

A deep silence fell between them. Rowan wished they could see each other. In their short time together, he'd neither agreed nor disagreed with her about her magical gifts. Nor had he shared a serious opinion on whether ancient myths might be built on even a small kernel of truth.

"Are you planning to leave soon? I don't think you should use that car." Huw's voice was strained.

"That car is my only way out unless I take Aunt Maya's ancient Oldsmobile, and believe me, it wouldn't have a chance in any high speed chase."

Need to know info. She could hear Griff's voice in her head. She'd shared too much.

"Rowan, an older car won't have any electronics like a GPS or other navigation tools that someone can hack into. In that respect, it's much safer for you." Huw's voice was harried, frustration and worry seeping through.

"You make a good point, Huw," Rowan said. "Listen, I don't want you to be late for the hike. Call me when you get back!"

"*Cwtch*, Rowan. Remember you're to come home to me one day."

"*Cwtch*, Huw. Take care and have a good hike!"

Rowan disconnected the call and looked up to see Maya standing in the doorway, shivering. "Oh, Aunt Maya! Sit. Let me make you a cup of tea."

Maya stepped into the kitchen, Rowan close behind, pulled out a chair and sat down. Her feet remained inside wet boots, but her coat hung dripping from a hook in the foyer. Rowan removed the afghan from her shoulders and wrapped it around her aunt, then put a kettle of water on to heat. "I'll be right back. I'm getting you dry socks and slippers."

Maya nodded. She looked exhausted, the stress aging her to a point older than her sixty-eight years. Her eyes were closed and her mouth set in a grim line. Rowan took the stairs two at a time, grabbing Maya's favorite slippers from beside her bed and a thick, warm pair of socks from her top dresser drawer. It must have been a very severe premonition that jolted her aunt enough to not only leave her bed but bypass her slippers. She slid her feet into them, religiously, each morning like a second layer of skin. Closing the drawer, Rowan froze. A photo of her mother and Maya sat on the dresser. They looked carefree and happy—two young teenage girls, the mountains and rolling hills of Wales behind them. Even in the low light from the bedside table lamp, the standing stones behind them were clearly Pentre Ifan. The piercing squeal of the tea kettle summoned her, and she moved quickly down the stairs, dropping the slippers and socks next to Maya before shutting off the gas flame on the stove. When she turned around, steaming mug in her hand with the string of a tea bag hanging over its side, Maya had changed her socks and slid her feet into the slippers.

"Thank you, Rowan," she said.

Rowan fished a spoon out of the drawer and honey from the pantry, then placed them in front of Maya, seating herself and waiting, silent, watching as the older woman slowly dropped the honey in the mug, stirred, then used the spoon to squeeze the tea bag's last bit of flavor. She sipped carefully, the steam from the drink clouding her glasses.

"You were speaking to Huw?" Maya's voice was surprisingly steady despite her appearance.

"Yes. He's heading out on a hike. The call only lasted a few minutes." Rowan reached across the table to touch Maya's hand after her aunt set her tea mug on the table. "Your hands are very cold. Would you like me to get a pair of mittens or gloves? I'm worried. You look exhausted."

Maya waved her arm at Rowan in obvious dismissal. "I'm old, not ancient. I'll go back to sleep and be fine in a few hours. I want to hear what you told Huw and what he said."

"You don't trust Huw?" Rowan frowned. Concern she wouldn't have had prior to four days of seeing her aunt's otherworldly abilities created a tightness in her stomach. "He asked how I suspected someone was outside—asked if I'd seen them—and said I shouldn't drive my car to meet Griff because it has GPS which can be tracked."

Maya nodded, her face relaxing a bit. "And what did he suggest you use in place of your car?"

"Your car. I said the only other car was your older Oldsmobile and he said that was safer because it had no electronics that could be hacked," Rowan said. "However, it won't help me in a high-speed chase."

"Did you give him specifics about your car? Is that why he said that?" Maya asked.

"No, I told him nothing about my car except that Griff provided it." Rowan sat across from her aunt and waited, all her senses on high alert. Her aunt appeared to be deep in thought. After a few minutes, Maya drank the last of her tea and stood, her hand on the back of the chair to steady herself.

"You asked me about Huw, Rowan. I don't know him. What I do know is someone is a Judas; someone let Jarrod's people know you're here." Maya turned and walked toward the foyer, stopping in the doorway. Her hair was a tangled mess, worry lines on her face. "We're safe for now. In the morning, we'll decide what your plan for leaving here should be."

"It has Pennsylvania plates. The car. That's how they confirmed it was mine." Rowan tried to stifle the waves of guilt washing over. The strain of her situation might be too much for her aunt. "Aunt Maya, I'm sorry to put your through this."

"Don't worry about me," Maya said, her voice firm, stronger than she looked. "I assumed that, unless Jarrod died, this day would come eventually, and I'm ready."

"Do you think I'm ready?" Rowan hoped uncertainty was not evident on her voice.

"You are as prepared as you can be. And it doesn't matter now. You have to go, regardless." Maya turned and walked away. Rowan could hear her aunt's footsteps moving steadily, deliberately, up the creaky stairs, followed by the rustle of bed sheets, then silence. She needed sleep too, but her nerves were jangling and on edge, making it impossible. Her mind sifted through who might have betrayed her. Obviously, Maya distrusted both Gemma and Huw but that could be overprotectiveness. What about Maya's neighbors? Could they be trusted? Rowan sighed, realizing it was unlikely the neighbors had any idea who Jarrod was or that Rowan was visiting. It was possible no one had betrayed her. Jarrod's relentless stalking had finally paid off.

"Mom? Talk to me . . . please." Rowan held the stone, feeling it pulse lightly.

"Your magic is meant to achieve more than saving yourself or protecting Griffith." Elin's voice was faint, resting gently in Rowan's ears and mind.

"I'm going to win my freedom from his stalking, his obsession." Rowan kept her voice low.

"Winning requires a finish line beyond which a new world is waiting if you can step over that line intact, whole. The stakes are higher than you understand. Strive. Aspire to more than Huw. The gift you've been given is deeply rooted. Reach inward to grasp it fully—then use it."

"That's much too large a concept to embrace," Rowan whispered into the darkened, seemingly empty, living room.

Exhaustion moved across her in waves. She waited, but no sound touched her ears except the movement of the wind outside, spinning snow artistically in all directions.

This was often how her conversations with her mother evolved. They were rare and ended abruptly, leaving her bereft and tired. Rowan climbed the stairs to the guest room. She'd barely crawled under the covers and laid her head on the pillow before she fell asleep.

Jarrod

Jarrod smiled, a warm flush of power running through him. Multiple windows were open on his computer browser, allowing him to check Google Maps and weather reports coming from the western end of New York in tandem. His source had done well, leading him to the Jamestown, N.Y. area, where Rowan was, apparently, snowed in, possibly with an aunt who'd somehow eluded his research. His source said the aunt, Maya, lived alone and was somewhat eccentric. Could she also be imbued with the same talents as her niece? Jarrod was convinced it was the elegant piece of blue quartz around Rowan's neck that bestowed those magical gifts upon her. Now he waited for Derrick's arrival, still irritated by his initial response.

"No one by that name ever came up in our searches," Derrick had said when Jarrod relayed the new information regarding Rowan's aunt. "How good is your source?"

Jarrod took it as a backhanded slap, delivered because information from his sources, in the past, led nowhere.

"Boss?" Derrick startled Jarrod. He'd silently let himself into the office. "Your source is excellent. We found her at a spiritualist community of psychics and mediums near Jamestown called Lilydale. She's holed up at the home of a Maya Edwards."

"You're sure?" Jarrod tapped his fingers on the desk.

"The car in the driveway is a black 2017 Honda CR-V registered to Griffith Campbell and purchased two weeks ago. He doesn't need the car. He primarily works from home or walks to an office, and he has a very nice BMW as well as a Jeep he can use otherwise. Unless we see his girlfriend driving it around, I think he bought it for his sister to use. We checked the garage in his building, and it's not there," Derrick answered. "We're as sure as we can be."

"The back roads are challenging after such a huge snowstorm but are doable with an all-terrain vehicle or a ski mobile. Not sure we could extract her and transport her that way. Barreling into a small, private community with any big vehicle will raise suspicions." Derrick added.

Jarrod nodded. He'd surmised as much himself. "Even if we had a snowplow, in these smaller communities they know who plows for them and may even have a private contractor."

"Do you expect more intel coming from this source?" Derrick cracked the knuckles on his hands; a clear indication he was sorting out all options.

"Yes. I expect more soon, hopefully intel on when she's planning to leave her current location," Jarrod confirmed. "I'm sure she plans to meet her brother somewhere between New York and Pittsburgh."

Derrick's face broke into a large grin. "We can catch her en route."

Jarrod snorted with derision. "Because that plan worked well in the past?"

Jarrod watched Derrick, familiar with his facial and physical responses. He looked comfortable. He must have another card to play.

"We hacked the car's GPS, which no one disabled, and it shows a drive from Griffith's place in Pittsburgh to the aunt in Lilydale." Derrick exuded confidence.

Jarrod nodded, satisfied, and gave Derrick a rare smile. He could feel it in his bones. She would be standing in front of him soon.

Derrick crossed his arms over his chest. "I sent someone in on cross country skis with clear instructions not to cause any disruption. Their assignment was to put a tracker on the underside of her vehicle. Now we wait."

Mobile phones for both men rang at the same time. Derrick stepped away to answer his call, while Jarrod swiped right on his phone and lifted it to his ear.

"Yes?" He listened. "Good work. Keep me informed. A deposit will be made to your account today."

Derrick returned, his face red with frustration, flexing his fingers in and out of a fist.

"What happened?" Jarrod asked.

"Somehow they figured out there was a tracker on the car and removed it," Derrick said. "I don't believe in psychics. Any possibility your source is a double agent?"

"No possibility. The stone in that necklace Rowan wears has paranormal qualities. I want that magic working in my favor." Jarrod leaned back in his chair, arms crossed. "Her brother is leaving soon. My source says he took a few days off work. Let's assume he's not going on vacation and is meeting his sister halfway. Figure out her route, and make a plan."

Derrick gave Jarrod a mock salute and stood, heading for the door.

"Derrick?" Jarrod waited until the man turned to look at him. "Don't fuck it up this time."

Griffith

The minute he opened the door to Pamela's, his nose was assaulted with a tumult of wonderful smells, his eyes with splashes of aqua and peach everywhere—from the sign outside to the walls, chairs, and ceiling inside. Rows of 1950's style tables were overshadowed by two walls filled with pictures of people—famous people, local patrons, and family photos of Pamela's owners and their families. Modern platinum strip lights glowed, positioned below an inlaid ceiling.

Huddled on 21st street in the famous Strip District, Pamela's was known for its crepe style pancakes and as a favorite of former President Obama. It was always packed with people exuding a happy, energized vibe. Griff moved toward a table near the window where Henry sat reading the small white laminated menu while steam flowed upward from a cup of coffee.

"Parking is a pain here on the weekend," Griff grumbled, waving to the waiter and pointing to Henry's coffee.

Henry shrugged and grinned. "I took the bus."

"Nice," Griff responded with a laugh. "I'm leaving here and heading north to meet Rowan."

"That's what I need to talk to you about." Henry handed Griff his menu and leaned forward, arms and elbows folded on the table.

The waiter interrupted them, dropping a second menu for Griff.

"I know what I want," Henry said. "You need a few minutes, Griff?"

Griff shook his head. "Two eggs over easy, bacon, rye toast, potatoes, juice, and coffee."

"Blueberry hotcakes," Henry said. "And a coffee warm-up please!"

Griff scanned the diner for familiar faces. Only strangers surrounded them. Noise was at the right decibel level, without being annoyingly loud, to keep their conversation private. He watched Henry do the same room scan. "Know anyone here?"

Henry shook his head. "No, but I'll keep an eye while we talk."

"You observed or heard something." Griff didn't ask. It wasn't a question. Henry was a no drama guy, and it was highly unusual for him to call for an emergency meeting.

"Both. They know where she is."

Griff clenched his hands, trying to control the panic rising in him.

"Is she with your aunt in a psychic community in New York?" Henry was expressionless except for a slightly raised eyebrow.

"Shit. Shit, shit, shit," Griff whispered. He looked out the window for a moment, trying to regain composure.

"I'll take that as a 'yes.'"

"What did you hear or see?"

"Went out to smoke. I put my earbuds in, hoping to look like I was listening to music—I wasn't—and stood a little closer than normal," Henry said. "They were talking about intercepting her. They didn't say her name, but I figured it was your sister. Then Derrick, the leader of the special security team, as Jarrod refers to them, came out and said they'd be leaving in an hour."

"After Derrick went back into the building, one of the guys said the tracking device they planted failed. They figure she's onto them. Derrick ordered an early departure to ensure they could follow and intercept her." Henry stopped talking. Their food had arrived.

"This was yesterday? And they were sure she was leaving today?" Griff looked down at his food, his appetite diminished by the news.

"I don't think they were sure when she'd leave. They planned to watch the tracker, but once it was removed, they assumed she was spooked enough to leave quickly." Henry cut his pancakes and added syrup while talking. "Can you tell her to stay put?"

"It's not safe for her either way. Once she makes it to the public shopping center parking lot in Erie where I'll be waiting, we'll leave the car, and I'll hide her at a friend's condo here for a few weeks." Griff barely tasted his food as he sorted through his original plan. "My friend is out of town. The place isn't far from mine."

"They all have weapons." Henry was digging into his food while Griff took a few bites, mostly moving things around on his plate.

"Rowan promised not to stop on the way," Griff said. "My handgun is in her glove compartment as a precaution."

"Rowan doesn't carry any type of weapon for defense? I'd think after years of running, she'd be well armed."

Griff snorted in derision. "She thinks she can use her magical powers to defend herself.

"Not good," Henry said. "These guys are serious. They mean business."

"Worst case scenario, they get to her. Think they'll take her to that weird room near your lab? The one you caught them building?" Griff switched to eating at least half his plate as quickly as possible. He needed to get going, but it might be the last time he ate for a while.

"Just guessing, but I think it's likely," Henry said.

Griff was both sickened and relieved that if she didn't make it safely to him, he'd know where to look and Henry would be nearby.

"One guy asked Derrick when they'd be back," Henry said. "He has a date later. Derrick said if all went according to plan, they'd be back early evening after the employees were gone."

Griff took a last gulp of coffee. He opened his wallet and laid enough money on the table to cover breakfast, tip, and then some. "I'd better get going."

Henry nodded in agreement. "I think the sooner the better."

"I'll hit the bathroom, then I'm gone. You handle the check."

"Griff?" He turned to see Henry's face, filled with concern. "I'm here to help you."

Griff patted his friend on the shoulder and walked away. No amount of hurrying or assuring himself that things would be fine could remove the sickening feeling in the pit of his stomach. Someone tipped Jarrod off. Rowan called him yesterday to tell him about finding the tracker on her car which, fortunately, had been removed. He doubted it had been Henry, The information Henry offered today he could have kept to himself if he were playing both sides. Somewhere there was a listening device, an app—a monitoring device that he'd missed. Or Rowan wasn't sticking to the need-to-know rule.

Rowan

"Text or call me when you reach Griffith," Maya said.

Rowan could see unease on her aunt's face, her arms crossed over her torso as if she needed to hug something to stay calm. They stood in the foyer, Rowan's suitcase and backpack on the floor next to her as she pulled on her winter coat and gloves. She'd agreed to meet Griff in the parking lot of the Millcreek Mall in Erie. It was a reasonable drive for Rowan. She'd leave the car he loaned her and go with him back to Pittsburgh. A large, busy parking lot would deter Jarrod's people from approaching her or trying any type of kidnapping attempt.

"I've spoken to my connections, and I have a few things to tell you," Griff had said during their call. "I think we should confront Jarrod together with law enforcement backup."

"He has connections there, Griff. I'm not sure that'll work." Rowan clung to the belief, after years of eluding Jarrod, that he had politicians, law enforcement, and others in his pocket.

"You watch too many movies, Ro," Griff answered. "I'm connected to a lot more people on the federal investigative level than Jarrod. He has things to hide. We can leverage that."

"Okay, I trust you," Rowan conceded.

"Don't stop anywhere, Rowan. Go straight from Aunt Maya's to Erie."

"Is Gemma still at your house?" Rowan asked, hoping it would be only Griff and her when she arrived.

"No. We had a little falling out over her request to move in permanently," Griff answered. "You'll stay in the condo of a friend of mine who's on vacation and asked me to check in on his cat while he's gone. This should be over before he's back."

"How can you be sure they won't follow you? That somehow you won't be forced off the road?" Rowan shivered at the image this conjured in her mind.

"I shut off the GPS in my car." Griff's relaxed, confident tone washed over her, lowering her anxiety but not her surprise. "Give me some credit, Ro."

"No one knows where we're headed besides you, me, and Aunt Maya, right?"

"Unless you told Huw. Gemma's been asking a lot of questions about you lately." Griff sounded irritated and uncomfortable. "I told her you were in Wales on a photo shoot."

"Huw knows I'll be with you. That's it. Should we talk about why you don't trust Gemma?" Rowan tried to control her desire to laugh. Griff notoriously came up with these types of reasons—excuses, in Rowan's opinion—before breaking off a relationship with a woman.

"We can talk about it when I see you."

"Three hours from now. In Erie. Love you, Griff." Rowan's heart was full, grateful for Griff and Maya. She wished, fervently, she could share her location and next steps with Huw.

"Yep. Ditto." Griff had disconnected the call.

Rowan tried to hold on to that good feeling and quiet the tension that encircled her. Her instincts were on high alert. She wasn't sure this day was going to go well. A dark foreboding hung over her, leaving her uneasy. Maya's face reflected her own thoughts.

"I'll text or call you the minute I'm in Griff's car," Rowan said. "I promise."

"If anything goes wrong, remember you don't need this." Maya touched the stone laying quietly on Rowan's sternum. "Your strength comes from within. Have confidence in yourself. Travel within yourself and tap your own capacity and gifts."

"I've learned an incredible amount from you in a short time, Aunt Maya." Rowan wrapped her aunt in a hug. "If it comes down to me, alone, with only myself to rely upon, I'm confident I'm equipped to handle any situation because of you."

"You're never alone, Rowan." Maya placed both hands on Rowan's cheeks and kissed her forehead. "A mother's love remains, even when she's unseen. Elin's love for you is eternal."

Now, twenty minutes into her hour-long drive to Erie, Rowan cursed herself for forgetting to use the bathroom before leaving. Discomfort from that extra cup of coffee she'd consumed was becoming painful. She could hear Griff in her head warning her not to stop anywhere, but she didn't think she could hold it another forty minutes. Signs for a service plaza had begun appearing. She'd have to stop and take her chances with the hope that a busy place filled with people would be safe for her.

A few minutes later, she pulled into the Angola service plaza. All the parking spots near the front door were taken and the parking lot was half full. Rowan assumed many people, like her, were crawling out of the vestiges of the snowstorm and hitting the road. She eased the car into an open spot as close to the building as was available. She was parked beside a large minivan which obscured a view of her by others. Not an optimum situation, but her bladder was about to explode. She prayed that the line to the toilets was short. Pulling up her hood, she exited, locked the car ,and jogged quickly into the building. There, an ever-shifting group of humanity bundled in coats and boots moved to either the food court or the restrooms. The wails of children and the hum of voices drifted around her, but no one stood out as if they were watching her. She followed a small group of women into the restroom, listening as they discussed a destination in Ohio. She stood quietly behind them, head down over her phone, shifting from one foot to the other to keep from losing control until a stall opened.

Ten minutes later, as she scanned the parking lot from the rest stop window, she clutched her necklace and called for her mother.

"Rowan, you're about to find out what you're made of."

"No kidding. Not helpful." Rowan frowned. "Is it safe to go back to the car?"

"We're all tested in this life. Until a person faces real pain, danger, or trauma, they don't truly know what they're made of—they can only assume. In the land of conjecture, many an error has been made and exposed in the harsh moment when reality hits."

Rowan waited but heard only the noisy sounds of people coming in and out, moving around her. With a sigh, she left the building, Elin's cryptic remarks swirling through her head. A gray Jeep much like Griff's sat to the right of her car, the van still parked to the left. Startled, she paused, distracted, then shook her head. Of course Griff wasn't here. The stone vibrated against her in a strange way. She smelled danger, but nothing around her appeared unusual. Rowan's boots crunched on salt and snow as she approached her car, eyes on the Jeep, its tinted windows hiding the interior. She stopped next to her car, her gaze sweeping the parking lot, before pulling out her keys and opening the door. She continued to watch the area around her from the windows as she slid into the driver's seat. Locking the doors, Rowan exhaled a sigh of relief at both the lack of discomfort in her bladder and the safety of her car. She leaned forward and placed the key in the ignition. A tiny prick on the right side of her neck caused her to look over her shoulder. A hooded figure, hypodermic needle in hand, was in her back seat. Panic surged through her. Rowan pointed her fingers at the attacker, intent on using her powers to defend herself. Then everything went black.

Jarrod

"We've got her. On our way." Jarrod smiled at the confirmation from Derrick. Finally, Rowan would belong to him.

"She's unharmed?" Jarrod trusted Derrick, but the people he hired weren't always careful.

"Yes, she's fine. She'll sleep for a while, although we do have her hands and feet bound, as a precaution," Derrick answered. "One of the guys has a pretty serious burn on his hand from trying to grab her necklace."

"Idiot! I thought you told them NOT to touch the stone around her neck. It's to be removed, carefully, when she arrives." Jarrod slammed his palm on the desktop in frustration. The sleeve of his white shirt, gold cufflinks flashing, slid upward, scar exposed as pain shot through his hand.

"I told them, boss. They didn't listen. He needs medical attention."

Jarrod could hear the guy moaning in the background. "If he wants medical attention, drop him off at an ER and keep going. He's on his own due to his stupidity."

Derrick was silent for a moment. Jarrod suspected the

order caused an internal battle. This is why Derrick would always be a gun for hire. He couldn't cut loose the dead wood and keep moving.

"Okay. Got it. We should be there before she wakes up." Derrick ended the call before Jarrod could respond.

"You'd better be," he muttered aloud to himself.

He clicked an icon on his laptop. An empty room appeared, its walls clean and freshly painted white. A double bed with a white coverlet and assortment of pastel-colored pillows dominated the center, positioned against one wall. An oval braided rug covered part of the floor where a couch, coffee table, and floor lamp had been placed. In the corner was a door to a bathroom that contained a shower stall, toilet, and small sink. Pale blue towels hung from a rack. Across from the bed, on the opposite side of the room, was a window that looked out into an empty hallway and a door with state-of-the-art security. Jarrod smiled. He'd enjoy watching her. It would take time to break her down until she came to him willingly, but he would have the necklace with its magical stone today. He was cognizant of the fact that he couldn't touch it, but without the necklace, he was sure Rowan would be helpless.

He closed the laptop. Standing, he stretched his five-foot-four frame and turned to face the window behind his desk. Trees covered with snow lent an ethereal beauty to the landscape. His company was headquartered on the north side of Pittsburgh. Jarrod walked to a mirror on the far wall near the door and inspected himself, something he rarely did. His hair, its color a drab brown, was thinning, foretelling a future in which he would be bald. In college, he'd overheard a woman he'd dated tell her friends he was "kind of mean and homely".

"Women don't care about looks," Jarrod told his reflection. "It's money and power that attracts them."

Making the statement aloud to himself did little to lower his insecurities where Rowan was concerned. She was the most frustrating woman he'd ever met. The Tom Ford suit, the diamond-studded cufflinks, exuded a power and influence only she was immune to, her disinterest insulting. What was the key to winning her over?

Jarrod's cell phone rang. The screen displayed "Private Number". He smiled, swiped right, and lifted the device to his ear. "Good morning, Senator."

He listened, murmuring in agreement several times. "We're much further along with MyShadow than expected. I'm heading down to the lab in a few minutes to check its progress. I anticipate it will be ready before the election."

A few minutes later, after saying goodbye, he pocketed his phone and walked toward his office door, intent on checking MyShadow's progress himself. Senator Harrison Cherrington III, known as "Trey" to his family, friends, and constituents, faced a tough re-election battle. Trey had never worked hard for anything. Willing, from an early age, to walk across others, if necessary, to get where he wanted to go, he sailed through Ole Miss, graduating with honors and only a few scandals involving young ladies. All of which were quietly taken care of by his late father, the first Senator Harrison Cherrington. That said, he wasn't a stupid man. Jarrod was careful when dealing with the senator.

Jarrod swiped a small gray token against a pad in the elevator, then chose the ground floor. He exited, moments later, into a cool, subterranean corridor with pristine white walls and soft, sound-absorbing beige carpeting. Turning left, he pressed his badge against another keypad and stepped inside the lab in which an elite group of Marrone Industries employees worked on projects they were paid handsomely for, but which signed non-disclosure agreements ensured they could never speak about inside or outside the company.

Quiet music played, a backdrop to a hum of voices. Groups of employees were huddled around various laptops.

Silence ensued once they noticed him. A tall, lanky man with a graying ponytail and faded tattoos on his forearm stood and walked toward Jarrod.

"Henry." Jarrod nodded, taking the man's outstretched hand and giving it a cursory shake. "Thought I'd stop in and check on progress. Got a call from one of our investors."

"We think we've completed fine tuning the original MyShadow. We're testing now." Henry crossed his arms over his chest, his gaze on the group in the far-right corner of the room. It annoyed Jarrod that Henry rarely made eye contact with him. He didn't care if it was the result of dislike; it was disconcerting. "Huw Evans's original creation was stellar. It's meant we didn't have to tear it down and fully rebuild it to meet your specifications, but honing the changes and meeting stringent testing requirements have had ups and downs."

Jarrod believed Henry to be a careful man, a smart man. Outwardly, he looked like an aging hippie, but inside he was brilliant with technology. That, plus the leverage he had over the man, made Henry a perfect choice. When he'd mixed his talent with his need for activism and landed in trouble with the law for hacking, the prison time, a pile of debt, and an ex-wife who demanded regular alimony and child support payments left him vulnerable and unable to find work. Leverage of any kind always created a comfort zone for Jarrod.

"I have some potential buyers in the political arena." Jarrod watched Henry raise an eyebrow, a look of surprise flashing briefly across his face. "When will it be ready?"

Henry finally looked at Jarrod directly, his mouth in a tight, angry line. He appeared to have a comment resting on the tip of his tongue. As Jarrod waited, Henry's face carefully closed. Not even a muscle twitched. "I believe we can test a prototype in March."

Jarrod nodded. His eyes scanned the room again. "Show me what you have."

Henry waved to a young woman in the left corner, her sheet of straight, long black hair hanging like a curtain. She and the three bearded guys huddled around a laptop screen with her looked up in unison. She stood, her petite frame covered with ripped jeans and a T-shirt heralding the singer, Pink. The men turned quickly back to the screen, but she walked forward, eyes focused on Jarrod in a stare that was both bold and curious.

"Joanne Chen." Henry smiled at the young woman. "Meet Mr. Marrone."

She extended her right hand and smiled. "Jo Chen. Nice to meet you, Mr. Marrone."

"Nice to meet you as well." Jarrod gave her small, birdlike hand a squeeze. There was an energy about the girl he liked and not in his usual dominating or lascivious way. The fact that she didn't appear to be afraid surprised and intrigued him. "Jo, I'd like a demo of MyShadow. See for myself how it's coming along."

Jo turned with a wave of her arm that indicated he should follow her and quietly headed back to the corner of the lab where she'd been seated, stopping at a table next to the one she shared with her co-workers. A few quick introductions left Jarrod convinced she was the leader in this group of introverted, smart tech geeks. Jo opened her laptop and proceeded to log in, using her phone to complete the multi-factor authentication. Jarrod pulled up a chair and sat next to her, preferring not to hang over her shoulder.

"Henry recommended we choose people with very public profiles because there is more available material to use as we work to accurately capture voice, gestures, etc. Of course, this is for testing only." Jo's fingers moved quickly across the keyboard as she spoke. "We also created a test using you, Mr. Marrone. We hope you don't mind. You would be the best person to determine whether our work accurately captures you."

Jarrod shifted in his chair, crossing his legs and arms, hoping his face masked his discomfort. Protesting now would only delay the project. "That's fine, although I prefer your focus be on people with a larger public persona."

Jo nodded, then with a few fast clicks of the mouse, opened a folder and suddenly the President of the United States appeared. Jarrod uncrossed his arms and legs and leaned forward. As the replication of POTUS spoke, Jarrod caught his breath at the stunning level of accuracy. An older gentleman with years of experience, the President was often soft-spoken but firm.

"Prototype one is the president as he is today, allowing us to work on synchronizing lip movements with audio and capturing the facial nuances and head motions that give it authenticity and a high level of realism," Jo explained, closing the file and opening another folder. "Prototype two begins to alter the president. Again, we focus on holistic facial dynamics—eye gaze, blinking, emotion in facial expression, and the items mentioned in the prior prototype."

Jarrod watched in awe as another identical version of the president now spoke in a somewhat shaky voice, his wrinkles deepened. The overall impact inferred the man was deteriorating. Missing words, mixing up concepts, and appearing to lose focus at times rounded out the impression of significant decline in the most powerful elected person in the world.

"Good work. Very impressive." Jarrod leaned back and smiled.

Jo then opened two more files, one of a well-known congresswoman and the second of a popular motivational speaker, each time showing both a real and a tweaked version.

"We train the deep fake on a series of real-life videos to

produce a high-quality product," said Jo. "Trained face encoders are used on a 3D image to extract... what we need."

She paused. Jarrod could see her sorting words in her mind to ensure she explained in an understandable way. He gave her what he hoped was an encouraging smile.

For a final demonstration, Jo opened a file of a deep fake version of Jarrod. Her right foot jiggled up and down in contrast to her seemingly calm demeanor. Jarrod twitched, panic shooting through him. Where it had been enjoyable to watch the pantomime of others on the screen, it was altogether different when he was on display. "No negative second version?"

Jo's face now laid bare her concern. He should tamp down on what he was sure was coming across as fury and soften his tone. "I know you told me to expect this, but it was a shock. It wasn't my intention to snap at you."

"I understand," Jo answered, relief spreading across her face although she continued to clasp and unclasp her hands while shifting slightly in her chair as if backing away from him. "There's no negative version of you, Mr. Marrone. It was never a consideration that we go in that direction."

Jarrod exhaled, allowing his heart rate to slow. He stood, facing Henry, his back to Jo. "The deep fake file of me is to be deleted. Do I make myself clear?"

"Yes, sir." Henry answered, eyes averted from his staff, his gaze focused on Jarrod.

Jarrod turned and walked away. He could provide the senator with the information he was waiting for once his hands stopped shaking from the realization that even he could fall victim to the very thing he was creating to inflict harm on others.

Griffith

Griff's heart was in his throat, his stomach in knots. Rowan should have been here over an hour ago. He'd waited in his car such a long time that the mall security detail was starting to drive by more often. Maya was frantic. She'd called him checking to see if Rowan had arrived, only to discover she hadn't. He'd reassured her he'd find out what happened, but she kept saying "He has her. I'm absolutely sure."

Griff nearly hung up on her. He couldn't manage a bunch of witchy premonitions and magic talk in the middle of a crisis. "As soon as I know, you'll know."

> Griff: Where R u?

> Henry: leaving work soon. Why?

> Griff: R was a no-show.

> Henry: Shit.

> Griff: contact me if u see her?

> Henry: Keeping an eye out

> Griff: later.

Griff willed himself to suppress his emotions and think coldly and rationally. He couldn't chance losing Henry. He needed him now more than ever. He shifted the car to drive and moved out of the parking lot toward 79 South, intent on reaching Pittsburgh. "Siri, call Rick."

The car phone began dialing. Rick answered on the third ring. "Griff? What's up?"

"I think Jarrod Marrone kidnapped my sister." He heard the catch in his voice, his hands shaky as he gripped the wheel a little harder.

"Are you sure? That's a federal offense." Rick's no-nonsense business voice helped Griff focus.

"Yesterday, she found a tracking device on her car. She's been staying with our aunt in a small village in western New York. Today, she was to meet me at the Millcreek Mall in Erie." Griff took a deep breath. "She never showed up. My aunt hasn't heard from her. Calls from me are going to voicemail."

"Where are you now?"

"On my way back to Pittsburgh. I'll swing by Marrone Industries and take a look."

"Don't . . . listen to me. Let me check for you. I'll send an agent to trace her path from your aunt's and see if there was an accident. What's the make and model of the car she was driving, and where does your aunt live?"

Griff relayed the information quickly. "The car's in my name."

"Stay clear of his company headquarters, Griff. He knows who you are, and he has security cameras. You could endanger her by showing up there."

"Okay, I hear you. But I'm not sitting on the sidelines if he took my sister." Griff's anxiety evolved into white hot anger.

"You still have a man on the inside?" Griff could hear

Rick's fingers clicking on a keyboard, probably sending out orders to his agents to run a check for Rowan.

"Yes. It would look suspicious if he went in on the weekend. He gave me a heads up that he was fairly sure Jarrod had located Rowan and his people were going to follow her."

"Head home, Griff. Stay by the phone. We'll update you with what we find out," Rick said. "I need probable cause to ask for a search warrant."

Griff set the cruise control and surfed the radio for news channels. Maybe there was an accident. He wasn't sure which was worse, a car crash or being kidnapped by a sociopath like Jarrod. Unable to find a news channel, he asked Siri to call Maya.

"Griffith. Talk to me." Maya sounded both tense and out of breath, as if he'd caused her to run from another room even though he'd called her mobile phone.

"I have a contact in federal law enforcement. He's sending agents to retrace her steps to see if we can determine what happened to her," Griff said.

"Good. Let them look. You stay away from Jarrod . . . please."

"I'd like to confront him, but Jarrod knows who I am. Seeing me could increase the danger Rowan is in if he has her."

"He has her. I sense it, the same way I'd know if you were in danger." Maya's voice was firm, assured.

"Could we please cut the magic talk? I have full confidence in Rick. And I have a good friend who's on the inside at Marrone Industries." Griff took a breath, struggling to speak with empathy not frustration. "When I find out where he has her, I'll use every bit of my skills to rescue her and destroy him."

"Kidnapping is a federal offense, Griffith. Let the federal agents rescue her," Maya said. "You could get hurt, and I couldn't live with that."

A wave of emotion at her concern and love enveloped him. If he were a little boy, he'd cry and let her comfort him, but he was a grown man. There was no time for that. "The feds need probable cause to get a search warrant, Aunt Maya. I, however, am not as confined to procedure."

"Griffith, I'm painfully aware that you don't believe in the inherent powers of the women in this family, but Rowan can and will defend herself." Maya's tone was much tougher now, forcing him to listen. "I spent four days training her. Jarrod will rue the day he took her."

"I can't sit by and do nothing, Aunt Maya. And I sure as hell can't agree to rely on magic." Griff told her he loved her, then hung up quickly.

His fingers tapped on the wheel in anticipation of setting them on his laptop keyboard and going to work. With or without Henry's help, he was an excellent hacker. He would access every inch of Jarrod's business and life to free his sister.

Rowan

Rowan opened her eyes slowly. Dry, crusty material had accumulated in the corners. She'd been awake for a few minutes, listening, trying to orient herself to her surroundings one sensory evaluation at a time. Silence encircled her. A light floral and lavender scent touched her nose. She was lying on her side on a double bed, her hands and feet free and unbound. She was shoeless but fully clothed. The walls were painted white. The bedspread beneath her was a lightweight quilt. A mild irritation emanated from the chafed skin around her wrists where she must have been bound. Rowan sighed in relief. She could tell she hadn't been hurt in any other way. A quick scan upward showed cameras monitoring her from several angles. She assumed the room was full of them. The setup reeked of Jarrod.

She turned onto her back, swung her legs over the side of the bed, and sat up. Momentary dizziness caused her to grab a fistful of the quilt and mattress edge. Her mouth was dry and her head a little foggy. It would take time for whatever they'd drugged her with to wear off.

"I'm with you." Her mother's voice. She shook her head

slowly from side to side. It must be the drugs causing her to imagine what she needed most in this moment.

"Don't speak. You're being watched."

Rowan raised her left hand to her throat. Her necklace was gone. Her body shook with fear, anger, and confusion.

"You don't need the stone. Use your gift."

Rowan took a deep breath. A glass of water in a plastic cup sat near her bed. Her mind raced. *Outthink them,* she told herself, silently.

She stood, leaning against the side of the bed until she was no longer shaky. The room consisted of three walls with a glass front that opened through one door positioned to the right of a long window. Beyond was an empty corridor. To the right side of the bed, a dark green love seat upholstered with plush material graced one wall. A coffee table in front of it held a vase of blue and white hibiscus centered on its dark, polished wood surface. Angled to the right of the love seat was a large armchair with a pattern of pink flowers, the green leaves matching the couch. A floor lamp stood beside the chair, the setup cozy, as if she would be entertaining a guest for morning coffee. The image made her nauseous. A smaller lamp sat on the nightstand. She picked up the water glass, turned, and walked to the end of the bed, keeping a light touch on the frame, her balance still uncertain. Outward from the left side of the bed, a small area extended from the wall with a door but no ceiling.

That bastard created a gilded cage. Rowan nearly ground her teeth with fury at the realization. She walked to the small, enclosed section and opened the door. Inside, directly ahead, was a shower stall, its clean subway tile and sliding glass doors beckoning her. To her left was a toilet and to her right a sink. She'd need to determine where the cameras were if she were to use the toilet or the shower.

Rowan poured the glass of water into the sink. She rinsed

it out with soap from the dispenser and dried it with a towel. Once clean, she refilled the glass with tap water and drank in long, slow gulps, refilling it again and then splashing cold water on her face before stepping back into the bedroom. That should send him a message. She would never trust him.

The water eased the lightheaded sensation. A rack with several dresses in her size stood next to the wall to her left. Sexy, slinky dresses. Not her style. She opened the drawers of a small dresser next to it. Sexy lingerie filled the first drawer. The next had casual clothes—yoga pants and what looked like tight T-shirts. A fierce wave of disgust followed by the desire to fight back arose in her, wiping out her earlier fear. Careful not to touch the clothing in case her internal ferocity set them on fire, Rowan closed the drawer and stepped back. Jarrod's weakness was on display here. He'd laid out his warped dreams of her in carefully stacked clothing she'd never give him the satisfaction of seeing her wear.

On a smaller table, beside the chest of drawers, was a coffee maker and two ceramic mugs. A variety of Keurig pods and plastic spoons lined its lower shelf. *Yes, coffee. That's what I need.* A little caffeine and her senses would be razor sharp. Rowan removed the container filled with water from the back of the machine, emptied it into the bathroom sink, and refilled it with water from the faucet. Choosing a dark roast coffee pod, she put one of the mugs in place and pressed the button to brew a cup. Rowan looked at the second coffee mug. Across the room, two champagne glasses sat on an end table near the couch. Apparently, Jarrod planned to spend time in this cage with her. She struggled to tamp down the wrath that threatened to strip the tenuous control she now maintained. She would allow him no hint as to her capacity for powerful magic until the moment when she used it against him.

She picked up the second coffee mug, walked across the room, and grabbed both champagne glasses. Then, looking directly up at the security camera, she threw the coffee mug against the windows, watching it shatter. That answered her question about whether they were made of shatterproof glass or not. She then took the champagne glasses and slammed them against the inside of the trash can until they cracked and broke. Rowan collected the pieces of broken mug and dumped them on top of what was left of the glasses. That should send Jarrod the message that she wouldn't cooperate with his sick fantasies. Turning back to the camera, she flipped up her middle finger.

A small refrigerator, the kind commonly found in a college dorm, was next to the table with the coffee maker. Opening the door, she found creamer, several containers of yogurt, and pre-cut fruit. All appeared to be in sealed, unopened containers, but she checked them, one by one, before removing the creamer and pouring a little bit into her coffee. Returning to the sofa, she placed the water glass on the coffee table, and then sat down and quietly drank the coffee, letting its caffeine and heat chase the remnants of the drug-induced fog from her brain and open her circulation. Coffee consumed, Rowan lay her hands on her knees, closed her eyes, and centered her mind and body in the way Maya taught her. She moved each toe, finger, limb, and then her entire torso slowly until her body and mind were completely activated. *"Use every resource. Your mind, body, magical gifts, and past experiences. Bring them together. Remain focused."* Maya's voice filled Rowan's mind as clearly as if her aunt was in the room.

Rowan opened her eyes, her muscles tight, tense, expectant. She had no intuitive sense of how this would end, but she was ready to fight back. Her modeling career taught her how to survive on a limited amount of food, a skill she'd continued to leverage as a photographer in order to travel light. The yogurt, fruit, and coffee creamer could keep her going for longer than anyone but Griff would believe. She'd spent many days in the hot desert climate of the Middle East on photo assignments, sometimes living out of tents or in rentals with less than consistent running water. She could go for a long time without a shower or change of clothes. He wanted to watch her shower and put on his choice of clothing? Not happening. Hell would freeze over before she'd touch that lingerie.

Suddenly, the lights flickered. Crackling noises came from various locations in the room and bathroom, then everything became dark. She heard the door to her prison unlock and she stood, stepping in that direction. The backup system re-locked it a second before her hand touched the door handle. Lesson learned. She'd be faster if it happened again. Being startled had cost her the possibility of escape.

"Rowan!" The sound of her mother's voice caused her to turn quickly, frantically scanning the dark for any sign. *"Over here."*

Rowan moved toward a faint glow to the right of the love seat that created enough light to keep her from tripping. Within the feeble glimmer was Elin's blurred, delicate outline. "Mom?"

"Shhh . . . speak quietly. Hear that crackling noise? Find each location. Each is a camera watching you. I've caused interference, but it won't last." Rowan moved quickly, listening. She identified five cameras in the small space, two in the bathroom.

"Creep," she mumbled to herself. "I'll take care of his spying."

"No," Elin's voice was stern but fading. *"Use this knowledge when an escape opportunity arises. Learn to disrupt the electrical system. Use your powers to make Jarrod think it's a common glitch."*

"Stay with me," Rowan whispered, pleading. "I can't call you without the stone. What if my magic isn't strong enough to escape?"

"Your magic is stronger than you can imagine." Elin's apparition dimmed. *"Believe in your own power. My love is always with you."*

Rowan gasped when Elin disappeared. She clutched her chest, feeling a full-on panic attack. Her breathing was erratic, her body frozen in place. The lights flickered. A hand landed softly on her shoulder and she turned, hoping to see her mother. It was Jarrod, moving his hand from her shoulder to her back. Raw hatred coursed through her. Her fist landed squarely on his right eye and her knee slammed into his groin.

"Don't ever touch me, you disgusting jerk!" Large strong hands pulled her arms back and held her in place as Jarrod moved closer. Partially turning allowed her to see a big muscular man. His Rolex watch scratched her wrist where he'd clamped down on it.

"I'll touch you and you'll like it, Rowan," Jarrod said, his face flushed with anger, his eye swelling. "Or should I call you 'Nora Edwards'? Yes, I know about your fake name."

Rowan spit on his face. She watched him wipe it with his fingers. He smiled and advanced toward her again, his fingers touching the top button of her shirt, toying with it as if to loosen it. It was a power play to scare her, to establish control.

"I have your magic stone. Without it, you're helpless. I own you." He ran his fingers down her neck and between her breasts, then stepped back, his face smug, contented. "Derrick, strip her. She won't be allowed to wear clothing for the next twenty-four hours."

Rowan's anger turned to ice. *Your magic is stronger than you can imagine.* Twisting her head, she caught a glimpse of zip ties as Derrick released an arm and extracted them from his pocket. She hovered her free hand over Derrick's upper arm and pushed hard with her mind before he could grab both of her arms again and tie them. Raw energy coursed from her to him. She didn't pull away when he screamed, letting go of her, but kept the pressure on. He fell to the ground, his body convulsing. Jarrod moved forward to grab her, but his short stature meant Rowan towered over him. With the same surge of energy, she reached down and placed her hand around his neck, closing her fingers on his windpipe, and then pushed. He flew backward, landing near the windows. She advanced toward him as he lay, prone, a wave of violent energy running through her, oblivious to the opening of the door until, suddenly, a sharp pain exploded across her shoulder. The force of the blow knocked her backward. She stumbled, dropping into the armchair. Guns were pointed at her by several men, one of whom had obviously hit her with the hard butt of a rifle. Standing slowly, she put her hands up, keeping her back to the wall.

"Don't shoot her!" Jarrod screamed between intermittent cries of pain.

They remained frozen in a violent tableau until men Rowan assumed were medics, but who displayed no standard EMT patch or badge showing local health services affiliation, arrived with stretchers. They loaded Derrick and Jarrod onto the beds. One put his fingers to Derrick's neck, shook his head, then pulled a sheet over his entire body. Jarrod struggled to sit up, his nose bloody, one eye swelling, refusing a medic's request to lie down.

"Bitch," Jarrod hissed, running a hand through his hair. "You'll regret this."

His agitation was palpable. She stared at him in a way she hoped appeared brave and unflinching, praying her balance would hold. Her knees shook, but in a voice that was clear and loud enough for everyone to hear, she said, "Don't ever touch me again, you filthy creep. You can flush your crazy delusions down the toilet. I despise you."

Jarrod's mouth was set in a grim line, his eyes flashing with fury as the medics moved him into the hallway. He pushed against them, unwilling to be taken out on a stretcher. Rowan imagined it was as much from her actions as it was embarrassment she created in front of his employees. A tall, thin man with a graying ponytail and wire-rimmed glasses was standing in the hallway, behind the jumble of gun-toting security guards and medical personnel, quietly watching.

"What are you doing here, Henry?" Jarrod snapped at the man, forcing the medics trying to wheel him away to stop.

Rowan couldn't make out all the words in the man's response. It sounded like "security," "asked to check an outage." The man gave Jarrod an easy, casual shrug and stepped out of the way in deference to the medics.

"You witnessed nothing here, do you hear me? Nothing," Jarrod yelled at Henry, although Rowan was sure it was meant for everyone from the gunmen to the medics to the guys checking the cameras and security in her cage.

For a brief second, as the crowd spilled from the doorway into the hall, Henry stepped toward the window and made eye contact with her. He raised two fingers, crossed them, and tapped the chest area over his heart three times, then he left, walking quickly down the corridor and out of sight. *Griff.* Henry had given her the secret symbol known only to she and Griff. It was a childish thing, a silly code made for the clubhouse in the backyard that their father built for them. It was never used for anything serious . . . until now. Rowan slowly lowered herself onto the armchair, both physical and emotional exhaustion causing her to tremble. Her head pounded from stress. She exhaled, closed her eyes, and hugged her chest to slow the shaking in her limbs. Griff had an inside man. Henry took a big chance by slipping in during the chaos. She hoped the lie he told protected him. Henry would tell Griff she was here. Knowing Griff, he'd work out an escape plan that involved hacking into the building. Fine, she could use all the backup available, but she wasn't going to wait for her brother or anyone else. She would get out of this cage on her own, hopefully without additional violence.

She'd killed another human being. Justifiable, yes, but knowing in theory she was capable and seeing the result, a dead man who—although despicable—had family somewhere, affected by her actions, left her shaken. He might not be the last if she were to escape. Rowan lay on the couch, her hands clenched over her heart. She was a killer. Every inch of her wanted to sob until the pent-up tension from her actions was spent, but she wouldn't give Jarrod the satisfaction. She'd never show weakness. Derrick was the first, but if he was not the last, she hoped she hardened inside in a way that made a terrible but necessary act easier.

"Mom?" Rowan kept her voice to a whisper, hoping the cameras would only see her lips moving. "I lost control. I killed a man."

Her words were met by silence.

"I need you. Stop disappearing. Stop leaving me." Rowan's voice choked. She covered her eyes with her sleeve. "I'm alone without you, and I can't do this alone."

"Physical death is never the death of a mother's love." Rowan sat up. There was no glow. No lights flickering or electronics crackling.

"Cwtch, my daughter."

Cwtch, Mom.

She closed her eyes and gathered her strength.

Jarrod

He winced with pain after inadvertently turning his head too quickly. The area on his neck where she'd choked him with superhuman power ached. He'd cursed her repeatedly, to the point where he had no words left. She would pay for this. He'd spent the last few hours making arrangements for Derrick, assuring what family he had, along with the coroner and local law enforcement, that his heart attack came on suddenly and he died before help could arrive. The rest of Jarrod's security team and the medics hired from a private company received a generous cash bonus in return for signing a non-disclosure agreement.

"How soon can we move her?" Jarrod looked at the man in front of him, trying to remember his name. Clint or Clay. Something that sounded like that. He'd been part of Derrick's team and looked hungry for a promotion.

"A crew has been working to prep the new location. We'll need to sedate her."

Jarrod watched as fear settled on the man's face. "Send her spiked food."

"Well, that's the thing. She won't touch anything that isn't sealed, and she's only taking water from the tap."

The sound of an incoming text erupted from Jarrod's phone. He held up one finger to the man in front of him, then tapped the phone and read.

> Source: G knows she's missing. Suspects you. Running search of ur properties.

He responded with a simple thumbs up emoji.

"Security system at the new location may have been hacked." The man in front of Jarrod pointed to his phone, then ran a hand over his dirty blond crewcut, revealing a skull and crossbones wrist tattoo. "We'll need to keep her here a little longer."

"Shit. Check to make sure it was a hack." Jarrod may have underestimated Griffith Campbell's cybersecurity abilities. "In the meantime, limit the people with access to her. Allow one person to deliver food or check on her, someone who may be able to gain her trust. We'll need that when it's time to sedate and move her."

Jarrod watched the man drum his fingers on the arm of the chair. Derrick's men were rough around the edges, possibly ex-criminals. He didn't want them to touch her. It had to be someone softer, someone who appeared to have been forced into the role against their will. Someone Rowan would see as a possible ally. A woman? He thought of Jo Chen. Too young, too ethical. Henry? Maybe.

"Check with the cleaning staff. See if there's someone willing to take on a special assignment for extra money. The person will have to be on call and willing to stay silent about Rowan." Jarrod leaned his chair back slightly, closing his eyes. His hand throbbed with pain. "If no one fits the bill, then I'll talk to Henry."

He opened his eyes and gave the man a hard stare. "Don't screw this up."

The man nodded, stood, and began walking toward the door.

"What's your name?" Jarrod called after him.

"Clay, " he responded, head half-turned back to Jarrod.

Jarrod took note of the tight, angry look on Clay's face before he pulled open the door and left. Wearing his emotions on his sleeve wasn't a good thing. It smelled of ego and lack of self-control. Derrick wouldn't have given a crap what Jarrod called him as long as he paid him.

Griffith

Henry: R here. Sealed room. Ground fl near lab. Gave signal.

Griff: U saw her?

Henry: 👍

Griff: Safe channel?

Questions were piling rapidly in his mind.

Henry: Private hotspot with MFA. 👍

Griff breathed a sigh of relief. Henry hadn't changed. He'd set the most secure route possible before communicating.

Griff: She's okay?

Henry: Yes. Jarrod hurt. Derrick dead. Guard says R did it. she's a badass.

> Griff: Derrick . . . head of security? No way she killed him.

> Henry: apparently she did.

Griff sat back, stunned. Rowan had no weapon and, even if she'd packed one, they would have taken it. She fought back and killed a man, at least that's Henry was claiming. His hand hesitated over the phone. He wanted to call Maya, but he didn't want to hear this was Rowan using mystical powers. He remembered she'd taken a series of self-defense classes from a certified black belt. Maybe Rowan surprised them and managed to get a weapon from the security guard.

He should call Rick and confirm that Henry had seen her. But what if Jarrod lied, said they'd caught her illegally accessing the building and she'd shot and killed an employee. Jarrod was slick, and it would be his word against Henry, an ex-con. Odds were good they'd move her quickly to another location

> Griff: Can u get to her?

Griff held his breath, hopeful.

> Henry: Maybe. Saw security code entered. But might set off alerts.

> Griff: Give me the code.

Griff waited as seconds ticked by. The silence in his office and on the screen was increasing his level of stress exponentially. Should he call Henry and ask what was up, or would that create additional stress for his friend?

> Henry: Not yet. Spy on ur side."

Griff froze. Unconfirmed suspicions were one thing. Henry's tone displayed certainty.

> Griff: Who?

> Henry: Not sure yet.

> Griff: Can u find?

> Henry: JM phone dropped in scuffle. Hooked up to droid kit.

> Griff: An Android? Perfect. Are you in?

> Henry: Read texts. Can't fwd or copy. Need 2 return phone soon.

> Griff: Who is it? 😠

> Henry: Don't confront.

> Griff: The hell I won't.

> Henry: Think. Breathe. Use them. share false info.

Griff's rational mind agreed that flushing out a rat too soon opened up risk and offered no benefit. His emotions were in a different place altogether.

His phone made a second beep. There it was. The name. Griff gripped the arms of his office chair hard enough to break them. It was that or throw the entire chair against the wall. He breathed in and out, willing his mind to take charge.

> Griff: Agreed. Use for false info

> Henry: Text says moving her in 48 hrs.

> Griff: Here's what I need.

Griff quickly typed a list. A security badge for an office cleaning person would be easy. But he imagined Henry's panic at his request for the deep fake prototype files.

> Henry: Give me until midnight.

If Henry pulled this off, Griff would owe him more than he could ever repay.

> Griff: Got ur back. Meet at ur house tonight.

A thumbs up emoji appeared. Griff waited. The screen lay silent. He was ready to give up when three ellipses began moving.

> Henry: Text when leaving. See u then.

He could park a couple blocks from Henry's apartment and wait until he was sure his friend was home and neither of them had been followed. The bar and restaurant meetings were now too public. Once he learned more from Henry, he'd build a plan, loop Rick in, and free his sister before the next life lost was her own.

Rowan

She lay on the small couch for a long time. She'd whispered a plea for her mother but received no audible or visual response. A man was dead. Rowan struggled to process that fact. Griff would tell her the guy deserved it. Maya would tell her she'd done what was necessary. But she'd been out of control, her body merely a tool once the magic overcame all rational thought. She would have killed Jarrod too if the guards hadn't stopped her. Confidence in her ability to turn this power on and off at will was shaken.

Jarrod would retaliate. Lying on the couch, sad and scared, wasted precious minutes. Despite thinking that making herself unappealing to Jarrod by skipping showers was a good idea, a hot shower would clear her head. She sat up slowly before standing. She'd expected to be shaky and lightheaded. Instead, strong, powerful sensations coursed through her body.

Rowan removed her hoodie and stepped into the bathroom. She would shower as quickly as possible, with her clothes on. Setting the water temperature as hot as she could tolerate, she stepped into the shower, grabbed the shampoo, and rapidly washed then rinsed her hair. She shoved hands lathered with soap under her shirt and down into her unzipped pants, turning her back on the cameras. Minutes later, after doing her best to wring the water out of her shirt while wearing it and towel-dry her hair, she stepped out of the bathroom and onto the carpet, still dripping. Using her full power had changed her. The muscles in her arms, legs, and back were taut, primed, ready for action. Her senses, even her skin, tingled.

Rowan opened the refrigerator and removed a yogurt container and a small bottle of orange juice. Plastic spoons sat in a cup nearby. She couldn't afford to be physically weak. She'd seen a small portable fan behind the armchair, possibly left by the workmen or maybe meant for her. She dragged it out from behind the chair, plugged it in, turned it on, and stood in front of it, hoping to at least partially dry while she ate. She smiled, knowing Jarrod would see she'd worked around his perverse setup.

Griff would do everything possible to rescue her, but she couldn't sit back and count on someone else. She must save herself. Maya was right. Her powers were exceptionally strong. She needed to think strategically about how to use them to escape.

The timing, the route, and where she and Griff were to meet had been known only to Griff, Maya, and her. Was it luck or did someone give Jarrod enough information to ensure his thugs were right behind her? It couldn't have been Huw. She resisted the thought. If she allowed herself to accept even the possibility of a betrayal by Huw, she would start crying.

"I can't let my emotions rule," Rowan whispered to keep her decibel level below security monitoring.

She tossed the empty container in the trash can, then dropped a pod in the coffee machine, pressed the button, and listened to it gurgle in response. Returning to the fan, she waited quietly, assessing her cage. Everyone had entered the hallway from somewhere to the right of her door. She'd heard a thud after they locked her door and left the hallway, then a few beeps. She could damage both doors and escape, but the minute she did, an alarm—possibly a silent alarm—would go off. She had no idea how to get out from a point beyond the second door, or even what she would find once she emerged there. How many of them could she fight at once? The full extent of her powers lay untested, but dismantling the security system was outside her ability. Rowan vowed that, if she got out of this predicament, she'd figure out how to update her magic from medieval level to modern technology.

My backpack. Where is it? She'd had it when she exited the rest stop on the highway. Long ago, she'd taken it apart and created a hidden, padded section. If someone checked the backpack, a lithium battery would seem to be stored in that area instead of a small burner phone. Would they have found it or solely rifled through her wallet and personal items, then tried to access her laptop?

Picking up the mug of hot coffee, she walked slowly around the edge of the room, mentally cataloguing everything, looking for anything she might have missed coming out of a drugged sleep that she could leverage. In the left corner, what looked like an intercom was installed on the wall. She stood quietly, the coffee increasing her heart rate, sending blood to her brain and throughout her body. Stepping forward, she pushed the red button on the intercom and waited.

"How can I help you?" A woman's voice, soft with a slight rasp that gave it a gravelly tone. Rowan was surprised.

"Could you please have someone deliver my backpack to me?" Rowan kept her voice friendly but firm.

"Ahh . . . I'm not sure that I can do that." Rowan noted the hesitation in the woman's voice. She wasn't in charge and not confident enough to make the decision alone, or at least make it sound like the decision was hers to make.

"To whom am I speaking? What's your name?" Rowan added an edge to her tone.

Silence.

"That backpack has my toiletries and a clean change of clothing, which I need." She'd been around demanding divas in the fashion world long enough to play the part if needed.

"You've been provided with all the toiletries and clothing you need." The woman sounded snippy now, her frustration showing.

"I've been provided with very low-class, drug-store-level products and tacky clothing I wouldn't be caught dead in," Rowan said, letting an imperious tone slide into her voice. "I'm accustomed to using specific brands for my hair care, including my favorite comb and detangle spray, and lotions I prefer. And I'm not wearing the slutty clothing left here for me."

"Well, you'll have to lower your standards and make do." Rowan smiled. The woman was thoroughly pissed off now, and it was probably taking all her self-control not to use the B word, which is what she was most assuredly thinking about Rowan.

"Put Jarrod on the intercom. Now." Rowan would meet that B-word expectation. She was flying by the seat of her pants here, but a deep-seated indignation motivated her to continue. Any woman who participated in helping scum like Jarrod and his men keep a kidnapped woman trapped in the basement of a building was disgusting.

"Mr. Marrone is not available. You'll deal with me, and you will not get the backpack."

"Eventually, when Mr. Marrone is back from the emergency room . . . which, by the way, is where I'm going to make sure you end up at some point . . . he'll come to this room. I'll then proceed to tell him that he cannot have what he wants from me unless he fires you and gives me my backpack."

Rowan paused. No sound came from the intercom. "I have something he wants, and you don't. He'll do anything to get it. If I don't get my backpack, it will be your loss, not mine." Rowan hit what she assumed was the "off" button to cut the conversation before the woman could say another word.

She doubted her little tantrum worked. Hopefully, she hadn't caused deeper scrutiny of the backpack. She could only wait and see if, after the woman stewed for a while, she'd end up more scared than angry and comply. In the meantime, Rowan needed to figure out how to contact Griff with all these cameras watching her if she did get that phone.

Rowan stepped back into the bathroom. She needed to use the toilet. Disgust at having to do this in front of security cameras made her want to scream, but there were some things —this being one—she couldn't avoid. The bathroom door opened inward. If she kept it open, the toilet sat behind it with no cameras directed to that area. The cameras were in the shower, one facing into the shower and the other angled toward the sink, right next to the shower. The toilet was the only blind spot in the room, provided the door remained open. She dropped her bare butt onto its seat and sent a silent thank you to the construction team who had built in this modicum of privacy. What they were assigned to build had to have struck them as bizarre, no matter what they'd been told its use would eventually be. There was a possibility, if she closed the door, that one camera would record part of her. She'd have to keep the door open, listening for anyone to enter from the hallway through the main door. If she could get that phone, she could text Griff. He could disrupt the one thing she couldn't—the security system.

Rowan heard the click of the main door as she hit the handle to flush the toilet. She washed her hands, stepped out into the larger room, and smiled. Her backpack, looking slightly damaged, sat inside the door. Its black exterior was dirty, one zipper broken. Aware the cameras were recording her, she hoisted the bag onto the bed and opened it. It was obvious they'd rummaged through her belongings. Her Brinks safety bar and her shoes were missing, as was her laptop, but a quick squeeze where the battery should be and she was rewarded. The phone was still there. Rowan sent a silent prayer that it remained charged. Playing to the cameras, she lifted her shampoo, conditioner, and lotion out and walked into the bathroom, setting them in place. She grabbed a towel and walked out, toweling drying the ends of her still-wet hair. The fan had been a slight help with her now damp clothes but not her hair. The phone was in a plastic bag, which meant she could hide it beneath the toilet lid.

Her mind raced as she dropped the towel on the left half of the open backpack and sorted through her clothing. If she put clean clothes on in the corner where the toilet sat, Jarrod would quickly deduce that she'd found an unmonitored spot. She might have to put on a show, but for the phone it would be worth it. She chose a pair of clean underwear, her favorite worn and comfortable Henley waffle knit shirt, and the second pair of trail pants Huw convinced her to buy. Gratitude that she'd rolled up the multi-pocketed pants and added them at the last minute when packing filled her. Her sweatshirt, along with the boots and puffy winter coat Huw purchased for her were missing. If she escaped, she'd have only the hoodie, socks, and hopefully dry ground to run on.

As she sorted through the clothes, she reached her hand under the towel and unsnapped the small opening she'd created at the bottom of the battery compartment. She slid the plastic bag with the phone out, leaving it under the towel. She now had a small pile of clothing topped with deodorant and her makeup bag. She laid the clothes on the towel, keeping it messy to ensure she could slide the plastic bag inside the towel before lifting the entire stack and heading to the bathroom.

Taking a deep breath, Rowan put the stack of items on the unfolded towel, then reached with her left hand, encircling the stack, tucking the plastic bag inside the towel and lifting towel and clothes with the phone sealed inside. She walked to the bathroom, left hand holding the pile, and put her deodorant and makeup bag on the sink. Then she put the toilet seat down and set the pile of clothing with a towel on it.

Closing her eyes, Rowan focused her mind and spoke in a whisper. *"Women of my ancestors please help me now. Hide me."* A pull on her right arm caused her to turn, arm up, finger pointing at the shower without forethought. Hot water began running, full blast, steaming the mirror over the sink. Rowan shut the door and smiled. It hadn't occurred to her, earlier, that steam would cloud the security cameras. She barely counted to ten and the tiny bathroom was filled with steam. Keeping her back to the cameras, she leaned forward, slipped the plastic bag out from the towel, lifted the toilet lid, and set the bag inside. With small, quick movements, she stripped off her wet clothes and dressed in clean, dry clothing. Concentrating, she pointed her finger at the shower, and it turned off.

Cool! I wonder if I can use that trick to unlock doors. A cloud of steam followed Rowan back into her cage from the bathroom. She dropped her dirty clothes on the floor. She needed to keep playing the diva for whoever was watching. Her favorite wide-tooth comb sat in the open backpack, and she was pretty sure she'd packed a couple of hair scrunchies in there. She walked over to the coffee maker and inserted a new pod, setting the mug underneath. She would need to load up on liquid to create a reason for another trip to the toilet. Spraying her hair with detangler, she grabbed the comb, a scrunchie, and a clean pair of socks, sat down on the small couch, and began untangling her hair while contemplating her next move.

Griffith

Henry's apartment was a large flat in a neighborhood primarily populated with elderly people who had arrived long ago as new immigrants. Mixed within this population were single mothers, divorced fathers, and a few graduate students. His block sat between an emerging neighborhood where gentrification was pushing out the poor and an edgier area that experienced its share of crime. Still, the small one-way street held its own and offered Henry living quarters he could afford with a level of privacy.

Griff stood in the shadows created by Henry's building and hit the buzzer, quickly stepping inside the foyer as the door lock released. Built in the early 1900's, it was solid red brick, sported a new roof, had absolutely no attractive landscaping, and came with a landlord who lived in another state. Griff assumed the building would be sold once gentrification reached Henry's street, but for now, it allowed him the ability to get back on his feet and save money. Jarrod paid him well. Griff listened as Henry unlocked three deadbolts before the door swung open and he stepped inside.

"Hey. Sorry it's cold in here. I turned up the heat, but it'll take a few minutes for this old place to get warm." Henry's coat remained zipped. Griff followed his example. The updated electrical wiring meant more to Henry than heat and insulation. He didn't need to worry his expensive electronic equipment would blow the fuse box or start a fire.

The decor was minimalist. Furniture, most from second-hand stores or IKEA, filled enough of the roomy flat to keep it looking lived in. Thick area rugs in warm fall colors and a few pictures of Henry's daughter made it more inviting. The rugs were purchased to mute sound. The tenant in the flat below Henry's was a middle-aged man who mostly kept to himself but had, on occasion, been a little too curious. Henry told Griff he'd run a quick test to see if the rugs served their purpose by knocking on his neighbor's door to ask if any of his mail had inadvertently landed in the man's mailbox while his daughter was on the phone in his own flat. He was relieved to hear no more than a soft hum, her words muffled beyond recognition.

Griff sat on one end of the worn brown couch, and Henry seated himself at the other end, laying what looked like hand-written notes on the coffee table

"I scanned the rooms for monitoring bugs with a radio frequency detector before you got here," Henry said.

"You still do that?" Griff grinned, both amused and admiring the thoroughness born of paranoia. "Find anything?"

"Nothing, but considering the secrecy around my work and who I work for, I don't take chances." Henry looked stern, serious.

"Start at the beginning. What happened today? You look twice as stressed as I feel." Griff unzipped his coat as the room became warmer. "Beers in the frig?"

Henry nodded. Standing, he removed his coat and headed to the kitchen, returning with two cans of Iron City beer.

"I'm not sure, specifically, what happened." Henry took a swallow of beer and leaned back on the couch, resting his head for a moment before sitting up straight again. "I was in the hallway, heading to the bathroom, when the elevator doors opened and a medical team with stretchers, followed by a few members of Jarrod's special security team, went flying by and opened the door to the hallway in front of that room . . . the one I told you about."

"They propped the door open," Henry continued. "When I heard Jarrod yelling, I slipped into the crowd, trying to stay hidden behind the others. I'm pretty nondescript and used to being overlooked. It helps me blend in. It's how I survived in prison. Anyway, Derrick was lying on the floor. They loaded him on a stretcher and covered him—body and face—with a sheet. Jarrod was obviously in pain. There were deep red marks around his neck and the beginnings of a black eye. He was cussing up a blue streak. Yelling at people to never mention this . . . that they'd seen nothing."

"Where was Rowan?" Griff clenched his hands together, waiting.

"Sitting in an armchair in the room . . . the cage . . . holding her head. Two guys had guns pointed at her." Henry shook his head as if he was still processing what he'd seen. "As they rolled Derrick's body out, I heard a medic say it was a heart attack. Jarrod was halfway out of the room, struggling to get off a stretcher while the medics worked to keep him on it. I tried to hide behind the crowd, and that's when I saw a phone and pocketed it. I had no idea at the time it was Jarrod's. It must have fallen when he backed into the hallway. He looked at me and yelled 'What are you doing here?' I had to think fast."

"Man, that must have been wild. What did you say?" Griff tried to visualize what Henry had described. What would happen to Rowan if she'd actually been responsible for the death of another person?

"I told him someone said the security system malfunctioned and they needed help. He yelled at me, and others, to get out of there. Rowan was standing now, watching them leave. As quickly as possible, I gave her the signal you showed me, then followed the security team out the door." Griff patted Henry's shoulder in silent thanks. "I stood next to the last security guard as he punched a code to lock the door to her hallway. I memorized the code."

"Your team didn't see any of this?" Griff hoped at least one witness to Rowan's plight might call the authorities.

"The lab is soundproofed. They had no idea," Henry said. "They thought I'd gone to the restroom. No questions when I returned."

"I'm grateful for your help. I know you're taking risks." Griff said. His own voice exuded a level of exhaustion that matched Henry's.

"I've owed you for a long time. Although, I might need your help finding a new job when this is over!" Henry gave a small laugh. "What's the plan for the spy?"

"Feed disinformation." Griff was sure his anger came through loud and clear.

"Okay, let me give you what you asked for earlier and then we can talk about what lies to feed Jarrod." Griff watched as Henry reached into his backpack and pulled out a security badge. He tapped the picture Griff had asked him to insert and raised an eyebrow.

"Better you don't know. She's one hundred percent trustworthy." Griff wasn't about to endanger Maya further by telling anyone she was going in undercover. He'd argued against it, and she'd told him he could help her or she could do it on her own. He'd assumed she meant by using magical powers he believed existed only in her head. Not a good idea, so he'd insisted on bringing her into the plan his way.

"Can I help with whatever you've asked her to do?"

"Keyloggers." Griff gave Henry a wicked smile and watched his friend laugh. "She'll be on the hunt for someone who leaves their login credentials exposed and then I'll remote in and attach a keylogger. Unless you can get me login information for an IT employee?"

"Out of my reach. Sorry."

"And the passcode to the security door?" Griff expected Henry to reach into his backpack again and pull out a portable jump drive with the information he needed.

"Griff, my friend, you'll be surprised, probably laugh at my choice here. It's going to mean a little manual labor, but I did it out of caution. A couple of the young people on my team are not only smart but want to impress Jarrod." Henry paused, shuffling the papers on the coffee table into a specific order.

"Hmmm . . . now I'm curious," Griff replied.

"I wrote a lot of information, including the code, on paper, although I have a few things on a portable drive for you," Henry said, a grin on his face. "Sometimes old school is the right school!"

Griff laughed while pulling a laptop out of his backpack. "That's both mad and brilliant. And a pain in the ass, but okay, give me a minute to create an encrypted folder with multi-factor authentication requirements, then we go through what you've got and I'll type."

"I thought you'd find being my executive assistant amusing." Henry chuckled.

"Very funny." Griff gave Henry a playful punch in the arm.

"Time to get serious," Henry said. "Most of what I wrote down comes from Jarrod's phone. I ran a last check of his text messages, installed ICU spyware, and left his phone in the men's bathroom on my floor. I figure the cleaning staff or anyone he sends looking for it will find it and be none the wiser. By the way, they're going to move Rowan."

"Where?" Griff asked, panic gripping him. "I assume you're giving me access to the spyware app?"

"I don't know where they're taking her," Henry said. "On his phone, he only uses a passcode, no biometrics, and the code is his birthday. All information I'll give you, along with access to the app. I don't think he'll figure it out. Security monitoring is weak for a company that's selling software."

"Probably difficult to get good people to work for him." Griff completed setting up a secure folder. "If everything goes according to plan, he won't figure it out until he's locked up."

"Wherever they're taking her, it's not completely ready, but you don't have much time," Henry said. "I know you. You have a plan. Can you share it with me?"

"It's all about timing, and it will be dangerous. If it doesn't work, I want to limit the fallout on you." Griff paused, uncertain how much to share. He needed Henry, and sometimes knowledge protected a person, other times it put them in a difficult position. "I told you the feds are investigating Jarrod. They think he and Senator Cherrington are planning election fraud to move the senator up the political ladder."

"Whoa!" Henry let out a soft exhale. "That makes sense regarding the deep fake project he has us working on. He thinks your sister can be convinced to assist with this plan?"

"She wouldn't. No amount of drugging her or trying to win her over will work, but Jarrod's never understood that," Griff said. "He can't see beyond his obsession for her and for amassing power."

"From what I witnessed yesterday, she does have unusual powers. Jarrod must be thinking that with her and his relationship with the senator, he can rise to new heights," Henry said.

"Who knows what he thinks," Griff snapped, angrily. "He'll be grateful to be behind bars when I'm through with him."

"Best place for him! Speaking from experience, he won't survive long there." Henry closed his eyes, rubbing his temples as if exorcising bad memories before reaching into his pocket and handing Griff a USB drive. "The deep fake examples are on here. There's a prototype of a deep fake of Jarrod, but it's rough. Needs work."

"Thoughts on what tweaks are needed?" Henry's expertise could cut the time it would take to polish the prototypes.

"Work on the algorithms that connect high-quality video synthesis and the low-latency requirements needed for real-time applications," Henry said, then laughed. "I see the look on your face. I'll explain. Latent space is the head and facial movements. When working on the prototype, consider all possible facial dynamics—eye gaze and blinking, lip motion, etc. The synchronization between the audio and lip movements, expressive and emotive facial dynamics, and natural-looking head poses needs to be precise. It's not quite there."

"I know Rowan. She won't wait for me. She'll try to get out on her own." Griff popped the drive into his laptop and began downloading to the secure folder. "Let's hope her efforts don't collide with ours in the wrong way."

Griff typed Henry's advice along with key information in his notes. He then went to the administrative website for the ICU app Henry uploaded to Jarrod's phone. "Cute name for a monitoring app . . . ICU! I'm in his phone. Good work. I'll send a targeted phish when I get home. If he clicks, I'll be able to install a RAT and access his laptop too."

"A RAT for a rat. Nice." Henry smiled. "Did you choose QuickConnect?"

Griff remembered times, as a student, when Henry put a remote administration tool or RAT in place as a learning activity for Griff.

"Yeah . . . I know there are a bunch of remote access tools, but I prefer QuickConnect."

"Anything interesting on his phone?" Henry had removed his coat and was sipping a beer, letting Griff rifle through his notes and pull what he needed.

"Not yet. I'll work on this later." Griff was determined to scour Jarrod's phone even if he was up all night. A notification popped up on the app. "Spoke too soon. An activity notification popped up."

Griff clicked in. Jarrod had received a text message.

> G knows she's missing. Suspects you.
> Running search of ur properties.

"What do you see?" Henry looked at the clock above his faux fireplace. Griff followed his gaze. Two o'clock in the morning. They were both weary and in need of sleep.

"A text. Letting him know I'm running a search of his properties," Griff said.

"You'd better check your own devices." Henry said.

"Disinformation. I planted it hoping you were wrong about who's reporting to Jarrod." Griff let a flash of dread roll through him and exit his exhausted body "Don't worry, my phone is locked down."

"Once I'm in Marrone Industries's system, I'll work on a disruption of sorts where the employees see Jarrod supposedly speaking to them via the screens around the building at the same time a fire alarm goes off and security doors malfunction," Griff continued. "The goal is to leave IT and physical security consumed with managing chaos, allowing Rowan to slip out into the crowd of employees exiting the building."

"That'll require specific timing . . . and it's problematic,"

Henry said. "It's a good plan on such short notice. Good, but it's not perfect. My team may recognize the deep fake as their work. They might intercede."

"I have that possibility covered," Griff replied. "I can't share details with you."

Henry yawned, rubbing his eyes. "Can you give me an estimate of when this will go down?"

"Not yet." Griff slid the laptop into his backpack and zipped it shut. "I hope by tomorrow, this time, she's free."

Henry picked up the papers, walked to the kitchen, and turned on the gas stove.

Griff put on his coat, hat, and gloves while he watched Henry carefully burn his notes, washing the ashes down the sink. "Not much chance of sleep for me. Heading out now to let you get a few hours rest."

Griff waved, opened the door, and headed down the stairs into the cold early morning air. He had his work cut out for him. If only he could speak to Rowan.

Rowan

Rowan had enough coffee and water in her to float a cruise ship. Hopefully, her minders wouldn't come running if she was in the bathroom longer than normal. A flood of relief spread through her. The phone was still fully charged. Sitting on the toilet, she sent Griff a text.

> Rowan: It's Ro. Txt from burner. Got ur message.

She checked for the third time that all sounds were muted on the phone. She said a silent prayer that he was available.

> Griff: Answer. Dog #2. Name

Rowan rolled her eyes. Griff and his security questions.

> Rowan: U, Chas. Me, Chester.

She admitted to herself that Griff's name for their second family dog was a good choice.

> Griff: Working on it. Aunt 2 help u. Trust guy who gave u my signal."

> Rowan: Henry. JM said his name.

> Griff: JM moving u bc of dead guy

> Rowan: When?

> Griff: Not sure yet.

> Rowan: G2G

Rowan shut off the phone and slid it back into the bag. She wanted to ask more questions, but she had to keep to short stretches of time. She flushed the toilet to cover the sound made while lifting the toilet tank lid and hid the phone inside. A minute later, hands washed, water cup refilled, she sat down, pretending to rifle through one of the fashion magazines on the coffee table. "Aunt" meant Maya. Rowan's father was an only child. She had no other aunt. But how could Maya access this securely locked cage? Her aunt had special powers, but Rowan didn't think they included out of body experiences or walking through steel doors.

She hoped Griff trusted Henry out of confidence, not sheer need. He was the only person who could have told Griff that Derrick was dead. The click and beep coming from the door startled her. Every muscle in her body tensed. It took a deep breath and fierce determination to control the desire to jump up from the couch. She left the magazine lying casually across her lap.

A small cart with what appeared to be cleaning supplies, a small vacuum attached to the top, closed doors on its lower half, rolled into the room first, followed by a petite, older woman, her shoulder-length gray bob covered by a bandana scarf, sensible sneakers on her feet. Her uniform top had a name tag below a company crest and fell to the top of comfortable looking black yoga pants. There was something familiar about her. Rowan waited for the woman to look up and face her. When she did, Rowan struggled mightily to keep from allowing an exuberant smile to cross her face.

"Hello. I'm Evelyn. I'll be here every day to clean and to replenish your food supply." Maya smiled at Rowan, making sure the cameras could see her. She perfectly mimicked an American accent, all trace of her Welsh roots vanished.

What Rowan heard inside her head was far different. *"Rowan, can you hear me? We practiced this. Try to answer."*

"It's nice to meet you, Evelyn. Don't let me get in the way of your work." Rowan dropped her head, pretending to read the magazine. She and Maya had practiced telepathy, but now Rowan struggled to concentrate. She closed her eyes and focused, shutting out everything around her, pushing the words out from her mind. *"I hear you, Aunt Maya."*

Rowan lifted her eyes. Maya was taking her time unhooking the vacuum and pulling a long-handled duster from the cart. She opened the doors to the bottom section of the cart and removed several cartons of yogurt and orange juice, placing them in the small refrigerator.

"Griff's friend got me the badge. It was luck I was chosen to clean here."

Rowan stifled a laugh. She doubted it was luck. More like Maya and her magic.

"I need Griff to hack the security system and turn it off. The rest I can do myself." A mild throbbing from the intensity of the telepathy began climbing through her left temple. Maya's head probably hurt too.

Maya pulled a covered plastic container from the cart and placed it on the coffee table with napkins and utensils. Rowan could see what looked like roasted vegetables and tofu with brown rice, hot enough that the clear top on the container was clouded with steam. It smelled delicious. Her stomach rumbled, and she set the magazine down beside her. She looked up at Maya who nodded approval.

"I'm going to vacuum. I hope you don't mind the noise while you eat. Then I'll clean the bathroom." Maya plugged the vacuum into a wall socket.

"I can eat this?" Rowan's hands clutched the edge of the couch cushions staring down at the mouthwatering food.

"This time, yes. The day they plan to move you, no. They want you trust the food and to trust me." Maya's back was to her as she quickly vacuumed the small area, then returned the vacuum to the cart and headed for the bathroom, Rowan's wet clothes over her arm.

"They can't see me on the toilet with the door open. A phone's in the tank." Rowan removed the cover on the food container, inhaling the smells of soy and teriyaki sauces, and began eating. She watched Maya disappear into the bathroom. She could hear water running in the shower and the sink. The food helped the pressure in her head subside. She heard the toilet flush and hoped Maya had left something for her in the bag there. She'd finished more than half of the food when her aunt reappeared and began dusting quickly.

"Did you enjoy the meal?" Maya asked with what looked like a nervous glance at her watch.

"They want me to befriend you. Appear wary." Rowan heard Maya, the telepathic words making her head begin to ache again. She assumed the glance at her watch was Maya indicating her time was limited.

"Yes. You can take the container." Rowan hoped her tone sounded dismissive and disinterested.

"Not going to finish it?" Maya asked.

"Thanks, but I've had enough." Rowan leaned back and picked up the magazine. She hoped the ibuprofen she normally kept in her backpack was still there, and that it hadn't been replaced with narcotics.

"Have you spoken to Huw? Can I trust him?" Rowan pushed against the headache to send the telepathic message. Watching Maya pick up the container and drop it into the trash bag hanging from her cart, she grappled with a pain in her heart nearly equivalent to the pain in her head. *"Someone told Jarrod where to find me. Was it Huw?"*

Maya looked directly at Rowan, her eyes searching Rowan's as if gauging how to respond. *"Rowan, I..."*

The door to the room opened and a man, heavily muscled with a scar on his right cheek, entered. "You can leave now," he said to Maya.

The telepathic thread between them broke with his words. She watched Maya nod and push the cart through the open door, turn right, and move forward. She heard a beep and assumed Maya had opened another door in the hallway with her badge.

"I'm Clay, " the man said. He was looking at her in a cocky but menacing way. "You'll be dealing with me now. Don't try any shit with me like you did with Derrick."

Rowan wished she could use her powers to toy with him a little bit. Despite his arrogant stance, a palpable level of anxiety emanated from him. But the headache was far too intense for her to waste what little energy she had. She needed to lie down and recuperate, preferably after swallowing a couple ibuprofen tablets.

"You can leave now . . . Clay, " she said, mimicking the tone and words he'd used with Maya, smiling at him in what she hoped looked like a cat eyeing a mouse for dinner.

She watched him open his mouth as if to have the last word, his face flushed, mouth in an angry line. Good—she could get to him with words only. The sensation of emotional discomfort coming from him increased. His hand appeared unsteady, jerking and causing him to fumble as he opened the door and left the room.

Rowan stood up. Her legs were shaky. She stretched her arms a little, giving herself time to get her balance and bearings. Thump, thump, thump. She rubbed her temples. Her head pounded with each step she took toward the bathroom. Maya had hung her wet clothes on the towel rack and over the shower stall. She tucked herself back onto the toilet and out of sight, twisted her body, lifted the tank with one hand, and pulled out the bag. She stifled a laugh, pocketing a small, travel size container of her favorite brand of ibuprofen. Maya had been at this telepathy thing long enough to anticipate what Rowan would need. The upper-right corner of the phone screen indicated the battery was at seventy-five percent. Not bad, but she'd need to be careful.

> Rowan: Cleaner + meal. gone now.

> Griff: 👍 2morrow—breakfast ok 2 eat. Lunch no. I can see.

> Rowan: Got it! Time 2 go?

> Griff: 3 pm.

Rowan sent a thumbs up emoji, shut off the phone, slipped two ibuprofen into her mouth, and flushed the toilet, quickly replacing the bag with the phone under cover of the noise. At the sink, she splashed her face, then cupped water in her hands and drank it. She filled her cup and took another drink. Three o'clock tomorrow. Rowan hoped he'd understood she was asking when he'd unleash whatever he was planning to help her escape. Griff always had a plan.

Rowan needed sleep. She had no idea what level of strength she'd require to escape, but she was determined to be ready for the fight that lay ahead.

Rowan

"Jarrod's on his way. Wake up, Rowan! You can't be asleep when he arrives."

"HURRY, ROWAN! WAKE UP NOW!"

"Mom?" Rowan could hear her mother's voice. Her sleepy eyes were hard to open, as if they were glued shut. A wave of urgency, physical as well as mental, pushed her upright. She swung her legs over the side of the bed, rubbing her eyes.

The room was dark. She heard a beep and click in the hallway. She turned on the nightstand light at the same moment she heard the second beep and click, then watched the door to her cage swing open. Jarrod stood there staring at her while the door closed behind him. Two bodyguards waited in the hallway. Rowan yawned, picked up her water glass, locked eyes with him, and took a long, slow drink. He held an object in his hand.

"Come any closer and I'll repeat what I did in Paris." Rowan said, keeping her voice pleasant but firm.

"I'm here to talk, nothing more." Jarrod slid whatever he was holding into his pocket and took a step toward the couch.

"Really? Because I think you logged into your many spy

cameras, watched me sleeping, and decided you'd come down here and do . . . I don't know . . . something creepy, perverted, illegal?" Rowan glared at him. "Oh . . . wait, you already did something illegal when you kidnapped me. Take whatever you slipped into your pocket out and lay it on the floor by the door before you sit in the armchair." Rowan wanted to stand, but she needed more water to steady herself.

"It seems you don't fully understand who's in charge here, Rowan." Jarrod's smirk was annoying, but it sent a rush of energy through her.

She remembered Maya's advice. *"Keep it simple, Rowan. Don't leave yourself drained and tired."* Rowan sorted through the many lessons she'd learned.

"Are you serious, Jarrod?" Rowan laughed. "Do you have any idea how pathetic you are? A grown man who can't get a girl to date you without forcing yourself on her? I'll bet your only option is to pay for it."

She watched his face turn beet red. She'd hit a nerve. Maya had taught her that in a state of anger, embarrassment, and humiliation, the other person was more vulnerable. Their blood pressure was up, their vision slightly clouded, and their ability to act rationally hampered. She had to stay cold, calm, and alert. Rowan breathed in gently through her nose and exhaled, relaxing her muscles. Preparing.

"You'll come to want me, Rowan. You'll see what an amazing life filled with power and money we can have when we join forces." He was near the couch now, closer to her, but he remained standing. Despite his words, apprehension and uncertainty emanated from him toward her. He had backup forces in the hallway, but in this moment, in this room, she was in control.

"I could care less about money or power. You've stalked me for years. I've shown no interest, and yet you can't get that through your thick head." Rowan took another deep breath to quell the hatred instinctively rising within her. She'd wanted to say this to him for a long time, but if she didn't keep her own emotions under control, she'd become distracted. "No matter what you do . . . drug me, force me . . . trap me. I will never, ever want you. I will never respect you. I will never love you."

Jarrod yanked from his pocket what looked like a patch. Rowan stood. If he planned to put a drug-laden patch on her while she slept, he'd come to regret that decision. Jarrod waved his arm, motioning for the two guards to enter the room. With them was Clay, the man who'd hustled Maya out earlier.

"Hold her down." Jarrod pointed to Rowan.

"Want to end up like Derrick?" Rowan crossed her arms over her chest and stared at the guards in a way she hoped unearthed their deepest fears. She didn't want to be responsible for another death. This time she'd remain steady, using her mind to stay a step ahead. Clay looked unmoved, but the other guards were clearly frightened.

Rowan tossed a few tricks around in her head. She remembered Maya inflicting pretty severe indigestion upon her. She was confident she could successfully pull it off. If she failed, she'd make the rug in front of them catch fire, dousing it quickly with the overhead sprinkler system.

Clay began moving toward her, his face grim. "I told you before, you're not pulling that shit with me."

Rowan gave him a big smile. Despite his words, he approached slowly. She whispered a chant, mimicking Maya, and pushed the words from her mind to her solar plexus, then raising her arm, left palm outward, released a burst of energy.

"What the . . . ?" Clay bent over, grabbing his abdomen and then his crotch. A large wet spot appeared on the front of his jeans, the smell of urine permeating the room.

"You bitch!" Clay screamed, clutching his stomach in pain, his face red with shame and wrath.

"I have no idea what you're talking about," Rowan said. "For such a tough, grown man, I'd think you'd be past peeing your pants."

Clay turned and ran toward the door, yanked it open, and disappeared into the hallway. It took all of her self-control to keep a straight face. She smiled at the two guards, noting the panic in their eyes.

"Get out, Jarrod." Rowan used her strongest, most authoritative tone. "You and your weaklings need to leave."

"You keep playing your little parlor tricks, Rowan. See where it leads. I don't have to house you in a nice place, offer food, keep you alive." Jarrod's pompous tone matched his body language. He no longer emanated fear, only arrogance mixed with displeasure.

"You call a cage a 'nice place'? Drugging me part of 'keeping me alive'?" Rowan struggled to tamp down the fury rising within and maintain control. "You expect, after doing this, I'll what? Find you attractive? Think you're a good guy to be with?"

"You'll get over Huw Evans." Jarrod smirked.

It hit her like a punch in the gut. How had he found out about Huw? Her hands twitched. She shoved them in her pockets, hoping to look casual, unaffected by his comment, while her stomach twisted in knots. "If you drug me enough, I won't be of sound mind, and then these powers of mine that you want so badly won't work. Think about that before you come in here with your evil ideas."

"You make a good point." Jarrod looked pleased with himself, satisfied and sure he'd flipped the game on her and was now in charge. "Maybe I'll remove Huw from the picture ... permanently. If you don't cooperate, that is."

Rowan stared at Jarrod, every muscle and cell in her body pulsating. He couldn't be allowed to see her vulnerability, her obvious love for Huw. She had to dominate and punish him.

The power rising within her came with the realization that not only could she kill him, but a part of her desired to cut his life short. Working to bury Jarrod's reference to Huw and the insinuation that came with it, she channeled Maya's training.

Instill fear without stepping over the line to evil. No matter what he says or does, you have magic, and he doesn't. You're a good person, and he's not. When uncertain, call for your mother and the women of your ancestors.

Rowan inhaled slowly through her nose. She envisioned herself at Pentre Ifan, facing the goddess and the many women who had come before her. "Be with me, help me," she whispered.

Rowan could see Jarrod had moved a few steps closer to her, the drug laden patch in its wrapper held tightly in his hand. He must think the threat to Huw meant she'd weakened, that she'd give in, folding to his wishes like a lamb to the slaughter.

"That was a weekend fling, Jarrod," Rowan said. "If Huw knows you, then he's not for me. I could care less what you do to him."

She focused on the section of the rug near Jarrod's foot and pushed from her mind through her arms to her hands. Pointing a finger from each hand at the rug, she drew a half circle, starting to Jarrod's left and moving in front of him then to his right. A half-ring of fire appeared between them, its crackling sound and instant heat both dangerous and exciting. She smiled, watching Jarrod cough from inhaled smoke and run toward the door, his arms waving frantically as a spark jumped to the bottom of his expensive trousers. She could wait until the sprinklers in the ceiling kicked on and put the fire out, but that was risky. Once Jarrod exited into the hallway, she pointed her finger upward at the sprinklers. Water descended, soaking the carpet and extinguishing the flames.

The air quality in her cage wouldn't be good for a while,

but she'd made her point. A fan behind a vent in the upper part of the wall kicked on automatically and pulled smoky air from the room. Rowan's eyes were stinging. She walked to the bathroom and turned on the overhead fan there. The watery tears streaming down her cheeks were more than a reaction to the smoke; they sprang from a deep sorrow at the possibility that she'd been wrong about Huw. Terror that Jarrod could easily blow poisonous gas through those vents made her gut muscles clench. There were no masks of any kind in this room. She'd pushed hard today. Jarrod might be weak, but Clay wasn't. Rowan inspected the carpet. A thin black arc remained like the beginnings of a magic circle—the kind she imagined would have been drawn for a ceremony by a medieval druid priest, or perhaps a powerful witch.

Rowan shook her head to remove those thoughts and wiped her eyes with her sleeve. She might be a witch, but she was also a woman in a dangerous situation who, without her magic, would already have been taken advantage of in ways she preferred not to think about. Tired from her efforts and lack of sleep, she moved the armchair in front of the door, knowing it wouldn't stop them from entering but at least would create enough noise to wake her up. Rowan climbed onto the bed, tissues in her hand, and sobbed, releasing the anguish she'd tamped down. She didn't care if they watched her crying. The longing for Huw mixed with the hurt and pain that she may have been horribly wrong about him crushed every part of her being. She prayed for sleep, and when it came, fitful and filled with sad dreams, she gave in to it.

Griffith

2:30 P.M.

Griff parked his car between two large company trucks at the far end of the Marrone Industries lot. He needed to be here, as close to Rowan as possible. Should his plan fail, he'd do whatever it took to intercede and save his sister. Once the alarms went off, Rick and his team would monitor local law enforcement and follow them inside. But Griff couldn't sit at home behind a computer screen like the Wizard of Oz. Tethering his laptop to his phone or a hotspot allowed him to work from his car. If confronted, he'd claim to be waiting for one of the employees.

The company's landscaping consisted of bare bushes that wouldn't flower until spring, leafless trees, and rows of still-colorful but wilting chrysanthemums. At two-thirty, regardless of weather conditions, Henry said he always exited the building for his afternoon smoke. Griff could see him sitting on the curb next to an unlabeled Mercedes-Benz Sprinter cargo van. It was a silent signal that this was the vehicle Rowan would be loaded into at 3:00 p.m. He picked up binoculars to get a better look at the men standing next to the cargo van on the opposite side from Henry. A man with a scar on his cheek and gelled, slicked-back hair fit Henry's description of Clay, new head of Jarrod's private security detail. The men appeared to be arguing. Texting Henry could put his friend in a difficult position if he hadn't silenced his phone. He couldn't be the first to message. Henry now bought into Rowan's claims of magical powers. Unlike Griff, he was sure Rowan could escape with or without their help.

> Henry: R did something. Guards scared.

> Griff: Thx. Need 2 know more.

> Henry: Hazmat suits—to extract her. drugged her food.

> Griff: She won't eat it.

> Henry: Clay says if not, he'll drug her himself.

> Griff: ☹

> Henry: thinks R's a witch. afraid 2 go in & take her.

> Griff: 😄

> Henry: Clay wants 2 punish R.

> Griff: For what?

> Henry: Humiliating him. Will be accident en route 2 new location. R in serious danger.

Griff watched the men tuck what appeared to be rolled-up white Hazmat suits under their arms and walk from the van to the building. What had Rowan done to earn the title of witch? Henry quickly pocketed his phone and lit up a cigarette. Griff wasn't one to pray much. He believed in technology, science, and his own brain and two hands. As fear swept over him, he closed his eyes and sent a fervent prayer to the God of his childhood that his hastily cobbled-together plan would work.

> Griff: 10 minutes 2 chaos. Help R run if you can.

He watched Henry pull the phone from his pocket, look at the screen, then stand and begin jogging toward the building. Griff's fingers clicked across the keyboard, checking that each piece was in place. Timing was everything. Ten minutes was more like ten hours right now, but the perfectionist in him waited.

Rowan

2:45 P.M.

Maya had arrived an hour earlier with her cleaning cart and food. With a small shake of her head that told Rowan the food wasn't safe, her aunt set a container on the coffee table. The tempting smell of what appeared to be pasta primavera was enticing.

"I'll be back to pick up the container when you've finished," Maya said, voice loud enough that the surveillance team could hear her.

"Don't bother. You can take it now. I'm not eating it." Rowan didn't want Maya in the middle of whatever was about to go down. She hoped her aunt would take the food and leave.

Maya shook her head slightly again. After she left without the food, Rowan moved the armchair back in front of the door, then sat on the couch, inhaling the meal's mouth-watering aroma while trying to decipher why her aunt refused to allow Rowan to defiantly return it. She stood and walked toward the small refrigerator. Glancing at the bathroom, she frowned. Maya had left the door closed. This kept the bathroom completely dark, invisible to the cameras. The lights would go on automatically when Rowan stepped inside. Had Maya left a present in there for her?

Rowan turned the knob on the bathroom door, opened it slightly, then stepped inside with her back against the inside of the door in an effort to keep from triggering the sensors that turned on lights. Standing in the dark too long might mean security would become suspicious. If Maya left something, it was in the toilet tank. Maybe closing the door was meant as a signal to Rowan. She stepped forward, and the light above the sink turned on but it was very dim. She could see two bulbs but only one was working. Rowan smiled. She stepped into the shower, and it remained dark. Maya had given her the gift of privacy. It wouldn't last long. She turned on the shower, quickly stripped off her clothes and hopped in, the heat and steam saturating her pores. She longed to make it a leisurely experience, but she couldn't. Quickly washing her hair and body, she then shut off the shower and reached for a towel on the rack on the shower's sliding door. It took less than a minute to pull her clothes into the darkened shower and put them back on before stepping into the light emanating from a single bulb above the sink. Now refreshed and awake, she noticed a small object on the back of the toilet. She dropped onto the toilet seat, then reached behind and smiled when her hands closed in on two protein power bars. She ate one while seated, tucking the other in the pocket of her trail pants. Flushing the toilet, she stepped back into the light and opened the door, exiting into the larger room of the cage.

Rowan stood while eating the last container of yogurt, her wet hair still dripping but pulled back into a ponytail. She heard Clay curse her from the other side of the door. His attempts to open it were thwarted by the armchair, which remained immobile. She smiled at him and waved. She was emanating energy at a very low level to hold the chair in place.

"Move the goddamn chair." Clay and his team looked

hilarious in white Hazmat suits. Rowan assumed they'd decided this was an effective form of protection against her.

"I'm not done eating," Rowan replied. Clay turned slightly, eyeing the people with him, his suit half unzipped. That move showed Rowan he wore a Kevlar vest. This might be more difficult than she expected.

"You're done, alright," Clay said, his voice menacing. "It's time for you to leave. We can do this peacefully or we can do it the hard way."

"Maybe I prefer the hard way." Rowan was stalling for time, hoping Griff would trigger whatever was coming and make it easier for her. She was sure that, somewhere in that big white outfit, Clay had a hypodermic needle. She threw the empty yogurt container in the trash and pointed at the chair, moving back several feet with her magic to allow the men to open the door and step inside.

"What time is it?" Rowan asked, keeping her voice calm.

"What do you care?" Clay asked. She heard the man behind him mumble "almost three" from inside the Hazmat suit. Clay glared at the offending team member.

Although she exuded an air of confidence, Rowan had no idea what her best move should be. Griff said three o'clock. There was a lot Clay could do in five minutes.

"If I didn't know better, I'd think this was a Ghostbusters reunion." Rowan laughed dismissively. The angrier Clay became, the higher the probability he'd make a mistake.

"This is the end of the road for you, witch." Clay icy tone told her this was it, the battle she'd prepared for. She'd leave in one piece or, by days end, join her mother in the afterlife.

"You think those cute white suits are something I can't work around?" Rowan directed the comment to the men behind Clay.

Clay raised his hand, and the men behind him pulled guns from their suits. Rowan looked down the barrel of three

Glocks with silencers. The man on the far end was emitting huge sensations of panic. His hands were shaking. She focused on his gun the way she had on the knives in Maya's kitchen. Raising her hand as if to protect herself, she sent as much pressure as possible. The gun flew out of the man's hand and across the room, hitting the wall as he screamed in pain, grabbing his wrist.

"One down, two to go." Rowan glared at Clay and raised her hand toward the remaining guard, who was visibly shaken.

As she sorted options in her mind, the door began opening and the cleaning cart pushed its way into the room, breaking her focus. "No, no . . ." she whispered to herself.

"What are you doing here?" Clay yelled. His voice, from the inside of his Hazmat head gear, took on an echo-like quality. "Get the hell out!"

"I'm scheduled to pick up her food and clean the bathroom," Maya replied.

Rowan marveled at her aunt's calm demeanor but she, too, wanted Maya gone. Griff should have known she was too old to be sent into a situation like this.

"It's okay. You can come back later," Rowan said.

Maya looked at her watch and then smiled at Rowan. Without another word, without telepathy, her look confirmed it was three o'clock. Suddenly the lights flickered and the electronic door lock began beeping. A screen perched on the wall above the tiny refrigerator that Rowan had assumed was a television, although she'd found no remote, lit up with Jarrod's face announcing the evacuation of all employees. A bomb scare. Brilliant idea, Griff. Rowan stifled the urge to laugh.

The room suddenly went pitch black, the only glow emanating from a small light perched on Maya's cart and faint emergency lighting in the hallway. It was enough for Rowan to see Clay step toward her, hypodermic needle in one hand, gun in the other. He froze as his team members cried out then fell, unconscious, to the floor. Rowan could see Maya's hand outstretched toward them, trembling with the exertion it had taken. Before Rowan could react, Clay turned, took a step backward, and plowed the needle into Maya's neck. Rowan watched her aunt clutch her heart and fall next to the cart. She moved forward, torn between fighting Clay and rushing to Maya.

"I've had enough of you," Clay said, facing her once again. "The only place you and your magic tricks are going is to the grave."

Arms at her sides, trying to remain still, Rowan lifted the fingers on both hands upward and pushed forward from her mind with all the strength she could summon. Instantly his gun fell out of his hand and Clay went sailing backward through the air, hitting the wall behind him. She dove for his gun only to realize he'd recovered quickly and grabbed a gun belonging to one of the fallen guards. They stood, weapons pointed at each other. If she raised her hand, or even a finger, to send a bolt of magic, she was sure he'd pull the trigger and maim or kill her. Rowan whispered a call to her mother and the women of her ancestry, unsure if, without her necklace, they'd receive her message.

Suddenly, a soft glow radiated in the room but the lights remained off, unchanged. Rowan looked over at Maya then down at her own hands, but the energy wasn't coming from either of them. It appeared to be coalescing directly behind Clay. Suddenly, the Hazmat cover flew off his head. He half-turned, elbow up and ready to slam into whoever was behind him. Rowan could see confusion and sheer fright on his face. She should shoot him now and be done with it, but she didn't want to kill another human being. She pointed the gun at his leg. As she was about to pull the trigger, Rowan looked above Clay's head and smiled. Bearing the look and stance of a warrior was her mother, white-hot sparks of energy around her, floating several inches above the floor.

"Drop down, behind the chair." Rowan heard Elin's voice, but Clay appeared to hear nothing. He was frantically shooting at Elin. A thick rope of iridescent color slipped around his neck. Rowan recognized what Elin was planning to do mere seconds before a bullet zipped within an inch of her ear.

"Now, Rowan. Down." Rowan refused, pointing her finger at Clay's wrist and sending waves of hard energy until he dropped his gun and reached for his neck, trying to grasp a rope he could see and feel but not touch. She wanted to plug her ears, to buffer herself from the terrible sounds of Clay choking. Remaining still, she pointed her finger at the gun, causing it to slowly slide toward her until it sat at her feet. She heard a heavy thud. Clay lay silent on the carpet, Elin floating above, the magical cord coiled and tucked onto a belt around her waist.

"Is he dead?" Nausea rose from Rowan's stomach to her throat. Death, no matter the necessity, still didn't sit comfortably with her.

"No, unconscious. He'll stay that way for a while." The aura around her mother was fading. *"Leave, Rowan. Maya needs help. She'll be with you or with me when the sun sets tomorrow."*

Rowan looked from her mother to Maya and back again. "You saved me. I should have been able to save myself."

"You would have been fine without me, but I couldn't stand by, knowing you could be seriously hurt." Elin's translucent hand touched her heart, and she smiled. *"You're strong, my daughter. You're a warrior now. Tried and tested. You're ready to defend yourself and protect others. Take up the mantle of the women in our family, and carry our power forward."*

"Who will continue to teach me?" Rowan looked at Maya, unconscious on the floor.

"Unlike me, you'll live a long life. One day you will teach your own daughter." Elin looked fuzzy.

"Don't leave, Mom." Tears ran down her cheeks.

"My love surrounds you, unseen. Death is not a barrier to the love for a child." Elin was gone as quickly as she'd appeared. Rowan took a deep breath, wiped her cheeks. She stepped over Clay's body and around the two still-inert guards to reach Maya.

"Aunt Maya?" Rowan put her hand to Maya's chest. She was alive.

Rowan tried to lift her aunt, but despite being a small, spare women, unconscious Maya was dead weight. She'd moved the chair. Could she move an entire body onto a cart without damage? Her right arm out, palm facing her aunt, she pushed with her mind to overcome the pressure and sharp pull in her shoulder as she began lifting Maya upward. Maintaining focus, she draped her aunt across the utility cart.

Griffith

2:50 P.M.

Griff watched Jarrod lower himself gingerly into his soft, leather office chair. He appeared to have a bandaged left ankle, calf, and left hand. He smiled, hoping the asshole was in pain. He had full access to Jarrod's laptop, including its camera. Jarrod opened the app attached to camera surveillance of Rowan. Ten minutes remained until Griff unleashed chaos.

"We can do this peacefully or we can do it the hard way." Griff heard a man's voice off-camera, and his gut muscles twisted, his tension level rising. The man must be in the hallway. Griff could only see Rowan in the room, alone. She appeared to be eating food from a carton and looking toward the door.

He heard Rowan say, "You think those cute white suits are something I can't work around?" She raised her hand, pointed it at a chair, and without further movement on her part, the chair slid away from the door. Three men dressed in Hazmat suits entered the room. They raised guns, pointing them at Rowan. Portions of the conversation were muffled by the Hazmat head coverings, plus Jarrod talking over them, cursing at what he saw. Suddenly Rowan raised her hand and one of the guns went flying across the room, the guard who had been holding it screaming in pain.

Griff sat, frozen, his usual denial submerged under a level of astonishment. An old memory from his childhood emerged. It was Rowan raising her hand in exactly the same way and sending a man in a suit standing outside their screen door flying into the yard.

"Holy shit, Ro!" Griff glanced at the upper right corner of his laptop. Five minutes until remote ignition of his plan.

As he watched, the door to Rowan's cage opened. The front of a yellow cleaning cart appeared.

"Dammit, what the hell is the cleaning lady doing there?" Jarrod shouted at the computer screen in front of him.

Griff sighed. He'd told Maya to stay away. Two minutes to go. He'd shut off Jarrod's laptop first. He typed in a command and hit enter. Jarrod's screen went black. Griff heard him frantically clicking the keyboard, trying to reboot without luck as he moved from Jarrod's laptop to the surveillance cameras inside the building, unleashing the deep fake of Jarrod onto every television monitor across Marrone Industries. He held his breath, waiting through the lag time between release and when it would appear on the company television monitors.

"What the hell?" Griff took a second to enjoy the look on Jarrod's face as the video began before he cut off the phone lines. Employees began streaming out of the building. It should be complete chaos inside by now. Griff heard sirens in the distance.

He opened the app on Jarrod's laptop to check on Rowan and Maya. There was a weird glow, a shape, in the darkness. Something looped around Clay's neck followed by a sound like he was choking. Maya lay on the floor. Rowan stood facing Clay and holding a gun, but she was talking to the effervescent shape. Griff heard a ping and transitioned to the screen where he monitored Jarrod's phone. Anger coursed through him as he watched a text to the person who had betrayed Rowan appear. Every part of him wanted to jump in and reveal himself, out himself to the traitor. He couldn't say a word because he'd turned all the information over to the FBI with the assurance both Jarrod and his spy would face kidnapping charges.

> Jarrod: Office hacked. Security down. Was this G?

> Source: I don't know.

> Jarrod: I pay you to know.

The screen lay silent. No ellipses.

> Jarrod: Text G. Tell me where he is right now!

So, Jarrod suspected he'd engineered what was happening. It was the last time the arrogant bastard would tell others Griff wasn't someone to worry about. Jarrod would live to regret underestimating him. The requested text came through on Griff's personal phone. He waited, silent, half furious and half satisfied that soon this nightmare would be over.

Griff smiled. If timing unfolded as he'd envisioned, they'd both be in handcuffs soon. His phone pinged again. This time it was Henry.

> Henry: deep fake files? Use of latent space 2 disentangle facial dynamics top notch! Facial expressiveness, appearance, dynamic nuances. Amazing. Whose work?

> Griff: Is R OK?

Griff needed to shake Henry out of his natural desire to talk tech.

> Henry: Brilliant optimization of algorithms.
> Employees believe it's JM.

> Griff: Later. What about R?

> Henry: Hang on. Pushing team 2 leave.
> They suspect deep fake. want to check.

Jarrod

2:50 P.M.

Jarrod lowered himself gingerly into his soft, leather office chair. He now had a bandaged left ankle and calf, thanks to Rowan. The part of him that imagined what magic like hers could do to make him more powerful was now in a battle with the part of him that wished he'd never kidnapped her in the first place. He opened his laptop and navigated to the icon that accessed the camera surveillance of her room in time to hear Clay say, "We can do this peacefully or we can do it the hard way."

He smiled at the determination in Clay's voice, thinking he might have misjudged the man. He was tougher than Derrick, less afraid despite evidence of Rowan's powers. Rowan stood facing the door, behind an armchair, hair wet, no makeup, barefoot, and looking beautiful. She created longing and rage in Jarrod.

He heard Rowan's voice. "You think those cute white suits are something I can't work around?" She raised her hand and the armchair moved, seemingly of its own volition, letting Clay and his men into the room. Moments later, the door to her cage opened again. Frowning, he focused on who would be entering the room at a crucial moment like this. He could see the front of a yellow cleaning cart.

"Dammit, what the hell is the cleaning lady doing there?" Jarrod shouted, eyes glued to the screen.

Clay must have forgotten to tell the cleaning staff to stay away until Rowan was removed. A simple error, and yet Jarrod experienced a twinge of concern, a gut feeling that something else was wrong here. Once Rowan was on her way to another location, he'd find out who this cleaning person was and fire her.

Suddenly the screen went black. Jarrod clicked his mouse and keyboard, frantically trying to reboot, but it remained blank. He stood quickly, wincing at the pain, intent on checking the situation for himself. Before he managed to step away from his desk, the internal company monitor on his office wall suddenly turned on. Jarrod found himself watching a video of what appeared to be him speaking to employees.

"What the hell?" He stepped out of his office where his executive assistant was hastily throwing her personal items into a tote bag.

"Why didn't you warn me first?" she said before she ran to the stairwell. He could hear her feet moving down the steps, then the steel door closed. Silence surrounded him.

He walked back into his office, a million thoughts tumbling through his mind. Who could hack his entire company system, including the deep fake file only the team in his secret lab had created? The file he'd told them to delete. If the lab team had turned on him, they would pay dearly. He picked up the phone to call security, but the line was dead. It must be chaos on the lower floors.

Jarrod stood in front of a large window in his office watching employees stream out of the building while police, fire, and ambulance vehicles pulled into the parking lot.

Whoever did this was not only a brilliant hacker but very thorough. But why?

"Rowan. That's why." Jarrod walked back to his desk and picked up the mobile phone lying there. Texting with a bandaged hand was frustratingly slow, but it wouldn't take many words to get to the bottom of this mystery. Jarrod's fury was rising. He had no idea what was happening in Rowan's cage. Was she trapped without power? Had Clay gotten her out before this madness began? Or, worse, had she escaped?

He was sure he had Griff to thank for this stunt. Jarrod grabbed his badge, then stuffed his car keys and wallet in his pocket. He needed to get down to the lab and assess the situation. A ding came from his phone.

> Source: G not answering.

> Jarrod: Find him.

> Source: Wait. Someone's at the door. Might be him.

Jarrod stood, silent, watching the screen for a few seconds. When nothing came through, he opened the office door and walked to the elevator. The elevator door opened, but instead of an empty car, he faced men and women in police uniforms, FBI jackets, and army fatigues. His heart sank, sweat breaking out as panic overwhelmed him.

Rowan

3:05 P.M.

Rowan heard beeps coming from the other side of the door in her hallway. She had Maya draped across the cart and had moved the cart outside the cage. Now she focused on the second security door, ready to fight off whoever was about to come through.

"Rowan?" She heard her name called softly. It was dark, but she was fairly sure the man who stepped through the door was Henry. He used his phone as a flashlight, and she breathed a sigh of relief.

"Griff sent me." Henry stretched his hand forward and grabbed the other end of the cart. "What happened in there?"

He scanned the room through the window with his phone, the light resting on Clay's inert body. "Dead?"

Rowan shook her head. "Unconscious."

"Then we need to get moving before he wakes up." Henry held the security door open as Rowan pushed the cart forward, and out into the hallway in front of Henry's lab.

She could see sweat dripping down the back of his neck. Was it stress or was Griff playing with the temperature controls?

"Henry, she's my aunt and she's barely alive," Rowan said.

She watched Henry pause, his face thoughtful, then he opened a side door to the cart. Looking in, she was surprised to find it empty.

"You get inside the cart," Henry said. "I'll say she pushed her cart into my hallway and collapsed in front of me, which is why I'm delayed. We'll get both of you out of here."

Rowan nodded. She was tall but flexible. She tucked herself tightly into the small space. Henry shut the door, and she listened as he pushed the cart toward the elevator. There was a bell-like sound followed by the elevator door opening. The cart moved, and minutes later, Henry exited onto the first floor.

"Have you seen Rowan Campbell?" Rowan heard a man's voice, the shuffling of multiple feet surrounding the cart.

"No idea who that is." Rowan wondered if Henry was talking to law enforcement. If that was the case, they were safe. He could open the door and let her out of the cart. He must have reservations.

The change in temperature from warm to very cold indicated they'd left the building. She banged on the door, and Henry opened it. Stepping outside, she shivered. The parking lot was fairly empty. A few employees and members of the media huddled behind yellow tape. A bomb squad van was parked closer to the building. Henry began pushing the cart toward an ambulance. Rowan sighed with relief as paramedics moved toward them, quickly lifting Maya onto a stretcher. She could see legitimate EMT badges on their jackets.

"Her name is Maya Edwards. I'm her niece." Rowan shivered in socks, wearing a hoodie but no coat.

"Can you tell me what happened to her?" One of the paramedics wrapped a blanket around her shoulders as he spoke.

"She was trying to help me escape the building. Jarrod's head of security had a syringe and injected her. She fell over, unconscious." The paramedic's stunned face told her the quick explanation inferred quite a bit more than he'd expected. "I don't know what drug he used."

"She has no identification on her," the paramedic answered. "Can you provide your name and documentation for her? You said she was your aunt?"

"I'm Rowan Campbell." Rowan heard a sharp intake of breath as the paramedic connecting monitors and IVs to Maya paused, staring at her in shock. "I can find her information and bring the identification with me to the hospital. It's probably in her car which should be parked nearby. I don't have a phone number to provide, but I can meet you there."

"Where are you taking her?" Henry asked.

"UPMC Passavant in McCandless." As the paramedic shut the ambulance door, turned on the siren, and headed out of the parking lot, Griff appeared, walking toward them. He wrapped her in a hug, giving Henry high five.

Her eyes watered, and a wide range of emotions filled her as she held her brother. Yet, the only thing that emerged from her mouth was "I'm freezing!"

Griff laughed. "I've got a coat, boots, hat—all in my car waiting for you."

"Griff, we need to go back inside." Rowan gestured toward the building. "Jarrod took my necklace."

They watched the swarm of police, firefighters, and Army National Guard, the journalists calling to them for information.

"You're kidding, right?" Griff said. "Your name is all over the news."

He handed her his phone, and she gasped as a series of headlines, all variants that contained her name and the word 'kidnapped,' swam before her eyes.

"So that's why the paramedic looked surprised," Rowan said, handing the phone back to Griff. She hugged herself to fend off the chilly air. "My blue quartz necklace is somewhere in that building."

"Either Henry or I will get it for you tomorrow," Griff said.

Rowan shook her head. "You know that no one can touch it but me."

Henry appeared thoughtful, considering her words. "If it will hurt me to touch it, won't it have the same effect on others?"

"I see your point." Rowan conceded.

Griff stuck out his hand to Henry and they shook. "Thank you, my friend."

Rowan smiled at Henry. "Thanks, Henry. Maybe next time we'll meet under better circumstances."

"For what it's worth, Rowan, I think you could have done this yourself," Henry gave her a little smile and a wink.

"Not a chance." Griff said, with a laugh. "Just kidding. Come on, Ro. We need to get to the hospital."

Rowan followed Griff to his car. She looked back toward the building and realized Henry hadn't moved. He remained standing, smoking a cigarette and watching them. She gave him a thumbs up. She could have escaped on her own, but it had been easier—with fewer casualties—having Griff dismantle security. At the car, Griff handed her a puffy black winter coat. Once she was inside and seated, he passed a bag to her with a black and white checked woolen scarf, socks, and boots.

"Maya must be parked nearby," Rowan said. "Her identification is inside the car. I might be able to unlock it. Could we find it and give it a try?"

"I booked her a rental car." Griff said. "I have the spare key fob, and I think I know where she parked."

"It was terrifying, seeing her come in right after they'd aimed loaded guns at me." Rowan's voice shook with emotion. "She tried to help, but Clay plunged a needle into her. I don't know what he gave her."

"I told her it wasn't safe . . . to stay away," Griff answered. "The plan was you'd get out on your own with help from Henry."

Rowan twisted the end of her scarf, wishing Griff was aware of his true connection to Maya. She hoped it wasn't too late for the two of them. "Hey, why the abundance of law enforcement swarming the parking lot and building? Did you convince them the bomb scare was real?"

Griff chuckled, his voice softening to a level of relaxation. "The police are there to check the building, but the feds are there for Jarrod. They should have arrested him by now with cooperation from the police. I texted Rick you were safely out of the building."

Rowan was quiet for a moment, letting the knowledge that Jarrod would be behind bars sink in. "That must have been the guy who questioned Henry, asking if he'd seen me. Henry never let on that I was in the cleaning cart. I wonder why?"

"Henry has a natural aversion to law enforcement, particularly to federal agents," Griff said. "He did time for hactivist type stuff."

"Ahh . . . he does seem tech nerdy enough to be a hacker. I wouldn't have pegged him as an activist though. Too serious."

"Prison changes people." Griff turned the car onto a tree-lined, residential street. "Let's see how Jarrod likes being in a cage. I doubt it will have the same positive change it did for Henry. And I imagine his lawyers will have him out on bail in no time."

The car stopped and she leaned forward, peering through the front window. They were parked behind what she assumed was Maya's rental car. Rowan opened the door as she spoke, stepping outside. "Why didn't you let Rick find me himself?"

"I didn't know what he'd find," Griff answered. "I didn't want you blamed for killing someone."

She watched him open Maya's car door and reach inside, extracting a tote bag.

"You'll need to give a statement to the authorities, Ro. Plus, you should call Huw, let him know you're alright." Griff dropped the tote bag on her lap once they were back in his car. He handed her his phone.

"Huw?" His name rolled out of her mouth more curse than question. "We can't trust him, Griff. Jarrod dropped Huw's name like he knew him personally."

Griff remained silent. She sensed his thoughts churning as she lay her head back against the seat and closed her eyes. She needed to put the emotions she'd bottled inside for days to rest —the worry about Maya, the dual suspicion and longing for Huw, all sat like pent-up steam in a pressure cooker. She'd fought, she'd won, she'd survived. But Jarrod had means and opportunity. Her magic was her only real security. Magic she now understood and could fairly consistently control.

"It was Huw who took a deep fake of Jarrod that Henry provided and improved it. He did it for me . . . and for you, Rowan." Griff turned on the radio, scanning channels until he landed on the news, then pulled away from the curb.

A reporter's voice filled the car. "We're here at Marrone Industries in the North Hills in what has been a bizarre turn of events. A bomb scare turned out to be a hoax, but sources tell us former fashion model and Pittsburgh native, Rowan Campbell, was allegedly being held against her will in the basement of the building. Sources confirm that CEO Jarrod Marrone has been arrested as part of an apparent federal investigation of both his business dealings and connection with Senator Harrison Cherrington, as well as the alleged kidnapping of Rowan Campbell. Calls to Campbell's brother, Griffith, to confirm Marrone was holding his sister hostage have gone unanswered. Pittsburgh police confirmed that globally recognized fashion model, Gemma Gallucci, romantically linked to Griffith Campbell, was taken in for questioning earlier today. She's suspected of assisting in the disappearance of Rowan Campbell. Tune in to our eleven o'clock news for updates on this evolving story."

Rowan stared at Griff, mouth open in shock. "Gemma? Gemma was Jarrod's spy?"

Griff nodded, a flash that could be anger or pain crossing his face. "Henry hacked Jarrod's phone and caught her. I fed her disinformation and confirmed she was texting Jarrod."

"Why?" A stab of remorse that she'd nudged Griff to make a more solid commitment to Gemma filled Rowan. "I thought she was genuinely in love with you."

Maya's words of distrust surfaced, her instincts obviously better honed than Rowan's. The puzzle pieces floating in her head linked together one by one in a dance of clarity. Griff turned into the hospital parking lot. Thankfully, news media weren't present. A good sign that no one had been tipped off about Maya or suspected where Rowan might be. The longer she could dodge the media and the authorities, the better.

"My commitment and trust issues have expanded, and it'll be a long time before I'm in a serious relationship again." Griff turned to look at her, his face stern. "You need to call him. Henry helped me get access to the work being done in his lab, but it was Huw . . . he's brilliant, by the way . . . who made the incredibly lifelike video of Jarrod and then worked with me to get it out in one push to all the internal television monitors."

Rowan nodded in acknowledgment. She refrained from telling Griff the bomb scare was helpful, but she was already successfully fighting her way out when it happened. She would have escaped on her own. "Why did Gemma do it? I don't understand."

"She needed the money. Her family's restaurant business was going under. A bankruptcy filing salvaged parts of it, but they'd borrowed from shady characters at a high interest rate and couldn't get themselves off the hook." Griff looked stoic, no signs of sorrow. She guessed he'd run through his feelings when he first learned of Gemma's betrayal and then tucked them away, deep inside himself. "Gemma's assignments were less frequent post-Covid. I contacted her agency. Apparently, she went outside her contract often to make extra money and then showed up late and tired to scheduled assignments. She was an easy target for Jarrod."

Rowan squeezed Griff's hand. "I'm sorry this happened to you."

"Call Huw."

Rowan fished Maya's wallet out of the tote bag and handed it to Griff as he opened the car door. "You get her information to hospital registration. After I call Huw, I'll meet you inside."

Wallet in hand, Griff exited the car and started jogging across the parking lot.

Rowan stepped outside. The cold was less stringent, its bite a little softer, with her new coat and boots. Standing next to the car, she blew warm breath on her fingers and then walked into the hospital lobby and settled herself in a chair. The time difference meant she'd wake Huw, but she longed to hear his voice. Sadness for Griff mingled with relief that her suspicions about Huw were unfounded.

"Hello?" Huw's sleep-laden voice wrapped her in joy. "Griff... is she safe?"

"Huw... it's me. I'm calling from Griff's phone." Rowan's smiled, her eyes damp.

"Rowan, thank God! Are you alright?"

She closed her eyes, listening to the rustle of bed sheets as he moved, wishing she was there. "I'm fine. Nothing a good meal and sleep won't cure. Aunt Maya wasn't as lucky."

The joy of hearing Huw was tinged with sadness for Maya, creating both pain and pleasure in her heart.

"What was Maya doing there?"

"I'll fill you in on everything later. I'm sorry I woke you up in the middle of the night."

"I'm glad you called. You're safe. I can finally sleep well."

Gratitude filled her, listening to the relief mixed with love in his voice. "I wish I were there with you." Rowan smiled, a tingle running through her body.

"Ahh, but then neither of us would be getting much sleep, now would we?" Huw chuckled. "When will you be back in Wales?"

Rowan was silent a moment. She longed to return immediately, but with Maya hospitalized and a full investigation underway regarding her kidnapping, she wasn't sure she was free to leave. "I miss you more than you can imagine. But I need to stay here a while . . . for Aunt Maya and Griff. Plus, Jarrod's been arrested and they need my statement regarding the kidnapping."

"Griff told me about Gemma . . . and about the authorities investigating Jarrod. He thinks Jarrod planned to use MyShadow for unethical purposes. I'm not surprised." Huw sounded tired. Rowan heard him yawn. "How's Griff? Gemma's betrayal hit him hard."

Shame washed over her. Penitent that she'd harbored even slight suspicions of Huw, her heart craved the release of confession, but her mind pushed her to let it go. Nothing good would come of unloading her remorse on him. "Griff's fine. It'll be a long time before he trusts again, but I have faith he'll find the right woman one day."

"Hmmm . . . yes. The right woman." Huw's voice was softer now. "Come home to me, Rowan. I love you."

"*Cwtch*, Huw," Rowan answered with a smile. "I love you too. Go back to sleep."

"Talk soon," Huw said.

She ended the call imagining his head on the pillow, hair tousled, the steady breathing and the smell of him as she spooned her body next to his. She was finally free to stay in one place, to build a life with someone.

Rowan walked through sterile white hallways, past staff in their blue or gray scrubs, and entered Maya's room. She sensed Elin nearby, although there was no evidence of her mother's spectral presence. Maya looked peaceful lying in bed, strands of white hair fanning across her pillow, framing a face in gentle repose. If not for the insidious beeping of the monitor, she could pass for a patient merely sleeping and able to wake up at will. Rowan sat on a small, hard chair next to Griff.

"Ro? Everything okay?" Griff asked.

"Yes. I woke him, but it was good to hear his voice," Rowan said. "He asked when I'll be back . . . in Wales."

"That's your plan?" Griff gave her an amused smile.

"I told him I'd have to see what happens with Aunt Maya. And I'll need to give a statement to the authorities." Rowan handed Griff his phone. "But wherever Huw is, that's where I want to be right now."

Griff nodded, pocketing his phone, his face serious. "The doctor said if Aunt Maya wakes up, it will be a long recovery. The next twenty-four hours are crucial."

"If she wakes up?" Panic surged through Rowan. "Are they saying she might not?"

"She might not make it, Ro. They think she had a mild heart attack, and when she fell, she hit her head in such a way that she has swelling in the brain." Griff put his arm around her shoulder. Rowan leaned in, head on his chest, tears bubbling up in her eyes.

"Oh, Griff. She put her own well-being on the line for me and now . . ." Rowan's voice cracked, a sob escaping. "There's something Aunt Maya should tell you, but seeing her like this makes it much harder to know whether she'll ever be able to do that. I think it's on me to share her secret with you."

Griff grabbed a box of tissues on the nightstand and handed them to her. "What is it?"

Rowan wiped her eyes. Facing Griff, she touched a lock of unruly hair lying across his forehead, nearly covering one eye. His brows scrunched in that familiar way she loved. He was laser focused on her, waiting.

"You're in need of a haircut and shave," Rowan said, tenderly rubbing her hand against his cheek.

The scruff on his face, at least three days old, said he'd ignored anything above the basics in hygiene to work night and day for her. She dreaded adding to his stress by telling him he might lose a mother for the second time in his life.

"Ro? Spit it out." Griff hated dancing around a subject. Rowan would need to get right to the point, rip off the Band-Aid, and then be there to support him.

"What she told me is going to be difficult for you to hear." Rowan looked down at her hands for a moment then up at Griff, holding his gaze. "Maya is my aunt. However, she's your mother . . . your biological mother."

"Rowan, I've seen enough to accept you and Maya have some type of magic. But this is a little crazy, don't you think?" He waved his hand dismissively. She was familiar with that response. She'd seen it many times when trying to convince him of things he'd rather not hear. "Maya's lonely. She never had children and she loves us like her own."

"Aunt Maya told me she had an affair with Paul Marrone. She and Mom were pregnant at the same time. She broke off the relationship and disappeared, hiding at Lilydale." Rowan slipped her hand into Griff's. "Mom went there in January. They went into labor at the same time. There was a bad snowstorm, but a midwife was able to get to Aunt Maya's house. You were born healthy, but my brother was stillborn. To protect you, Aunt Maya and Mom switched babies before going to the hospital. They paid the midwife for her silence."

Griff was mute, his face pale, his body very still. He shook his head from side to side, opening and closing his mouth, speechless.

"One day you were in a store with Mom. Paul Marrone was there. You look like Aunt Maya and Mom . . . but you have his dark, curly hair and unusual dual eye colors. He became suspicious and hired an investigator." Rowan paused, watching Griff. "I know this is tough, but don't go into denial until you hear me out."

"Dad has dark, wavy hair. That's no indication." Griff's hands were balled into fists.

Rowan placed her hand on his and uncurled his fingers, feeling the struggle within him physically enter her body.

"Why would I need to be protected from Paul Marrone? Or from Jarrod? He would have been a teenager when I was born." Griff was obviously seeking logic, the story difficult to absorb.

"Well, you won't like this part. Mom went there because she and Aunt Maya wanted a reading from a medium. The medium told them Jarrod was a danger to Maya's baby." Rowan waited, expecting a dismissal now that a psychic medium had been brought into the story. Griff's face was flushed, his eyes watery. His usually tough exterior had sloughed off and left him looking like a vulnerable little boy.

"I can't lose her . . . aunt or mother," Griff said, his voice gruff and filled with sorrow.

"Let's not go there. Not yet." Rowan whispered a few

words of an ancient incantation that came to her suddenly, although she'd never heard it before. A sense of calm, like a sedative, moved from her body to Griff's. He exhaled, the muscles on his face relaxing.

"Whatever you did, I'm better." Griff gave her a heartbreaking smile. "Okay. Finish the story. I'm listening."

"Marrone discovered two babies were born that night—one lived and one was stillborn. He must have paid the midwife a lot of money for the truth, but he confirmed you were Maya's son and, he assumed, his." Rowan pulled her hand away from Griff's and sat back. "Do you remember when he came to the house? The day Mom died? You were very little and frightened."

Griff looked at her, his expression intense. "That memory came back to me when I hacked Jarrod's laptop. You raised your arm at the guard, knocking the gun from his hand. I had a quick flash of you—arm up, hand out—and then a man outside the screen door flew through the air, landing in the yard. I told Dad later, and he told me to forget it, that it never happened. He said I had a big imagination."

"I panicked. I was a teenager with no understanding of my own abilities. Mom told me to always protect you." Rowan smiled. "He'd come to take you. My reaction was instinctive."

"Someone once told me everyone has their own superpower." Griff crossed his arms over his chest. "In that cage, you learned you have powerful magic, didn't you Ro?"

Rowan hesitated; her mind and her instincts were not in agreement on this. "I learned to believe in myself, to be confident that I'm a powerful woman with no need to rely on a necklace or another person. The magic was always there. Once I opened my mind and heart and accepted that fact, I set it free. Aunt Maya helped me remove my fear and trained me to defend myself. In that cage, I learned the real superpower is me. That confidence and belief in myself lets me accept and control my magical gifts."

"I admit, I didn't think you could escape without me," Griff said.

"I think it would have been much harder and taken much longer—and more people may have died—if you hadn't done what you did. But I could have done it alone." Rowan eyed him with amusement. "I'm grateful for your help. The lesson, Griff, is together we're unstoppable."

"Agreed, Ro." Griff chuckled. "If what you're saying is true . . . that I'm Paul Marrone's biological son . . . then why didn't Jarrod come after me?"

"Aunt Maya broke into the investigator's office and destroyed all the evidence. Several years later, Paul's brother, Ray, discovered a few handwritten notes and decided confirming the information meant he could cut in half the percentage of Marrone Industries Jarrod would inherit." Rowan took a deep breath. The next part of the story was still hard to comprehend. "Maya confronted Ray and, when angry words passed between them, she lost control of her magic for a second. She caused Ray to have a heart attack and die."

"She covered her tracks and went home," Rowan continued. "Jarrod found Ray's file with the notes and set out to determine which of us was a threat to his control of the company. When he approached me in Paris . . . well, I inadvertently used magic to push him away. That must have convinced him it was me."

"You . . . and Jarrod . . . as, what? A power couple?" Griff shook his head in disbelief.

"From things he said while I was in that cage, I think so. I was surprised at my lack of remorse when I stretched my powers and attacked Jarrod and others." Pride filled her at the memory of Jarrod's bandaged hand and the acrid smell from the ring of fire she'd created. "I became a warrior in that cage, Griff."

"I kept thinking of you as trapped with no options until Maya showed up." Griff said. "Apparently not!"

"Mom was there. Not all the time, but she spoke to me and appeared a few times, and she taught me a couple tricks." Rowan smiled, her heart filled with longing for Elin.

"Admittedly, things have happened today that I can't quite explain, but Mom showing up?" Griff reverted to his usual dubious look at her claims of paranormal activity.

Rowan moved her free hand toward the overhead lights and they flickered, the room going completely dark for a few seconds, then with a flick of her wrist, they came back on. "Like that."

"Very cool." Griff sat still for a minute, looking at her as if he were taking in an entirely new person and deciding whether he accepted the change. "I guess I have two mothers and Dad is, well . . . what exactly is Dad? Does he know? What should I do with this, Ro?"

"He knows. Aunt Maya told him at Mom's funeral." Rowan could see that full import of her words hadn't sunk in yet. "Griff, you're the rightful owner of one half of Marrone Industries. Possibly all of it if Jarrod goes to jail."

"Who's gonna believe that and hand over a multi-million-dollar company to me?" Griff rolled his eyes at her before closing them and leaning his head forward, rubbing his neck, legs stretched out in front of him. He looked completely exhausted.

"Aunt Maya will wake up. I'm sure of it. She'll confirm the story . . . or perhaps there's a way to find DNA evidence." Rowan patted her brother on the shoulder. "We'll find the original investigator. Maybe the midwife. Don't worry about that now."

"What if Maya doesn't make it?" Griff's voice sounded as

if he were choking. She could see tears in his eyes. "You want me to believe you have magic, Ro? Then use it to heal Maya."

Maya's voice filled her head. Rowan could see her aunt, wiggling her fingers, cautioning Rowan about healing others even as her words came back to her. *We can do more than defend or attack with these hands. It's the wonderful part of the gift we inherited. If we focus, we can heal.*

"Maya told me our magic can be used to heal. I'm willing to try." Rowan grasped Griff's hand as he stood, reaching out to him.

"Aunt Maya told me it's part of my responsibilities to always guard you because you're destined to do a lot of good in this world." Rowan touched his cheek, locking her gaze with his. "What do you think about that?"

"I think she has a bias in my favor." Griff's face reflected concern despite his lighthearted tone. "If you try your hocus pocus, will you endanger her? Make it worse?"

Rowan shook her head. "I don't think so. We'll do this together, Griff."

"I wish Mom . . . I mean your mom, Elin . . . were here to help," Griff said. "Wow! Weird. I guess she's my aunt. Even stranger, you're my cousin."

Rowan looked around the room as if anticipating Elin's return, but there was no light, no voice in her head. "I was sure I'd never be happy without Mom. In that cage, I discovered she's with me . . . always . . . because a mother's love never dies."

Rowan smiled. A picture was forming with near cinematic precision and clarity in her mind, the pieces coming together as if pulled from the four corners of the earth to create a solution. She tapped the many generations of women who came before her, culling the knowledge needed to heal Maya.

"You have a weird look on your face, Ro." Griff dropped her hand and crossed his arms over his chest, taking a step back from her. "Don't do something bizarre, like a spell or whatever it is you're concocting in your head."

"I'm not a witch, Griff."

"Yeah. I think you are."

Rowan laughed. "Uggh . . . such a small, common word that will never encompass our rich history. You watch too many movies. No one's getting a black cape, riding a broom, or stirring a big steaming pot of stuff, dude."

"Quit getting defensive." Griff playfully punched her in the shoulder. "Geez . . . now every time I say anything, you'll be giving me your feminist pushback, suggesting I insulted generations of women."

"There's a beauty in the passing of power from one woman to another over the centuries and on into time, even if that power isn't laced with magic like the women in my clan . . . our clan . . . possess. Passing self-worth, knowledge, strength, and love from a mother to a daughter has its own special, eternal magic."

Griff hugged her, tightly. "Not sure how I can help you, but we have to try to save her. Give it a go."

"Griff?" Rowan placed her hand on his forearm. "Maya warned me not to let others see healing powers. It could result in unwanted attention. Let's be careful."

She grasped Maya's hand and Griff's at the same time. "Talk to her, Griff. She can hear you, and she loves you."

Griff leaned in toward Maya, speaking in a low voice. To anyone watching, they looked like a close family, supporting one another, perhaps praying over their loved one. Rowan closed her eyes and imagined she was at Pentre Ifan, the goddess in front of her with many dreamlike women spread out behind. Unfamiliar words echoed in her head and, without hesitation, she whispered them. Finished, she looked down at Maya. Her aunt's blue eyes were open—glassy and red-rimmed, but alert.

"It worked," Griff said, awestruck. He frantically pressed the call button.

A second before the room filled with medical personnel, Rowan heard him say "Mom" to Maya. The many monitors attached to her aunt reflected her response as her blood pressure rose and cardiac rhythms registered a strong pace.

Rowan stepped out of the room and into the hallway. This was Maya's long-awaited moment with her son. She and Griff deserved to be alone. Rowan wandered down the hall to a family waiting room. It was empty except for one nurse, gazing out the window, her back to Rowan. Before Rowan could sit down, the nurse turned and smiled at her.

"Mom!" Rowan inhaled a sharp breath and took a step forward, arms open.

Elin held her tightly, then stepped back, her hands on Rowan's face. "I'm proud of you. You accepted your powers and used them for good. To fight your magic is to deny one of the crucial elements in our alchemy . . . and the women in our clan, my beautiful daughter, are the alchemy of the world. Always embrace your magic and the responsibility it brings with it. Consider it a privilege."

"There's quite a lot that I still don't know," Rowan said. "Stay . . . please. Teach me."

"I can't. This is the last of the energy bestowed upon me by the goddess and the God of our faith to help you save yourself and acquiesce to your destiny." Elin's face was forlorn. Her hands dropped away as her image faded. "Never doubt that I'm with you whether you see me or not."

"I love you," Rowan whispered into the now empty space. She sat down, her body trembling.

"Are you alright?" An elderly man with a cane stood barely a foot inside the door, a Pirates ball cap on his head. "You were talking to yourself, and I see you're upset. I can find another place to wait."

"No, no . . . sit, please. I was sending out a little prayer. My aunt turned a corner and is going to make it."

"Ahhh, congratulations. I wish it were the same for my wife." The man's face drooped, mouth downcast, and his eyes filled with sadness. "She's all I have. We never had children."

Rowan clasped her hands, feeling an internal struggle rising within her. Could she touch his wife and heal her? What if she did and that information got out publicly? Maya had shown her how to transfer her magic through ancient words that, to Rowan, sounded more like chants. But they hadn't had time to practice before Rowan had to leave.

"Could I pray for her with you?" Rowan asked. He sat on a chair across the room. She'd need to sit next to him and hope he didn't mind her holding his hand.

"That would be nice. My wife would approve." He smiled at her. She stood and moved to the chair next to him.

Rowan held his hand, holding her energy in check, determined not to hurt him. "Close your eyes."

"Lord hear our prayer. Please heal . . . ?"

"Miriam," the man said.

"Please heal Miriam through your grace and mercy. Amen." She'd have to get a little better at drafting prayers on the spot. Unfamiliar words, in Welsh and English, floated through her mind, and she mouthed them silently, still holding his hand.

Rowan patted the man's shoulder. "Go hold her hand. Tell her you're here and you love her."

He nodded and pushed on the cane with one hand while Rowan held his other arm to provide support as he stood up. "Thank you. I feel better already."

"So do I," she whispered to herself as he walked out the door and into the hallway, every part of her body tingling with joy.

Rowan

CONWY, WALES

The early December air was crisp and cold. Rowan shivered as she punched the code into the pad to the right of the pink door of the vacation rental. The placard on the exterior wall to her left announced to passersby traveling the cobbled street that once upon a time it was the Signalman's Cottage and home to someone employed by the king. The tall townhouse, in a row of the same, sat within the walls of Conwy Castle, a magnificent structure dating back to 1287. She hoped it didn't have the musty, centuries old smell like the bookstore she'd stopped in on her way from the train station to the cottage to pick up a guide to the history of the town and its castle. She touched her necklace, gently. It had become a habit to reassure herself it was, in fact, returned and resting in its rightful place around her neck. Griff arranged for her to pick it up herself. She'd been relieved it was in a secure box and no one hurt themselves trying to touch it.

Rowan and Griff had insisted Maya be discharged to Griff's condo, not to her home, until she was well enough to manage alone. Living together, even for that short time, had been wonderful for the three of them. A distant cousin of

Paul Marrone's challenged Griff's assertion that he was the rightful heir to Marrone Industries. Griff hired a lawyer who moved swiftly to order DNA tests between Griff and remaining family members, and to collect statements from Maya, the now retired midwife, and the investigator Paul Marrone had hired. What Maya and Elin had done, long ago, was illegal. Rowan had no idea what the fallout might be for her aunt or the midwife, but she was certain Griff would pull every string available to protect them. It was hard to imagine Maya and the midwife, both elderly women, would be punished for a decision that had such a happy ending.

Rowan spoke to Huw every day for the first week, introducing him through video calls to Maya and even to her father, whom she could finally visit free of concern. Five days was as long as Huw could endure before he hopped on a plane and appeared in the doorway of Griff's condo.

"I couldn't wait any longer," he said, wrapping her in his arms.

Waves of love flowed through her. Huw was her definition of coming home, not to a place but to a person. Home could be anywhere in the world as long as they were together. Rowan booked a room at the Fairmont Hotel, where they stayed locked in for nearly two days, ordering room service until Huw demanded to see the city and Griff reminded her that Thanksgiving was only a few days away. It had been a long time since she'd celebrated Thanksgiving in her home country with family. Griff made it a magical experience, hiring a catering company, inviting Henry and his daughter to join them, and ending the evening with drinks and the spectacular view of the city from his condo.

"I wish I could stay," Huw said as they sipped wine, the multi-colored lights of the city's buildings and bridges sprawling out before them. "I've got to pick up Cooper from my sister. She leaves on a trip in two days. And I've got a small group hike on the books."

"I wish we could leave together," Rowan answered, kissing him tenderly.

"It's okay." Huw pulled her in, her head resting on his chest. "You wrap things up here, and then come to Wales. For good."

"I'll be with you in two weeks. One interview with national media and a deposition, then I'm free to go." Rowan sighed with pleasure as he ran a finger down her arm and clasped her hand in his.

"I need an exact date before I leave."

Rowan turned to face him. "What is it you have in mind?"

A mischievous smile filled his face. He leaned down to kiss her and then whispered in her ear, "A full-on romantic adventure."

"And will we be sightseeing or merely trying out different beds in various locations?" Rowan asked with a laugh.

"You'll have to show up to find out." Huw kissed her deeply, passionately. "I say we stop talking now."

Here she was, the second week in December, following the instructions Huw had provided, opening the door to this quaint cottage. He'd said he would meet her here tomorrow and they'd explore Conwy, then drive down the coast all the way to the Gower peninsula before heading to his home. Rowan tingled with excitement at the romance, the mystery, the sheer freedom ahead of her. She pushed open the door, hauled her suitcase inside, and found herself standing in a cozy living room with a fireplace. A kitchen area extended slightly beyond. Everything was modern and renovated, from the polished hardwood floor to the new appliances and cabinets. Beautiful blankets draped the chairs and couch, inviting her to wrap herself in warmth and comfort. A bottle of wine and two glasses sat on the coffee table. She smiled. Huw must have asked the host of their accommodations to add this inviting, alluring touch.

Polished wood stairs curved upward to her right, the ceiling above exceptionally low, especially for someone her height. She'd need to duck midway in order to keep from banging her head. Rowan picked up her suitcase and moved to step up on the first step when she heard a noise and froze. Jarrod could no longer reach her, yet she hadn't developed the ability to fully relax and stop looking over her shoulder. The sound was coming from a long narrow hallway extending back off the right side of the kitchen. She set her suitcase down, dropped her backpack on the floor, and began walking in that direction. Halfway down the small hallway, she located a bathroom to the left, on the end. She paused, silently waiting.

The toilet flushed, followed by a mild thud, and a man's voice said, "*Cachu*" in Welsh. Rowan smiled. Her knowledge of the Welsh language was limited, but a good and proper curse was in her small vocabulary.

She knocked on the bathroom door. "Did I hear a man say 'shit' in there? Did you maybe have a little accident?"

The door flew open and Huw stood before her, face flushed and filled with surprise, holding his left hand with his right. "You're early! I wanted to surprise you."

Rowan laughed. "Oh, I'm surprised! What happened?"

"This damn bathroom is too small," Huw extended his hand, a sheepish, embarrassed look on his face. "I banged it against the sink."

Rowan raised an eyebrow in amusement. She could see a bruise starting below his thumb. Placing his hands in both of hers, she summoned a little magic energy, rubbed his fingers, and then released. "Let's see if that helps."

Huw wrapped her in a hug. "Can I show you the bedrooms upstairs?"

"Absolutely!" She squeezed him fiercely in return, joy

spreading through every inch of her body. "And now that I've healed your hand, you can carry my bags up those stairs. But don't bang your head. I'm not sure I can fix that!"

"I didn't know people were this short a century or more ago," Huw grumbled. "The theme of our weekend might be 'mind your head.'"

"I stopped to pick up a guidebook to the castle and the town," Rowan said, following him up the narrow stairway.

"You don't trust a Welshman's expertise in his own country's history? I'll be giving you a personal tour." Huw dropped her suitcase and backpack on the floor of a decent size room with a double bed. Across the hall was a second bedroom with twin beds.

"Think of the poor signalman and his family who lived here and had to go all the way downstairs and to the other end of the house to use the bathroom." Rowan imagined a cramped life for a family here.

Huw roared with laughter. "Spoken like a modern American. You'll need to take your mind back a few centuries. There would have been no loo. Only chamber pots or maybe a small hut—the privy—in the backyard."

"Like an outhouse?" Rowan yawned. Jet lag was creeping across her body, leaving her brain foggy, her limbs tired.

Huw wrapped his arms around her, and she laid her head on his chest. "Tired?"

"I could use a nap to get my time zones adjusted." She looked at the bed with its inviting knit throw draped across the bottom. "Sorry. Not very romantic of me."

"You sleep. I'm going out to pick up food."

Rowan lay down on the bed, smiling as he tucked the blanket over her. Sleep came immediately. It was deep and dreamless, and when she awoke, refreshed, it was dark outside. At first, she sat up, disconcerted, alone, thinking it was the middle of the night. She could hear movements downstairs.

Her phone screen said four-thirty. During the three hours she'd slept, the winter sun set over the United Kingdom. Her stomach rumbled. She stood, pulled her messy hair into a clip, and headed for the stairs.

"What's this?" Rowan smiled at the spread of cheese, grapes, olives, and prosciutto between two empty wine glasses waiting to be filled. "Did I tell you I love a man who can cook?"

"Oh, no! This is a starter, then we're going out to a restaurant for dinner." Huw chuckled and leaned in to kiss her. He smelled of shampoo and soap, his hair still damp.

Rowan popped a carefully cut square of cheese in her mouth. "I was thinking shower first, then food, but my stomach is begging me to wait on the shower."

Huw poured pinot noir into their glasses, the dark red liquid welcoming her to what appeared to be the start of a wonderful evening. She heard the light patter of rain outside and walked to the front windows to take a look.

"It's raining. Should we stay in?" Rowan returned to the kitchen and watched Huw, relaxed, unhurried, sipping wine.

"Of course not. This is Wales. Rain comes with the experience." He smiled, and those blue-gray eyes she loved were mischievous.

For an hour, they discussed everything from Jarrod's upcoming trial to their sightseeing plans for the following day and beyond, grazing upon a careful and tentative imagining of permanence.

"I'm excited to see the castle," Rowan said. "Let's do the self-guided tour tomorrow. Take our time . . . stop when we choose."

"You're aware that this castle represents the final win of an English king over a Welsh king, don't you?" Huw's eyes twinkled with mirth. "I'm not sure how much we should enjoy the subjugation of our ancestors."

Rowan rolled her eyes and stood. "I'm taking a quick shower. Then let's get dinner before wine on a nearly empty stomach gets the better of me!"

Rowan insisted her picture be taken in front of the famous "Smallest House in Great Britain", which butted up against the castle walls as they toured Conwy the next day. She loved the leisurely, touristy experience of having all the time in the world to relax with the man she loved. They'd had lunch next door at the Liverpool Arms, choosing a corner seat near the fireplace where they snuggled together and shared sandwiches, fries, and ale. Its modernized interior didn't hide its history as the oldest traditional pub in Conwy.

"I love the view outside—the estuary, the castle, the fishing boats." Rowan kissed Huw on the cheek and leaned her head on his shoulder, warmed by the fire and their bodies tucked together. "I hate that the wind off the estuary makes it too cold to take in the view for long."

"We'll come back in the summer when the city is filled with tourists who block the view, but the weather is better," Huw said, causing them both to laugh at the irony of how best to enjoy a beautiful view in a tourist mecca. "You know, when Edward I took over Conwy and built his castle, he forced the Welsh to move across the river that protected the southern flank of the town. If they went north of the river they might be killed."

"Whoa, not a nice guy." Rowan imagined her ancestors living in a recently conquered Wales and shook her head.

"The river was the border. Border, in Welsh, is *cyffin* which eventually mutated to *gyffin* and left the area with the name Aron Gyffin. Nine hundred years later, it's still known by this name," Huw said. "It's a subtle reminder of the Welsh long memory regarding being excluded and the modern-day culture clash that continues between . . . let's say Celts and Brits. I packaged it that way to take into consideration the Scots and Irish, fellow Celts, who push back fiercely."

"Now there are Welsh-speaking schools, and the language is taught in all schools," Rowan said. "I'd like to try to learn it. I remember my mother and Aunt Maya using it for private conversations, but I was never formally taught to speak or read in Welsh."

"Hmmm . . . well, there are adult classes in the village. I warn you, it's the oldest language in its original form and tough to master if you don't grow up with it." Huw gave her a side hug and then waved the waitress over for their check.

"You speak and read, I assume?" Rowan loved learning new things about Huw. A lifetime wouldn't be long enough to get to know him.

"Yes. As children, our parents split languages speaking to my sister and me, one in Welsh and the other in English. That's how we simultaneously learned both languages." Huw stood, wrapping his scarf around his neck and pulling on his knit cap.

Rowan did the same. Jackets zipped, hats and gloves on, they stepped out into the December chill. Festive Christmas decorations were everywhere, brightening the shops and homes. They'd toured the town first, in agreement the castle should be left for last.

"You're wishing I'd agreed you could bring your camera?" Huw looked amused.

"I'm twitching to shoot photos of this amazing architecture and the views," Rowan admitted, looking out over the estuary from their spot high up on the castle wall. "But we agreed this is our day. Your phone will suffice. Tomorrow, I may come back with my camera."

She followed Huw to the interior of the castle, awed at

how well preserved it appeared to be. But it was the royal chapel that took her breath away. They were tagging along behind a guided group, listening to tidbits of history here and there while keeping to themselves. The stained glass windows —three long panels—were stunning.

"Commissioned and installed in 2012, the Medieval techniques of stained glass were used to create what you see today. The work was inspired by surviving medieval fragment panels kept in the archives of Llandudno Museum," the guide explained.

Rowan listened while taking in the story, depicted in the windows, of the Welsh Princes and their bloody struggles with Edward I, her hands longing to hold her camera. Huw was snapping photos with his phone, his focus on the depictions of mountain bikes and modern life. Rowan was drawn to the ancient stories, a mild energy flickering inside her. The figures depicted before her came to life, speaking to her although she couldn't understand their words. She wished she could identify which of her ancestors had been part of this period in history.

Lost in thought, she heard Huw as if he were at the end of a tunnel. "Rowan!"

She turned to look at him, the ghosts of the stained glass receding. The room was empty except for the two of them. Rowan shook her head a little, making sure she was back to reality. She looked at his face, expectant, loving, and experienced an overwhelming tide of emotions. Before Rowan uttered a word, Huw kissed her passionately. Neither of them heard tourists enter the room until they heard the sound of many hands clapping.

"Would one of you be willing to take our picture?" Huw said to the tourists.

He handed his phone over to a man who volunteered, and nudged her to a spot in front of the windows. Tears in her eyes, she inhaled the enormity of this moment. She'd made it through the dark years running from a stalker, the endless longing for her mother, and the fear and uncertainty about her magic, to find the strength to fight both Jarrod and her own insecurities. Best of all, while embracing the power within her, she'd found love.

"If we're going to explore this thing between us, I want to be your equal partner," Rowan said.

"I'd expect no less for us." Huw leaned in and gave her a long, slow kiss.

"I love you," she whispered.

"*Cariad au*," he replied.

Rowan smiled. It was a phrase she remembered her mother saying to her. It meant "precious love." Love that emanated from the man next to her throughout her being. A mother's love that surrounded her eternally, flowing from centuries of female ancestors, and extending beyond the confines of this brief, physical life.

Rowan

MUMBLES, WALES

A deep, abiding sense of being rooted, of finally fitting like a puzzle piece into the right place, enveloped her. She sat quietly in Huw's bedroom in a chair facing the village and Swansea Bay beyond, a soft wool blanket across her lap, hot coffee and Welsh cakes on the table beside her, watching the sun rise. She'd brought a level of joy with her from Conwy that created the sensation of floating on air and yet being, ultimately, anchored in a safe, solid future. She'd hoped that Griff, Maya, and even her father, could come for Christmas, but Maya wasn't well enough and her stepmother had made plans her father couldn't or wouldn't wiggle free of to make the trip. Griff was knee-deep in taking over Marrone Industries.

Christmas had been beautiful all the same. Jarrod's trial was postponed until after the new year, but his passport had been confiscated, and law enforcement tracked down and arrested many of his accomplices, including Clay, who had regained consciousness and escaped the day Rowan broke free of the cage. He was now behind bars. Rowan occasionally checked the internet for updates, but most of her information came from Griff. The best news had been about Henry. His job was intact. Griff had protected him from any potential fallout around Jarrod's arrest and, once he was fully ensconced as CEO at Marrone Industries, he planned to promote Henry.

"Penny for your thoughts." Huw slipped into the chair on the other side of the small round table and set his coffee mug down.

"Shouldn't you say something like 'a tuppence for your thoughts'?" Rowan gave him an amused smirk and was rewarded with a laugh.

She inhaled the morning sounds of birds singing, despite the cold outside, and cars starting as neighbors headed to work. "Maybe if we promise my stepmother she can meet someone from the royal family, Dad might be able to make a trip over here."

"And what will Shellebrity do when she discovers we can't keep that promise?" Huw let out a boisterous laugh at the thought. He'd met Shelly briefly, long enough to match the veracity of the joke with the actual person.

"Good point!" Rowan sighed. "We'll need to make friends with a royal. You'd better get working on it!"

"Ready to get back to photography?" Huw asked. He'd heard her arguing with her former employer who'd dropped her when she disappeared and, now that her story was all over international news, wanted her back for freelance work.

"Yes, but I don't want to be gone all the time chasing freelance assignments." Rowan reached over and touched his arm. "I can breathe here."

She was beginning her life again close to the ocean and Pentre Ifan, in a village she loved. The Gower Peninsula in all its fierce beauty offered endless photo options, as did much of Wales. She'd displayed a few pieces of her work on consignment in the local gift shops and was reconnecting with old friends in the world of photography.

"It doesn't mean you can't travel as much as needed to

pursue your career." Huw looked amused. "I have faith you'll always come back to our home."

"I've lined up places to have reproductions, framing, and more outsourced," Rowan said. "I need a quiet place—in town or in this house—to download photos after a shoot and work."

"I'm sure we can find a solution." Huw smiled and she inhaled the look of affection on his face that she never tired of.

"A new company approached me with an offer. I'd retain a good percentage of the profit, have primarily in-country assignments, and my work would be sold on greeting cards, as framed prints, and applied to other merchandise," Rowan said. "I'm thinking of accepting. I'll call the new line of items 'Goddess Art.'"

"Will you go back to your real name now that you're safe?" Huw's eyebrows raised in surprise.

"Nora Edwards has been my signature pseudonym as a photographer for such a long time it's become my brand." Rowan could see the look of both skepticism and concern on Huw's face. "I like keeping it for a bit of privacy."

"You don't truly feel safe? Is that the real issue here?" Huw reached across the table for her hand, holding it tightly.

"I'm safe with you, in this village, in this community." Rowan paused, hesitant. "I lived in fear a long time, Huw. I came into my own power, my self-confidence, these past few months by learning I can protect myself. I'll always choose caution. My guard will always be up in the outside world. But never here . . . with you."

Huw nodded, a serious look to the set of his mouth and the downward furrow of his forehead. "There's something I need to tell you."

Rowan became very still. She watched as he ran his hands through his hair, then clasped and unclasped them, a sure sign it was big news, and that he was unsure of her response.

"Griff and I were approached by both the U.S. and U.K. government security organizations to, on a per-case basis, run operations that, well . . . let's say, that flush out bad guys," Huw said, his words coming out in one big rush, his gaze intense and focused on her. "Griff's new role, as CEO, may create a conflict and he'll need to decline."

Rowan's heart clutched with fear. "This could be dangerous work, Huw. Have you said yes?"

Huw shook his head. "I said I'd consider it. I won't say yes unless you're comfortable with me returning to the tech world part-time and, honestly, undercover—and if you'll agree to work with me. Use your powers for good . . . isn't that what I've heard you say?"

Rowan let go of his hand, feeling cold from trepidation. She shivered with unease. Her mind flashed back to the cage, the smell of blood mixed with acrid smoke from the burned carpet. She'd used her powers out of necessity. Could she do it intentionally? Did she want to?

"I was hoping for a boring village life. You, me, Cooper . . . hiking, taking photos, cooking together, meeting up with friends." Rowan sighed. "Granted, I need to keep an eye on Griff. Safeguard him when needed, even though he'll never believe he needs help from anyone else."

"I'm sorry if it's cast a shadow, my bringing this up." Huw looked contrite. "They'd like an answer straightaway. But I can hold them off or decline."

"What would you do with the hiking business if you said yes?" Rowan's heart clung to her dream life while her mind sought a way to meet Huw halfway. She'd sensed a rise in his energy level when he spoke of the offer. It excited him. Their connection was exceptionally deep now. She experienced his moods and the shifting movements in his mind and body viscerally. Telling him this might frighten him. Better she keep her expanding magical abilities to herself.

"The hiking business stays as my cover, which is a relief because I love it. I don't want to give it up." Huw said. "The assignments would be random, perhaps only one or two a year. Plus a few meetings in London or D.C."

"Our life would be eighty percent normal. Your hiking, my photography, our village life, sprinkled with a few assignments," Rowan said, embracing the future vision as if it were a shawl she would happily wrap around her shoulders. "But twenty percent would be dangerous undercover assignments. Would we bring that danger back here . . . to our home?"

Huw smiled. "You said 'we.' If I accept, does it mean we'll be in this new adventure together?"

Rowan nodded. "I couldn't let you embark on this alone. Before you decide, consider this question: What happens when we have children?"

The smile dropped from Huw's face as quickly as it had appeared. Rowan was sure fitting a child into the exciting, new scenario in his mind came as a shock. He'd imagined himself back in the tech world he loved, possibly as a superhero saving the world from bad threat actors while tucked behind a computer screen and hunched over a keyboard.

"We were both robbed of a parent before we reached adulthood," Rowan continued. "I don't want that for our children. Unless you're not interested in having children?"

She watched surprise run across Huw's face as he shook his head. She'd blindsided him, which wasn't fair, but she couldn't give up every inch of her future dreams. One day there would be a little girl to pass her magic on to.

"I definitely want children. Being Cooper's father isn't enough!"

Rowan laughed. "Well, you know, I carry my mother's lineage. No promises there won't be a little witch in the mix. Are you ready for that?"

Huw maintained a serious countenance, a nervous twitch

appearing at the corner of his mouth. "I'm ready for whatever life with you brings, Rowan. Could I ask that we wait a year or two before children? And are you, in your unique way, asking me to marry you?"

Beads of sweat appeared on his forehead and upper lip. An anxious heat coming from this heretofore confirmed bachelor washed over her.

"I'll let you know when, if, I think that might be necessary," she answered, grinning at him in amusement as she watched him exhale, his body relaxing. "Maya often indicated my magic is a privilege that comes with responsibility, that my gift should be used for the benefit of others."

They sat in silence, finishing their coffee. Huw devoured a Welsh cake. The sun was up now and melting the frost on windshields and windows, creating dewy droplets on the bare branches of the trees.

"If you accept, I'm with you. We're partners in all things," Rowan said.

Huw stood and wrapped his arms around her from behind, kissing the top of her head. "I'm off to walk Cooper. You've given me a lot to consider."

Minutes later, Rowan heard Cooper bark, then the front door open and close. The sounds of singing birds and church bells blended in beautiful harmony outside. She opened the window a crack to let the sound cascade around her, through her, as a sharp, cleansing cold air filled her lungs.

"Thank you, Mom. I hope you're proud of me."

Rowan whispered a prayer, an old psalm she'd learned as a child, the blue quartz vibrating as the wind carried her words out into worlds both seen and unseen in tribute to the power that lies within all women.

Acknowledgments

The support of many people made writing speculative fiction for the first time possible. This book is dedicated to my friend of 40 years, Angie. She loved fantasy books and, sadly, passed away while beta reading this novel. I miss her every day - her wisdom, friendship, and love of good political jokes and great books!

Thanks to the Early Bird Writers whose daily support gets me going and keeps me writing. Thanks to beta readers Mora Durante Astrada, Lisa Peterson, Jen Sinclair, Kathy Dodson, Remo Hammid, Pam Stockwell, Deb Atwood, and Ann Menke for invaluable input; to Amanda Dove of A Dove Editing Services for a development edit and the "Rules of Magic" guide; to Kate Underwood for a first proofread, Lori Diederich for a final proofread, Kim Lozano Writing Coach for great input, and to Larch Gallagher Designs for the amazing book cover. Special thanks to Meagan Tudge and Charles Meaden for leading our hike to the old druid stones at Pentre Ifan.

Thanks to my friend, Justin Wright, threat intelligence expert, for pointing me to deep fake articles that helped me write that section as realistically as I'm capable of doing.

Last, but never least, thank you to my family. My mother, Shirley Roberts, my biggest cheerleader; Jim, Doug, Kathy, Dave, Dao, Wes and Tessa Roberts. And even though you can't read yet, Cori and Jet, I hope I leave you a legacy - not just of books written but to always follow your dreams.

About the Author

Janet Roberts is a former global leader in cybersecurity education. A member of Women's Fiction Writers Association and Sisters in Crime, she lives in Pittsburgh where she loves spending time on her porch swing. Learn more at https://www.booksbyjanetroberts.com

www.ingramcontent.com/pod-product-compliance
Lightning Source LLC
LaVergne TN
LVHW011759060526
838200LV00053B/3631